SELECTED STORIES

This selection of stories is drawn from the author's earlier selections *The Gorse Blooms Pale* (1947) and *Breathing Spaces* (1975). They are arranged in the chronological order of the periods of his life which, with varying degrees of directness, they reflect. The stories owe their original impulse to the desire to make the past live again even, and perhaps especially, for those who have not experienced it. They are each of them an act of creation and re-creation; attempts to repay a debt of gratitude for a life lived and to express a hope that, through the power of even a humble art, not everything need wholly die.

DAN DAVIN

Selected Stories

WELLINGTON
Victoria University Press
with
Price Milburn

LONDON
Robert Hale Limited

© *Dan Davin 1981*
First published in Great Britain 1981
ISBN 0 7091 9094 8

Robert Hale Limited
Clerkenwell House
Clerkenwell Green
London, EC1R 0HT

First published in New Zealand 1981
ISBN 0 7055 0684 3
Victoria University Press
Victoria University of Wellington
Wellington
with
Price Milburn & Company Limited
Post Office Box 2919
Wellington 1

Publication of this book has been assisted by
a grant from the New Zealand Literary Fund

Cover design by Lindsay Missen

Photoset by
Specialised Offset Services Limited, Liverpool
Printed and bound in Great Britain by
Redwood Burn Ltd., Trowbridge and Esher

Contents

III

Introduction

Introduction

The stories in this book are selected from my two collections, *The Gorse Blooms Pale* (1947) and *Breathing Spaces* (1975). I have arranged them, not in order of composition or publication, but in the chronological order of the periods of my life whose experience they, with varying degrees of directness, reflect. I have preferred this arrangement because of the illusion it may give of a simple narrative unity in time transcending the time movement of the particular stories. And I have excluded stories which are not set in New Zealand or among New Zealanders at war, in the hope of achieving a further unity of theme. The one self-indulgent exception is 'The Locksmith Laughs Last', set in New York. This I have included to give a hint of my more recent manner and to show an expatriate in a situation of double expatriation.

Between the two published collections there is an interval of eighteen years, a gap bridged by myself and some of the stories in the second volume. And, now that I have reached the age when the past cannot but be longer than the future for me, and the occasion of making this selection has arisen, I have been wondering how I came to write short stories at all and what I imagined I was up to when I began to write them. If there were time to spare, no doubt I could date the composition of most of them and, if my memory were better, I could perhaps recall some at least of the circumstances in which they were written and even what each of them was supposed to be saying and how far I thought each achieved its purpose. As it is, I can only assume that my guess, if worth making at all, is likely to be marginally better than anyone else's.

Everyone in our family was fond of stories, they were all mimics and raconteurs. To begin with at least, none of us were 'literary': my parents had had a minimum of schooling: my mother had been taken away from school in Makarewa, in spite of her schoolmaster's protests, by my grandmother and sent 'out to service' at the age of fourteen; my father had run away from school in Galway – he still used the word 'scholar' in the sense of someone who could read. We their children were educated in Catholic primary and secondary schools where religion tended to be identified with 'culture'. I recall that our English teacher, Brother Egbert, used to unroll a chart on either side of the classroom fireplace. One explained, in bold red type on yellow, the evils of alcohol and the other the evils of nicotine. These, he sonorously declaimed, were the best examples of English prose we could possibly encounter. And, for poetry, he found most moving his own verses on the death of Michael Collins. I still recall our embarrassment at the tears in his voice and eyes as, an ideal audience, he responded to the banal beauty of his own words and sentiment.

Apart from the charts and the recitation and the Penny Catechism, such scraps of literature as came our way were extracts in the *School Journal*, often rather good as I remember, gobbets in exam papers – it was here I first met Milton's Sonnet on his Blindness – a series of penny classics I disinterred in an old school cupboard, North's translation of Plutarch's *Lives* also found there, and a number of Clarendon cheap reprints of classic poems rescued from an old rubbish dump.

Our library at home consisted of *The Book of Irish Heraldry*, *The History of the Irish Struggle*, Harry Holland's *Armageddon*, and an old bound copy of Chambers' *Journal* for some year at the turn of the century. Since I was a fanatic reader – at the age of four I was discovered reading Zane Grey's *Lone Star Ranger* which a neighbour had lent to my mother during the 1918 influenza epidemic – this was hardly enough. So we borrowed from libraries, neighbours and friends and gobbled omnivorously – *Chums*, the *Boys' Own Paper*, *Magnets* and *Gems*, *Buffalo Bills*, the *Wide World Magazine*, Walter Scott, Sax Romer, Dickens, W.J. Locke, *East Lynne*, anything we could lay hands on. It was not until 1930 when I spent a final school year on a scholarship at Sacred Heart College in Auckland that, under the guidance of Brother Stephen, I came to have any ordered notion of literature; and even then Francis Thompson, Belloc and Chesterton, and Dennis' *The Sentimental Bloke* had a place in my esteem I would hardly concede them now.

I doubt if I was any better than my brothers and sisters or parents at actually telling stories and it is hard to say why I rather than anyone else in the family decided to become a writer. I do remember that I formed that intention very early, somewhere about 1925, and it was about this time that my skill in using words began to be noticeably better than my skill in handling figures. I also dropped an alternative notion of becoming an artist when a candid school friend pointed out that all my drawings of people tended to turn out self-portraits. I can still recall the relish with which I found myself introducing the word 'unostentatiously' into a school essay about a rugby match. I also remember, however, that then and for many years afterwards I felt that the time to attempt to write creatively would not come until I knew much more about 'life'. Till then my skills were used for passing exams and winning scholarships and it was not until my later years in Otago University that I began to write stories and poems with a view to publication in the university periodicals of that time. Otago was perhaps the most important of all my rites of passage. I met a good teacher, Herbert Ramsay the Professor of English, I made friends of different religions or none but people who took literature as something to be unself-consciously enjoyed; and I met my future wife. And my mind was by that time set on getting out of New Zealand by one means or another – preferably by winning a Rhodes Scholarship; for those were the days when one felt – or I felt – that to become a writer one had to distance oneself from an interfering and censorious ambience which would inhibit one's powers of expression and the courage of one's candour.

In those days I thought of myself as a poet to be, as well as a writer of stories and novels. I also had a polymathic urge, the desire to know everything – I could never understand why Adam hadn't picked the apple himself instead of waiting for Eve. I wanted to be a sort of renaissance man, something between Leonardo and Michaelangelo with a dash of Boccaccio, an ambition which now looks absurd, though like much of youth's absurdity, not altogether ignoble.

In Oxford between 1936 and 1939 I was perplexed. Not that I thought the time had yet come to write books but because of the conflict in myself between the determination to finish my degree and self-reproach at not fighting in the Spanish War. I consoled myself by thinking that the main war was still to come and that the Spanish War was only a curtain-raiser. From the egotistic point of view of my tidy mind it came tidily when it did come, just after my finals and my subsequent marriage. Assuming that I would be killed in France in 1940, since in projections of the future I have always preferred to assume the worst case, I thought it prudent to make a double bid for immortality by begetting a child and by writing a novel, even if prematurely. One of these involved less labour (for me) than the other but the total time of gestation was about the same. So between July and September and in the interval of being assigned to a regiment after volunteering, I wrote a good deal of verse, and a few short stories of which one was published the following year in *The Manchester Guardian*. (It appears in a revised form with the title 'Death of a Dog' in the present collection.) And I began *Cliffs of Fall* (1945) and another novel set in Paris of which I lost the manuscript in Greece in 1941. My first daughter was born in July 1940 and the novel finished about the same time.

A year in Cairo, 1941-2, when after being wounded in Crete and having a long spell in hospital I was seconded to GHQ military intelligence, gave me the chance to write again and I produced a good deal of verse and a number of short stories, some of them included in this volume. After my return to the

New Zealand Division there was little chance to write — though I made hundreds of notes for stories and novels, most of them now unintelligible. But I did manage to write a few stories when I was in England on leave in 1943. Back in Italy the following year, there was little one could do beyond observe and take notes. Towards the end of 1944 I was again seconded, to Intelligence in London. Now for the first time I came in touch with the fringes of literary Bohemia and even found I had a certain status in it through having published 'Under the Bridge' in Penguin New Writing and because my novel *Cliffs of Fall* appeared not long after my return.

At the end of the war I took a full-time job to support my family (now two and two-thirds of daughters) but counted on having enough energy and determination to continue writing. I wrote a war novel, *For the Rest of Our Lives* (1947), and finished enough stories to make the volume *The Gorse Blooms Pale*. But I had piously agreed to write the volume on Crete for the New Zealand official war history and this was to take up most of my spare time between 1946 and 1953.

Generally, my job began to soak up all my diminishing energies and I found I could get the continuity for novels only by using my exiguous holidays for writing full stretch. Now and then I was able to write a short story in odd fragments of leisure: if one had thought about it enough beforehand and caught one's moment to write, it was possible to begin and finish at least a first draft within a few hours.

Before the war I had planned to write a whole sequence of novels about New Zealand. After the war, the pattern became blurred and I had become a different man. But I have always found it difficult to abandon an idea once formed, even when its enactment no longer makes the original sense; and so I stuck to my purpose. Since my mind was set on New Zealand themes and themes of war, the stories I wrote at various times tended to deal with these themes also, though in later years I began to turn to the life now about me. Stories written in this later phase I have excluded from the present volume.

Looking now at the output of those years, and trying to make out what I thought I was about, I see that my stories, to make an egregious comparison, resemble the paintings of Graham Sutherland: each is basically an *objet trouvé*, eroded and worn by tides of experience, smoothed by long pondering and the affections of memory. I have tended to use the medium of a single consciousness because the brevity of the story does not admit of the complexities of witness available to the novel. Paradoxically, I have tended to use the first person narrator when I was departing from the literal facts of memory or of my own direct experience. It is my belief that, to be literature, a piece of fiction must combine a passion for the exact, the authentic, detail; some intellectual power which can organise the form and weight it with a central, though not necessarily explicit, thought; and a power of feeling, a spirit, which means that the story, while avoiding a moral, is fundamentally moral.

How far have I been successful? The judgement of that must lie with others. The only interest of the author's opinion is that, however subjective, it is an opinion which must have some starting point in the knowledge of what was being attempted. Authenticity I think I have on the whole achieved. The intellectual force is difficult to judge in a story because it is in its essence a simple thing and intellectual organisation or its absence are more readily discerned in structures more complex and ambitious like the novel. The feeling, the moral force, is I think mostly there and ultimately springs from the desire, perhaps not wholly an expatriate desire, to make the past live again even, and perhaps especially, for those who have not experienced it. For, in the end, the writer's drive is for creation, to make lives and people live, and in my own case it has been mostly re-creation: a debt of gratitude for a life lived, long ago, and a hope that through the power of art not everything need wholly die. And in a sense the stories I have here selected are not only an attempt at repayment but an apologia, a reminder to my country that to leave it physically does not necessarily imply desertion or estrangement.

D.D.

Selected Stories

I

Perspective

God blazed in every gorsebush
When I was a child.
Forbidden fruits were orchards,
And flowers grew wild.

God is a shadow now.
The gorse blooms pale.
Branches in the orchard bow
With fruits grown stale.

My father was a hero once.
Now he is a man.
The world shrinks from infinity
To my fingers' span.

Why has the mystery gone?
Where is the spell?
I live sadly now.
Once I lived well.

The Apostate

'Good-bye, Mum,' said Mick from the door.

Mrs Connolly put down her cup and looked up.

'Come here a minute, Mick,' she said. 'Did you clean your ears?'

'I have to go, Mum. I'll be late.'

'Come back and let me have a look at those ears.'

He came back over the coconut matting to her chair in the corner.

She put him between her knees and took his head in both hands. She turned each ear towards the light of the window and looked carefully. Her apron was wet and smelt damp. She had been clearing away their dishes before sitting down to her own breakfast.

'The Lord save us,' she said. 'You could grow a crop of King Edwards in them ears. Come here.'

She got up stiffly. She had been up three hours to make an early start on the washing before getting all the breakfasts. The damp was already in her bones.

In the scullery she wet a piece of the roller towel on her finger under the tap and scoured out each ear in turn. He wriggled impatiently.

'There now,' she said at last. 'We couldn't have you going off to school like that, a disgrace to us all.'

Released, he shot towards the door. She looked after him, smiling.

'Wait a minute,' she said.

He stopped in his tracks. Had she noticed the hole in his stocking?

She reached up to the high mantelpiece and brought down her small black purse. She slipped the two silver knobs of the catch past each other, looked in and sighed. She could feel him watching her. Well, it was little enough pleasure the poor kids had. She took out a penny.

'Here,' she said, and held it out to him.

'Oh, thank you, Mum.'

'Now, don't you go letting on to the others at lunch-time or they'll all be wanting one. And mind you don't spend it on trash.'

She sat down, tasted her tea and found it nearly cold. She reached for the big brown teapot.

Outside. Old Jack got up and wagged his tail, hopefully.

'No, Jack, it's only school today.' A hug of consolation.

At the corner of the house he looked back. Jack had not yet lain down again. He was sitting there on the back verandah, head on one side, brown eyes wistful.

There was no need to hurry at all, really, now that he was out of the house. It was only half-past eight and school didn't go in till nine. The sun was hardly up. As he came along Venus Street he could look straight into it through the five-barred gate of Scott's paddocks, lying low behind the mist.

The mist had made the frost light and there was just the faintest silvering on the footpath. It had kept the sun from getting at the spiderwebs on Basset's macrocarpa hedge, too. There were little wee beads strung along each fine thread.

You could hardly believe they'd been spun there so cleverly just to catch flies. But if you started at the outside and followed the lines they always led into the centre where the little spider was bundled up, waiting for the sun.

Still, there were some good spiders. They had crosses on their backs and they were blessed. Once their great-great-great grandfather had spun a web across the cave to stop the soldiers finding Jesus and His Holy Mother. It just showed you. And you should never kill a spider without looking first to see if it had a cross on its back. Besides, if you killed any sort of spider it always rained afterwards, though it was hard to see why.

Mick got tired of staring at the spiderwebs. He began to run. When he came to his favourite branch, the long one that hung out over the footpath, he jumped the way he always did to see if he could reach it. Today he just managed it. That was a good sign. He laughed as it showered silvery drops over him. It was a pity Paddy wasn't there to see. He couldn't get any way near the branch, though of course he was a year younger.

He looked at the little twig he had snatched. Queer how each little bit fitted so snugly into the others. Like little green knuckles. And what a nice green colour it was.

He crossed the gravel road and came through the cocksfoot to Scott's big gate. The withered heads of cocksfoot were hanging down under the weight of mist.

There was plenty of time so he'd take the short cut today. He reached up to the top bar. It was cold and slippery as if it had been soaped. His fingers left dull, steely ridges across the frost. Right from the top he jumped and landed with a thump. His schoolbag followed anxiously and clumped against his behind a second later.

A narrow track led through the paddock towards the railway bridge. There were no marks on the grass. Nobody had been through today yet. He was an explorer lost in the fog. His feet swooshed over the sheep-cropped grass, leaving patches of dark and sending little sprung showers of silver from the short, proud blades.

On the top of the rise he stopped. The mist was clearing. You could see the dark green gorse hedges meet at the corner just before the bridge.

Under the mist everything was green. He squatted on his haunches to look at everything. The mist of his own breath came out in front of him and melted away. Down in the dip a sheep coughed and the mist of its breath came out in a sharp puff.

The grass under his feet was green, shining where they had rubbed the white moisture off it. The sprig of macrocarpa was still in his hand, green.

He had a revelation. In a flash, like what happened to Saint Paul, only not frightening.

Green was the colour of God. It was the colour of the grass and of the trees and of the sea and of all the best things, of God's things. Green was the colour of Ireland. In Ireland, his father said, everything was green. Even the fairies. Green was Ireland's National Colour. And the Irish were the best people. Even here in New Zealand you knew that. And all the Irish were Catholics. Their colour was green. God's colour was green. That proved it. The Irish were God's green people. So their green God was the real God.

At first he only felt this. It was afterwards that he worked it out. After he had crossed the bridge, not stopping to watch the lines meet in a point this morning, but jumping down over the ditch and then following the creek bank.

Now he was wonderfully glad. He had felt glad before but without knowing why. This was different. He would have liked to have somebody to tell about it. But probably it was better to tell no one. He would just keep it inside him and walk about as if nothing had happened. While all the time inside him he knew that God was green and Irish and a Catholic.

It was still too early. The bell wouldn't go for ages. In the distance he could see the other kids playing outside the school, chasing one another up and down the bank and making slides. Usually he tried to get to school early to do this too. But this morning was different. All that didn't seem right somehow for a boy who'd just found out what he had.

He would walk round the block when he came out of the paddock into Islington Street and come into school by the main gate.

He got through the barbed wire fence and out on to the footpath. It was asphalt although there were still only a few houses in the street. His father said they'd made the road, thinking the town was going to grow there but it had stopped growing.

Up towards the main road houses were thicker. Men were coming out their front gates and getting on their bikes.

Mothers were fussing over their kids as they left for school. Most of the kids were Protestants. They'd very likely go to Hell when they died for singing:

> Catholic dogs
> Jump like frogs,
> Don't eat meat on Friday.

Then, when Mick and his friends sang:

> Protestant dogs
> Jump like frogs,
> Do eat meat on Friday.

both sides would pick up stones out of the gravelly road and begin to fight. But, of course, that was only in the evening on the way home from school.

He stopped outside Mrs Peak's store. There were pocket knives in the window, very sharp and shiny. The big blades were right open and the little blades half open. The Nest knives were best with their warm black handles and big blades that had a hollow scooped out of the top near the point and a sharp, lifting edge. When he was old enough to skin a rabbit his father was going to buy him one. His father's knife was very narrow in the blade because every Sunday after dinner he sharpened it on the oilstone to mend their boots. It had string wound round the handle.

The cheapest knives were three-and-six. But he only had the penny. So it was better to look at the pencils. There was a lovely, shiny box full of them, all colours. It didn't say how much they were.

He went into the shop. Mrs Peak leaned over at him, looking as if she'd like to eat him. She was fat and had a sort of musty smell.

'Well, what can I do for you, my little man?'

He stiffened. That was no way to talk to a boy who would soon be able to skin a rabbit and knew what God was like.

'How much are the pencils, please?'

'A penny each.'

So was a chocolate fish. Or he could buy a penny's worth of specked fruit and make the joke about not too many coconuts. Or a penny's worth of rosebuds. If he sucked each one instead of crunching it they would last all morning. Even after he'd given some to Tommy Stafford and Jack Bates. His mouth watered. He didn't really need a pencil.

But Mrs Peak had got the box out of the window.

'What colour would you like? There's a nice green one.'

Mrs Peak was a Protestant. It was like that word in the catechism, simony, for her to sell green pencils. But she couldn't know any better. She couldn't know it was God's colour. So perhaps it was all right.

'Or perhaps you'd like a red one.' She took out the red one and handed it to him. It was a wonderful pencil, round and rich and shiny, the colour of blood. He took it in his hands. He could see it in the class sharpener twirling and then coming out with the blood-red part ending in a smooth circle and then the reddish wood coming to a sharp, black point.

He sneaked a look at the green pencil again. It seemed a quiet sort of a pencil, not very exciting.

'It's a maroon red,' said Mrs Peak.

'I'll have the maroon one, please,' he heard himself say. Maroon had clinched it. His penny was warm and damp when he handed it over. He had been holding it in his pocket. The bell rang.

He just got to school in time.

At playtime he and Tommy Stafford and Jack Bates raced over to the park. In and out among the pine trees they chased each other. Then they sat down on the pine-needles to get their breath. The pine-needles were lovely and dry and tingly and you could smell them.

'Look what I've found,' said Tommy. He held up a piece of shiny stuff.

'It's only a bit of gum,' said Jack.

'It'll be kauri gum,' said Mick. 'I had an uncle who used to dig for it once up in Auckland. He used to put a long spike into the ground and feel for where it was.'

'Don't be silly,' said Jack, 'kauris don't grow down here.'

'Perhaps they did once and we are the first to know, all through my piece of gum,' said Tommy.

Jack was half persuaded. He got up and began to scuff among the needles to try and find a piece. If he could find any he'd believe it.

Something brown moved at the foot of a big tree. They rushed over. It flew in front of them, in desperate flights, a little distance at a time. It was a young thrush. Mick fell on it and caught it.

'We'll wring its neck,' said Jack. He was angry. First the gum and now the thrush. And he was the biggest, too.

'You'd be too frightened,' said Tommy. 'I wonder what it'd look like when it was dead?'

But Mick had the bird in his hands. He could feel its heart beating. Its eyes were bursting with fear.

'No,' he said. 'We'll let it go.'

'I want to kill it.'

'They do eat the gooseberries,' said Tommy. 'I've seen them.'

'No, we'll let it go. How'd you like to have your neck wrung?'

'Softy,' said Jack.

'Softy,' Tommy said after him. He was the youngest.

Mick could see they were going to rush him.

'The bell must have gone ages ago,' he said.

They hesitated. This was only too true. Mick let the bird go. It flew on to a branch and could hardly breathe for relief.

They all watched it for a second. They were glad it was safe now and they could say it was Mick's fault if anyone asked why they didn't wring its neck. They rushed back to school.

'Two cuts each,' said Sister Mary Xavier gravely. But when they told her how they'd caught a bird and let it go she didn't give them very hard ones.

They walked back to their seats with their hands in their armpits, pretending it hurt. The little girls' eyes were big with horror and respect. Little girls never got the cuts. They cried if they were just scolded.

Mick's wrist against his pocket seemed to miss something. He held his breath and tried to fight off the movement when he would know what it was. But he knew already, even before he searched. He had lost his maroon pencil. His eyes filled with tears. He bent his head down. The others would think he was crying because he'd got the cuts. He'd already been called a softy because of the bird. They were very critical about these things. Only poor old Jumbo Jones was expected to cry. That was because he was a real sugar-baby.

Through the moist mist the maroon pencil floated in a vision. The gladness had gone from the day.

But perhaps if he prayed to Saint Anthony, Saint Anthony would talk to God and get it back from him. Three 'Hail Marys' to Saint Anthony, that would do it. 'Hail-Mary-full-of-grace – .' Not so fast or Saint Anthony would be offended. 'Hail Mary, full of grace, the Lord is with Thee, Blessed art Thou amongst women – '

Religion was the last lesson before lunch. Sister Mary Xavier talked away. But Mick wasn't listening. He couldn't even play the game of seeing faces in the shape made by the damp on the plaster wall behind the nun. All the shapes kept turning into pencils. If only the bell would hurry up and go so that he could tear over to the pine trees and look for it.

What was that she was saying?

'And one of the most glorious of God's saints has said that it has never happened that anyone who prayed with all his heart for what he wished, provided the wish were holy, has had his prayer unanswered.'

Of course he'd find the pencil. Didn't that as good as say so? Better say another three though, to make sure. After all, the saints must be pretty busy. They'd need reminding.

'But, dear children, our prayers are not always answered the way we expect them to be. God who knows everything knows what is best for us. And sometimes he knows that what we pray for with all our hearts is not what is best for the salvation of our immortal souls.'

That was just like grown-ups. His heart began to sink. They always talked like that when they weren't going to give you something. Supposing it was not for the good of his immortal soul?

'But, be sure, my children, the prayer is always answered. If not in the way we expect, then in some other way and in the long run the best way. For God is infinitely good. Don't forget to bring your crayons for drawing this afternoon. Now repeat after me this prayer.'

He came back from the park. No thrush, no red pencil, nothing. Only an old piece of pine-gum.

He sat down in the sun by the porch door and opened his schoolbag. His lunch was wrapped neatly in newspaper. Jam sandwiches. He didn't like the way the jam soaked into the bread, even if it was raspberry. He'd save the corned beef one till last.

The others had all had their lunch and were playing marbles. He was glad he didn't have to talk to anybody.

As he picked the last shred of corned beef from his coat and pushed it down over the lump in his throat something in the pile of sawdust swept from the classroom caught his eye.

The end of a pencil was sticking out of the sawdust. A red pencil. A maroon pencil.

He kept quite still for a moment. Then he leapt.

The pencil was two inches long.

He sat down again. So that was God's answer.

But perhaps it was a punishment for not buying the green one? No, because he'd been afraid of simony and you couldn't get punished for being afraid of a sin. And anyway if it was that why should God give him a red one now?

'Be sure God will always answer your prayers somehow, dear children.'

There was no God. And He wasn't green either. And if that was the best He could do He could keep His rotten old pencil.

He threw the stub back into the sawdust.

The Vigil

It was a late summer afternoon. The cows had been milked and were out in the back paddock, lying down and chewing their cud or lazily cropping the short grass. The gorse hedges which ran down two sides of the paddock were a mass of gold and there was a thrush on one singing its heart out. Half-an-hour before, old Mr McGregor, the carter, standing up in his spring-cart had sailed down the road which marked the top end of the paddock to his milking and his tea. No one else would pass along it now.

The hens had been let out through the little square hole that led through the back fence from the fowl run. They were busy poking and scratching about in the dried mud which had been all soft and squelchy and impossible to walk on in the winter. You could still see the deep holes where the cows had walked, dragging their hoofs out of the ooze. But the holes were hard and dry now. Some of the hens were picking away at the very fresh light-green grass that grew round the ruins of the haystack. In the winter the cows used to wear the barbed-wire fence down trying to get at the hay. Now they didn't care and only the hens were interested in scrabbling about among the sticks and logs which had kept the stack off the wet ground.

The back gate leading to the garden was open and Mick sat there to keep the hens from getting in. He had the Catholic weekly and he was reading the 'Smile-raisers'. The best one was about a man writing to his girl to say he'd go through fire and water for her but not to expect him if it rained. At least that was the one that had made his mother laugh.

Then there was a lot of stuff about a writer on the literary page. He must be pretty bad because the editor kept talking about Liffey mud and the disgrace to the glorious literary tradition of Ireland. But it was hard to tell what it was all about. Some day when he grew up he would read all the books in the world and know all about everything, even about this writer.

After a while he got tired of reading about things he couldn't understand and he put the paper down. He began to feel hungry. It must be about tea-time and it was getting a bit cold. He lay on his back and looked up to try and see the lark he could hear singing. Soon he found it, the smallest little black speck in the sky. He watched it for a while and then sat up again to look at the hens.

Every now and then one would try to get past into the garden and he would frighten it with a long stick he had, to save getting up. Some of the hens didn't worry about the garden at all but were quite content where they were. But there were two cunning hens who never moved far from the gate and only pretended to be interested in what they were doing. As soon as he looked away they would make a dash for the gate. Hens as a rule were stupid, but when they were cunning they were even more annoying because somehow they were still stupid but bad as well. He collected some clods and when the two hens made him angry enough he pelted them until they scurried squawking into the gorse hedge.

Rosy, the one his father called the red cow, came up to the water-trough and stood there drinking. It was the trough they scalded the pigs in whenever they had a killing. Afterwards it used to be scrubbed out and brought into the paddock again. It was always a long time before the cows would drink out of it. But they'd got used to it again just now. It held a lot of water but even so it went down by inches when Rosy drank. At first she drank steadily, then more slowly, lifting her head and looking thoughtfully and sadly into nowhere, while long dribbles of water idled their way from her nostrils back into the trough. She was the biggest and boldest of the cows; once she had thrown a young bull which was pestering Strawberry, into a ditch.

It was high time his mother called him for his tea. It must be getting late. They didn't seem to care whether he got anything to eat or not. He tried lying on his stomach to see if he would feel less hungry that way. Then he saw Rosy staring at him sadly and he forgot about being hungry.

How was it that all cows had that sad look? When he had the sulks his mother used to say he had a lip on him like a motherless foal. But probably even a motherless foal couldn't look as sad as a cow, with those great big brown eyes.

Rosy perhaps had a right to look sad, though. Her calves were always bulls and so they were always killed. And even though she seemed to forget about it after a while and the other cows were very sympathetic she must have a sort of idea what would happen by now. And she was due to calve in another month because the last time she went to the bull his father had chalked the date up on the cow-shed wall. It was the same with all the other cows, too, because even when they had heifers they were taken away. They all knew what would happen but they couldn't do anything about it. Rosy was probably telling the two yearling heifers about things like that when she let them lick her.

She was a fine cow; not really red but nearly, and very glossy and shiny now with her summer coat.

It was getting very late and very cold. He could hear the other boys playing away up on the hill but he hadn't had anything to eat and he'd have to stay where he was or else the hens would get into the garden. His mother always said his father would have a fit if the hens got into the garden. That was the worst of having a father who was mad about gardens. Even Jack, the collie, knew better than to go galloping about in there among the potatoes and cabbages.

It was getting dusk as well now. He could hear Mrs Scott away in the distance calling to her kids to come in off the hill. They were lucky not to keep hens and a garden in their family. And there were McGregor's drake and ducks going off down the road from the peat swamp. He hunched himself up against the wall. His knees were so cold they felt all prickly with goose-flesh.

There was nothing more to think about. He had thought about hens and haystacks and larks and cows and gardens, and even if there'd been anything left to think about he was too hungry. The trouble was they'd forgotten all about him. They didn't care whether he went hungry or not. He often used to think he was an adopted child; now he was sure of it.

And his step-parents were trying to be cruel to him. Well, if nobody cared whether he starved or froze he would just starve and freeze. He'd stay sitting here forever and when they found him he would be all stiff and cold and then everyone would be sorry and his mother and father would be very ashamed while people criticised them for their savage cruelty and neglect of their sensitive child.

One of the innocent hens had been getting worried about the time and she now came towards the gate thinking it was the way back into the fowl-run. He threw a clod at her and caught her a terrific thump.

'What a noble-looking boy,' people were saying as they looked down at his young corpse stretched out on the bier. There was a calm, sad expression on his pale, drawn face; as of duty done. 'Some people don't deserve to have children,' one person said. 'What an intelligent, sensitive face,' said another. 'Like the sentinel at Pompeii,' said Father O'Duffy, who used to tell them about Italy. Beside the bier lay his faithful dog, Jack, with his head between his paws. Later on, when they buried him out in the cemetery between the railway and East Road, Jack would lie by his grave, the way Mr Manion's dog Glen did, and stay there fretting till he died.

Still no sign of anyone to call him. They'd be sorry but he wasn't going to let them off. He'd stay by his post. They needn't think he was going to put the hens in himself and come up to tea. If they were going to neglect him it wasn't his place to remind them of their duty to their child. Even if he was only adopted.

Just then Mrs Connolly came through the gate.

'Ah, there you are, sonny,' she said. 'What with getting

your father off to his late shift and getting the baby to bed I forgot all about you. Don't bother to shut the hens in. Paddy's had his tea. I'll get him to do it.'

He stalked small and dignified down the path in front of her, so that she wouldn't see him nearly crying.

But when they got up to the warm kitchen she said: 'Now sit down here in your father's chair next the fire and I'll make you a nice piece of toast and boil the brown hen's egg for you.'

As she cleared away the tea things to put back fresh ones he swallowed the lump in his throat and began to forget the tragic drama in which he was to have been the most important figure, though stiff and cold beneath the stars.

Milk Round

Mick stood back with the leg rope in his hand, while Ned pulled out the iron bolt from the top bar of the bail and let Strawberry's head free. But she was in no hurry to go out into the cold. She turned her head to look at them and rolled an appraising eye. The wisp of hay hung out on each side of her jaws like a moustache.

'Come on, you old scamp,' said Ned and he slapped her where the canvas cover came down over her shoulder. Strawberry accepted fate, turned fussily in the narrow space, her heels slipping and scraping on the wet concrete, and made for the door.

'Tell Mum I'm just going to put them up in the hill paddock and throw them a few swedes and then I'll be in for tea.'

'Right you are, Ned.'

Ned followed Strawberry out into the mud.

Mick picked up the two buckets. They were light enough for him to carry. Only Dolly and Strawberry were milking now and they were drying off, too.

In the backyard, the light from the kitchen window picked out the puddles in the asphalt. His father hadn't quite got the knack yet when he put it down and the surface was uneven.

Paddy was in the wash-house, doing the separating. He took it very seriously. It was only last Saturday that they had decided he was big enough to turn the handle all the way round and be trusted with the job.

'Just in time,' he said. 'There's hardly any cream coming

out now. The bowl must be nearly empty. You'd better go and get Mum to pour it in right away.'

'Who're you ordering about?' said Mick. 'I've got to measure out the milk for the customers first. Then I'll pour it in.'

'But you can't reach that high.'

'Can't I?' Mick swung the two buckets up on to the bench. Their father always made the buckets out of old kerosene tins and the light of the hurricane lantern winked back now from their shiny sides.

The empty treacle tins they used for billies were ranged up alongside, all clean and washed and ready. Mick got the pint-measure out of one and began to dip.

A good full quart for Mrs Campbell because she was a hunchback. And another bit extra because she was a widow and was poor and had four children. Only the bare quart for Mrs Crofts. She was so snooty just because her husband was a bank manager and her daughters took lessons in elocution. A good quart for Mrs Thomas because she had white hair and was always so nice. Well, perhaps a little bit more for Mrs Crofts; it looked a bit mean having her billy so exactly half full. Though she didn't deserve it.

'Hurry up,' said young Paddy. Even the skimmed milk spout was hardly more than a trickle.

Mick didn't answer but pulled the kerosene box up to the separator and began to pour what was left in the two buckets into the bowl. He could feel young Paddy waiting for him to slip.

The new weight on the pans made the handle stiffer to turn and the sound that came from the separator was different. Slowly the two spouts began to thicken again.

Mick had to reach on tiptoe to get the last of the milk out of the bucket. The box swayed dangerously.

'Be careful,' said Paddy.

'Oh, go to hell.'

'What was that I heard?' said Mrs Connolly, entering suddenly from the kitchen. 'I never thought I'd live to see the day when I'd hear one son of mine speak like that to another and the two of them brought up in a good Catholic home.'

Mick grabbed his billies and made for the door. His mother looked after him as he crossed the yard. It was a shame to have to send the poor kid out into a dirty black night like this.

From the corner of the yard Mick shouted back Ned's message. Jack, the collie, heard him and began to rattle his chain by the wood-heap. Mick put down his billies and went back. On the end of the chain Jack leapt and pawed at him. Mick undid the chain from his collar.

Together the two of them came out into the street. Jack raced away up the footpath and disappeared into the dark and the rain. He knew they were going left because they always went that way to save Mrs Thomas's for the last. And he knew he could run ahead for a while because it was two blocks to Mrs Campbell's.

Laden with its precious freight of gold dust the mail-coach moved slowly along through the narrow gully, a cliff on one side and on the other a steep fall to the river. Somewhere in front, Jack, the outrider, was scouting for bushrangers and would come racing back at the slightest suspicion of an ambush.

Behind the front hedges there were lights in the houses they passed. People little thought how out there in the night men were coming and going on dangerous missions so they might eat and sleep warm in their beds.

Jack was waiting for him at the corner by Macdonald's General Store. The shop was closed but by the street-light you could almost read the names of the sixpenny books in the side window. 'Deadwood Dicks', his father always called them, though none of them were ever about Deadwood Dick. They were mostly about how the money was found in Harry Trevor's pocket in the changing-room before the big match with Aston Villa and how it was proved he hadn't taken it after all and he was allowed to play and kicked the winning goal; or about how blood will tell and how Ralph turned out to be the missing heir to the baronetcy and the fortune; or what happened to Bill Cody in Dead Man's Gulch and the valley with the whitening bones.

That was Mrs Campbell's, the little house with the white picket-gate. You could always tell which one it was because she'd made the gate herself when the kids broke the last one swinging on it and the pickets were all different sizes.

They went round past the lighted kitchen window and Mick knocked.

'It's Mick with the milk, Mum,' called little Rose. She kept on holding the door open and smiled at him seriously. She was nearly six and the eldest.

'Come in, Mick,' called Mrs Campbell. 'Come in out of the rain. The boy's as wet as a shag,' she went on when she saw him. 'Won't you sit down there in front of the range while I wash the billy for you? And a good hot cup of tea would do you no harm either.'

'No thank you, Mrs Campbell.' The little room was nice with the range open and the children staring at him over the top of their plates, but he must be getting on.

'You'll have a bit of cake then,' she said. 'Just wait a minute now while I cut you a piece.'

His heart sank. He'd been afraid of this. Her cakes were terrible, all soggy in the middle and no currants. But there was no way of refusing because whatever you said it would really be because you didn't like her cake and that would show in your face.

The piece of cake stuck to the knife like an oyster, but he got it away without breaking it up. 'Thank you very much, Mrs Campbell,'' he said. 'I'll eat it on the way.' He couldn't look her in the face as he told her this but she didn't seem to notice. He backed out the door.

'Good-night, Mick, and don't go catching a cold.'

'Good-night, Mrs Campbell and thank you.' But he wasn't quite able to say: for the cake.

Jack was wagging his tail and kept jumping up for his share. But Mick made him wait till they got under the light. He looked at the cake. Its inside was a pale, sticky yellow. He threw it to Jack. Jack leapt and his jaws snapped on it. Then he seemed to think. He laid it down on the footpath and looked up meekly, anxious not to give offence.

'There you are, you see, Jack,' said Mick. 'And now we'll have to pick it up and hide it in Pratt's hedge in case the Campbells find it.'

They were getting near the Mortons' place now and they'd have to be careful. Last night those two Morton girls, like the great, stupid lumps they were, had thrown clods of earth at him out of the garden and some of it had splattered into the milk. Tonight he'd be on the watch for them. He bent down and picked up a good-sized stone from the loose gravel at the side of the road.

This was it, the house they were coming to now. Over the front hedge he could see the front door was open and there was a light in the hall. He shifted the two full billies and the empty one into his left hand. Their weight made the wire handles cut into the underside of his fingers. But it was best to have his right hand free. He whistled Jack back to heel.

As he came level with the hedge a clod was thrown over it and fell in the gutter just beyond him. Another followed. He could hear them giggling. They were behind the hedge all right.

'After them, Jack.'

Jack gave his rabbiting yelp and thrust in between the thick holly roots. The girls raced squealing for the door. Jack burst out behind them.

Mick craned over the hedge with his right hand back, ready. They appeared in the light, Molly, the fat one, first. She tripped on the mat and fell sprawling. Dora tripped over her and fell forward on her hands. Mick saw the blue stretch of bloomers and threw. Another angry squeal and tears behind it this time. Girls. He called back Jack and went on.

That meant their brother Howard would be waiting for him tomorrow night. And he was in the Sixth Standard at Georgetown School. Well, let him. He'd fix Howard, too. And Mick's father was twice as big as theirs. Or else he'd get Ned to come along with him. There mightn't even be any need for that. He could see Howard blubbering already and Dora running to the tap with a handkerchief for his nose and Molly saying: You shouldn't have hit him so hard. How was he to know you were so strong?

But Crofts' gate with the big brass number-plate and the cold concrete path suddenly came between then and now and he grew down to his ordinary size again. Even the few chrysanthemums that shivered there still in the garden looked as if they only stayed there because they were paid to and couldn't afford to go anywhere else.

A neat little girl about his own age with her hair stretched tightly back over her forehead and a ribbon in her pigtail answered his knock. She looked at him without speaking and called back over her shoulder: 'It's the milkboy, Mummy.' Then she tossed her head and went away.

Milkboy, indeed. If only she knew who he really was she wouldn't talk like that. But the dung on his cow-boots was more faithful and damning than his imagination. The sleeves of his coat were too short. But long enough to rub the drip from his nose before Mrs Crofts could come. He would have to wait till he grew up. Meantime he looked round to see that Jack wasn't running over the clean matting they had on their verandah. But Jack was skulking back in the shadows. He knew when he was welcome.

Mrs Crofts' bosom appeared in the doorway, a rampart not a haven. Her severe voice spoke from the battlements.

'So there you are. The milk last night wasn't fit for human consumption. It had dirt in it. When you go home tell your mother I'm not paying for dirt in my milk. I hope it's all right tonight.'

No good reminding her it was the best milk in town or she wouldn't be buying it. And what was the good of explaining about the dirt? If it had even been boys – . You couldn't say girls had done it.

He passed over the billy in silence.

The other little daughter peered out while her mother was getting the clean billy. She had dark eyes. Half curious, half derisive, she looked at Mick as if he came from a different world, the place where people who got wages and had dirty fingernails came from.

'Run inside at once, Doris dear,' said Mrs Crofts, coming back. 'You'll get a chill.' Listening to her voice now was like looking into a room with a fire. 'Here's the billy,' she added to Mick in the other voice and the door in that room slammed shut.

A pity about them, them and their chills. Soon she'd be like her sister and able to look at the people who brought their milk without seeing them at all.

Getting outside that gate was like changing out of your good suit when you got home from Mass on Sundays. Jack's tail was up again like a flag. If only those little girls weren't so pretty as well. That was what stopped you being as sorry for them as you'd like to be.

It was raining again and under the next street-lamp the gusty wind shook and swayed the circle of light. The spears struck out of the darkness and through the light, glittering at him. He bent his head and marched on against them, a Greek soldier advancing under the darkness of Persian arrows. They rattled against his armour and he shook the billies exultantly as he pressed on. Jack looked back and saw the gesture and raced on with the standard through the slain.

The corner before Thomas's two lights swung into the road. A dragon coming with glaring eyes to devour him and his faithful hound. Undismayed he went on to meet it and the glare in its eyes grew more terrible and he could hear its angry roar. But he had his good sword.

Just as it reached him it swerved to one side, unable to brave the certain death that waited in his right arm. By magic it changed itself into Mr Crofts' Chrysler and inside in the magic square of light he could see the magician himself, his hands on the wheel, the thin lips pursed up and the eyes staring on into the darkness beyond the rain.

At Thomas's Jack was waiting for him again. Together they went down the asphalt path with the trellis where they grew such lovely roses in summer on one side and on the other the garden where there nearly always seemed to be flowers. He held Jack by the collar. Solomon, the big black cat, might be sitting behind the lighted window. Last night Jack had left great muddy streaks on the paint trying to get at him but Mrs Thomas had said it didn't matter. Solomon was there again tonight and arched his back as he saw them pass. The stiff hair rose on Jack's back and he growled but let Mick hold him down.

'Ah Mick, what a wet evening it is for you,' said old Mrs Thomas. 'Stand up on the verandah out of the wet and I won't keep you a moment.' Her brown eyes smiling under the white hair made him feel quite warm inside. She went away to get the clean billy. He could hear the big laugh of her son Bob in there. He played for Southland and might be an All Black soon and rode a motor-bike. Alice was laughing, too, though you could hardly hear her, her voice was always so soft. He could tell by the sound of it her boy Geoff must be there. She always said hello to you in the street and wore silk stockings and smelt of scent.

'There you are, Mick,' said Mrs Thomas, handing him the billy. 'And here's something for you.' She stuffed an apple in his pocket.

'Thank you, Mrs Thomas,' he said. It was all right taking things from her because it would have been very nice to give her things, whatever things you gave to old ladies. A teapot, perhaps.

At the front gate again Jack turned round and looked up expectantly.

'I'm sorry, Jack, it's an apple and you know you don't like apples.'

Jack kept on looking, only he shifted his head from one side to the other.

'You know I always give you half if it's anything you like.'

Jack kept on watching him sadly.

'It's a terrible waste, Jack.'

Jack didn't move or take his eyes off his face.

Mick took out his knife and cut the apple in half. It was a Cox's Orange. He had to wipe the juice off the blade on his coat.

Jack's eyes were eager. Mick looked at him again, sighed, and threw him his share. Jack's jaws snapped and caught it.

He put his head between his paws, mumbling it. Mick began to eat his half, hurriedly.

Jack looked up and walked back to Mick, leaving his half in the gutter. He watched Mick eat his.

· 'No, Jack. You've had yours. I can't help it if you don't like it, can I?' He hastily swallowed the last of the core.

The two of them went on down the lane past the Ghost House to the barbed wire fence where the short cut started. Through the drops that made little rainbows on his eyelashes Mick could see the light in the kitchen, away across the empty section. Soon he'd be taking off his wet boots in front of the range and his mother would be wrapping her hand in her apron to get something hot for him out of the oven.

'Come on, boy,' he said to Jack who was nosing about in the gorse. 'It's Saturday tomorrow and we'll chase the rabbits then.'

Presents

The two boys were reading at the kitchen table. Mrs Connolly had set a place at the range end of it an hour before. Now there was nothing for her to do but wait and worry. From time to time she leaned her head to one side, though her hands kept shuttling the knitting-needles, and she listened. When no sound answered she would glance over at the boys and look down at the half-finished sock again, not sighing. They knew she had looked at them and knew why she hadn't sighed.

When the heavy step and the clicking of the bicycle chain came round the corner of the house they all heard it at the same time.

'There he is at last,' she said. 'So he'll be able to take you into town after all. Now out of here with you and let him have his meal in peace.'

Now that she wasn't worried any more her voice was sharp. They were afraid she was trying to get them out of the way to give her a chance to go for him. If he was in a bad mood that would make him worse. If he was in a good mood it might put him off.

'You wouldn't like us to give you a hand washing up the dishes?' Mick said.

'I know you and your tricks, Mr Long-ears. Run on into the sitting-room now, there's good boys. Your father and I want to have a talk.'

But they did not quite close the door.

'What on earth's been keeping you, man?' they heard her say. 'You know you promised those kids you'd take them in to see the Christmas shops tonight and they've set their hearts on it. Where on earth have you been? Is anything wrong?'

'Wrong, Mary? It's the terror you are for worrying. Of course there's nothing wrong. Why should there be anything wrong?'

That was like him, asking one question to answer another. And the voice sounded too cheerful.

'He's had a few in, all right,' Mick whispered.

'Shut up, Mick,' Ned said. There was talking again in the kitchen.

'Well, I only hope you haven't gone and spent that few bob in Joe Shields' pub.' She was poking the range fire to bring the kettle back to the boil and make fresh tea. You could tell from the noise what she thought.

'It's little enough the poor kids get at the best of times,' she went on. 'And you know how much money there's left in the house. Yet you're not content with filling them up with all sorts of talk about Christmas presents. No, you must go and spend most of what money there is down there in the town, buying drinks for strangers, I'll be bound, and forgetting all about your own family. It doesn't look as if they'll get much of a Christmas.'

'Now never you fret, Mary. I'll take them all right. We'll manage, don't you worry. It's not my fault the damn strike is on and you wouldn't be having me a blackleg, would you, Christmas or no Christmas?'

'It's not a question of that. You know I'd never ask you to go against the union. But I would ask you to do without a few beers for the sake of the kids.'

This was a facer. They were afraid he'd get wild. If he did they could say good-bye to Christmas Eve.

'That'd be asking more than you think sometimes, Mary,' he said, quite gently. 'When things are like this the days drag on a man. He thinks of what's best for his missus and his kids and the next thing he knows he's doing what's worst for them. It's the way things are.'

They heard her sniff in the silence. They knew by the sound of it she would be wiping her eyes now on her flour-bag apron. His chair scraped and they heard him get up. He would be putting his arms round her.

'Smooging won't get you out of it,' she said. But her voice was different from the words.

'The poor kids,' she said, 'what do they know about strikes? All they know is that it's Christmas.'

They walked along towards the tram stop, one on each side of him. Mick had the sixpence for the tickets in his hand and it was sweating. Part of him was still back in the kitchen. The sixpence had come out of his mother's black purse, not his father's pocket. Did that mean anything? And the strike was in his mind, too. Till today it had been quite exciting, something to tell the other kids. Having the old man at home was better still. When he wasn't digging the garden he'd tell them stories about when he was a boy in Galway or show them how to make cradles to catch birds. Everything he made always worked and the very first time they tried it they caught a blackbird and two ring-eyes. And every day he thought of something new that they might never have known about if he hadn't been on strike.

It was different today, though. He'd gone away straight after dinner and as the afternoon went on the fun just went out of things and they could tell from their mother's crotchetiness that she didn't like it and something was the matter. The way she kept looking at the clock at tea-time put it into their heads what she was worrying about and so they began to worry as well. The strike seemed to become quite a different kind of thing, not like a holiday at all.

Still, here they were walking along Centre Street with him and the tram waiting at the top of it to take them into town and see the sights. And he didn't seem to be worrying, not a bit of it.

'Got that sixpence, Mick?' he said when they stopped by the door of the tram. Ned had already climbed up the step and jumped in.

'You bet I have, Dad.' And he almost blurted out that he
and Ned had two more sixpences, one each that they'd saved
up. But that was still a secret.

'Góod for you, then,' And he took Mick's arm with one
hand and hoisted him right past the step into the tram. He
was very strong.

They got out at the main stop in front of Post Office Square.
There were lines of trams there, all lit up inside, empty ones
going off to get more people and full ones coming all the time.
There were lights everywhere in the streets and shops,
Chinese lanterns and strips of coloured paper. What with the
lights and the moon you could make people out right across
the street as clear as day, even though people said that Dee
Street and Tay Street were the widest streets in New Zealand.

'Come on,' their father said, and they crossed to the
Majestic side, opposite the Post Office. Behind them sand
crackers and bombs were going off in the square and you
could hear kids squealing with laughter.

'Can we go and see, Dad?' said Ned.

'Not just yet, Ned. I want to go round to Esk Street for a
minute and see a man.'

The two boys looked at each other. The Shamrock was in
Esk Street. Of course, Invercargill was a dry town now. Still,
even they knew you were supposed to be able to get sly grog at
the Shamrock. Once he was in there was no telling when he'd
come out. Christmas Eve didn't look much just then.

But he put a hand on the shoulders of each of them and
steered them through the crowds and Mick felt how kind he
was and how mean it was to be so suspicious.

'Now just wait on this side for a bit and have a look at the
shop-windows. I'll be out again in two shakes of a dead lamb's
tail.'

They watched him cross over and go in by the back way.

Ginger Timms went by with his father and mother. He was
blowing at a long paper snake thing that went in and out and
made a crackly noise. They turned to the window behind
them and he didn't see them.

The shop was a Chinese laundryman's and the window was

full of pink strings of crackers and roman candles. The centre piece was a big basket-bomb.

'I wish we could spend our sixpences on that,' Ned said. 'I'd like to buy the biggest basket-bomb there is and blow up Ginger Timms.'

'But he's not a bad joker,' Mick said.

'I'd blow him up all the same.'

Then they saw Ginger coming back. They crossed the road to the other footpath. It was darker because there was only the Shamrock and next to it the Rialto with its window full of second-hand furniture which nobody thought worth lighting up tonight.

'There he is,' Ned said.

He was standing just outside the Shamrock gateway with his back to the footpath. They recognised him by the way he stood with his hands in his pockets and his shoulders squared back. He was talking to someone just inside. As they got closer they recognised the voice. It was Joe Shields. They'd often seen their father talking to him after eleven o'clock Mass on Sundays.

'I'm sorry, Ned,' Joe was saying, 'but that's the best I can do. You know I'm only too anxious to lend a hand if only for old times' sake. But all the boys are in the same boat and this is the time of the year when we all feel it. I'll tell you what, though. If you get a chance later on, come back and we'll have something together.'

'That's all right, Joe,' their father said. 'I know you would if you could. Thanks all the same.'

The two boys were at the gate by now. Mick felt as if he'd dearly like to be somewhere else. Neither his father nor Joe Shields sounded quite natural, as if they wanted to get away from each other and at the same time didn't want to or didn't know how to.

Then Joe noticed them.

'So these are the two young sprigs, eh. Ned. Fine-looking kids too, aren't you, eh? But you'll have to be pretty good if you want to be as good as your father, won't they, Ned?'

He patted their heads. Then he stuck his hand in his hip pocket.

'Here,' he said, 'here's something for you.' He grabbed Ned's hand and put something in it, then Mick's. Mick could tell by the feel it was sixpence. He would look later and make sure.

'Thank you very much, Mr Shields,' they said.

'Well, good night, Joe,' their father said. 'And many thanks. A Merry Christmas, too.' His voice sounded much warmer now.

After they had spent Joe's sixpences on some sand crackers and a bomb each and had had some fun throwing the crackers at people's feet in Post Office Square they all sat down on a wooden seat next to the City Library. They were going to keep the bombs to let off next day after the Christmas dinner.

'Well now,' their father said, when he got back from the Gentlemen's underground, 'what would you like to do next? Would you like to come and help me buy your Christmas presents?'

They looked up at him with delight. Ever since the Shamrock they'd been convinced there weren't going to be any presents and had been making the best of the lights and the crowds and the sand crackers. And that was why they'd hung on to their basket bombs, so as to have something for tomorrow. Neither of them could say a word now.

'Come on,' he said, 'tell me what you want and we'll see what we can do. You first, Ned. What do you want for Christmas? Don't ask for a bike though. That'll have to wait for your lucky day.'

That made Ned laugh. The cheapest bike you could get was six pounds thirteen and six with guarantee.

While Ned was laughing Mick was knitting up his forehead. Would there be enough money for what he wanted? Better wait till Ned had had his and then if it wasn't too much and his father was still smiling he would be able to tell whether he should ask for something nice and cheap.

Ned knew what he wanted. 'I'd like one of those fountain pens Pat Rodgers has. They're only four and six at Playfair's.'

'Only four and six?' his father said. 'And what about you, Mick?'

Mick couldn't tell from the way he said it whether four and six was an enormous lot or whether it wasn't. Perhaps he just ought to ask for a pencil. But perhaps his father had the money after all and half-a-crown would only be a fleabite.

'I'd like a printing-set,' he said. 'They only cost two and six.' And he looked down so as not to see how his father would feel if he didn't have enough money.

'Well,' said his father, 'We'll see what we can do.'

All the way to Playfair's their father seemed to be thinking of something else. Once he stopped and talked with a man they didn't know and it looked as if he were asking the man for something. The man shrugged and threw his hands out sideways and said: 'Search me, Ned.' Their father shook his head in the queer, comical sort of way he had sometimes. 'Well, a Merry Christmas, anyway, Jimmy,' they heard him saying. He came back and joined them and they went on.

People were pouring in and out of Playfair's with their arms full of parcels. Everyone seemed to have a kind of dazed grin on his face and to be in a hurry to squash through one way or the other. But when their father went into a crowd there was always room somehow and it was easy if you kept close up behind him to follow along in the tunnel he made.

'Now where are those pens of yours, Ned?' he said when they got inside.

'Over there at the stationery counter.'

There were some real beauties, 'Swans' and 'Onoto the Pen' and 'Watermans' and kinds you'd never heard of with gold and silver all over them and places to get your name engraved. The four and sixpenny ones were in a big tray right at the front.

Their father picked up a beautiful gold one as big as a barrel and showed it to the girl behind the counter.

'Is this a four and sixpenny one?' he said, smiling at her.

The girl was very smart in a tight black dress. She was wearing a real pearl necklace and she smelt of nice scent. But

she must have been tired with so many people pestering her
and not able to make up their minds what they wanted
because she just looked at the pen and not at him and she said
'No,' a bit huffily. 'The tray at the front,' she added.

He smiled more than ever and took one from the tray. 'I
thought so,' he said. She looked at him then and began to
smile back as she wrapped it up in a bit of fancy paper.

'Which one is it for?' she asked, quite nicely.

'The big one.'

'So he's the scholar?'

'Oh, they're both scholars,' he said. 'Not like their father.'

'Better to be nice than clever,' she said with a special smile.

He held out a half-crown and a two-shilling piece and
wished her a good Christmas.

Mick was wonderfully relieved. His father really had had
the money and he'd been wrong again. Now it would be all
right with the printing set. And they'd get their mother a
present, too, and it would be a real Christmas.

The printing sets were on a shelf in the middle of the shop.
There were all sorts of other things as well and people were
pushing and shoving everywhere and asking how much this
was and how much that was and there weren't enough girls to
look after everybody and kids were blowing toy bugles and
wanting to practise with wheelbarrows and tricycles and their
mothers were trying to stop them. There was a terrible
hullabaloo going on.

Mick opened the box and showed his father how you fixed
the rubber letters into the stamp and how you could print
your name and everything.

'We'll make a printer out of you yet,' his father said, 'and
you can print the *Southland Times*. Now close it up and we'll try
and get out of this madhouse.'

They started to move over to the counter.

'I'll tell you what, Ned,' their father said, 'you and Mick get
out of the crush and wait for me outside. I won't be two ticks.'

The two boys made for the door. But on the way they
stopped to buy their mother the brooch they'd planned to get
with their shilling. And while Ned was paying Mick looked

through a gap in the crowd to the other counter. His father wasn't there. But Mick saw him going towards the other door and at the same time putting the printing set in his pocket.

They found him outside. When they explained what they'd been doing he said: 'That's good kids. And now I think we'd better get the next tram home.'

Their mother seemed even more pleased to see him than them. It was the first time they could remember seeing her kiss him in front of them.

'And what lovely presents,' she said. 'And a present for me, too. You shouldn't have been so extravagant, Ned. I didn't need anything.'

'You should know me better, Mary,' their father said. 'They saved up to buy you that.'

Mick went to bed that night with the printing set on the chair beside him. 'I don't care if he did pinch it,' he said to himself finally, 'it was better than if he'd bought it, in a way.'

Late Snow

Ned was still away at Uncle Tom's and wouldn't be back till
Monday. Paddy and young Matt had gone off to see Tom Mix
at the Civic. There was no one to tempt Mick out into the
uncertain sunlight of the early spring afternoon. Even in the
kitchen it was quiet because Nellie and Eileen were away at
choir practice and Saturday was always the day Mrs Connolly
went to the Rialto to sit in the old armchairs that never got
sold and listen to the auctioneer's jokes and talk with relations
in from the country about the price of poultry-food and butter-
fat or how young Johnny Nolan was letting his farm go to rack
and ruin taking that no-good Calaghan girl to every dance and
race-meeting in the country and she no better than a black
North of Ireland Presbyterian, and they say she drinks too.

So Mick felt fairly sure of getting in an hour's reading
without someone asking him to come and have a look at the
watermill he'd made or lend a hand cleaning out the ferret
cage or mow the back lawn or run up to the store and buy
some seedless raisins and a pound of almonds or whatever else
it was people always wanted you to do as soon as they saw you
trying to get a bit of time to yourself in peace.

They'd found the books this morning in the rubbish dump
at the gravel pit. They all had old Stott the lawyer's name on
them so he must have chucked them out when he moved over
to the north part of the town where all the nobs lived. They'd
been drying on the rack above the range ever since in spite of
Mrs Connolly's demands for all that old rubbish to be taken

out of the way of her cooking. And now one of them, the
Pageant of English Prose, was nearly dry and this little one, *The
Ancient Mariner* was dry enough to read. Mick had already
unstuck most of the pages without tearing them much. He'd
always liked the bits they read in *English Extracts*, painted
ships upon a painted ocean and we were the first that ever
burst into that silent sea and at one stride came the dark. But
this was the first time he'd ever come across it all in one piece
so now was his chance to see what it was all about.

Curled up here on the sofa by the window he scarcely heard
the occasional loud crack of the red pine log in the open grate
or the continual sizzling of gum at its ends. Even when the
corner of his eye caught the little jumps and starts of the wild
kittens under the macrocarpa hedge he didn't consciously look
at them. But he could see the long beard and glittering eye of
that old man all right and the wedding-guest wanting to get
away and wanting to stay at the same time like wanting to go
to the lavatory in the middle of a good picture. And all the
noise coming out the bridegroom's door like the day Molly
Killearn got married, with Uncle Jack's fiddle scraping up
inside and the women all gabbling and the men outside in the
wash-house tasting the jar of Hokonui that Tom MacDonald
had brought.

But he didn't hear his father's boots scraping on the mat out
on the back verandah or hear him cross the kitchen until he
was nearly at the sitting-room door. And by the time he did
hear the door was already opening and it was too late to curse
himself for not having thought of this and hidden on the roof
or in the hedge where no one would have thought of looking
for him. So here was the old man with some job for him,
picking over small potatoes for the pigs, chopping up oyster
shells for the hens or carrying round the hammer and a tin of
staples while they mended a fence.

But, instead of summoning him to any of these or saying:
'There you are with your nose stuck in a book as usual,' his
father just called to him and when he looked up beckoned him
with his head, as quiet and mysterious as if there was a baby
in the house he was afraid of wakening.

What was he up to now? Well, there was nothing to be done about it. The old man could put on a glittering eye, too, when he liked. Mick put the corner of the cushion in the book to mark the place and followed him outside.

By the time he got to the back verandah his father was already half way across the back yard and turned round only long enough to beckon Mick again. On they went, Mick still a few yards behind. But now he felt like a bather who once the water is over his knees thinks he might as well make a job of it and splashes flat on his belly like the rest. Besides they'd passed the back lawn and the hen-house so it wasn't that. And now they'd passed the potato shed so it wasn't that either. What was the old man up to? They went through the cow-shed and round the big wooden fence that cut the cow paddock off from the back garden.

The old man had fenced off the cow paddock this year and put it down in swedes and potatoes. You could see where he'd been working in the potato drills because some of the earth was freshly turned up and his shovel was still upright in the ground. Some job there then, probably.

About half-way along the back fence his father turned round and put his finger to his lips. Like a girl, thought Mick as he stopped to see what would happen next. But at that moment he stood on an old pile of potato shaws and they crackled under him. His father, who had got down on one knee and was looking through a knot-hole in the fence, turned his head to stare at Mick for a second. Not so like a girl. He got clear of the potato shaws.

But what was it all about? The old man was back at the peep-hole and grinning to himself. He wore no collar but the front stud was still in his shirt and you could see the black-green mark it had made against his neck. Size seventeen in collars he took. There were sweat patches spreading from under each side of his upper arm. With the sleeve rolled up and the thick flannel rolled up underneath so that the big vein on his arm was swollen and green against the muscle. An enormous arm. Like a chunk of red pine. It must be something pretty interesting to make him stop working. You usually had a job to get him away from his shovel till it was dark.

His father moved over to make room and signed to him to have a look. Mick got down and squatted on his heels. He screwed up one eye and peered through.

On the other side of the fence and about ten yards away was the manure heap, all ready to be spread. At the base of it there was a round hole and from the hole little showers of black earth were being thrown back. As Mick watched the showers came faster and thicker and thicker. Finally the glossy hindquarters of Darkie, the half-tame black rabbit they'd brought home from Waimatua when she was a bunny, appeared. As she worked back out of the opening heaving the earth clear you could see her pads all wet and velvet.

When she was right out she sat up on her hind legs and listened. Mick could see her nostrils and whiskers twitching. They seemed to keep time with his father's breathing and his own. As if the same breath went in and out of them all. Her eye was wilder and more watchful than usual as she looked around the garden.

At last she was satisfied. She looked down at the dark earth heaped around her and set to work distributing it evenly, smoothing it away till the only sign left of her work was the hole.

Mick's father was nudging him. He pretended not to notice. Darkie finished spreading, sat up and looked and listened and then went back into the hole. The earth began to shower out again but this time it fell further inside the opening, almost blocking it.

Another nudge from his father and Mick nearly fell over backwards. His father took his place at the knot-hole.

Suddenly from away on the other side of the garden Mrs Connolly's voice called:

'Ned, are you there, Ned? Would you like a cup of tea?'

'Damn,' said Mr Connolly. He straightened. 'All right, Nellie,' he called back. 'I'm coming.'

'She's frightened Darkie away,' he said to Mick.

They looked over the top of the fence. Darkie was sitting under the wreckage of a winter cabbage. Her nose was twitching but her knees were tucked under her as if she'd been there all the afternoon.

'The cunning of the creatures,' said Mr Connolly. 'She knows it'll be warmer under the manure heap than anywhere else in case there are any more frosts.'

And when Mick came to think of it, often in the sun after a white frost you could see steam coming out of the manure heap.

'Well,' said his father apologetically. "I thought you might like to see, you being fond of animals. But don't tell your mother about it. You know what she's like about having young animals running round the house.'

It was a few weeks later that the snow came. The night before, Mr Connolly had shaken his head when he came in.

'I don't like the look of it, Nellie. There's a ring round the moon and it's cold enough for snow.'

'But surely it wouldn't go snowing on us now, Ned, with the garden coming along so nicely and the earliest lambing they've had for years.'

'I don't like the look of it all the same. I think one of you boys had better come up with me after tea and we'll put the covers on the cows.'

'It's all right, Dad,' Ned said. 'I didn't like the look of it much either, so Mick and I put them on when we'd finished milking.'

'You did then? Well, good for you, son.' He had his boots and collar and tie off now and sat down in his chair by the fire. His wife had already taken the big plate of steak and onions and fried potato from the oven and set it in his place.

And sure enough, when they woke in the morning it was to snow. Paddy and Matt were delighted and watched it out the window from the bed. They didn't have to get up yet. But it was a different matter for Ned and Mick. They had to get out into it to attend to the cows. In the kitchen Mrs Connolly had been up since six.

'A dirty morning,' she said. 'This'll put the country back a step. I felt sorry for your poor father this morning, up at five to get off on that early shift. Still, he'll be back in time to get a good lunch and it may clear.'

Mick left Ned pulling out turnips from under the snow-covered heap. It was always his job to cut them up for the bran mash while Mick brought the cows down from the hill. This morning they were standing at the gate ready and miserable, with their backs to the driving flakes. They set up a roar when they saw him. No trouble today trying to get them past the fresh grass that grew on the roadsides.

After the milking they decided to leave them in the home paddock with enough hay to keep them going for the morning. Cutting it with the snow slithering in clots from the top of the stack was their last chore of the morning. Then, quite suddenly, they began to enjoy the snow. Before long all the boys of the neighbourhood were there and the cows chewing away at their hay watched the snow-fights thoughtfully and listened to the shouting.

But by afternoon Mick was tired of it. Ned had got him and Paddy out into the back paddock after dinner to make an igloo. It was good fun at first. But once you got the walls over a certain height and wanted to make them curve towards the centre, they kept on falling inwards. It became a back-breaking job instead of a game. Only Ned's determination kept them at it. Even then they gradually began to feel it was his igloo, not theirs. And there was a bitter wind, with a bite of hail in it.

Skinny Dunick came along the back road with his dog, Rover. He was Paddy's great friend.

'Where are you off to, Skinny?'

'Over to Mason's bush to see if we can get a rabbit. We'll be able to see their tracks in the snow. Why don't you come? Bring Jack.'

Ned was squatting on his haunches and frowning as he tried to work out some new way of balancing the blocks. Paddy saw his chance and bolted, Jack after him.

'Hey, come back here, young Paddy, where are you off to?' But it would have been too hard to catch him in that snow.

'No guts, that's the trouble, Mick. A fat lot of rabbits they'll catch, them and their tracking. Any rabbit in his senses'll stay in his hole today.'

And so would anyone else, Mick was thinking. He kept thinking too of that fire in the sitting-room. But how was he going to get there? Poor old Ned was so set on building his igloo. And the more failures he had the more stubborn he got. He'd be there till it was time to get the cows in. But you couldn't very well go away and leave him. He always thought you felt the same way as he did about things. And if you didn't he'd make you. Unless Mick could think of a good excuse he'd be stuck. There was no good trying to make a break for it. Ned would be on the watch now and that two years extra made him faster and stronger.

'Mick! Mick, where are you?' His mother's voice. He could see her over the top of the fence, standing by the woodheap where the gooseberries began.

'Women,' said Ned bitterly. 'Why the blazes can't they leave us alone. Pretend you don't hear.'

'Mick!'

'She can see us,' said Mick. 'I'd better go.'

He set off towards the back gate.

'Come here, Mick,' his mother said, as he crossed the yard. 'Go in and put on your Sunday coat. I've been thinking it's time you had a new one and I might see something nice in town today.'

'Are you going to town in this weather, Mum?' he said when he came back, the jacket looking very clean against his torn shorts and dirty boots.

'I've got to. I promised poor Mrs O'Neill in the hospital I'd see her today and it'll be very miserable for the poor creature there in this weather if no one comes and she so bad with the gallstones. So I might as well stop off in the town, while I'm at it. Now, let's have a look at you. Yes, it's much too small for you, you're coming out in all directions like a squeezed sausage. A size bigger we'll need. Perhaps two sizes.'

'Now, Mum, I don't want all the other kids laughing at me after Mass on Sunday and saying: Is your old man in bed?'

'Don't speak like that about your father. You'll get what I

think's good for you. The rate you're growing you need every-thing too big or it'll be the ruination of us all, keeping you in clothes. It's elastic jackets and leather pants you ought to be wearing.'

But he could tell she'd remember what he'd said all the same.

There was always a great scene before they got her away, what with remembering the buttons to be matched, and the prescription for Eileen's cough, and the final discussion about the new frying pan, and Nellie's new ribbon, and the instructions about keeping a good fire on in the range and not dreaming and letting it go out on them, and the search for the tram time-table and the trial trip out the door and the hurried rush back again and: 'You'll miss that tram, Mum,' and: 'I can't go without my purse, can I, now where did I put it?' But at last they got her safely away.

Mick looked out the window. Sharp against a sky that looked like a bruise he could see Ned toiling in the snow with all the grimness a hopeless job called out in him. He had forgotten all about Mick. He was used in the end to being left alone with the impossible.

Mick dropped back the corner of the curtain and looked round the kitchen. Nellie and Eileen had the cookery books out already. No doubt what they were up to. Making toffee. That'd keep them busy for a while.

All the same, after he'd put a new log on the sitting-room fire, he hid their music under one of the mats just in case they took it into their heads to practise 'Little Brown Bird' or 'She is Far from the Land' again.

And then he shut the door and got out *The Ancient Mariner*. He knew parts of it by heart now. The great thing about it was that it was so easy to remember the bits you liked and they gave you something to think about when you were milking or going head on into the rain as you followed the cows. Every time he came to the albatross he thought of the stuffed albatross in the museum upper gallery and that led on to the lovely humming-birds in the glass case and all those different-coloured moths you never saw in New Zealand. And then there were the swordfishes and sharks and of course the jawbone of a whale that was hung in the centre and looked like a gigantic wishbone. Or if you read about the wedding-guest that led you on to the time all the kids went to the tin-canning when the Crowe couple came to live opposite – .

They seemed very quiet out in the kitchen all of a sudden. Not a giggle out of them. Then he heard why. The tramp of his father's cow-boots. Coming towards the door, too. By the time he got the window open it'd be too late. Under the sofa? Hopeless, he'd be seen from the door.

The door was open now, anyhow. His father was beckoning him out. Had he ever been to sea? He never talked much about that time just after he left Ireland. What was it this time? There seemed to be a curse on him every time he tried to read. He got up and followed.

In the garden the snow lay heavy, drifted against the fences. Only under the cabbages and the gooseberry bushes, now just turning green, there were wet, black patches. The apple trees seemed sorry they had taken the spring at its word.

But his father didn't look left or right. The first time Mick had ever seen him walk along the path without stopping to look at something and see how it was getting on, or mutter to himself about trying shallots there next time or putting in a bit more lime.

They stopped at the manure heap. Sickly yellow snow covered it, with sodden black corners sticking out here and there. And today you could see the opening to Darkie's burrow. A week or two back after the young ones were born she'd sealed it up and only used to open it for herself. But now either she'd opened it or the weight of snow had broken it in. The opening was full of dirty snow-water, dark, dirty-yellow. The heat of the manure must have melted the snow.

Half on the surface, half under it, floated a baby rabbit, its eyes still closed, drowned before it ever saw the light or knew the colour of snow. The rest of them would be drowned inside.

Mick didn't dare look up. His father hated them to cry.

'Look,' said his father.

Under a desolate cabbage Darkie was crouched on a bare

black patch of earth. Her nostrils were twitching and her sides were moving in and out. Her eyes were velvety and dark, the old wildness out of them.

Mr Connolly went over and picked her up. It was the first time she'd let herself be caught for ages.

'I'll take her in and put her by the fire to warm,' he said.

It was very cold. Mick felt embarrassed. As if what they felt about Darkie separated them and they were afraid to look at each other.

He watched his father go towards the house. What was to be done now? He couldn't go back to the albatross. The girls would be talk, talk, talking about Darkie.

He got through the hole in the back fence. Ned was still digging away.

'Where the hell have you been?' Ned said as Mick came up. 'I think I've found the way to do it. Just give us a hand with this bit, will you? We'll have to get it done before milking time. Then it'll freeze solid tonight.'

Death of a Dog

'Now stop your arguing and get to bed,' said Mrs Connolly. 'It's long past your bedtime already and your father's too tired after his late shift to listen to any more of your nonsense.'

'But it's not nonsense, Mum,' said Ned. 'Jack didn't mean to bite her. It was her own fault for teasing him when he was eating.'

'No, I don't think he really meant to, Mum,' said Eileen. She looked over at the boys placatingly. But they only looked back at her grimly. Too late for that sort of talk now. Why hadn't she left poor old Jack to have his bone in peace? Or if she had to go teasing him why couldn't she shut her mouth instead of rushing up to the house as if all the devils in hell were after her instead of just a bit of a bite on the knee. Anyone'd think it was a rattlesnake the fuss there'd been with their iodine and poultices and all the rest of it. Women!

'It was a nasty bite, though,' said Nellie. Not that she meant any harm. She just liked a fuss and she was too stupid to see it was practically asking for old Jack to be killed, talking like that.

'I don't care what you say, the dog will have to be shot.' Mrs Connolly had made up her mind and nothing could shift her. The worst of it was that if she'd made up her mind the opposite way she'd have been just the same. She'd get it into her head that they thought they could talk her into thinking black was white and once she got that way you couldn't even convince her black was black.

'The neighbours have been complaining long enough,' she went on, 'and the poor postman hardly dares come in the gate. And now he's bitten one of our own there's no telling what he'll do next. He'll be having the law on us, that's what he'll be doing, and before we know where we are we'll be getting a bit of blue paper. The dog'll have to be shot, that's all there is to it. And let that be an end to it.'

The boys looked at their father. He liked Jack. Surely he wouldn't let this happen. There was a silence. He was always slow to speak.

'Now, Ned,' said Mrs Connolly, 'don't you go being soft with those boys. I've told you and told you there's no good bringing dogs home to these boys. A dog with boys for master has no master. They'll always cock him up and end by spoiling him the way they have with Jack. We've been threatened with the law over him already and if you don't do something this time it'll be the law we'll have.'

Mr Connolly turned his chair at right angles to the table and rested his weight on his left forearm as he faced them.

'Your mother's right,' he said. And he looked down at his plate where the fat was already beginning to thicken about the remains of his chop.

That was final. There was no hope that way.

'It's no use,' said Ned, as soon as the lights were out. 'We'll have to find some other way.' Mick and he were sitting up in the double bed they shared. On the other bed Paddy and Matt were sitting up against the wall with the blankets wrapped round them.

'Couldn't we take him out to Manion's farm,' Paddy suggested, 'and get them to look after him till the storm blows over?'

'No good,' Ned decided, after a moment. 'They've only got sheep and he's a heeler. Besides, we couldn't get him out there in time. It's too far.'

'I'll tell you what,' said Mick. 'Why not get up as soon as it's light and take him up to the bush. We could tie him up there and take turns smuggling food to him.'

'That's it,' Paddy broke in. 'And the day after tomorrow's Saturday. We could take him on to Manion's and get young Joe to look after him for us.'

'You know, I think that's it,' said Ned, and they all began to feel suddenly that it was reasonable. For if Ned thought a thing was all right it was all the same whether it was morning or night time he would do it. He wouldn't forget about it in the morning or say it was hopeless.

'Won't Dad be wild when he finds out,' said Matt. 'I'd like to stay with Jack up in the bush and he could catch rabbits and I'd cook them and there'd be no need to come home or go to school or anything.'

'You shut up, young Matt,' and Paddy jogged him with his elbow. 'This isn't a silly kids' game. It's a matter of life and death.'

Ned and Mick began to feel uncomfortable. This sort of talk made it sound less like common sense.

'All shut up now,' said Ned, 'and get to sleep. You won't have so much to say in the morning.'

The moon had come up. Away in the distance Black's retriever began to bark at it. Then came Jack's bark answering. The last time he fought the retriever Mick had to hold him by the collar while Ned prised his jaws open with the handle of the rabbiting adze. Mick's memory worked back through all that long list of fights and his eyes filled with tears. But they weren't going to let him die.

The retriever had stopped barking. Through the open window you could hear Jack's chain clink as he went back to his kennel.

Thinking he was smothering Mick woke. Ned stopped shaking him but kept his hand over his mouth and gestured towards the other bed.

'We won't wake them,' Ned said. Remembering everything, Mick got that hollow feeling in his stomach again that was always the same no matter what you were sorry or afraid about. It was better to be asleep. But you had to face the day.

'Hurry,' Ned whispered. 'I think I slept in a bit.'

They went out to the kitchen and took their boots from the super-heater cupboard where they'd been drying. They sat down and began to lace them up.

In the bedroom off the kitchen there was a heaving and a long, low yawn like a groan. They looked at each other. But it was too late. Mrs Connolly came out in her nightgown to light the fire.

She looked at them and looked at the kitchen clock. It was not quite six.

'You're early on the go this morning, aren't you?' she said.

'Oh, well, we were awake so we thought we might as well get up and get the cows,' said Mick. He was quicker than Ned at that kind of thing – Ned always went red. Mick could tell he was going red now the way he was bending down over his boots.

While she was getting the kindling out of the oven they slipped out and round by the wood-heap where she couldn't see them.

Jack jumped wildly up at them. But Ned caught at his collar so the chain wouldn't make a noise. 'Down, Jack, down,' he said. He unslipped the chain from the collar. It was to look as if Jack had got free by himself. They'd use an old leg rope to tie him up when they got there.

They followed the line of the gorse hedges so as not to be seen from the kitchen window. Once they were on the grass road it was all right. Jack had calmed down, too, as if he sensed there was something up. He kept quietly in to heel though the dew was full of wild scents and you could smell the spring coming.

But it was taking longer than they thought it would. There was a ghost of mist still loitering in the peat-hollow beyond the frog-pond, though the first roosters had long since had their crow. Ned kept taking out the five bob watch they'd bought out of the rabbit-skin money. It was his turn to wear it this week.

'You know, Mick,' he said. 'We're too late, we'll never make it and get back in time for the milking. It's my fault for sleeping in like that.' But he kept on hurrying on towards the edge of bush, still so remote beyond the mist.

'I'll tell you what, Ned,' said Mick. 'What about the old underground hut? We could tie him up there for today. And then tonight after school one of us could take him on the rest of the way. The old man'll never find him there.'

'I'm not so sure. You know how shrewd he is. But there's nothing else we can do. If we're late back they'll smell a rat anyway. Yes, that's what we'll do.'

They turned half left and climbed towards the clump of gorse on Faraway Hill. The year before they had all set to work digging the underground hut. By the time they had dug down to the yellow clay the others had deserted. But Ned had kept on with the big mattock till it was deep enough. Only by then the summer was already gone and the rain coming. And the very first time they had lit a fire in it to boil eggs and potatoes the roof had caught fire. But the gorse round it had not caught and the place was still well hidden.

They fastened the rope to the heavy manuka pole which had held up the scrub roof. Jack sat down in the middle of the dugout and looked up at them, wagging his tail.

They patted and hugged him and then climbed out. He looked up at them and put his head to one side.

'Good-bye, Jack. We'll be back tonight, so don't worry. You just chew away at that bone and wait for us.'

They set off for home, bringing the cows with them.

It was a longer, drearier morning at school than it had ever been before. Brother Athanasius's jokes had never been so feeble, Mick thought. And though he had no difficulty with the correction of sentences and remembered about Cromwell and the massacre of Drogheda and got his answers to the questions from the Pink Catechism right word for word he was beaten by Dennis Beaton at mental arithmetic. It was easy enough to do things you liked but when it came to long tots it took more effort to be the best. And when you thought of poor old Jack and that winter's night when Dad first came in out of the rain and put down his railway lamp that had a red and a green and an ordinary glass in it and took out of his big overcoat pocket the fat little black and tan puppy, well, it was pretty hard to keep your mind on figures then.

'I don't know what's the matter with you today, Mick. Tell him the right answer, Dennis.'

And there were the times when they came home from the Bluff Regatta or the railway excursion to Queenstown. As the whole family came trudging up to the gate with the empty picnic baskets and their mother wondering if the fire had kept in and if the hens had got into the garden there Jack'd be, waiting for them behind the gate, his nose stuck through the pickets to see if he could get a scent of them coming down the road or hear their voices. And when they opened the gate he'd be nearly frantic with excitement and go running round himself in circles, grinning and trying to catch his own tail. So that even their mother couldn't help showing her smile, though she always pretended not to like dogs, dirty big beasts running all over the house with their great, muddy paws, carrying the Lord only knows what germs.

'Yes, Brother Athanasius. By the four marks of the Church I mean that the Church is one, she is Holy, she is Catholic, she is Apostolic.'

Jack taking them as far as Scott's paddocks on the way to school and looking after them from the gate as they went on, the morning wind stirring in the plume of his tail. Jack on Saturdays watching them pump up the bikes and following them down to the ferret cage when they went to put Snowy in the sugar bag for the day's rabbiting. And trotting home behind them at night, tired and tireless, after the day's wild runs among the biddy-bids and tree stumps, and the splashing in the peat-swamps and the stampedes in the gorse, and sometimes the rewarding snap as the rabbit doubled and the pattings and congratulations, and the flung carcase for him to worry and crunch while they took up the nets and stowed away the skin, stabbing their knives in the crisp, grass-covered ground to clean them. And the hawks hovering overhead, and the sun dropping cold towards the mist which sidled out of the bush and swamp, and at last the ride back with their voices reaching only a little way into the dark and after the head wind and the miles a glimpse of the light in the kitchen window, seen from Oteramika Road across the wetness of McGregor's Flat.

Jack, the great fighter, who walked Georgetown stiff and proud as a boxer and met every strange dog, no matter what his size, with bristling hair and whose teeth came flashing and fast behind his challenge. Jack in whose reputation they could have walked from one side of the town to the other, wrapped in it like a cloak.

And now perhaps they'd already seen the last of him.

'And now all join with me in saying the midday Angelus.'

As they came down the creek and across the paddocks they reassured one another while their hearts sank lower and lower. Whatever happened there'd be trouble, that was certain.

'Now, remember, you kids,' said Ned. 'Not a word out of you whatever he says. He can't kill us. Anyhow, it's me that'll get all the blame, being the eldest. But he might try to worm it out of you. All you two need say, Paddy and Matt, is that you had nothing to do with it. That's not telling a lie, really, because you didn't, you only had something to say about it. But it's me and Mick he'll go for and me mostly, worse luck.'

When they came round the corner of the house the first thing they saw was the rifle. It was leaning at an angle against the kitchen door. Mr Walsh's .32, the one they always borrowed for the pig-killing.

They went in and sat down on the form their father had made to hold the four of them at meal-times. Their mother was rushing to and fro with hot plates. She hardly looked at them and you couldn't tell what she was thinking. Their father must be still down in the garden. They knew his shift ended at ten that morning. No sign of the girls so no way of finding out what was brewing.

They'd planned to say nothing till the subject was mentioned. But as they bent over their soup-plates they didn't have to look to see the rifle still standing at the door. Had he found Jack and shot him? Or had he borrowed the rifle and then not been able to find him?

A shadow darkened the doorway. He wiped his boots on the old potato sack and came in. He crossed to the fireplace and sat down. Mrs Connolly put his soup in front of him. He took up his spoon and began. There was complete silence. Mick felt as if the rifle was leaning on his brain.

And now the stew. He went on eating. He was waiting for them to ask.

At last the strain was too much for him. He finished his meal and stood up. Four pairs of eyes followed him up, fastened on his face where it stood level with the mantelpiece.

'Thanks for digging the grave for Jack,' he said. 'It saved me a lot of trouble, just having to fill it in. You didn't think Mr Walsh was watching you when you went up the road, did you?'

Four pairs of eyes looked down at their plates. Not even Matt whimpered. They weren't going to let him have the satisfaction of seeing any tears. They didn't know the jeer came from a heart as sore as their own. Worse, because it couldn't let itself be sorry.

'I'll say this for him, he was tough. It took three bullets.'

'That'll do now, Ned,' said Mrs Connolly. 'You've killed their dog. Isn't that enough without tormenting them about it?'

He looked at her, astonished and hurt. It wasn't the first time she had acted as if he were wholly responsible for what they had decided on together.

But the boys weren't fooled. No speeches from her would make them forget her part in it. It was just like her, trying to change sides when it was too late. At least you always knew where you were with him.

They trooped out in silence. If they hurried there was time to get up to Faraway Hill before they had to go back to school.

Part of the dug-out was filled in. You could see the fresh yellow clay piled up in one corner. Soon the gorse would grow over Jack and the rabbits would burrow there and he'd never know.

They said nothing to one another and avoided one another's eyes till they were well on their way back down the grass road again. But to themselves they were saying: 'Good-bye, Jack. We won't forget you.'

After they had thrown stones on Mr Walsh's roof there was nothing for it but to go back to school. As they climbed through Scott's big gate one after the other, Ned smiled a bit, suddenly.

'Three bullets it took. And the old man's a good shot. He was a great dog all right.' And that was their first taste of comfort.

Roof of the World

The coast was clear. Mrs Connolly had gone off with Eileen to the Paddy's Market for the Saint Vincent de Paul Society. And their father was on the Dunedin express run.

Their mother had left them to do the washing up so as to make an early start and Ned was to do the churning. Mick and Paddy finished first and left him grinding grimly away — he never stopped the way they did to lift the lid to see whether the butter had come when they knew very well it hadn't.

First of all they went down the garden and filled their pockets with gooseberries. Then they went round the far side of the house where there was a narrow strip of lawn between the house and the macrocarpa hedge but where nobody ever went much because it wasn't sunny. They had a look at the wild cat's kittens but didn't come too close — Mick still had scabs from the scratches he got the last time. Then they climbed up on the wooden tankstand, took hold of the rim of the round, corrugated iron tank, and hauled themselves up to where they could reach the roof guttering. From there it was an easy matter to get right up on the roof.

For a while they sat side by side with their feet dangling over, squashing the inside out of the gooseberries and throwing the skins into the open tank. When they had enough they began to chase each other with the ripe berries they could no longer be bothered eating.

The clatter of their hobnailed boots on the roof brought Ned out on to the verandah below.

'Hey, you kids, cut out making all that noise.'

'Ned,' called Paddy, 'sling us up Dad's bike pump, will you?'

'What do you want it for? I will if you promise not to go squirting me.'

'I promise.'

Ned got the pump from its shelf at the end of the verandah and flung it up to where Paddy knelt in the gutter, looking down into the yard. Paddy caught it neatly.

'Come on, Mick,' he said. 'Let's fill her up and lay an ambush for the postman.' He walked over the roof to the tank, his boots grinding on the iron and making shiny lead streaks through the red paint. He leaned over the tank on his stomach and filled up the pump.

Mick watched with a certain lassitude. He was thinking of the two frogs he had put in the tank the year before with the idea of starting an aquarium. Then he had forgotten about them and by the time he remembered they were floating belly-up on the surface. The water had been too far below the lip of the tank that dry summer and they had not been able to get out and have a rest. They couldn't have had much to eat either. They still haunted him from time to time and at the moment the thought of that murderous failure left him with no heart for squirting the postman. Besides, the postman mightn't have any letters and if he didn't he wouldn't need to come within squirting distance. Even if he did have any letters they'd probably be bills. Or perhaps there'd even be something from the police about Mrs Quelch's broken window.

A sparrow perched on the macrocarpa hedge opposite. Without moving the rest of his body Mick felt in his pocket and pulled his shangeye out gently by the prong. But the leather pouch coming out after the prong dragged a small mirror as well. It fell on the roof with a clatter. The sparrow swivelled a beady eye, twitched its tail and was off. Mick put the shangeye in his pocket. Then he bent and picked up the mirror. He had pinched it and a comb lately from Eileen. They were useful when you went swimming; though why he'd got interested in combing his hair lately he didn't bother to ask

himself. Now he studied his face in the mirror and felt his chin
musingly. Nothing there yet. Ned had nothing either, though,
even though he was two years older.

He sighed and put the mirror back in his pocket. Then he
turned to look at Paddy who was now crouching just at the
front of the slope which ran up to the front-room chimney.
From this position he overlooked the path by which the
postman would have to come.

Mick had an idea. On hands and knees he began to crawl
up the slope to the peak of the gable, putting his feet against
the lead-capped nails so as not to slip. At the top he lay with
only his head showing. His spread weight and the roof nails
against his toecaps stopped him from slithering down again.

On the other side of the road Mr Pratt was in his garden,
digging weeds out of the lawn with a queer-shaped fork. Mick
took out his mirror and manipulated it to catch the sun. The
trapped light began to dance obediently about Mr Pratt's
head. Mr Pratt moved and the reflection played on the grass
below his face. He straightened himself up slowly with one
hand on the small of his back in the 'Every Picture Tells a
Story' position. He looked about him puzzled. The light
flashed in his eyes and then as he began to track it to its source
Mick disappeared behind the gable.

When Mick took another look Mr Pratt was bending over
his weeds again. Once more the light began to dance in front
of him. But Mr Pratt knew his neighbours and this time he
managed to stoop right down and look between his legs
towards the most likely place.

It was too late to bob down so Mick stayed where he was
and grinned. Mr Pratt grinned back and shook his fist.

Well, it was no good trying to trick him any more. Mick
looked around for fresh victims. And there was the postman
coming along from the direction of Stone's house.

'He's coming, Paddy.'

'Yes, I've spotted him.'

The postman crossed the road towards their front gate, the
light from Mick's mirror frisking about his eyes. The front
gate clicked and he came down the path. Paddy let him go out

of sight to the front door. They heard the lid of the letterbox rattle and the postman blew his whistle. As he came into sight again on the path Paddy let fly with the pump. The water squirted in a long leaping then dying stream, falling short except for the first few drops.

The postman, his face red with the heat and his heavy black uniform, turned and looked up to see their laughing faces.

'At it again, you young devils,' he said. 'I've a good mind to tell your mother.'

He went out the front gate and they could see as his head bobbed along the front hedge that he was grinning. He wouldn't tell.

They joined forces again at the bottom of the slope just as Ned's head appeared above the tank. When he had climbed on to the roof they could see he was carrying their mother's best umbrella. His face had a solemn, absent look.

'What are you going to do, Ned?' asked Paddy.

'I'm going to try out this parachute stunt. I reckon that if I put the umbrella up and jump off holding it I ought to float down gently. Be interesting to see whether it works or not.'

'But it's a hell of a height, Ned,' said Mick.

'Can't help that. If you don't try a thing out how can you ever tell whether it's going to work or not?'

This convinced Paddy. He sat down with his legs hanging over the edge and resting on the tank rim. Mick was still sceptical but he sat down too.

'He might break his neck,' he murmured anxiously to Paddy. It was no good arguing with Ned, though. When he was like this you just had to wait and see what happened.

Ned had put up the umbrella and taken his stand near the edge of the roof. He seemed to be thinking.

'Go on, Ned, what are you waiting for?' said Paddy. He could already see Ned floating gently in the air. And he was impatient for it to come to his turn.

'Got to wait till the wind's just right,' Ned said. There was no wind of any sort this late summer day; but neither of them for a moment doubted that this was what he was waiting for.

Ned took a deep breath. 'Here goes,' he said and jumped.

Both hands above his head and holding the umbrella he dropped like a stone. Not expecting to fall so fast he fell badly with his legs too stiff and then tumbled over on one shoulder. He lay there.

'Are you all right, Ned?' Mick called.

Ned sat up red in the face. 'Of course I'm all right,' he said, when he got his breath back.

'Well, that's the end of that, I suppose,' Paddy sounded very glum.

'What do you mean, end? You can't say a thing won't work if you only try it once.' He picked up the umbrella, closed it and climbed back on to the roof.

'The wind might have been wrong, or anything,' he explained as he opened the umbrella again. He wet his finger and held it up. Then he pulled it down again, looked at it, considered. 'It's from the east,' he said. 'I'd better go off at an angle this time.'

He turned half away from the tank side and jumped again. He went down as fast as the first time, only his feet, they noticed, landed the right way and took the force of the fall up to his bent knees.

'Give us a go, Ned,' said Paddy. 'You're probably too heavy. I'm the lightest so it'll probably work with me.'

'It's a bit high for you to be jumping if it doesn't work,' Ned said doubtfully. 'After all, you're the youngest.' But he climbed up again with the umbrella.

'Mick ought to try next,' he said.

'But I don't reckon it'll work whoever tries it,' Mick said.

'Go on, you're frightened, that's what,' Paddy said.

'I am not,' Mick said. 'I'll give her a go if you like, Ned. But I still don't believe it.'

'Frightened,' said Paddy.

'I'll show you if I'm frightened,' Mick said. He got to his feet, walked along the edge, stopped to get his balance, and then jumped without any umbrella, landing neatly with bent knees and bottom sinking to his heels.

'Well, anyhow, let's have a go,' said Paddy.

Ned looked at him approvingly. There was something

disloyal about what Mick had done. It took the excitement out of the thing a bit. So he warmed Paddy's faith. 'It'd be interesting to see if it worked with someone lighter. But I don't want you to get hurt.'

'Don't you fret your fat,' said Paddy. As he was two years younger than Mick he had developed a reckless competitive courage long since.

'All right, then. Here you are.'

Mick had climbed up again by now, feeling rather guilty though still sceptical. But it was plain from the way Paddy looked, standing on the edge under the open umbrella with a blissful look on his face, that he didn't doubt for a moment it was going to work for him and that he would float like thistledown.

Paddy jumped and hurtled down as fast as Ned had done. On the way down he dropped the umbrella but it took no longer to land than he did.

'My turn now,' Mick said.

'But it's no go, Mick,' Ned said. 'You saw the way the umbrella fell. It's too heavy. Hold on, Paddy. I'm coming down.' Not bothering any more to climb by way of the tankstand he jumped down on to the lawn.

Paddy was already on his feet, bouncing around, disappointment forgotten. 'I did a jolly good jump, didn't I, Ned. It's the first time I've ever jumped from so high.'

'Yes, very good, Paddy. But come on in to the wash-house and I'll show you my new water-mill. It's got much bigger paddles than that other one that wouldn't go. I think it's going to be a real beaut.'

They disappeared round the tankstand. The umbrella still lay on the grass.

Mick jumped down, too. Just like Ned. Never did anything just for fun. If it didn't work he lost interest until he'd thought up something new.

Still, you could never be sure. Perhaps it might work, after all, especially now when no one was looking. Though of course it wouldn't.

Mick took the umbrella and climbed back on to the roof.

Perhaps the distance wasn't great enough to give the parachute a chance? He climbed up the slope to the peak of the gable. That was a good ten feet higher. But it was also a good ten feet higher than he'd ever jumped before. If the parachute didn't work he might break his neck. It made you giddy to look down.

He looked down, all the same. It made him dizzy with a queer feeling in his stomach. Of course the damned thing wouldn't work. And there'd be no one there to pick up the pieces. They wouldn't even believe that he'd ever jumped from so high. So if he didn't break his neck this time he'd have to do the jump all over again to make them believe him. And he'd never get away with it twice.

Just like Ned to get him into such a mess and then clear out without even bothering to watch. Well, he had to go through with it now or he'd never be able to look himself in the face again.

'Hail Mary, full of grace,' he began to gabble as he jumped. The umbrella gave no support. The green ground shot up at him. He just managed to get set in time for the landing. His knees came up at him but he managed to throw himself back just before they hit his chin and he lay on his back with the breath knocked out of him.

'I knew I was right. Just another of Ned's stupid ideas,' he thought, forgetting how until the moment he jumped he had believed right inside himself that this time it would work and he would float down like a spider on a thread. He felt himself over to see if any bones were broken.

The Tree

It was well after three when Ned and Mick finished bagging
the potatoes. Ned got the big stable broom and Mick held the
sack open, just below the lip of the doorstep. Leaving only
streaks of fine dust behind it on the floor and a wet patch
where the heap had been, Ned's broom swept in front of it all
the rotten potatoes and the ones that were too small to be any
good. Then the two of them caught the sack by an ear each
and dragged it into the fowl run. The hens scattered in front of
them but when the sack was upended and emptied they were
soon back and picking in the mess, grabbing special little
morsels for themselves and scuttling off to eat by themselves.

'Well,' said Mick, looking at his hands all smeared with dirt
and rotten potato, 'that's that. A good Saturday afternoon
wasted. It's too late to take the ferrets out between now and
milking time. What on earth shall we do now? There's over an
hour to put in before we can bring the cows home.'

Ned felt the challenge. 'We'll soon think of something.
Come on and we'll wash our hands first anyway.'

In the wash-house Ned rinsed his hands under the tap and
dried them on an old sugar-bag apron of his mother's. While
Mick took his place at the tap he sat on the separator bench.
His eyes ranged around the walls and fixed on the crosscut
saw suspended by its handles from two nails above the copper.

'I'll tell you what, Mick,' he said. 'We'll cut down the tree.'

'What tree?'

'The macrocarpa tree, of course. The old man's always

going crook because the thrushes and blackbirds roost there and come down and gobble up his blackcurrants. Well, he'll get a surprise tomorrow when he comes home and finds no tree.'

Mick looked at him doubtfully and then at the saw. The handles made you just itch to get to work on something with it. But he hadn't any grudge against the tree.

'And afterwards we can cut it up for firewood. It'll keep us going for weeks,' Ned went on.

Mick still hesitated.

'Of course, it isn't the easiest thing in the world to cut down a tree. You've got to make them fall the right way and that's easier said than done. You remember how old Andy Keogh brought that big broadleaf down right on top of his own kitchen. Only the real bushmen can do it properly.'

The word 'bushmen' did the trick. Mick climbed up on top of the copper and lifted the top handle off its nail so that Ned could pull the saw out from the wall. They carried it, a handle each, out through the backyard and past the woodheap. The sun caught it as it rippled between them. It made a noise like steel water. There was something fierce about it, like a stallion. It couldn't wait to get at the tree.

They walked down the path and between the rows of gooseberry bushes, long since picked. From his post at the rear handle Mick looked over to the corner of the garden. The trunk of the macrocarpa tree reared up from behind the wooden fence and spread its broad green hands. It had been there longer than he could remember. It was alive and they were going to murder it. Still, it was only a tree.

Ned unlatched the wooden door in the broad fence and it swung back by its own weight on the leather hinges. They took the saw through and came up to the tree. Looking up they caught glimpses of the sky through its deep green darkness.

'It leans outwards,' Ned said, 'so we'll start on the fence side. When she crashes she ought to fall just by the gorse hedge.'

They crouched one on each side of the tree and ran the teeth of the saw to and fro until it had cut through the bark. When the colour of the sawdust had changed from dark brown to white they stopped.

'Now remember,' Ned said, 'we've got to keep the saw exactly level or otherwise it'll start sticking and jamming as soon as we get properly into it.'

Mick looked up at the banked darkness and then back down the trunk to the brief white scar where the teeth had begun to bite. It didn't seem possible there was any connection between what they were doing and the life of the tree.

Ned was spitting on his hands. 'It stops the blisters coming.'

Mick spat on his hands too.

They looked at each other along the flat, malevolent saw. Ned's eyes were solemn. They were always like that when he was set on something. It was their way of showing excitement.

'Now,' Ned said.

The saw worked to and fro between them. The white sawdust trickled down below the cut, filtering at first into the cracks in the bark and then, as these filled, sliding straight down and heaping in a little pile at the foot. The teeth ripped and tore closer towards the heart, greedily.

All through milking Ned was making plans. As soon as they were old enough they would get a job at Port Craig. They would be known as the boldest bushmen in the south and as a team they would beat the Aussies at all the axemen's carnivals. Nick milked away in silence and felt the sting in his blisters each time he squeezed.

'Old Con Kelly says you can always tell a bushwhacker by the shape of his arm muscles, the way they're long and supple and not bunched up like the muscles of a man who works with the shovel. We must have a look at ours after we're finished and see if it's made any difference. And we'll get Dad to take us to the Tuatapere sports next year and watch the crosscut competitions. We must try our hands with the axe, too, later on when the trunk's dry enough.'

But listening to Ned wasn't quite the same as working with him on the other end of the saw. It didn't get across to you the same. By the time they had put the cows up, brought the milk to the wash-house, separated and come in to find their mother was home and supper ready, most of Mick's ardour had vanished.

'Did you boys finish picking those spuds?' asked Mrs Connolly.

'Yes, Mum.'

'And how is Strawberry? Does she show any signs of springing at all?'

'Oh yes, she's getting a real big bag on her. I reckon she ought to be about due in a week or two from now,' Ned said.

'Here, Mick, bring over your plate and have some more fried potatoes.'

Mick held out the plate.

'What's the matter with your hand? What's that, is it a blister, you've got there?'

Mick looked down at his hand and then looked over at Ned for his cue.

'Yes, we've both got blisters,' Ned said, holding up his own right hand.

'And what have you been up to to get blisters?'

'We've been sawing down the tree.'

'What tree?'

'The old macrocarpa tree. It's a surprise for Dad.'

She looked at Ned, then at Mick, and pursed her lips doubtfully. 'People don't always like surprises,' she said.

But she went on dishing out tea for the others.

'What do you want to cut down that lovely old tree for?' asked Eileen. 'It wasn't doing any harm to anybody.'

'That's all you know,' Mick said fiercely, for this was what he had been coming to feel himself.

'Well, what harm was it doing?'

'It was a real pirates' nest for all the birds that pinch the fruit.'

'The worst pirates live in this house, not in the poor old tree,' she said meaningly.

'And it was choking all Dad's plants with its roots,' Mick said, and then was silent with surprise; for this was the first time he'd thought of that for a reason.

'A fat lot you care for Dad's plants. Look at the fuss you made the other day when he was going to hit that awful new dog of yours for chasing the cat over them.'

'Oh, shut up, Eileen,' Ned said. 'We're cutting the tree down and that's all you need to know about it. You look after the flowers and leave trees to the men.'

'Cissie Francis is going to be a boarder in Saint Dominic's, so Mrs Francis told me today,' Mrs Connolly said quietly. And Eileen thought no more of the tree.

'We'll have to hurry if we're going to get it finished before dark,' Ned said.

Mick had begun to hope that they would wait till tomorrow to finish the job. He should have known Ned better, though. And he wasn't going to complain about the blisters if Ned didn't.

So they fitted the saw into the cut again.

'There's not really any need to push or pull, you know,' Ned said, the next time they paused to get their breath. 'All you have to do is just keep it going and the teeth cut in of their own accord.'

'I wonder if it'll fall the way we want it to.' Mick got up and pretended to study the lie of the tree. His back was very stiff.

'She'll be jake, don't you worry,' Ned said without getting up. Mick bent down again, on one knee this time to see if it was any better that way.

The saw went to and fro.

'What are you jokers doing?'

They looked up. It was Tinny MacEwan from next door.

'Just sawing down this old tree,' Mick said casually.

'Can I have a go?'

'Mick might let you have a turn at his end. He's getting a bit tired, I think.'

'I am not.' Mick sawed away harder than ever.

Tinny walked round the tree. 'You're well past halfway. I'll tell you what. What say I get a rope and see if I can lend a hand, giving her a good tug?'

Ned didn't care much for the idea. It didn't sound the sort of thing they would do up at Port Craig. But it was getting dark and he was more tired than he would admit. 'If you want to, you can. But you'll have to hurry. She'll be down in a minute anyway. Get a legrope out of our cowshed.'

In two minutes Tinny was back with a rope and up the trunk. He tied it to a limb near the trunk and came slithering down it.

'Which way do you want her to fall?' he asked.

'She's going to fall between the fence and the end of the gorse hedge.'

Tinny took his rope out, found it was too short, got another legrope and tied it to the first. He walked out and began to take the strain.

Ned eyed him jealously. 'Watch out she doesn't come down on you now,' he said. 'Come on, Mick, a little more and the job is done.'

Just then there was a tearing and cracking. The gap above the buried saw-blade began to widen upwards. Then the branches above began to heave and sway as if they were trying to regain their balance. It was as if the sky was moving. Watching, Mick suddenly felt as if it were someone like his father beginning to fall. It was the first time he had ever known something permanent change.

'Come on, Mick, let's finish her off.'

They tore to and fro with the saw. Tinny grunted as he strained and hauled on the rope. Suddenly he dropped it and began to run. Mick looked up at the tree. It was listing. And then, seeming stationary, as if it were the world that was shifting and not itself, the tree toppled. The earth came up and met it, absorbing its crash in a smashing softness of broken minor branches that heaved and writhed as if they were alive, while the larger branches that now spanned an incredible stretch of ground bounced at the edge of a green sea. One branch had caught the gorse hedge and a shower of gold followed it down.

Tinny was on the other side, grinning and cheering. Mick looked at Ned who had straightened up and was now staring gravely at the fallen tree.

'There,' Ned said, 'just where I wanted it to fall.' He picked up his end of the saw. 'We must rub this with an oily rag before we put it away. It's a good saw.'

It was still not quite dark when Mrs Connolly and Eileen came to have an awed look. Then they went away again. Tinny was called inside by his mother to finish his homework. Ned and Mick took the saw in, oiled it, and hung it up once again on its nails. They went inside then and Ned began to read a copy of *Wide World*. But Mick could not settle.

Soon he was back at the tree. He looked at the stump. Its surface was smooth except where the jagged pieces on the further side stuck up like stalagmites. Near them drops of gum had begun to exude. Like tears, Mick thought. Like blood.

He and Ned would never climb up into those branches any more, never sew together their father's sacks and make hammocks where you could lie with a book listening to the life going on under you and hearing the world breathe in the wind. Never again sit up there remote with nothing but a green roof between yourself and the sky, feeling the strong, living tree move gently under you. The birds would never nest there again and he would never wake in the morning to hear them singing there. Something that had challenged the sky was gone.

Mick sat on the stump, staring down into green branches. Then he felt someone standing beside him. He looked up. It was his father.

'It was the only tree I left when I cleared the section,' his father said. 'Later on I always meant to cut it down but somehow I didn't want to. It was a good tree.'

And Mick saw that what had added to his own past was taken from his father's.

Goosey's Gallic War

In the last few weeks of that summer Goosey's Roman army had been getting a bit beyond a joke. When the Saunders family first came to live in the house next door, we had merely kept up a routine surveillance, checking on the kids' doings through knot-holes in the wooden fence, and we'd decided that Goosey and his swarm of young brothers were mad but harmless enough. Their old man was a returned soldier who'd been at Gallipoli and in France too, people said. He was a black Orangeman, I heard my father tell my mother, and a tiger for the drink, and he had a bad tongue on him. We were told to have nothing to do with the kids. Not that we wanted to. They went to the Georgetown school anyway, which was Protestant, and we looked down on them as strangers, and there were enough of us on our own to keep ourselves amused. It wasn't likely we were going to rush to make friends with this red-headed lot.

Later on, though, Goosey and his bunch began to branch out. Their old man was working on some unemployment scheme, and so he was away a lot, going round the country gassing rabbits for the Government at ten bob a week or working on the new road up at Lake Te Anau. Their mother was a bit of a streel, our mother said, and she didn't have much control of the kids, especially in the long summer holidays. So they'd be out of the house as soon as breakfast was over and ranging round the countryside. The trouble was that before long they began to find their way into all our favourite territories. We didn't have the feeling that the gravel-pit, Metzger's Bush, the Faraway Bush, Heidelberg Hill, or Lyons' Swamp belonged to us in peace any more.

The next thing we knew was that Goosey had made himself a suit of Roman armour out of old sheets of corrugated iron. He pinched his father's steel helmet and his bayonet too. He armed his brothers in much the same way, except that they only had wooden swords and javelins instead of the bayonet and they didn't have proper helmets, only cardboard ones. There were some other kids from Georgetown school as well as the three young brothers in his gang and they built themselves a sort of Roman camp in Murray's paddock. Goosey used to drill them in front of the camp every morning before taking them out on manoeuvres.

We watched them from our hut in Mr O'Dea's trees and there was really something rather impressive about the way Goosey would lead them in a charge on Murray's cows. The cows would be feeding, their heads down and all facing in the same direction towards the wind. Goosey's army would march towards them in artillery formation, with a few light-armed troops skirmishing on each flank with shangeyes. When they got within about thirty yards of the cows, Goosey would give the word of command and the two files of infantry would peel off into line of battle. Then another word of command and the slingers would let fly over the heads of the infantry with stones from their shangeyes. At the same time the infantry would hurl their manuka javelins and then charge, swords drawn. Goosey would be a few yards in front, waving his bayonet and shouting. The cows would look up gaping with their great eyes and wondering what on earth was happening. Then their tails would go up and, before it could come to close-quarters' fighting, they'd turn round and bolt for it at the lick of their lives, udders swinging from side to side.

Goosey used to call a halt then and regroup his forces and give them a short, martial speech, praising their valour and sometimes awarding a leather medal for some conspicuous act of courage beyond the call of duty. After that, he would give an analysis of the action and explain the lessons to be learnt from it.

Goosey himself didn't look all that impressive, if you just saw him in the street in his schoolclothes. He had red hair like all that family and his father kept it close-cropped to save paying a barber. Everything he wore had obviously been bought at a jumble sale or handed down by his big brother who was too old for playing soldiers, had a motor-bike and a job in a garage, and was chiefly interested in girls. Goosey's legs and arms were long and thin and his body was short but not stocky. His eyelashes were pink and every part of him you could see was covered in freckles. His neck was too long and he carried his head forward. His nose and his eyes were the things that struck you, though. The nose was a great hooked thing with a white patch on the bridge where the skin was too tight for the bone, like a clenched knuckle. The eyes were a pale blue and they stuck out of their sockets as if they were straining to get round the nose. He had an expression like a goose looking up a bottle, my father said. But they were fierce eyes, a fanatic's, and the grown-ups were fooled by the fact that he wasn't clever at school and didn't have much to say when they were around. In fact, Goosey lived by the imagination and there was something extreme in the way he acted out his loony notions which made him able to impose himself on other kids. They mightn't like being bossed around but the fact remained that when Goosey was about no one could complain that there was nothing to do. He always thought up some mad scheme and he made it seem so real that they just couldn't help getting interested and tagging along, if only to find out what was going to happen next.

Well, we kept a pretty sharp eye on Goosey and his army, thinking that they were up to no good, but there wasn't any real trouble until Goosey's father, Duncan Saunders, complained to the police that our big red cow Rosy had been loose in the Oteramika Road one night and had tossed him and his bike into the ditch. None of us believed it, of course. We just thought he'd been tight and had ridden into the ditch and then thought up a cock-and-bull story. Or else he'd had the DT's, we thought, and had seen a horned beast which he'd taken to be our placid Rosy but which was really a foul fiend imagined by himself out of all that Presbyterian stuff he'd probably been taught as a kid.

Unfortunately, though, other people had seen Rosy on the road that night. It was true they were Protestants but then so were most people round our part of the town and we knew perfectly well that quite a few of them, most of them in fact, wouldn't tell lies any more than we would. Not in a court of law, anyway, and that's what it came to. For Duncan sued my father and there was a great old fuss. In the end the case was dismissed but we were given a warning that we must make sure our fences were all right and that the cows didn't get loose.

The whole thing caused a good deal of bad blood, one way and another, and of course religion got mixed up in it. When we passed some of Goosey's lot, if there were enough of them to feel safe, they'd call out 'Catholic dogs jump like frogs' and that sort of stuff. And we had a few things of our own about black Orangemen and so on. A sort of feud built up and after a bit we had to make sure that none of us was ever out in the paddocks by himself or up in the bush.

One evening my young brother and I went up to get the cows and found them looking very wild in the eyes and sweaty in their coats. And we spotted the rearguard of Goosey's Roman army withdrawing behind a gorse hedge. The cows didn't let down their milk easily that evening and my mother was puzzled why they gave so little. We didn't tell her what the reason was but it wasn't hard to guess what had been happening.

When we put the cows up in the hill paddock that night, my elder brother said it mightn't be a bad plan to take a look round the fences. And, sure enough, we found someone had taken down the Taranaki gate on the side that led to the Oteramika Road, the one we didn't normally use. So we put it up again and tied it round with so many strands of barbed wire that it would be a bit of a job for anyone to get it open again.

Then he and I went home and had a council of war with our two younger brothers. Ned, that was my elder brother, said envoys would have to be sent to Goosey to protest against the attack on our cows and the sabotage of our fence and discuss whether it was to be peace or war. I was in favour of peace, because it.was going to be a hellish nuisance if you couldn't go out to mind the cows while they fed on the grass roads and you read a book under a tree or in the dry ditch without being in danger of an ambush. But my two younger brothers were all for war and Ned said that probably the only way to get peace was to give Goosey's army a thrashing that would teach them a lesson.

So it was decided that Ned and I would go as ambassadors that very evening after we'd had tea.

Goosey's headquarters was in a big red shed in the far bottom corner of their garden. In the days when whoever lived in the house used to run cows and keep a couple of draught horses, this shed had been divided into two, one part for the horses which you got at through a half-door, and the other part a cowshed open at the front.

When the time came Ned and I climbed over the barbed-wire fence and went up the track towards the red shed. There was a gorse hedge on our left, which hadn't been cut for years, and on our right was the garden with a lot of blackcurrant bushes and raspberry canes run wild. Duncan Saunders never bothered about the garden and it was pretty over-grown.

We knew Goosey had sentries posted because we could hear them moving level with us on the other side of the gorse hedge and caught a glimpse of a blue jersey hiding in the bushes on the right and of a bow and arrow trained on us. When we got within a few yards of the shed the ones who'd been behind the gorse came out in front of us. They stood there in a row with their hands on their swords. As well as Goosey's younger brothers, there were big Tony Tansley from the house beyond, Soapy Stone the boy from the orphanage whom everyone was sick of being sorry for, and Nuggety Daniels who was Goosey's chief lieutenant.

'Where do you think you're going?' Nuggety said.

'Where's Goosey?' Ned asked.

'What do you want to know for?'

This didn't seem to be getting anyone anywhere, what with one side asking questions and the other asking some more, and I was thinking of trying some other sort of diplomacy when suddenly Goosey stood up behind the half-door, opened it and came out. He was wearing his full armour and he passed through his men and stood in front of them about a yard from us.

'What do you want?' he said.

'You were chasing our cows this afternoon,' Ned said.

Goosey frowned. He didn't like Ned's choice of phrase. 'We were conducting a punitive expedition,' he said.

'Call it what you like but as far as I'm concerned it was chasing our cows. And I'm not going to have a pack of bloody kids chasing our cows when one of them's in calf and the rest are in milk. Or any other time, for that matter.'

'You aren't, aren't you?' said Goosey. 'We'll have to see about that. Are you prepared to give hostages or guarantees for their conduct in future? If so, I'm prepared to grant them an amnesty.'

'Even if we wanted your silly amnesty,' Ned said, 'it wouldn't be much use when you start leaving our gates open so that our cows can get out and get into trouble on the roads, frightening the wits out of drunks who don't know a pair of cow's horns from the devil's. So you know what you can do with your amnesty. You'll leave our cows and fences alone.'

'Or else what?'

'It boils down to this. Either you promise to leave our cows alone or your army of kids is going to take a thrashing. I give you fair warning.'

'Then it's war,' said Goosey.

'Call it what you like. But you aren't going to like it when it comes.'

'I give you safe conduct back to the frontier,' Goosey said. 'After that, watch out, that's all.'

'To hell with you and your safe conduct,' Ned said.

'I've given my word and you won't provoke me to break it,'

Goosey said, with maddening dignity.

'Come on,' Ned said to me.

We walked back down the track. The hairs were standing up on the back of my neck. As we'd been talking I'd seen the rest of Goosey's army forming up in the open front of the shed. They all had bows and arrows except a few who had airguns. The arrows were only long dock stalks but they had nails in the heads and I'd used them often enough to know that they could hurt. There were a few of them with shangeyes, too, and a stone from one of those could hit hard. I'd once killed a rabbit with one.

I wished Ned would walk a bit faster but he strode on at a deliberate pace. I wanted to look back to see whether they were following us but couldn't very well with Ned alongside me. He wouldn't have thought much of that.

We got through the barbed-wire fence. As soon as we were on our side I heard the airguns go off and the whine of BB pellets past our ears. And stones fell round us and a dock arrow hit me in the back.

'You have been warned,' Goosey shouted after us.

Back in our cowshed, we found reinforcements had arrived – Les Stokes and Denis Wood. Ned grinned when he saw them. 'Good,' he said. 'Now we can have a proper go at them tonight.'

I still thought it wasn't too late to make peace through some neutral envoy and on a basis of territorial division. I pointed out that were far more of them than we had on our side and some of them had airguns.

'Don't you worry,' he said. 'Once we get to close quarters we'll soon fix them. Now listen. Here's what we'll do. Goosey will be more or less expecting us any night from now on and the longer we wait the better chance he'll have to build up his defences. So we don't gain anything by waiting. I guess he'll put the blokes with the airguns inside the closed part of the shed because they don't need much room. He'll put the small kids with shangeyes on both sides and the big ones in the middle watching the main track. They're the ones that count,

Nuggety and big Tony the most. So they're the ones to go for. Soapy will just skedaddle, it doesn't matter about the little kids.

'So Martin and Les and I'll go up the middle. Denis can go on the gorse hedge side and Matt up through the garden. They can keep the kids busy and stop them from pelting us while we take on the big jokers in the middle.'

'What about me?' Pat said. He was our youngest brother and only ten. But he'd have had a fit if anyone suggested leaving him out. And he wasn't a bad shot – he even used to kid himself he was a better shot than I was.

'You follow on behind Matt and get behind a bush with your shangeyes and plenty of stones. You're the best shot and if you watch the windows and the doors you can keep the airguns down. Then when we make our big charge at the finish you join in with us.'

So then we collected all our ammunition supplies and weapons. We all had bows and shangeyes, the bows made out of strong lancejack and the shangeyes with strips of rubber cut from old lorry tubes. Mine had a willow prong notched for everything I'd killed, two notches for a rabbit and three for the hawk I'd once stalked in a swamp.

In case of emergencies we'd been collecting ammunition for a good while back, ever since we got suspicious of Goosey's gang, in fact. We had piles of stones specially chosen from the river gravel, nicely round and shiny and just the right size. And we'd been raiding the old man's toolshed for special flat-headed nails that just fitted into the dry dock stalks that we'd picked from the lower paddock. The nails gave the arrows the weight they needed at the business end to make them shoot accurately and hit hard.

There was still plenty of light to see by and we wormed our way along behind the board fence where we couldn't be seen from the Saunders' place. Then we crawled out and got into position behind an old log. Denis wriggled through a gap on to the gorse hedge side and Matt and Pat managed to get behind some bushes in the corner of the Saunders' garden without being spotted. By this time the light wasn't so good and we would have to get going pretty quickly before it was too dark to aim properly.

'I can see Nuggety and big Tony and Goosey in front of the shed,' Pat called over to us, just loud enough for us to hear him. 'No sign of Soapy, though.'

'Right,' Ned said. 'When I say "Go", everyone can shoot off all his arrows. We're close enough and it's no good taking the bows with us; they'll only get in the way once we get to close quarters and start putting in the stoush.'

We waited for a bit to make sure everyone was ready. Then Ned called out 'Go'. We all jumped up so as to be able to see and started loosing off our arrows. Stones began to fall all round us and you could hear the airgun pellets pinging past. This went on for a couple of minutes and then Ned shouted, 'After them'.

The three of us raced up the track towards the shed, Ned in the middle. We could hear kids squealing on the other side of the hedge and could see some more of them running back towards the shed from the garden, Matt and Pat after them.

Then big Tony and Nuggety were coming towards us. I felt a sharp pain in the flap of my ear and realised I'd been hit by a BB pellet but I didn't care by then. I was feeling full of a queer sort of artificial rage and when a stone from a shangeye hit me next, full in the chest, I didn't care about that either. Next thing I knew Nuggety was in front of me, waving his sword. I went at him hard and got him with my shoulder just below the ribs. He doubled up, properly winded, and I grabbed his sword from him and broke it. I looked round and saw that Les had big Tony on the ground and they were rolling over and over. Ned was in front of me and Goosey was in front of him with his bayonet out but backing away as Ned came at him. Other kids were coming out of the shed to help but at that moment Matt and Denis came out on either side of the track and began to let fly with their shangeyes. The kids all ran back into the shed.

I looked round to see how Les was getting on. He had big Tony on his back with his arms pinned but Nuggety had got his wind again and was going to the rescue. I ran in front of

him, grabbed an arm and tried the flying mare the way my
father had taught me. It worked like a dream and Nuggety
went sailing over my shoulder into the gorse hedge.

Ned was still driving Goosey backwards step by step
towards the shed. But the bayonet looked pretty ugly and I
could tell Ned wasn't sure whether Goosey wasn't mad
enough to use it. So Ned just kept after him, waiting for an
opening. Suddenly young Pat darted out of the currant bushes
and dived for Goosey's legs. He wasn't big enough to bring
Goosey down but Ned saw his chance, rushed in past the
bayonet and hit Goosey on his breast-plate with the heel of his
fist. Goosey went down with a crash and couldn't get up again
because of his armour and because Pat was still hanging on to
his legs. His helmet had fallen off and rolled away.

Ned grabbed the bayonet from him and threw it into the
hedge. Then we left Goosey still on the ground and charged on
towards the red shed. Though the three champions were out
of action Goosey's discipline was strong enough to keep the
others in action and stones and airgun pellets were all round
us. Ned got to the shed first and charged with his shoulder
against the half-door. It broke open and we were in. All the
kids except Soapy who was too fat had bolted by now out
through a hole in the back wall and the fort was ours.

'I surrender,' Soapy said.

We looked back down the track. Pat had left Goosey so as to
be in at the death with us. Goosey was sitting up and rubbing
his head. Nuggety had got out of the hedge and was trying to
help him up. Les had let go of big Tony and they were
standing grinning at each other, not knowing what to do next.

I ran back and got my favourite bow from where I'd left it. I
went over to Goosey, who was standing up now.

'I have a message from my sovereign liege,' I said, 'Richard
the Lionheart. It says: "To Robin Hood, of Sherwood Forest.
My servants tell me that you have fought nobly in the cause
against the usurper John and the caitiff Sheriff of Nottingham.
In token whereof I send you by the hand of herald this bow.
Keep it and continue to do good service, succouring the poor
and pillaging the unjust rich".'

A light came in his eyes. A new vein of fantasy in action had been opened. Besides, it was a very good bow. He held out his hand and took the bow.

'You may tell your master that I shall gladly be his ally. And he can count equally on my brave lieutenants, Little John and Friar Tuck.' He looked at big Tony and Nuggety and I could see they had caught on and were quite happy with their new parts.

'Have you read the books about Robin Hood and all that?' Goosey asked me.

'Some of them,' I said. 'But there are one or two I haven't been able to lay hands on.'

'Come and take a look at mine,' he said. 'I've got them hidden in the wash-house.'

Ned leaned over the half-door, watching us and grinning.

When we got to the door of the wash-house, we heard grown-ups talking and laughing somewhere in the house. Goosey put his finger to his lips to indicate silence and signalled to us to follow him. Ned had gone back home but all the rest of our side were with me and Goosey. We went round the side of the house and peered through the window into the front room. To my amazement I saw my mother and father sitting in chairs round the fire-place. Mrs Saunders was talking to my mother. They were holding glasses of wine of some sort and eating seed-cake. Our sister Norah was sitting on the sofa with Jim Saunders, Goosey's big brother. They weren't drinking or eating but were just looking at each other, as far as I could see. And Mr Saunders and my father were standing by the mantelpiece with glasses of beer in their hands.

Mr Saunders spotted us kids staring in through the window and came over. 'Bring in your cobbers, if you like,' he said to Goosey. 'I'm just showing Mr Connolly my souvenirs.'

We went round to the front door and trooped in. The things were all spread out on the sideboard, all sorts of medals and ribbons, a German helmet, a gas mask, a big shell-case, a belt with 'Gott mit uns' on the buckle, and a whole lot of other stuff.

I can't say my father seemed to be taking a great deal of notice and the women just weren't interested. Norah and Jim didn't seem to realise there was anybody else in the room at all.

'Those are my father's medals that he won at the war,' Goosey said to me. 'Was your father at the war?'

'No,' I said and I almost wished he had been, though he'd often said he was glad he had too many kids for anyone to expect him to fight in England's war.

'We'll open another bottle,' Mr Saunders said to my father.

My mother never missed a thing. 'Now, now, Ned,' she said. 'Remember you're on early shift tomorrow morning.'

'Never mind about that, Mary. It's not every day we have an engagement in the family.'

And that was the real way that Goosey's family and ours turned out to be allies in the end.

The Basket

They heard the clump of the wooden latch on the back gate.

Mrs Connolly looked up from the range which she was blackleading on her knees. 'Who's that, Nellie?'

Nellie put down the knife she was polishing and looked out behind a corner of the lace window curtain. 'It's Mrs Fox. She's just coming across the back lawn.'

'Blast the woman. Hasn't she got more sense than to be coming round here this time of a Saturday morning, of all mornings, pestering me with her blather and me with the housework to do and the dinner to get ready?'

She got up and flurried into the bathroom.

There was a knock at the back door. Nellie opened.

'Good morning, Mrs Fox. Come in. Mum won't be a minute.'

'Oh, and I won't come in just now with your mother busy and all. I just came over to give her back the basket she lent me to carry the vegetables in the other day.'

'Come in, then, Mrs Fox, come in.' Mrs Connolly had emerged from the bathroom, drying her hands on the roller towel as she came. She had taken off her sugar bag apron. 'You must excuse the kitchen being in such a state, Mrs Fox, but we were just having a little clean-up.'

'Och, Mrs Connolly, and I won't be coming in interrupting you at all. I just wanted to give you back your basket for fear you might be needing it.'

'Nonsense now, come in and have a cup of tea. You'll be

after catching a cold traipsing across those wet paddocks.'

'It's too much of a trouble it would be for you, surely, Mrs Connolly.'

'Not at all, now, not at all. Nellie and I were just going to make one, weren't we, Nellie? Run out and get a little kindling, Nellie, and we'll have the kettle boiling in two shakes of a dead lamb's tail. Sit you down there now, Mrs Fox, and make yourself comfortable.'

'You're too kind altogether, Mrs Connolly. If you're sure I'm not disturbing you?'

'Of course not, woman, of course not. What's the matter with you at all? There now, you see, the kettle's on and it'll be boiling in a moment. And how's Mr Fox?'

'He's well enough. Though he's not the man he was. He's ageing and it's a disease has killed stronger men than him before today. And how's your husband?'

'He's very well, thank God. Sure he's so well that if he gets a cold he thinks he's dying. He's as strong as a man of forty. I wish I was as good on my feet.'

'It's a strong healthy woman you are too, Mrs Connolly.'

'Well, I can still cook him good meals and wash and keep the house clean. There's the kettle boiling now, Nellie. Take it off and make the tea. Is it two teaspoonfuls of sugar you'll be taking, Mrs Fox?'

'Thank you, Mrs Connolly. It's the good cup of tea you make, that's certain.'

'There's no comfort like a cup of good strong tea. It puts strength into your bones.'

'You're right there, Mrs Connolly. Many's the long day I don't know how I'd have got through if it hadn't been for a good cup of tea. And have you heard that young Nellie Flaherty and Johnny Brogan are to be married? And them so young. I don't know what they're going to live on, I'm sure.'

'The Lord will provide, Mrs Fox. Perhaps it's better for the young folk to get married and be happy while they're young. It steadies them too, I always say.'

'And that's true for you now, Mrs Connolly. I was only a slip of a girl myself when I was married and many's the hard

trial I had soon after, what with Frank taking to the drink so
hard and all.'

'Never mind, Mrs Fox, you can look back now and say: It
was a hard life but I lived through it and was true to my man
and brought up his children in the love of God.'

'True for you, Mrs Connolly. It's a rare comfort for an old
woman to have a chat with you in the butt-end of her days,
and you with the good heart and the good word always for
another's troubles. But I must be going now and getting something ready for Frank to eat when he comes back from the
town.'

'No hurry, Mrs Fox, no hurry at all.'

'I must be getting away, just the same and many thanks to
you for the good tea and the kind words. It's lucky you are,
Nellie, to have such a mother.'

'I'll walk down to the back gate with you, Mrs Fox. Nellie,
just be finishing off those knives and have the potatoes on for
the men's dinner. And keep an eye on the fire. I'll be back in a
minute. We'll walk through the garden way, Mrs Fox.'

They crossed the square of asphalt, went by the wood-heap,
still shrunken from last winter's fires and not yet the great
mass of roots and red slabs it would be by the onset of the
next.

The garden flourished with the vigour of a disciplined
jungle. Beans reared massively up their poles into the air like
muscular sailors swarming up the rigging, rows of peas dizzy
with height twined perilously on to the sticks they had
outgrown and stretched their tendrils into space like the hands
of greedy children. The cabbages squatted fatly on their stalks
each rapt in an intensity of bulging growth. Delicate and
succulent the lettuces folded their modesty into tempting balls
and complacently awaited ravishment. Beetroot, carrots,
parsnips, onions, spring and spanish, alternated their serried
parade on either side the narrow path. Most impressive of all
was the rhubarb, whose coarse, veined canopy of leaves almost
concealed the huge, red-streaked stalks beneath, through
which pumped the rich sap almost visibly.

'Sure, Mrs Connolly, and it's a gift of God your man has for making the world grow. Just look at the wonder of them cabbages.'

'Perhaps you would like a cabbage to take home with you, Mrs Fox?'

'It would be a shame to be cutting down one of God's miracles.'

'That's what Ned is always saying. He spends all his spare time growing things and yet he would have them all flowering away to seed if you would let him, rather than cut them. But we'll take one from the corner there and he won't notice it. That big yellow fellow over there with the heart of a bull on him.'

She felled the giant, cutting him close to the ground and covering over the butt of the stalk with soil, guiltily. But she grew bolder.

'And a few sticks of rhubarb he would never be missing. I don't know why he grows it, I'm sure, since there's only him and me that eat it. None of the others will look at it.'

'It's too good you are, Mrs Connolly.'

'Don't be talking, woman. What good is it if not for the eating?'

The rhubarb also fell to the knife, the broad voluptuous leaves were cut off and left to grow grey in the sun.

'And some carrots and parsnips to mash up for your man's dinner. You can't beat the good, fresh vegetables.'

'There never was woman had such a good neighbour as you, Mrs Connolly.'

'Sure, aren't we all neighbours, Mrs Fox. The good food is all the better for sharing. Perhaps you would like some spuds as well. The King Edwards have done wonders this year.'

'Now, Mrs Connolly, it's too much you have given me already. And haven't we potatoes at home?'

But already the spade was under the roots and the fat white potatoes lay on the upturned ground, naked and born.

'It's poor ground you have over there and the likes of these would be hard to find. Take them if only to try them.'

'Och, Mrs Connolly, and the woman with the heart like yours deserves the grand husband God gave her.'

'Don't be talking now. I'll just run back and get you the basket.'

She came back with the big wicker basket and it was loaded full.

Mrs Fox passed out through the little gate in the fence.

'Goodbye to you now Mrs Connolly, and may the Lord repay you for I can only give you the thanks of a poor old woman.'

'Get away with you now and if ever you're in need of a few vegetables, just be letting me know.'

Mrs Fox went over the paddock picking her way through the cow-pots. Mrs Connolly came back by the garden. She was drying her eyes furtively. They were wet with her own generosity and Mrs Fox's poverty.

She came into the kitchen. 'Poor old woman. It's the hard life she's had, Nellie, with that lazy old drunkard of a husband of hers and little enough to show for the long years of slaving for him, now that they're coming into the years of old age.'

'Have you been giving away Dad's vegetables again, Mum?'

'And what if I have given her a miserable old cabbage or so that would have gone to seed otherwise? And don't you be telling your father she was here or he'll be down in the garden complaining as if it was murder I'd done. And haven't you done those knives, yet, my lady Jane, dreaming here all the morning and doing nothing? The devil take that old wretch of a woman coming round here destroying my morning's work with her blathering, and me with a houseful of men will be home in an hour roaring for their food like a pack of wild things. And bless me if she hasn't gone away again with my basket.'

Growing Up

It was late afternoon but the heat had not gone out of the day. Gorse pods still burst occasionally and their abrupt snap seemed to split the moments in two like the halves which went on twisting, the inner sides black and shiny and the outer silky and furred as a bee, even after their seeds had whirled out in an invisible arc to the future. Hidden in the sky the larks exulted, far above the paddocks which concealed their private future, the nest of four pale eggs. And on the edge of Murray's swamp the frogs croaked harsh praise of a world of sun and grass and water.

At Walsh's little house on the corner Mick and his father turned into Grass Road. They could see by the blue smoke curling above the macrocarpa hedge that old Mr Walsh was watching the passing of men and time from his usual ambush. When they came level with the pink-painted picket gate he took the pipe from his mouth and looked at them with faded blue eyes.

'She's had the calf all right,' he said. 'A fine stamp of beast she is, that cow.'

Without looking up Mick shared his father's relief that Rosy was all right, his annoyance that once again old Mr Walsh was there to rob them of surprise.

'Thanks then, Tim,' said his father. 'Yes, she's a fine beast.'

He didn't ask whether it was a bull or a heifer and Mick knew why. The old man would have told them already if he'd been up to see. So Mick's father didn't stop but walked on, hands in the trouser pockets he always had made well to the front, old waistcoat unbuttoned but held in place by the weight of nails and staples he always carried in case a fence needed mending. Old Mr Walsh replaced his pipe and continued to look out over the paddocks, rehearsing in his memory unspoken the calvings of the last sixty years.

'You couldn't have a boil on your bottom without that old fellow knowing it,' said Mr Connolly. He spoke aloud but to himself. Yet Mick felt bigger and older as he did the day his father first let him take Rosy to the bull.

They moved on up O'Donnell's hill. Now and then Rob, the new collie, dashed from the golden flare of gorse which crowned the right of the road, looked about till he saw them, waved his tail reassuringly and vanished once more after rabbits.

Away on the left, where the country dropped to the creek and the railway, an engine shrilled triumphantly, its brood of trucks behind it. It would soon be home.

'The four-thirty-five goods,' said Mick.

'That's right,' said his father. He took out his watch, looked at it, snapped back the cover and put it in his pocket again. 'She's up to time,' he added.

They left the road and jumping the dry ditch came to the gate, three strands of barbed wire nailed to three manuka poles. Mr Connolly lifted the wire loop from the head of the pole nearest the straining post. The gate folded back open.

O'Donnell's trees running along the crest of the hill cut the paddock in half and the dropping sun had thrown the nearest side in shade. Rosy would be on the other side of the crest where the grass still basked in warmth.

The macrocarpa trunks were bare as high as Mick's head. The cows had broken off the small branches and twigs, rubbing themselves there on days when the sun was too hot or rain made them take shelter. Wisps of hair clung to the rough bark. And the ground was dry there with little grass since the trees stole the rain. As they passed under Mick couldn't help looking up to where framed in the branches the sparrows'

nests were, so untidy outside, so neat and downy within. Last
year he would have been up there in the branches, counting
the eggs.

Rosy lay on her side, back towards them. She was between
them and the calf. She had lost all her winter hair and the sun
nestled warmly in the licked whorls of her roan summer coat.
She heard them coming and turning her head recognised
them. She got slowly to her feet and lowed anxiously. They
could see under her belly to the calf, also up now and teetering
a little on legs far too long for its body.

'Gosh,' said Mr Connolly, 'the kids didn't take long to find
them.'

And sure enough both Rosy and the calf had long daisy-
chains draped round their necks in garlands.

Rosy shook her head as they came up and moved round to
keep between them and the calf. The calf was licked and
clean.

'Well, old girl,' said Mr Connolly, and he slapped her on
the shoulder, 'so you made it all right. Just hang on here,
Mick and I'll see if I can find her cleaning. If she hasn't eaten
it already, the old devil.'

He began to walk about the paddock, searching the grass.
Rosy looked from Mick to the calf, all pride and fondness for
the calf, confidence and suspicion for Mick.

'It's here, all right, Mick,' called out his father. 'We'll leave
her in the home paddock tonight and you bring up a spade
and bury it in the morning.'

He came back and looked at the cow and calf.

'A bull,' he said. 'Pity, I hoped we'd get a nice young heifer
out of her this time. A strong little beggar he looks too.'

Mick watched Rosy compassionately. She was licking the
calf and each lick was a caress. Poor Rosy. She always had
bulls.

His father bent over, picked up the calf and slung it over his
shoulders. Rosy tossed her head and lowed, her eyes wild. The
calf lowed back at her. She rushed round to where the calf's
head was and began to lick it.

'It's all right, Rosy,' said Mr Connolly, bending his legs and heaving the calf further up his shoulders. 'We're just going home, that's all.'

They set off for the gate. Rosy followed just behind, lowing anxiously. She walked awkwardly with her full udder.

Rob came scampering over the hill, saw the procession, stopped irresolute, then followed behind Mick, subdued.

As they passed Walsh's house old Mr Walsh was still at the gate. He took out his pipe.

'A fine bag of milk she's got there,' he said. 'A bull, by the look of him. A pity, and him with a touch of the Jersey. It's a good cross for Southland, the Shorthorn and the Jersey. Well, you'll get five bob on the skin, I suppose.'

Mick glared at him and then looked back at Rosy. She didn't understand, luckily.

At the big wooden gate of the cowshed they stopped.

'We'd better get him in right away,' said Mr Connolly. 'If she gets used to him sucking her there'll be the devil to pay. You open the gate and as soon as I'm through nip in and close it so she can't get through.'

The door clumped to in Rosy's face and Mick slid the wooden bolt.

'That's the style,' said his father.

Rosy's roars came frantically through. The cows in the next paddock began to bellow in sympathy, recognising their common fate.

Mrs Connolly was feeding the hens, her sugar-bag apron caught up with the oats in its fold, her hand strewing out the grain in fistfuls. It fell like a rain of sunlight and the hens scurried about in a frenzy, their heads jerking up and down like the needle of a sewing-machine, their eyes always ahead of their beaks, their greed in advance of their eyes.

'A bull, Nellie,' called Mr Connolly.

'Poor Rosy,' said Mrs Connolly, 'such fine calves and never a one we could rear.' Then, as if ashamed of that softening or frightened of it: 'Well, I suppose the sooner it's killed the sooner we'll have peace and quiet again.' She pursed her lips and went on strewing the oats, mind closed against the sad bellows beyond the wall.

As Mr Connolly came with the calf to the lawn, the Scovy duck retreated with dignity and her family to the hedge. Molly, the ferret, left her young in the darkness of the inner compartment and climbed up the netting of the cage spread-eagled and pink eyes cold and curious.

Mr Connolly set the calf down on the dark of the rich, clipped grass. It stood there, doddering with its awkward grace. It had Rosy's colouring, only at the ends the hair deepened into the Jersey's tannish black. It was still wet from the mother's licking. It shivered a little. It was alone for the first time. Suddenly it gave a strong young bellow, startlingly strong from something so young. Rosy's answering bellow was prompt, desperate with solicitude.

'We'll have to get on with it, Mick,' said Mr Connolly. 'Fetch me the mall.'

Mick dragged the heavy mall from the tool-shed. His father hefted it above his head and put it down again. He liked the mall because it was heavy enough to make him feel his strength. Mick looked at the iron rings which bound each end of the wooden, barrel-shaped head. The calf's eyes were big and dark.

It stood shakily in the square of green. Two hands on the handle of the mall, Mr Connolly was leaning forward, muscles relaxed, watching the calf. His grey eyes were inscrutable. Mick felt the layers of feeling inside his father, the indifference – almost callousness – forced by life which held these necessities, under this the gentleness that puzzled at the necessity, the strength and weakness of man forced by life to give life and take it.

The cables of muscle and sinew on the heavy forearms rose and tautened, the biceps bulged against the rolled sleeves. Mick looked at the mall raised high above and behind his father's head. Would he be able to watch the down stroke? He must if he were to be grown-up.

The mall came swiftly down. Mick looked away. But his ears heard the thud.

When he looked back the calf was down. It had made no sound. There was blood at its ears and nostrils. His father was leaning on the haft of the mall, breathing more heavily. Red hairs, short and curly from the calf's head, red and tannish black, clung in blood not curving but broken to one of the iron rings. Mr Connolly was looking down at the calf.

'Poor little beggar,' he said. And then to Mick: 'I'll show you how to skin him tomorrow. You can have the skin. It's a good skin, worth five bob.'

But Mick was running up the path towards the house.

Mrs Connolly came back from the fowl-run. She looked down at the dad calf.

'It's a shame,' she said. 'But what else can you do? I've fed the pigs.' She went on towards the house.

'Bring the milk bucket back with you,' called Mr Connolly after her. 'She's got a big bag of milk on her and there'll be a nice drop of beastings.'

'I left the bucket in the cowshed,' she replied.

He put the mall back then went to the cowshed and barred off the opening so that Rosy couldn't get through to see her calf. He opened the wooden gate and let her into the bail.

'Poor old girl,' he said as he leg-roped her. But while he milked her, easing the great swollen udder, she kept her head turned towards him in the bail and from time to time she moaned.

'Perhaps you'll have a nice little heifer the next time,' he said.

In the kitchen chops were frying and you couldn't hear Rosy. Mick's young brother came in.

'What was it?' he asked.

'It was a bull so we had to kill it,' said Mick casually.

The Quiet One

The band concert was over and three of us came out of the Regent into Dee Street with the rest of the crowd.

'I could swear she gave me the eye,' Sid said.

'I'll bet she did,' Wally said. 'One look'd be all she'd need, too. Who did, anyway?'

'That sheila with the black hat on that was in front of us about two seats away. You'd be too busy looking at the statue of the naked Greek dame to notice, I expect. Anyhow she was just in front of me when we were coming out and when I pushed the swing door open for her she turned round and gave me a real grin. Look, there she goes.'

He pointed the way we were going, and, sure enough, we could see a black hat bobbing along a bit in front where the crowd wasn't so thick.

'Come on, boys,' said Wally, 'Here we go.'

'But, look here,' I said, 'I thought we were going to the Greek's.' All the same, I changed my pace to keep up with theirs.

'To hell with the Greek's. Who wants to be sitting down to eggs and chips when there's a chance of picking up a sheila, eh, Sid?'

Sid just grunted. You couldn't see the girl because of the crowd and he was staring straight down the footpath, towards where we'd last seen her. You wouldn't have needed to know him as well as I did to guess from the sour way his mouth was closed that he didn't fancy the shape things were taking much.

Wally was a tiger for the girls, and a good-looking joker, too.
And old Sid hadn't had the same confidence in himself since
the dentist made him have all his top teeth out. Wally didn't
give him much chance to forget about it, either, calling him
Gummy all the evening.

Not that there was anything in it for me, anyway. If there
was only one girl I wouldn't be the chap who got her, that was
certain. And, as a matter of fact, though I'd have been the last
to say so, I'd have been scared stiff if there'd been the least
danger of me being the one. I never really knew why I tagged
along with them those Sunday evenings. I must have hoped
some sort of miracle would happen, I suppose, and that some
sheila or other would fall for me and put me into a position
where one move had to follow the other in such a way that my
mind'd be made up for me. At the same time I was terrified
that just that would happen, knowing in advance that at close
quarters with a girl I'd be like a cow with a musket. Anyhow, I
needn't have worried. Nothing ever did happen and by this
time I think I was getting to realise, only I wouldn't admit it,
that nothing ever would.

That didn't stop me, though, from putting off going home
till the last possible moment in case some sort of miracle
turned up and when I finally left Wally or Sid at Rugby Park
corner of a Saturday or Sunday night I'd trudge the rest of the
way home in the rain or the moonlight, cursing myself and the
town and everything in it and wondering what the hell was the
matter with me, whether I was a different breed or what, and
why it was always me that was left, and thinking that in some
other country somewhere things mightn't be like that at all
and people would see what I really was instead of what I'd
always been.

So, with all that at the back of my mind, and Wally
rampaging alongside with about as many afterthoughts as a
dog has after a rabbit, and Sid on the other side getting down
in the mouth already at the thought that Wally was going to
pinch his girl, I didn't think much of the night's prospects.
The upshot'd be that Wally would get her all right and I'd
have to spend what was left of the evening at the Greek's

trying to cheer Sid up by encouraging him to skite about all the girls that had fallen for him and pretending not to notice how much Wally going off with this one had got under his skin.

Well, after a bit the crowd got thinner and most of them started to cross over to where the last tram was waiting, towards the Majestic side. So we could see better what was in front of us. And there was the girl all right, about twenty yards ahead, all by herself into the bargain, and pacing along at a fair bat. Good legs she had, too.

'I reckon she knows we're following her,' Wally said. 'The trouble is, there's too many of us.'

'That's right, Wally.'

It was very sarcastic the way Sid said it but that didn't worry Wally.

'Go on, Sid,' he said, 'don't be a dog in the manger. A fair fight and let the best man win, eh?'

Of course, that was just the trouble, the way Sid looked at it. It's always the best man who says these things.

Anyhow, before Sid could think of an answer, or before he could think of something that wouldn't have given away he knew he hadn't a hope against Wally whatever kind of fight it was, the girl started to cross the road and so, us too, we changed course like a school of sprats and over the road after her, only about ten yards behind by this time.

She stepped up on to the footpath on the opposite side of the road, us tagging behind like three balloons on a string. She looked behind just then and saw us.

'Now's our chance,' Sid said, getting quite excited and nervous, I could tell.

Wally didn't say anything but he took advantage of his long legs and he was up on the pavement a good yard in front of us.

It was darker on the footpath because of the shop verandahs and because the nearest street-lamp was a good distance away. At first I couldn't see what was happening, owing to the notion I had that if I wore my glasses when we were out on the pick up on nights like this I'd spoil my chances, such as they were; but I felt both Wally and Sid check. And then I saw what it was. The girl had stepped into a shop doorway and there was a chap there waiting for her.

The girl and her bloke came out of the doorway and walked off towards the other end of Dee Street, her hanging on his arm and talking a blue streak and laughing the way we could tell the joke was on us. And the bloke looked back, once as if he'd like to have come at us. But, seeing Wally and thinking he had the trumps anyway, I suppose, he turned round again and kept on going.

'Well, I'm damned,' Wally said.

'Foiled again,' Sid said. But he didn't sound narked at all, really, and I knew by his voice he'd sooner have had it that way so that the laugh was on Wally instead of on himself as it would have been if things had gone differently.

I was pleased, too, for that matter, though I couldn't help envying that bloke a bit with a good-looking girl on his arm and a nice new blue overcoat and Borsalino and never a doubt in his head as to where he was going and what he'd do when he got there.

Still, envying him made it easier to pretend I meant it when I cursed the girl up hill and down dale like the others. For it wouldn't have done for me to show I was really relieved. It was sort of understood that even if I didn't mean business like Wally and Sid I had to go through the motions just the same. They really weren't bad blokes in a way, Wally and Sid, because they knew all the time I wasn't a serious competitor and yet they always treated me as if I was, thinking I'd be hurt if they didn't, I suppose.

And I would have been hurt, too. Somehow, if there hadn't been this kind of agreement about the way we were all to behave, I'd have had to drop the game altogether. I could tell that, because when, as happened sometimes, other blokes joined us who didn't know the rules or didn't care if there were any and they began to pull my leg, I always pushed off after a while. Which was what these other chaps wanted, I expect. 'The Wet Napkin', I heard one of them, Ginger Foyle it was, say once after I'd gone and he didn't think I could hear him, because I hadn't got my glasses on, perhaps.

No, Wally and Sid weren't like that, especially Wally. They knew I was all right once you got to know me and, besides, I used to be able to make them laugh when we were by ourselves and get them to see the funny side of things they'd never have noticed if it hadn't been for me.

Well, anyway, there we were left standing in the middle of Dee Street and all cursing our heads off in the same way.

'Nothing for it but to go over to the Greek's,' I said.

'Listen to him, will you, Sid,' Wally said. 'Him and his bloody Greek's. And us all whetted up for a bite of something tastier than old Harry could ever put under our noses.'

I felt a fool immediately, because I might have known that was the wrong thing to say, the way they were feeling. Once Wally had got the idea of skirt into his head it wasn't easy to put him off. And Sid, for all I don't think he really liked Wally, would trail along with him all right, knowing that was his best chance. That was what fascinated him about Wally, he could always have what Wally didn't want. But it was what made him hate Wally's guts, too.

Besides, I suppose they felt I'd sort of broken the rules by not being keen enough and waiting a bit longer before giving up what we all knew was a bad job.

'Well, what'll we do now, Wally?' Sid said.

'Let's take a stroll as far as the Civic and back,' I chipped in, trying to establish myself again. 'You never know, we might pick up something.'

'That's more like it,' Wally said. And then, because he wasn't a bad bloke, a better chap in many ways than Sid would ever be, he added: 'After all, if there's nothing doing, we can always go over to have a feed at the Greek's later on.' Which showed he wasn't really fooled by what I'd said.

So away we went, down past the Majestic where Len Parry and Alec Haynes and all that bunch were as usual, pretending they were talking about who was going to win the Ranfurly Shield when all they were interested in really was the girls who kept scuttling by on their way back from the band concert. I took a look at the Town Clock on the other side as we went by and there it was, half-past ten already, one more

Sunday evening just about over and nothing happening, only the same old thing. Already everyone who had anywhere to go was going there and soon the only people left in the streets would be chaps like us who couldn't think of anything better to do and soon we'd be gone home too and the streets would be empty and another night would be gone out of a man's life and him none the wiser one way or the other.

'Was that your cousin Marty I saw all by himself in the doorway next that bloke who met the sheila, Ned?' Sid suddenly asked.

'I didn't notice.'

'It was him all right, poor bastard,' Wally said.

I pricked up my ears at that. My cousin Marty wasn't the sort of chap you talked about with that particular tone in your voice. He was rather a big shot in the eyes of our crowd. A good five or six years older than any of us, he must have been twenty-two or twenty-three, and he used to earn good money before the slump. A plasterer he was, by trade. But he'd been one of the first to be turned off when things got tough because, though he was good at his job, he had a terrible temper and was too handy with his fists. A big joker, he was, with reach and height, and they used to say that if only he'd do a bit more training there wasn't a pro in the business he couldn't have put on his back for the count. As it was he'd made quite a name for himself round the town as a fighter and once when I was at the barber's and got fed up with the way slick little Basset kept taking me for granted because I didn't know what was going to win the Gore Cup I'd managed to get in casually that Marty was my cousin and after that Basset could never do enough for me.

'What do you mean, "poor bastard"?' Sid was saying.

'Didn't you hear? The trouble with you, Sid, is you never hear anything now you've got your teeth out.'

'Come on, come on, know-all. What's it all about?'

'Yes, what was it, Wally?' I asked; for I could tell Wally was wishing he'd kept his mouth shut, knowing Marty was my cousin.

'Well, it's only what they're saying, Ned, and there

mightn't be anything in it, though I have noticed Marty hasn't been about much lately. You know how you'd always see him and Dulcie Moore round together of a Saturday and Sunday night?'

'That's right,' Sid said, glad to get in on the inside again. 'I saw them coming out of the Rose Gardens about two in the morning the night of Ginger Foyle's keg-party and they were always at the Waikiwi dances together.'

'Well, they say he put her up the spout. And then he got some old dame who hangs out in Georgetown to fix her up. Of course, that's happening all the time all over the place, you know, and nobody ever thinks a thing about it as long as no one gets caught.' This was for me. 'But the trouble this time was that something went wrong and she got blood-poisoning or something, and now she's in hospital and they say the johns have been at her all the time beside her bed trying to find out who did it and who was the man. But so far she won't say and the odds are she won't pull through.'

'Jesus,' said Sid. 'I thought he looked a bit down in the mouth.'

'Wouldn't you be?'

'But, look here, Wally,' I said, 'who told you all this?'

'I heard Marty's crowd, Jim Fergus and all that lot, talking about it yesterday after the game. And when I was shaving in the bathroom this morning and they didn't know I was there, I heard Mum telling the old man about it. It was her that told that bit about her not being expected to live.'

We'd got as far as the Civic and turned back by this time and the crowd was getting very thin by now, everybody making for home, feeling much the way I'd been feeling, I expect, that they might as well be in bed as hanging round. Only I didn't feel like that any more. Things happened, sure enough, and even to people you knew, even to your own family, near enough.

Sid and Wally kept talking about it all the way back up Tay Street. It was queer the way they seemed to get a sort of pleasure out of discussing it. And what was queerer still was that I liked hearing them talk about it. It must have been partly how old we were and partly the town we lived in. You felt the place wasn't quite such a dead-alive hole, after all, and you felt you really were grown up when things like that, terrible things but things all the same, happened to people you even knew.

Anyhow, just as we got to the Bank corner, two girls came round it the opposite way and we almost banged into them. While we were dodging around them to let them pass and show what gentlemen we were they cut through between me and Wally and we could hear them giggling as they went on.

'Sorry,' Wally called back in an extra-polite voice I hardly recognised, he could put on the gyver so well when he wanted to.

'Don't mention it,' one of the girls said and giggled again.

We stopped at that and Sid made a great show of lighting cigarettes for us while we all had a good dekko back to see what the girls were up to.

'They've stopped in the doorway next the jewellers,' Wally said. 'Come on, Sid, here we go. We're home and dry.' He was so excited he forgot to pretend I was in on it, too.

The two of them cut back the way we'd come, like a couple of whippets at first and then as they got closer with a sort of elaborate stroll as if they might just as well be walking that way as any other. I followed after them, trying to catch up and yet not to catch up. I knew I ought to have gone away. There was no good just tagging on, being a nuisance. But I kept following, all the same.

'Hello,' Wally was saying as I came up to the doorway. 'Going anywhere?'

'What's that got to do with you?' the girl who had called back to us said.

'Well,' Sid said, 'it's getting late for girls to be out by themselves with all the roughs there are about this time of night and we thought you might like to have an escort on the way home.'

Sid could always talk well when it came to the pinch, especially if he had Wally with him. I of course couldn't say a thing, being as nervous as a cat, although I knew already that it didn't matter much what I did, me being only the spare part.

'You know what thought did,' the girl said.

'Come on, Isobel,' the other girl said. 'It's getting late.'

'Will you have a cigarette, Isobel?' Wally said. And he took out his case. It was the one he kept his tailor-mades in, not the one he used for home-rolled ones and butts. In that light you'd have taken it for silver.

'Don't mind if I do.'

'Come on, Isobel,' the other girl said again.

'Now, Jean, don't be an old fusspot. There's heaps of time really. Why don't you have a cigarette, too.'

'That's right,' Wally said, and so Jean took one from the case, a bit nervously, I thought.

'We don't even know your names, do we, Jean?' said Isobel when Sid had flourished his lighter for them. You could see them trying to get a look at us while the flame was there. But of course we had our backs to the street-lights and they couldn't have made out much what we looked like.

'That's easy,' Wally said then. 'I'll introduce us. My name's Wally Radford and this is my friend Sid, Sid Cable. And this is Ned.'

'He's a quiet one, isn't he?' Isobel gave Jean a nudge and giggled at me.

I tried to think of something very witty to say, the sort of thing that would have come to Wally or Sid in a flash. But I couldn't think of anything at all and I could feel myself blushing. I hated that Isobel then. It was always the good-looking ones that made me feel most of a fool. The other one, Jean, I didn't mind so much because I could tell by her way of giggling that she was nervous, too. She wasn't anything like such a good-looker, though.

There was a bit of a silence then. They were all waiting for me to say something. When I still didn't say anything I felt them all just give me up. Wally got into the doorway close to Isobel and tried to get his arm round her. She kept fending him off and looking at him and then at Jean in a way that said as plain as a pikestaff: Wait till afterwards when we can get away by ourselves.

Sid was talking a blue streak to Jean so as to give her a chance to get over her shyness, I suppose, and to shut me out of it and make me see I was being the gooseberry, in case I didn't see it already.

There was nothing to do but leave them to it. I was only holding Wally and Sid back from doing their stuff, hanging round like that.

'Well, I must be getting along,' I said.

'Why don't you come with us?' Jean said. Her voice sounded quite scared. But I could tell Sid wasn't going to get anywhere with her and I wasn't going to have her use me as an excuse to keep him off and then have him putting the blame on me next day.

'I'd like to,' I said, 'but I live up the other end of the town.'

'OK, Ned, good night,' Wally said in an offhand sort of way and Sid said good night too, in the friendly voice he always used when you were doing something he wanted you to do. That was one of the things Sid liked about me, that I always did the expected thing. It wasn't one of the things I liked about him.

So I set off by myself up towards the Bank corner again, feeling like a motherless foal, as the old man would have said. I thought I'd better give them plenty of time to get clear and so I decided I'd walk a few blocks up Dee Street and back again.

The town clock was pointing to nearly eleven by now. All the crowd that'd been in front of the Majestic was gone and Dee Street was as empty as the tomb except for a bobby standing in the library doorway over the other side, just in case there should be a row at the Greek's, I expect.

Seeing the Greek's lighted windows gave me the idea of going in for a feed, after all. But it was pretty late and I couldn't face going in there all by myself, with the blokes eyeing me and guessing what had happened. So I crossed Esk Street and went straight on up.

But it wasn't nearly so bad being by yourself when the whole street was empty like that and you didn't have to wonder what people were thinking about you. I quite liked striding along under the shop verandahs as if I were going nowhere in a hurry and listening to my heels hammer on the asphalt and seeing my reflection pass dark on the windows. It was better feeling miserable by yourself and not having to put up a show any more. Or else the kind of show you put up when there was no one but yourself to watch was more convincing.

'Hullo, Ned.'

I stopped in my tracks and looked round to see where the voice came from. Then I saw him. He was in the same doorway that the sheila had met her bloke in earlier on. He was standing there, all stiff like a sentry, and in that light you'd have thought his eyes were black they were so dark. A Spaniard, he might have been, with the long sideboards halfway down his cheeks and his straight, thin nose, that had never been broken for all the boxing he'd done.

'Hullo, Marty,' I said.

He didn't say any more, just went on looking at me. I didn't know quite what to do because it struck me it was probably only the suddenness of seeing someone he knew that had made him call out and probably he wished he hadn't now. Besides, knowing what I did, I felt uncomfortable.

I went up to him all the same, not knowing how to get away without it looking awkward and as if I'd heard about his trouble and was dodging off so as not to be seen with him.

'Have a cigarette,' I said and I produced a packet of ten Capstan.

'Thanks.'

I lit them for us both and when that was over there I was still stuck and unable to think of anything else to say. The only things that came into my head sounded quite hopeless compared with the things he must have on his mind.

'All the crowd gone home?' I said in the end, for lack of anything better.

'Suppose so,' he answered and took a puff of the cigarette. Then he added in a voice so savage that it gave me a real fright. 'Who the hell cares what they've done? Pack of bastards.'

I didn't say anything. I was trying to work out what he meant by that. Had they done the dirty on him and talked to the johns? Or was he just fed up with them?

He gave me a look just then, the first time he'd really looked at me since I stopped.

'You've heard all about it, I suppose?'

That stumped me properly. I didn't want him to get the idea the whole town was talking about him. Especially as that was what they were probably doing. I was scared of him, too. He'd be a bad bloke to say the wrong thing to.

'Heard about what?'

'You know.' He'd guessed by the time I took to answer. 'About Dulcie.'

There was no good pretending. 'Yes,' I said. 'How is she?'

He didn't answer but he kept on looking at me in the same queer way that he had been looking at me before. And then, as if he'd been sizing me up, he got down to what was on his mind.

'Look here, Ned,' he said. 'What about doing something for me?'

'All right,' I said. 'What do you want me to do?' My heart was in my boots because I didn't know much about the law but I felt sure this was going to be something against it.

'It's like this. I can't ring the hospital to see how she is because the johns are there and they keep asking me my name and they know my voice, too. What about you ringing for me?'

'All right, Marty,' I said. 'But what'll I say if they ask who I am? If I give my name they might come poking about home trying to find out what I know about it.'

'Say your name's Eddie Sharp. That's a friend of her young brother's and it'd be quite natural for him to ring. Will you do it?'

'I'll just see if I've got any pennies.'

We walked back towards the Post Office square. But the john was still in the library doorway and so I told Marty to go back to the place where I'd met him and wait for me there.

The john gave me that hard look that policemen give you but I went straight past him without giving a sign of how nervous I was. It was being so sorry for Marty that made me able to do it, I think.

'Southland Hospital,' a woman's voice answered when I'd got the number.

'I want to inquire about a patient, Miss Moore, Miss Dulcie Moore.'

'Will you hold on, please?'

There was a lot of clicking at the other end and I could hear whispering. Then a man's voice answered.

'The patient died an hour ago. Who is that speaking?'

I didn't answer. I just rang off and came out of the phone box.

How was I going to tell him, I kept asking myself as I went back past the john, hardly noticing him this time.

Marty was standing in the doorway, just as he had been the first time.

'How was she?'

There was nothing else I could do. I out with it.

'She died an hour ago.'

He stood there without saying a thing, just looking at me and yet not seeing me. Then he took a deep breath and his chest came out and he stood even straighter.

'So that's how it is,' he said. 'She's dead.'

I didn't say anything. I just stood there, wishing I was anywhere else in the world.

'If only I'd known,' he said. 'Christ, man. I'd have married her a hundred times, kid and all.'

He stopped. His mind must have been going over and over this ground for days.

He gave a laugh suddenly, such a queer, savage sort of a laugh that I jumped.

'If it'd been twins, even,' he said.

I had enough sense not to think that I was meant to laugh at that one.

'And those bloody johns sitting by the bed.'

'Did she come to?' I asked.

'Yes, she was conscious a lot of the time. But she wouldn't talk, not Dulcie. Not her. She was all right, Dulcie.'

Then there was silence again. I didn't know what to do or say. It was getting late. They'd have locked the door at home and there'd be a rumpus if they knew what time it was when I came in. How queer it was: here I was in the middle of something that really mattered and worrying about what my mother would say if she heard me climbing in the window.

All the same I wanted to get home. And then I had to admit to myself it wasn't really that. It was that I wanted to get away from Marty. I think it must have been the first time I was ever with someone who felt as badly as he was feeling.

'I remember her,' I said. 'She was a stunner to look at.'

'Wasn't she?' Marty said. And the way he said it made the tears come into my eyes.

'Why don't you walk my way?' I asked him. If he did that I could be making towards home and at the same time wouldn't feel I was ratting on him.

'No, I'm not going home yet,' he said.

I shuffled from one foot to the other, wondering what to do next and a bit worried what he would do after I'd gone.

'We always used to meet here,' he said. 'In this doorway.'

'Oh,' I said. 'Well, look here, Marty, I've got to be getting home now.'

'That's all right.'

I tried to think of some way of saying how sorry I was. But there was no way of saying it.

'Good night, Ned,' he said, and then, as I began to walk away, he called out: 'Thanks for doing that for me.'

So that's how it is, I was saying to myself all the way home. That's the sort of thing that happens once the gloves are off. And by the time I'd got to the front gate and opened it with one hand on the latch to stop it clicking and sat on the front verandah to take my shoes off I think I'd taken it all into myself and begun to wake up to how we only kid ourselves we can tell the good things from the bad things when really they're so mixed up that half the time we're thinking one thing, feeling another, and doing something else altogether.

That Golden Time

Castle Street was empty, as empty as that other space towering vacantly overhead towards the stars. The emptiness, the way his heels rang on the asphalt, was satisfying, emphasised his aloneness. A man alone, alone late at night with no one to say he should be home in bed. A man making his way home from the arms of his mistress. And the clear, frosty night a splendid setting for his solitude.

Mistress, it wasn't quite the word really. It didn't go somehow with a girl you'd met at the Town Hall dance only a week before. She was too far from names like Roxana and Pompadour, the canopied beds, the whisper behind the fan, loud feet on the stairs, the sudden hush of the nightingales and a quick escape into the moonlit garden. No, the slang words suited her better – sheila, skirt, tabby – gin in the dark of the doorway and, distant in the dance-hall, the band playing 'I'm Dancing with Tears in My Eyes'.

Still, she'd fallen for him, and when you didn't know any better you had to take what you could get. She did have a room at least, a flat really. And when they were away from the others she was quite gentle and hadn't laughed at him. Of course he looked older than he was. But it was the first time for him, you couldn't get away from that. She must have noticed.

But he didn't want to think about her. She was only the essential partner in the thing. The important fact was that now he knew. And out here in the lonely silence of the street he could piece into the mosaic this final stone.

So that was what it was like. In itself, nothing so very wonderful. A relief certainly, after the tension and desire. An event really, an epoch. But in itself, nothing so very wonderful. A disappointment? Well, yes, in a way. But an adventure, a stage in knowledge. A step across the threshold. He was closer to being a man. Was a man, in fact. Of course, he wasn't fool enough to think that at seventeen you could know everything. But at least he knew more than he had known. He had had one of a man's experiences, even if it wasn't much, not all it was cracked up to be. He'd been drunk and he'd had a woman. Not too drunk luckily. Or perhaps he had been? Perhaps it would have been better if he hadn't drunk so much? Alcohol was a sort of anaesthetic, wasn't it?

With academic deliberation the university clock boomed a warning note. Like old Prof. Evans clearing his throat to speak. To announce that Catullus, in spite of his sensuality, it could not be denied was a great poet. A pity that in a society as corrupt as that of the late Republic his experience should have been almost necessarily licentious, that the manners, he might say, the mores, of the time made it natural that he should express himself in a licentious way. One might almost grant him the excuse of inevitability since he inevitably reflected the morals of his time. 'To hold the mirror up to Nature – '. And, after all, even in Shakespeare – . And then, also, one must remember that he did not have the benefits of revealed religion. We must make allowances. And he was young. A passionate pagan – .

The Professor sighed, troubled perhaps by a vague resentment that Catullus, in spite of his professors, should be living still, while he, Professor Evans, M.A. of his University, Elder of the Church and confident of everlasting life, should stand here, dead, and forbidden by a lifetime's hebetude to expound the paradox. He sighed again: 'Well, we must get on with the reading. Lesbia's "Sparrow". Will you begin, Miss Macpherson?'

The clock, an old man's echo, struck its three strokes in empty pomp. But its reverberation, a quavering afterthought, still vibrated over Miss Macpherson's well-conned reduction of a light Latin fancy to Presbyterian prose.

Vivamus, mea Lesbia. The waters of the Leith, telling their own less even time, smoothed the rugged jutting of Miss Macpherson's earnest face, abolished her horn-rimmed glasses and Lesbia's passionate paleness burned from the water. Night and the clock's ponderous warning sombred daylight's shallow stream into the depth and passion and mystery of all dark water still and flowing.

Yet, perhaps the Professor and Miss Macpherson were right. Or the sparrow. Tonight's experience had more of his swift flurry in the gutter and casual aftermath of adjustment than it had of Lesbia. Lesbia herself perhaps had only been the hen, lent false feathers and the fine sheen of passion by a poet's frustrated frenzy. And that frenzy itself but a more complex kind of mating call.

> *Nobis cum semel occidit brevis lux*
> *Nox est perpetua una dormienda.*

The night at least was magnificent and, as for the final sunset and the single timeless sleep, that remained to be seen. Or never to be seen.

But he wasn't really being fair to Catullus. Let sparrows observe sparrows. Men must watch the fate of men. The whole point of a love poet lay in the love. And he could hardly claim to have been in love with Lily, God forbid.

So perhaps he still didn't know.

Lesbia had left the water, dismissed to the enigmatic past. Lily's friendly face, pale in the naked overhead light as putty, in the light of the lampshade pink as her own brassières, passed along its prisoner's walk of expression from anxiety as they tiptoed up the stairs and past the landlady's stertorous room, to nervous and giggling triumph as they sat on the bed and canvassed with a show of argument the inevitable understood, to complicit eagerness which she masked by bending to her shoes and releasing her choked feet to irrelevant cheerfulness, through all these stages till at last, nervous and heart hollow, he saw again under the half-closed lids the eyes fixed across the enormous distances beyond which we see nullity when, alone except for the company of another guilty body, our desires cling to their desperate ecstasy, alone.

Surely he had got some truth out of it then? But if truth were beauty and beauty truth? Too bare an equation surely, when the two were one and that one not beauty. Catullus and Keats were more fortunate than he. Or less impatient? Or were they wrong?

Anyhow, he'd got some truth out of it. Even if one man's truth were another man's poison he knew something he hadn't known before. He could face these poet chaps more on their own ground now. He was different from what he had been. He looked up from the stream, its dark film now empty as the street, to the University's Presbyterian gothic. It might have given him Catullus but he was one up on it now. What would old Bacchus Evans think if he knew where he had been? And all the class which would mouth poetry tomorrow as mechanically as prayers. Masked behind his face he would savour secret laughter.

The clock voiced with the quarter its brief disapprobation. Time to be making for home. A quarter past three. It would be good to be back in his digs, alone in his room, that first base from which he had set out to wrest from the city knowledge and freedom. It was there on many a lonely night that he had pored over the map of the unknown and measured his adversaries, ignorance and fears. He would go back there now and mark in the new line, the new frontier.

He moved on, fingering still the outlines of his experience, minutely scrutinising it for missed significance, suffering already his first intimations of the speed with which the memory of the senses fades, till what is called pleasure depends on the word it first created for reality while the urgent detonation in the nerves can no more be recalled than the dead bones of poets can arch again the pulsing sap from which their passion flowered. And he learnt for the first time the disgust that seeps into the place of passion which, engendered in the brain, passes along the blood, goes and leaves a vacuum untenanted by tenderness or love.

The house stood out white against the dark of the hill. But its whiteness was blank and unlit. The Buchanans were always early to bed. The door was locked. They must have thought he was in bed too. He crept round to his ground floor window. Mrs Buchanan was not tolerant of new moralities. The window was ajar as he had left it. He climbed cautiously in.

He switched on the light. He was breathing a little hard, from climbing in. And this was his moment. There might be no crowd for his triumph but he did not want anyone else. Triumph is better enjoyed unwatched. One's own jealous observation is a sufficient audience, a sufficient adversary. The most formidable even, since here visors are lifted, motives and vanities admitted and disasters plain.

Yet he paused before facing the mirror, as a man pauses before looking to see what cards he has drawn, or before opening a letter long awaited. Now he was to see the lines that drink and debauchery had cut in his face. He was to see what it looked like to have changed. He squared his shoulders and turned to the mirror, to see and confront his manhood.

The face that he saw was young, its imaginary beard carefully shaven and tomorrow's instalment of the fiction not yet visible. The mouth was full but its line firm. The eyes were steady, perplexed, inquiring, very young.

It was the face with which he had set out that evening, nerved for the momentous stride into maturity. It was the face of an intelligent youth of seventeen, only now a little tired.

He studied it a long time. Then he put the mirror down. He felt very tired. It was late. And he had not prepared his Cicero for the morning.

Still, he had done one thing. He was no longer a virgin, anyway. He had the laugh on the rest of them, say what you like. As for the Cicero he didn't need to bother about that old windbag. His tirades were never unpredictable. He could do it at sight, easily.

He picked up the mirror suddenly, as if to catch it off its guard. The face was obstinately the same. He saw what looked like a blackhead and became intent on removing it.

Lily had a bad complexion. Fastidiously he banished her memory from the mirror.

The clock struck the half-hour as he got into bed.

A Happy New Year

It was New Year's Eve that night so we'd got the milking over early and had tea. Everyone else was up at the house and getting ready for the party. But I never was much of a one for parties. Not that kind of party anyhow where you sit round the sitting-room that the women have suddenly started calling a drawing-room and the girls are all dressed up and it's: 'Will you have a glass of port, Mrs So-and-so?' and: 'You'll take a drop of whisky, I expect, Mr So-and-so,' but the girls never get squiffy and you can't lay hands on enough yourself to get over feeling a sawney and wishing the whole show was over.

So I just sat outside the door of my hut and watched the cows in the front paddock going it to get a good feed in before they settled down for the night. The sun wasn't quite down and the air was as clear as a bell. Away up high you could see some gulls flying as if they were in a hurry to get to wherever gulls go and you could hear quite plainly the sheep calling to one another away behind on the ridge. In fact it was one of those evenings when you begin to feel sorry for yourself in a quiet kind of way and wish you had someone you could explain to about how you really weren't a bad chap. Only it'd have to be a girl because when it comes to that kind of thing a man just laughs.

So in a way it was a kind of distraction whenever my big toe gave a jab where young Jackie Brass put a .22 bullet through it when I took him out on Christmas Day to try his new

Winchester on the rabbits. Not that I was worrying much: it was healing up nicely and I'd been on quite a fuss the first few days what with Phyllis Brass coming and smiling at me and bringing me cool drinks and Mrs Brass, who wasn't a bad sort really, feeding me up like a fighting cock and as pleased as Punch with me because I'd said it wasn't Jackie's fault.

Still, for all that, it was a bit of a curse tonight. If it hadn't been for the old toe I'd have been down in the township at the New Year's Eve Grand Dance and there'd have been plenty of booze going and there was a sheila I had my eye on. So there I sat and I was thinking to myself it was about time I stopped going to all these hops anyhow and never staying put in a job more than a few months and never writing to that nice girl I used to have in North Auckland before I came down South and spending all my dough on what I could drink. After all, a man can't stay a rouseabout all his life on other blokes' farms. What the old man used to say to me about chaps who didn't have a spark of gumption in them except for getting in on a hand of poker or a bottle of whisky or a girl, kept coming back into my head. And I got to thinking of all the other New Years I'd known and how in the old days before the depression a man used to think each New Year was going to be different but now they were all the same. By that time I'd stopped looking at the landscape and was looking down at my feet, one of them in the cow-boot and the other in the old gym-shoe which was turning green at the edges with grass and cow-dung and had a hole cut in it for my sore toe to stick out.

So I didn't see old Jack Brass coming at me and didn't hear him either because he was always a bit of a creeping Jesus the way he walked. Not that he was like that in other ways. It was just that the Missus had put the fear of God into him about walking round the house like a great clodhopper and he'd got into the habit of walking as if the ground would object. He had just enough money to die a few years younger than he might, poor old Jack, from worry. He'd have been all right if he wasn't married. Or perhaps he was better the way he was. Having sheep and cows and land and kids to worry about stops you from worrying about yourself, I suppose. Anyhow, for a boss he wasn't a bad boss. It was pretty hard not to see good in a bloke with a daughter like Phyllis, in any case.

'Hallo, Len,' he said, 'all on your lonesome?'

'Yes,' I said.

'Why don't you come on up to the house? Phyllis has got some girl friends coming and the two young Bretts from across the river are going to come over.'

'Thanks all the same, Jack,' I said. 'Don't feel much like it tonight.'

He took a good look at me and then looked back towards the house. I could see he was up to something.

'Come on over to the stables,' he said.

There was some sort of mystery on but I could see by the way he was purring and frightened at the same time it was a pleasant one.

'O.K., Jack,' I said. And I got up and hopped alongside of him. When we got inside he shut the bottom half of the stable door which made it pretty dark because the evening was getting on by now. The big rumps of the team were sticking out from their stalls and you could hear them snorting and blowing their lips about as they dug into their chaff but you couldn't see their heads.

Jack stopped looking out the top half of the door and came over to where the big barrel of chaff was in the corner. I sat down on a heap of sacks. Jack fished a big bottle out of the barrel.

'You know what the Missus is,' he said. 'Been saving this up for a long while.'

I thought I'd better not follow up that one about the Missus so I asked him what it was.

'Just the best, that's all, Len,' he said. 'You know I don't often touch it but what with the party and you looking so down in the mouth I thought a taster wouldn't do us any harm. Here, help yourself.' And he held me out the bottle and a mug.

I poured out a little one on the bottom.

'Go on, man. Make it worth your while.'

Well, I thought, why not? I tipped the bottle and filled up

the best part of the mug. More than I meant to, as a matter of fact.

'Drink her down,' he said.

I couldn't see what the colour was in that light and didn't care much anyhow so I just upped the mug and down she went.

He reached for the mug. He had the bottle already.

'What do you think of it?' he said.

I was still getting my breath. It was raw Hokonui, if I'm any judge, and about as strong as anything that ever came out of the bush.

'Pretty good,' I said.

He had put just a bit in the mug, not half-way. I began to feel a bit ashamed at having hogged so much. He drank his down.

'Good stuff,' he said. You couldn't tell whether he knew it was Hokonui or not. He was so innocent in some ways he might have thought it was Scotch. But he was as cunning as a Maori dog, too, and he might have known bloody well but just not be giving anything away unless he had to.

'Have another,' he said.

I took the bottle and the mug. This time I was only going to have a polite one. But then I thought: It's too late to start getting polite now. So I filled her pretty full again. And away it went.

This time I noticed he filled it right up to the top himself.

Well, after that we got to talking and in the end he began to tell me how worried he was about Billie. Billie was his brother. He lived in the hut behind the stables and lent a hand on the farm. Good worker he was too, hard as nails and though he wasn't as big as Jack, who had bones on him like a swamp-plough, he was a tough bit of goods. Only he was a terror for the booze. He wouldn't just go on a lash for a day or two like most of us and then sweat it out. He often kept at it till it laid him on his back in the DT's.

'You haven't seen him at all today, have you?' Jack asked me.

'Not a hair of him.'

'He ought to be home any time now. He's not the man he was and he's been knocking it back since two days before Christmas. I don't know where he's getting the dough from, either. He must have spent what I gave him by now.'

This was news to me. I'd always thought Billie had some of his own. He generally seemed to have plenty. What with this and the booze I began to think Jack was a pretty good sort of joker.

'He can't keep off it once he starts, poor old Billie,' said Jack. 'If it hadn't been for that he'd have owned this farm today.'

'That a fact?' I said, not wanting to seem interested.

'Yes,' he said. 'He's older than me, you know, and the old man left him the farm. All of it this side of the river, that is. The rest came with the Missus. I worked the farm for him while he was away at the war. But when he came back and took over things were going to rack and ruin. It was the war changed him, I suppose. He didn't seem to care a brass farthing for anything except the booze and talking about the war with his old cobbers. They were all the same, those returned men. Well, in the end we bought him out with Cissie's money, Cissie and me. We'd just married. Billie went off on the swag for a few years, him and Joe Hoskins who's the baker down in the township now. Then they turned up again and Billie asked if he could stay on. Cissie thought he'd probably do better on his own. But I said yes, of course.'

'Jack! Where are you, Jack?' I could tell Mrs Brass must be standing at the back door. That was the way her voice always came when she called, round the bend of the macrocarpa, with a grinding edge to it like a train.

'Coming, Cissie,' Jack called back. 'You'd better come on up with me,' he went on. He'd got a bit bolder now and he was resting the bottle on the leaf of the door. There was just enough light for me to see it was pretty well cut. So I got up off the sacks and went over to him.

'I don't think I will, thanks all the same,' I said. And all the time I must admit my mind was back fossicking in the chaff barrel to see if there was any more. Bottles are like fleas:

where there's one there's two.

'Come on,' he said. 'Phyllis'll be disappointed if you don't.'

He was a nice chap all right. But of course, that was the whisky talking. He knew I didn't have a bean. Mind you, the way he liked Phyllis, if she'd been set on having me he'd probably have given in. But the way the Missus liked her was different and she'd have had plenty to say. And she'd have won the way her type always do. Anyhow, that's not the way I do things. I'd sooner be without money than marry for it. Still, it was nice of old Jack. And Phyllis was a nice girl, too.

'All right,' I said. 'I'll be right on up as soon as I've changed my boot and put on a tie.'

It soon turned out I'd guessed right what sort of a party it would be. So there I was stuck in a corner under the picture of a Newfoundland dog Phyllis had painted when she was at school. Mrs Brass was very proud of that picture but you could easily tell Phyllis had never seen a Newfoundland dog. Opposite on the other wall was that picture of the wild horses when they see the lightning. Jimmy and Peter Brett on the sofa underneath it, dressed up to the nines in their blue suits and Christmas-present ties, looked a bit like wild horses themselves the way their eyes goggled at Phyllis. Only they seemed to like their lightning since that was what they'd put on collars for.

Phyllis was full of beans, of course. Who wouldn't be, with the three of us gaping at her and the two girl friends from the next-door farm pretty well chosen so as not to put her in the shade? And Mrs Brass sitting up as straight as a swingletree in a bolster and smiling away as if it was her we were after. So it was in a way, I suppose. Women with daughters are like that, I think, with the glazed look in their eyes and a smile at the corner of their mouths so you can tell by the way they take a dekko from time to time at their own old man that their minds are skipping back twenty years or so and they're having it both ways.

Not that it stopped her from keeping a pretty close eye on things: but then they're all the same and even the youngest of

them can take your hand away from her knee, pick up a point
from Jean Harlow's hairdo, wish you were William Powell
and keep that soulful look in her eye all at the same time. And
work out how much you paid for the seats too and decide to
marry you at the same time as she's thinking how mean you
are and how men are all the same – except William Powell, of
course.

So after a while Mrs Brass thinks it's time Phyllis showed
off how well they taught her the piano at the convent.

'Won't you play us something, Angela?' she says, knowing
very well Angela hasn't brought her music.

Angela swallowed down the bit of seed cake she'd just
nibbled. 'I haven't got my music with me or I'd love to. But
surely Phyllis will play for us. She plays so beautifully, doesn't
she, Jean?'

'Yes,' says Jean, who was a bit better looking and didn't
have to be quite such an enthusiastic friend.

Phyllis dickers a bit but of course she finishes by getting up
and saying she's going to play a thing called Offenbach's
'Barcarolle'. The Bretts goggle a bit more and Jean, who
can't play and has her eye on young Jimmy Brett, looks tight
about the mouth. But Mrs Brass is as proud as a full money-
box.

I notice old Jack's head has begun to jerk, though, and his
pipe's gone out and after a while his eyes go dead on him and
his head sags like a top-heavy stook. Then up it goes again
with a jerk and he stares wide open in front of him as if he
daren't look to see if anyone has noticed.

By this time I was feeling pretty desperate for a drink myself
and I didn't care much for this kind of game. Too young for
me. I wasn't as shook on Phyllis as all that. The trouble was,
though, she knew I was the only half-hearted bloke there so it
was me she was after. She was pretty young still and it narked
her that everyone was eating out of her hand except me. Of
course, if I'd been able to kid myself a bit it might have been
different. But I knew enough to know that that feeling inside
only seemed to be the sort of thing the blokes in the pictures
are supposed to feel. I knew bloody well that if her legs and

waist and breasts and face had been different I'd have felt different too and I wouldn't be thinking what a lovely character she had. Anyhow, supposing I had begun to play round and get keen, half my attraction would have vanished. And she was only a kid. She wouldn't have to wait round long before a better sort of joker than me would turn up.

Well, she got through the 'Barcarolle' business all right and it wasn't bad either. Sort of suited the way I was feeling. Then there was a lot more polite talk and she began to sing 'Danny Boy' while Angela, who seemed to have got over her caraway seeds and having no music, accompanied.

Just as the song finished we heard a voice outside roaring away at the same song, taking her off. Mrs Brass looked at Jack and Jack looked at her and both looked at me. The Bretts and the two girls looked at their feet and Phyllis pretended to be looking at her music though I could tell she had her eye on me. It was Billie, all right.

This was just my chance. So I got up, looking very indignant, and said 'Excuse me a bit, would you.' And I had the satisfaction of making everyone feel I was being the gentleman and doing them a favour. Only I'm not sure Phyllis was fooled.

Billie stopped roaring as soon as he saw me, which was just as well because he'd just started on 'My Lady of the Boudoir'. He gave me a great whack on the back. 'Thought that'd fetch you,' he said. 'Come on over to the hut.'

As soon as we were in the hut I knew this was a worse jag than I'd ever seen Billie on before. For one thing Joe Hoskins was flat out on one of the two bunks already. When he saw me his eyes gave a roll and his Adam's apple moved up and down under his sunburnt skin like a rat under a sack. But that was about all he could manage. Billie looked better but his grey eyes were bloodshot and had a queer glitter in them and a week's growth didn't help his looks at all. His hands were shaking too, just a little but all the time. Ripe for the DT's, I thought to myself.

'Poor old Joe,' says Billie. 'I put him down here to cool off.

He's got to get his pies into the oven before four o'clock tomorrow morning. But can't let a man ride his horse across the river in that state.'

Joe's eyes opened and he said something thickly. Pies was the only word I could catch.

'Poor old Joe,' says Billie. 'He knows I won't let him down. Not after the way you carried me back that night, eh Joe? Me and Joe left together with the first draft and we came back together, too. Good old Joe. Plenty of time for the pies, Joe. Have a drink.'

We were sitting down on the other bunk by this time with a mug each and were hoeing into some Hokonui. Like a real old soldier Billie had fixed himself up pretty comfortable in that hut, rough but snug.

Well, things were pretty good and Billie showed me all over again how he worked his system of strings so that you could switch out the light from the bed and pull a bottle and mug from under it if you had a hang-over and didn't like getting up. But then he got to talking about the war which is a thing that always makes me a bit uncomfortable with old soldiers. They get to poking the borax at everyone who was too young to be there and everyone who was old enough but didn't go and they sing songs no one else knows and tell yarns you know are probably lies but you can't say so because it's not the thing to contradict a returned soldier, not with him drunk anyway and as tough a customer as Billie.

And sure enough Billie was no exception, because after he'd pulled out his old kit-bag and shown me the bits of shrapnel they took out of his shoulder and the bullet they'd got out of his leg and the French and German newspapers, yellow as cheese and dated 1918 and full of chaps that only Billie and blokes like him knew about any more, nothing will do but he must make me try on a German helmet he had and as a matter of fact it didn't suit me badly either. But when I said 'Donner und Blitzen' the way my old man used to say it for fun Billie suddenly gets a notion that I'm a German and comes at me with his old bayonet. I didn't like the look in his eye at all and I wasn't too fly on that gammy foot of mine but I took the weight on the other foot and the next minute I had the bayonet and threw him on the floor. Still, things didn't look too good so I said:

'A Jerry could never have done that to you, Billie.'

'By God, you're right,' he said and Joe said 'Pies,' from the bed.

'Don't worry, Joe,' Billie goes on. 'No, Len, it'd take a better man than a Jerry to do that. Why don't you marry Phyllis, Len. You're not a bad sort of joker.'

That knocked me back a bit, especially as girls' names usually bring trouble when chaps are drinking. They get a bit touchy then and they suddenly get shocked and on their high horses about things they know perfectly well when they're sober but don't think about.

By this time Billie was back on the bunk again with his head in his hands. When he took them away I saw there were tears rolling down his cheeks. Jesus, I thought to myself, he's got a crying jag on now.

'What's the trouble, Billie,' I said. 'Have a drink.'

He pours out a drink without saying anything. And then I see he isn't crying any more but working himself into a flaming rage about something. I didn't like to kick the bayonet out of sight for fear of starting him off again, but I kept my eye on it.

'Yes,' he says. 'You ought to marry her. She likes you and you're not a bad joker. Of course, those greedy bastards over at the house would never let you. She'll marry more land if they have their way. But I don't see why I shouldn't have my say, God damn them if I don't.'

'I don't see why I shouldn't have mine either,' I said. 'Nobody's asked me what I think.'

'It's the least I could do for her,' he goes on.

I didn't like the drift of this at all so I changed the subject. 'I don't see why you've got such a down on them,' I said.

That started him off properly.

'No,' he says, 'but I do. No Jerry could do to me the things my own family have done to me, my own bloody family that

Joe and me saved from the Jerries back there in the bloody trenches.'

Joe stirred a bit and started muttering about pies again.

But Billie was still chewing the rag. I thought I'd better get out because I could see something was coming and I didn't want to be mixed up in any of this family stuff.

'I reckon I might be able to get Joe on to his horse now,' I said.

'You leave Joe where he is. I'm not letting Joe get buggered about by any bloody fly-by-night rouseabout. Where would he be better off than with his old cobber? Or are you against me too? Are you on the side of those bastards up at the house, lording it with their drawing-rooms and their la-de-da parties?'

'I'm on nobody's side, Billie.'

'That's right and nobody's on my side. Except poor old Joe here and he's in the rats. Just a couple of poor old returned men that nobody wants after we slogged out our guts in the trenches for them.'

'That's all bull, Billie. Everyone likes you.'

'So they bloody well should, the way I've been a door-mat for them all my life.' He took another gulp. You'd have thought he was quite sober if you couldn't see his eyes. 'Look here, Len,' he said. 'You're not a bad joker.'

'Aren't I?' I said.

'No, you're not. But I'll tell you what. You're a bloody fool all the same. Otherwise you'd do what I say and marry that girl. But you're just a bloody fool. I suppose you think Jack's not a bad joker, either?'

'Well, yes.'

'And you think the Missus is all right, too, don't you?'

'Yes,' I said.

'Well, let me tell you something. It's time you knew just who you're dealing with if you're going to marry Phyllis.'

I let that one pass. He'd have forgotten all about it in the morning.

'Well,' he went on, 'when I went off to France I owned this

farm. And I was engaged to Cissie.'

'Uh huh,' I said.

'Naturally us boys didn't feel much like settling down when we came back. It seemed pretty tame. Well, we got to boozing round a bit, Joe here and me, and we kept a couple of racehorses. And the next thing we knew I had to take a mortgage on this place. And a bit after that the bastards were going to close on me. Cissie was pretty keen on me but she's no bloody fool, too right she isn't, and she's got some of the skinflint blood of that old man of hers in her. You know how mean he was and how much he left when he died. Well, you don't, but it was a hell of a lot. Anyhow Cissie knew a thing or two and she was dead scared that me and the booze between us would send her dough after mine. To cut a long story short she pointed her gun at Jack instead of me. Of course, he goes down like a rabbit. She had looks in those days. So Joe and I went off on the swag for a while and the end of it all is that she and Jack get married and buy up my mortgage. And so here am I, just the poor bloody drunken relation.'

'Still, Billie, you asked for it. A man's got to grow up. It's every man for himself these days.'

'Perhaps we just didn't grow up out there, some of us. It wasn't every man for himself the night Joe carried me in, my bloody oath it wasn't. But you don't know the half of it.'

He gulps down the rest of his whisky, fills her up again and stares at the floor.

'You don't know the half of it,' he says again. And I can see his mood getting blacker and blacker on him.

Suddenly there's tap at the window. We looked up and we could see Jack peering in through one of the broken panes.

'Did you take my bottle, Billie?' Jack says. Not nasty at all but just as if he'd like to come in and have a bit of real company. We must have looked better than we felt.

'Of course I took your bloody bottle.' Billie is on his feet and making for the door. 'Why shouldn't I take your bloody bottle? Haven't you taken everything of mine.' All this in a sort of scream.

'For Christ's sake, be quiet, Billie, you fool. They'll hear you up at the house,' Jack said, as he met Billie at the door.

'Let her hear if that's what you're frightened of. There's a thing or two she wouldn't like you to hear.' And at that he takes a swing at Jack, misses and falls back inside.

Jack and I soon had him back on the bunk and tried to quieten him down. The noise had wakened Joe and he was muttering away about his bloody pies. Once we had Billie by an arm each we didn't quite know what to do and I for one felt a bit of a fool sitting there, hanging on to him.

'What do you mean, Billie, there's a thing or two she wouldn't like me to hear?' Jack said then.

Billie looked at him and you could see he was almost out of his mind with rage the way some chaps get with the whisky, especially Hokonui.

'I'll tell you what,' he said. He stopped and then he out with it. 'She wouldn't like you to hear Phyllis was my kid, would she?'

There was a long pause, not really long but it felt long. At the end of it I knew Jack wasn't going to crown him. He let go Billie's arm and you could hear the bunk creak as his weight relaxed on it. You couldn't tell whether it was sheer surprise that had knocked him or whether it was something he'd guessed all along without knowing it.

Nobody said anything or looked at anyone else. Only old Joe kept grumbling in his stupor.

Then Billie spoke and his voice was quite different, sort of flat and dry.

'Yes, Jack,' he said, 'and I never meant to tell you. Cissie was in pod when you married her. She knew it, too, but she knew I'd never be any good. It wasn't her fault. I talked her into it one night when we were still on together. She thought it might help keep me off the booze, I suppose. Anyhow it didn't and she soon thought better of it. She knew you were the better man. So did I, for that matter, and told her so. That's why I pushed off with my swag that time. We never said anything to you about it because we thought you were more likely to be a decent father for Phyllis than I ever would be. So you were. So you are, Jack. As for me, I couldn't even hold my bloody tongue. I'm sorry, Jack.'

'It's all right, Billie,' said Jack. He got up. 'I've had everything of yours,' he said. He looked at the whisky bottle and gave a kind of grin. Then he went out.

'Pies,' Joe was muttering again.

I limped over and started to get him on my back.

'I'll do that,' Billie said. 'At least I can get my old cobber home.'

From the door of my hut I watched him get Joe across the saddle and ride down the tussock slope towards the river.

Things would either remain the same or get better or get worse, I thought. But it would be better for them not to have me still around when I knew so much. Up at the house I could hear Phyllis's high voice calling goodnight to the girls. The Bretts would be seeing them home.

The next day I'd collect what Jack owed me and get a lift down to the township. I could put up at a pub. New Year's Day was as good a day as any to be on the move again.

II

Below the Heavens

Already, just before dawn, Trevor and Red were awake. They had pooled their blankets ever since the weather got cold and slept together for warmth. They lay there now beside the slit-trench, listening to the rain patter on the ground-sheets they had spread over the blankets and watching the light filter gradually through the trees.

'Come on, you lazy bastards, off your backsides. Jerry's going to pay a call today.'

That was Joe coming off guard and waking the section posts. They could hear the groaning and cursing come closer as each man crawled from his blankets and got ready for the day.

When Joe reached them they were already sitting up. Trevor rubbing his thick black hair, Red pulling through the rifle he had kept dry under the blankets.

'What sort of shift did you have, Joe?'

'Absolute bastard. Raining all the bloody time.' He shook himself and the rain from his gas-cape sprayed them. 'These gas-capes are a godsend. Though I doubt if they'd keep out much gas.'

'Anything exciting, though?' asked Red.

'Nothing much. We could see fires burning over Katarini way and we thought we heard tanks in the distance. Kept hearing noises in the bush, too. But it always turned out to be the odd bird or lizard or something. Bloody cold it was, too.'

'Well, we weren't much better off. Blankets were as wet as a sponge. What's happening about breakfast?'

'Shorty's going over to Platoon HQ at seven to get some tea and some hot grub. The boss says hang on to the rations you've got as long as you can in case things get a bit sticky. Mac says bring your dixies along to his hole. One at a time, about half-past.'

'OK.'

Joe turned and climbed up to the track. Trevor and Red were already in their hole. Trevor tenderly removed his gas-cape from the Bren and put it on over his greatcoat. Red was stowing the blankets wrapped in the ground-sheets into a hole in the side of the trench where the water couldn't reach them.

'At least a man doesn't have to get dressed when he wakes up these days,' said Trevor.

'No point in shaving, either, for whoever's funeral it's going to be.'

'It'll be theirs,' said Trevor.

Down in the valley and away to the left there was a rattle of small arms' fire.

'Christ, boys, d'you hear that?' Joe was on his way back from the posts on the right.

'She's der Tag, all right,' Red called back, grinning.

Trevor was still listening. 'Bren and rifle,' he said. 'The boys must have spotted something.'

He tucked his Bren into his shoulder and looking down the sights tested for the hundredth time his field of fire.

'God help the Heinie who pokes his nose into our little neck of the woods today,' he said. 'This bloody rain has put me into just the right mood for them.'

'I could do with a smoke,' said Red.

'Sit back and have one then. I'll keep an eye open. They can't come up on the left without running into 13 Platoon. If they come up the front it's chicken-feed. And Bill and Scotty won't miss much on the right.'

Red tucked the tails of his greatcoat between his heels and squatted. The rain streamed down his gas-cape and plopped, missing the greatcoat, into the water which, red from the churned-up clay, reached to their ankles. He rolled a cigarette.

'Silver Fern,' he said. 'Only the best, that's all. What a godsend that parcel was. A man needs a bit of decent tobacco what with all this rain and Jerries about.'

'Go easy on it, boy. We don't know how long it's got to last us. We'd better roll racehorses.'

'Plenty here, Trev, plenty. How's time?'

Trevor pulled back the sodden sleeve of his greatcoat.

'Seven fifteen. Quarter of an hour yet.'

'I'll finish this smoke and take over from you.'

'OK.'

It was now broad daylight. The mists had shrunk back into the valley. On the hillside where they were, the last shreds had gone. The rain still came down steadily, checked at the foliage above them, then gathering into little streams and runnels ran down the trunks, or, the pools on the leaves brimming over, dropped in irregular, heavy plops. On the ground it soaked into the leaf-mould beneath the trees. But where there were gaps it gathered on the trampled clay, hesitated and then, taking courage with volume, streamed down the slope to the gully.

Trevor, arms folded against the parapet, watched along the Bren barrel. A shrub from which they had scooped out the inner branches screened both him and the gun from the front without obscuring the view.

His eye kept roving the ground before him. It sloped away steeply down to the fields in the valley. Though trees broke the view before that. They were relying on surprise and close range. But they had had time to cut away the young saplings for the first couple of hundred yards and lace the stumps with barbed trip-wires. A pity the ground was broken in three or four places by old grass-grown terraces, high enough to hide a man. And a couple of shallow water-courses, full only when the snow on Olympus was melting, cut the ground vertically. Just out of grenade reach ran the main barbed wire. Nobody could cross that without being seen. And nobody would.

The main snag was the deep wadi on the left. But Mac had posted Shorty and his cobber there. And Charlie had his mortar ranged on it.

Then there was the ground on the right, the most broken, with a lot of low cover and big rocks. But Bill and Scotty would cover most of it. They'd have to keep their eyes peeled and watch the rest themselves.

'O.K., Trev. You hop off and sample the scran. I'll look after the little vixen.' Red slapped the butt of the Bren. Trevor turned squelching in the trench and clambered up on the ground with his dixie.

Left alone, Red took up Trevor's position. The rain streamed from his helmet to his shoulders. An occasional drop ran down the front of his helmet and fell from there to his nose, tickling him till he wiped it off, or slithered chillily down his neck. His feet were cold in the wet boots and he was hungry. But he was only half aware of these things. He was nervous and excited. So der Tag had come, what they'd been waiting for. Jerry was going to get what was coming to him today. But inside he felt all tensed up. Not all hunger, either. Well, they'd show him today. He licked his lips, still hot with the strong tobacco, and dry.

He started. Firing again. Down on 13 Platoon front. Thank Christ he wasn't down with them. Too much of a good thing. Bloody sticky position they had. The firing continued, bursts from a Bren and the slower shooting of rifles. Then silence again.

But now, away over on the left battalion front, artillery opened up. Our twenty-five pounders, it sounded like. Jerry was bound to tackle the main pass road first. The firing reverberated among the mountains behind, the ground vibrated.

He heard tramping behind him. Trevor was on his way down from the track, dixie held in front of him, steam coming out of it.

'Heard the firing down 13 Platoon way so thought I'd better get back. Nothing doing yet?'

'Not a bloody whisper. Think it's OK for me to go up?'

'Yes, right as rain. Not that there's anything right about this bloody rain.'

'What's for breakfast?'

'Beans.'

'Oh, beans. Well, I'll be back.' Red nipped out of the trench.

'I'll be back like a shot if I hear anything,' he called from the track.

'OK.'

Trevor was at the Bren again. There was no change to the front. Now that Red was gone the silence was taut, in spite of the rain. The birds which had been so noisy yesterday were quiet. Without taking his eyes off the front Trevor gulped occasionally at his mug. Today was the day. He counted on doing a bit of killing today. It was not so very far from here his father had been killed, at Gallipoli.

Not a sound in front. Nothing moved. Only the water trickling over the clay down to the wadi or dropping into the trench beside him. And on the left somewhere the artillery blasting away. Must be the Maoris. They had all the luck. Still, you never knew. They always used to say after the last war: When Jerry's quiet, watch out. Yes, the old man would get a shock if he could see his son now. Same old game. Same old Jerries. Only worse. Well, God help any that came this way today.

Red came dodging down, grabbing the trees as he went, partly for cover, partly to keep his footing.

'What d'you think you're doing? Playing Red Indians?'

'No good being a fool,' Red flushed. Their first battle, men were still sensitive about courage.

Trevor caught the angry inflection. 'OK, redhead. You're quite right.'

The morning wore on like the rain, steadily, without hurrying. From time to time there was firing in front. Then it would die down, quiet as before. Sometimes the sun struggled through for a bit and an occasional ray probed through the trees. Now and then they heard planes fly overhead but could not see them. They knew by the sound they were not ours.

'A fine bloody spring,' said Red. 'Just like the West Coast. Nothing but rain for days on end.'

'Doesn't matter much. Rain won't kill you.'

'Back in old Greymouth, though,' Red went on, 'a man'd be sitting in the pub with a schooner under his nose. Or a rum and raspberry I'd have today. Think of it, a rum and raspberry.'

'A whisky would do me. Going to be any tea for lunch?'

'Boss says we'd better drink from our water-bottles. Thinks there's bound to be something doing before long. Think of it, water. And I could have been drinking rum and raspberry.'

'I suppose too much of that was what made you volunteer.'

'Well, I was a bit plastered. But the whole town was, that day.'

'Did you hear anything then?'

They listened. A few yards in front a big tortoise hobbled out of the bracken, thought better of it and shuffled in again.

'Bloody old I-tank,' said Red. 'What about a bit of bully? How's time?'

It was after midday. Red took a haversack from the hole in the bank.

'Bully, I suppose,' he said.

'What else is there?'

'Bully.'

'I'll have bully then.'

Red opened the tin and set it in front of them. They dug in with spoons, alternating it with bites of biscuit. When the dry mixture was too much for them they swigged from the water-bottle.

Firing again. More to the front this time. And there was a mortar going as well.

'That must be old Murphy with the mortar,' said Trevor. 'Things must be getting a bit more willing down there.'

But, though it lasted longer, the firing died away again.

'A bigger affair,' said Trevor, 'but it hasn't come off or there'd be grenades flying.'

'Trust old 13 Platoon.'

'We'd better watch out. Sounds as if they're maybe working round to this side.'

They bent over their weapons, both watching now. The rain gathered in the bully tin, turned the remaining shreds of meat to a dirty, wet grey.

'See that?' said Red. 'I thought I saw a chap dodge behind that tree.'

'You did. But hang on. Where there's one there's more. Let them get in close.'

'OK.'

They waited. Nothing more happened. Red could hear Trevor's watch ticking beside him. The rain kept falling.

Suddenly the Jerries broke ground and came running up the slope. At the same time from somewhere to the right a Schmeisser began to fire. The bullets thudded into the bank behind them. But they didn't hear. Red's first two shots went wild. The next ones were better. Trevor swept his gun across the line of Jerries and back, firing automatic. As he swung back to the right he tried to catch out of the corner of his eye a sight of the Schmeisser. But it was too far right.

The enemy disappeared.

'Gone to ground,' said Red.

'Dropped down behind the first terrace.'

They watched their front closely. Two Germans lay in front clearly visible and didn't stir. They could see the bracken waving where another had fallen. Trevor sent a short burst after him. Close to the cover the enemy had first broken from a man jumped up suddenly and ran back. He had only five yards to go. His right arm hung stiff. Red sent a shot after him. But the man reached the cover. The bracken where the other had fallen waved again. They caught a glimpse of him as he dropped into the water-course. Not worth a shot. He was safe now.

'Those two seem to have got away all right,' said Trevor.

'There's two that won't move again, though,' Red replied. 'I fired five rounds. How many did you?'

'Best part of a magazine. Too much.' He had already changed the magazine. He was watching the ground to the right. The Schmeisser had stopped firing. There was no sign of movement.

'I make it four still in front,' said Red.

'So do I. But there must be more around.'

There was rifle fire from the post on their left.

'That'll be the others coming up the wadi,' said Trevor.

'Listen.'

They could hear the Jerries in front, talking quite loudly. They listened intently.

'Buggers are talking German,' said Red. 'Can't help it, I suppose.'

'They're trying to distract us.'

As Trevor spoke there was a burst of Schmeisser just over their heads. It came from the right again, but much closer.

'You bastards,' said Trevor. 'Can you see them, Red?'

'They're behind the rock, just over there. Can't see a target, though.'

'You watch the front. They must be going to rush us.'

Trevor took a grenade from inside his battle-dress blouse, pulled out the pin, held it a moment, stood up suddenly, sideways in the trench, and hurled it in a high, curving lob. It dropped behind the rock and exploded. The Schmeisser ceased.

But Red was firing. Trevor jumped back to the Bren. The Jerries behind the terrace had come up when the Schmeisser began and were racing up the slope. As he looked one fell. Two more had come out of the gully and were covering them. There was firing from the posts on the left and right. An attack all along the front.

'Take the two on the right,' said Trevor. He was firing single shots now. Take your time, take your time. He fired at the one furthest on the left. The man fell but got his rifle forward and began to fire back. The first shot snipped a twig beside Trevor. Trevor could see only his head and shoulders. He sighted carefully and fired. The man's face became a red blotch, his arms collapsed from the elbows and stretched out in front of him, the rifle dropped between them and his head sank on to its stock.

But the man in the middle, a big fellow, was almost up to the wire. He was carrying a stick grenade. He jumped up on to the last terrace before the wire. He swung his right arm with the grenade. It might just reach them. Trevor's bullet struck him just before the grenade left his hand. The German groped at his stomach with both hands, balanced drunkenly for a second, toppled backwards and vanished behind the terrace. The grenade burst in the wire, harmlessly.

The remaining Jerry was running back, leaping and dodging through the trip-wires. Trevor fired. Missed. As he fired again the man tripped on the last strand of wire and fell forward into the dry water-course. The bracken stirred as he crawled away.

The two Jerries on the left above the gully had stopped firing now there was no attack left to cover. As Trevor traversed the Bren to deal with them one leapt to his feet carrying a Spandau and jumped for the gully. Red fired. They could see by the jerk he was hit. But he got to the gully, slithering on the last foot of clay and leaving two yellow weals behind him. The firing from Shorty's post immediately began again.

'Got the bastard.' It was Shorty's voice.

Where the gun had been one man still lay, his face against the leaf mould, arms stretched in front of him.

'No more sausage for that bastard,' said Red.

They looked at each other, grinning.

'That'll teach the bastards,' said Red. His hands were shaking a bit now.

'Lucky for us they're bloody bad shots. That's six up to us, not counting the wounded and whatever the grenade did. We'd better watch out, though. They might be shamming.'

They watched their front. Five bodies were more or less visible.

'There's still the big bloke who had the grenade,' said

Trevor. 'But I think we can count him out.'

'And Shorty must have finished off the joker in the wadi.'

There was silence again on both their flanks. No sound but the dripping rain. Not a move from the bodies lying in front. Trevor and Red grinned at each other from time to time. Both kept going over the fight in their minds, seeing it all again with all the elation of men hitting out at last and hitting hard.

'Hans.'

'Christ, what's that?' said Red.

'Hans.'

'It must be that big bastard out in front.' Trevor did not answer, just stared grimly ahead.

'Hans.' The cry was urgent, piteous.

'Poor bastard,' said Red.

'Poor bastard be damned. If it wasn't him it'd be us.'

Silence again in front. But there was a slight noise behind them. Red whipped round, his rifle ready.

'It's the boss,' he said.

'How'd you get on?' came a voice from above.

'Got six, we reckon, sir. The rest bolted.'

'That's the stuff. The other blokes got a few as well, not sure how many. Are you all right?'

'Good as gold, thanks. Anyone hit?'

'Mac got a graze on the arm. Nothing much. They seem rotten shots.'

'That's what we thought.'

'Be no hot meal, I'm afraid, tonight. They might have a crack about dusk. If they do it'll be tougher now they know how strong we are. I think they were only trying it on. But they may feel further round.'

'Any news at all of the others, sir?'

'I haven't heard about the other battalions. Sounds as if they're having a lash over on the Pass road. Our other companies have all had a go. Thirteen Platoon's had the most trouble but they're holding on. They got poor old O'Connell.'

'Poor old Mick. And to think they wanted to keep him at base because of his feet.'

'Well, keep it up, lads. If Mac has to go back to the RAP you take the section, Trevor. And keep your eyes peeled tonight. I'll let you know if I hear any news when I come round later on tonight. Cheerio.'

'Cheerio, sir.'

The day crawled into late afternoon. The rain kept falling out of a sky which, where you could see it, was an unchanging grey. The silence grew deeper. From time to time the wounded man in front cried out. Often they caught the word 'Hans.'

'Must be some cobber of his,' said Red. But Trevor kept staring out in front.

'Hans,' the man cried again.

'God blast him. I wish he'd shut up,' said Red. 'Poor bastard must have it bad. And Hans has buggered off and left him. Where d'you think you got him?'

'In the guts, I think.' Trevor was not talkative.

The day wore on. Once or twice the artillery opened up. The shells feathered overhead, like a flight of birds, but invisible. The bursts were away to the front, hidden from them by the trees.

The mists began to creep up from the valley. The light became more difficult. They opened some more bully and ate in the rain. Their eyes kept seeing shadows which became bushes when they looked at them hard.

'Hans,' called the man in front. They both jumped.

'I'm going to fix that bastard,' said Trevor, in the middle of a mouthful of bully. 'Give me your rifle.'

'Christ,' said Red, 'don't tell me you're going out there.'

'I'm not going to stay here listening to him howling all night. You cover me with the Bren. I don't think there are many Jerries in front. Anyhow they're stinking bad shots. And the light's bad.'

Red felt sorry for the Jerry. But there was no good trying to stop Trevor. He watched him clamber out of the trench and sneak cannily from tree to tree. A bloodthirsty old sod, he thought. Poor old Jerry.

The rifle cocked and ready, Trevor came down on the German from the flank. He was sitting up against the stone terrace. At first Trevor thought he was dead. His eyes were closed. There was blood at the corner of his mouth. His legs were spread apart. His trousers were soaked in blood. There was blood all over the water-soaked ground. In the evening light it was a dark wine-red.

Got it in the guts all right, Trevor thought. He stood, slightly bent and looking down at the man. He had an uneasy feeling in his back that he might be shot at any moment.

The man's eyes opened slowly. He saw Trevor. Life struggled into his face.

'Hans,' he said and tried to smile.

Poor bastard. No joke, lying out there in the rain bleeding to death. With a bullet in your guts. Might have been him or Red, after all.

Christ, you couldn't kill a man in cold blood like that. He set the rifle down against the wall and began to take the emergency dressing from his pocket.

But when he bent down with the dressing the man smiled and shook his head. He closed his eyes, then opened them again.

'Zu spät, Hans,' he said. He pointed to the rifle and said: 'Schiessen.'

It was plain what he wanted. The only thing, too. Even if he could have been got up to the RAP he was a goner for sure. Trevor took the rifle and pointed it at his head. The helmet had fallen off. The fair hair was wet with rain. The eyes were closed. As Trevor hesitated again the man groaned. Trevor fired. The man slumped, then slid sideways. The shot echoed. He was dead.

Trevor ran quickly from tree to tree. It was almost dark.

'What happened?' asked Red.

'I gave the bastard "Hans".'

'You're a cruel sod, Trev. Did you rat him?'

'I forgot.'

'You're crazy. He might have had a Leika.' He pushed the tin of bully over.

Trevor dug out a spoonful, lifted it, looked at it, put it down again.

'No, thanks,' he said.

Under the Bridge

Black, opaque and in hundreds they interposed their darkness between us and the smiling Cretan sky, shattered the summer's peace with the death they carried, slew its silence with the roar of their engines and the punctuated thunder of the bombs. Each explosion overtook its predecessor's echo, and merged with it to make a perpetual rumble in the hills.

Sometimes a shadow would pass directly over us, swiftly, flitting and bat-like. The drone increased to a roar and the plane would follow, bullets streaming with the undiscriminating prodigality of rain. Like rain on a gusty day. How long since I had seen and felt rain, refreshing rain not deadly, from grey, unhurrying homely skies, not this lethal metallic rain.

Our hill overlooked the village on its left, on the right front the sea. The sea, smooth and untroubled, its calm a promise of permanence when this tumult should be silent, road home to the lands of rain. Crouched under the lee of the rock, nostalgia gripped me like a cramp, nostalgia for the past or for the future. Anything to be out of this moment where we were held by the slow, maddening pace of time. But not for long this mutiny of the heart. Madness to venture hopes on such a sea, to commit oneself to anything but a prudent despair. Try to save your life certainly, but within the bounds of decency and dignity. And not expect to save it. Fighting was easier, dourer in despair.

Nothing much to do till the air quietened down a bit. There

might be more parachutists to follow soon, the concentration was so fierce. But no; it was the town that was getting it this time. Our share was only the overflow. They were solacing themselves for their reverses on the ground in an orgy of undirected destruction, an orgasm of rage and inflicted terror. Clouds of dust and smoke rose tranquilly, unfolding and expanding with the leisure of time itself from crumpled homes and ruined walls. Flames groped up into the afternoon, their red transparent to the day and then, as their mounting impetus declined, filmy and water-coloured but still bloodshot.

Just outside the village where the last houses straggled like lost children, the road bridged a gully. I was watching the bridge. During raids the people sheltered under it. We had warned them to go away, not to wait. They were obstinate, they would not leave their homes. We told them the bridge would probably be hit, was a military objective, but the mere physical fact of its shelter, its mere bulk blinded them to its danger. They continued to go there.

That would have been bad enough. But now we all had a personal interest there as well. Angela and her grandmother would be there too. And Angela had somehow succeeded in making herself real to us in a way civilians are not usually real. The two didn't even belong to the town but had come down from their village in the hills. They used to help us with food sometimes and do the washing. There was something about Angela's smiling freshness, the beauty of her teeth and hands which made everything she did for us seem better than if someone else had done it. Seeing her made you notice how good the weather was and when you looked at the sea you would see how blue it was and the snow on the mountains inland would strike you in all its cold remote whiteness for it seemed the first time. On the old, leisurely standard I would have had time to fancy myself in love with Angela.

From where I was I could see the bridge perfectly. The gully ran out from the foot of our hill and in a straight line away from us till it passed under the road. You could not distinguish individuals. But you could see them praying. They were all kneeling under it, the women and the children and the very old men. You could see them praying, making the sign of the cross over and over again. Their fear was erect and dignified. For the hundredth time I admired the bravery of these Cretans, their steadfastness. Angela and her grandmother would be there too, like the others afraid, as who would not be, like them calm and accepting with a proviso of reserved revenge.

I felt so close to them that I was with them. I almost blessed myself too when they did. It was like the family rosary of long ago. But the devil 'who wanders through the world to the ruin of souls' sought bodies too. He was real and present. He was death, travelling with every bullet now broadcast from the air and guiding, too, haphazard chance, and the cool selection of the sniper's eye.

In spite of the intenseness of my presence with them I was aware too of the planes, could see them as one after another detached from the intricately weaving group and swept low with a rising roar over the prostrate village.

They would have been better off spread along the gully. But they might have a chance. The German hadn't yet bombed any bridges to my knowledge. Saving them for himself. But this was a side road. It wouldn't matter much to him. And today he didn't seem to care greatly where he dropped them: he was out to terrorise. By now the town couldn't be much more than a chaff of mortar and rubble among drunken walls.

From over the centre of the town a bomber came sailing out towards the bridge. Slowly, very slowly. Above the outskirts they began to drop, swift and glistening where the light caught them. I watched them. The first struck the edge of the town. A series of explosions among the scattered houses. I heard them only. I was watching the last. I don't think he particularly meant to hit the bridge. But it disappeared. The whole scene disappeared. It was as if I had become blind with smoke and dust instead of darkness.

I waited for it to clear. For reality to reassemble. The cloud settled into the grey-green olives in either side of the gully. The bridge was still standing. The bomb had fallen in the

gully, on the far side. I began to breathe again. And then I saw
that the group had changed. They were no longer kneeling.
Their small dark knot had opened out like a flower. There
were shapes scattered in a semi-circle this side of the bridge,
still. The bomb blast must have travelled along the gully like
an express train through a cutting. Still, I thought at first; but
after a while I seemed to discern movement. It was not a
movement of whole bodies, a stirring of limbs rather, of
extremities, faint and painful like the movements of a crushed
insect whose antennae still grope out pitifully with a hopeless,
gallant wavering to life.

This was the bare slope of the hill. The red clay showed
through the thin soil and the olives were few, thickening only
at the bottom. And the planes were as active as ever. It was
impossible to get down. And anyhow we had a position to
hold.

Afternoon became evening, since time moved even in that
eternity. And day diminished into dusk. The racket slackened.
Only an occasional rifle shot or burst of machine-gun
reminded the twilight silence of its brief tenure. Silence like us ·
and them was mortal.

I told the others I was going down. They were to cover me
across the open patch. I slipped out from cover and holding
the tommy-gun bolted for the olives. No firing, no vicious
swish of bullets. I made my way through the olives, along the
lip of the gully. The dusk was deeper in the olives. The hill
held its bulk before the sun.

As I approached the bridge I hesitated. I knew what I was
going to see. And there had been so much of it in these last
days. I stopped and listened. Not a sound. That eternal,
suffering grey of the olives, the agony immobilised of their
gnarled trunks anticipated and accentuated what must be in
the gully. The silence, the patient silence and the dusk, but
mostly the silence, were too much. It was silence of mangled
bodies, a silence of negation and death. There was no life in
the gully. Pain, perhaps, frozen into immobility, but no life. If
I should see it as well, bodies caparisoned in all the bloody
trappings of a violent death, blood and grotesque distortions

of the body's familiar pattern, it would be too much. Not as if it were new. The very familiarity of the distortion, the blasphemy of it, would prove final. I did not want to see any more. I did not want to see Angela, her grandmother, others I had known. Or supposing I did see them and did not recognise them?

But perhaps there was something one could do. I listened again. Not a groan or sigh. There was much to do, much fighting yet. One must fight for one's sanity as well as one's life. I hesitated. In sudden horror I knew there was something else dragging me to the edge. Appetite for frightfulness as well as revulsion. Death squatted within the hollow like a presence, its emanation came up, grisly, dragging at me. I felt the hair on the back of my head stiffen. I took two steps forward. My eyes saw but my brain would not see. I turned and ran.

At the edge of the olives I halted. My knees were like jelly, with a hot trembling. I waited. Then ran again across up over the bare slope. It was with relief I heard the bullets searing their tunnel through the air. At the rock I turned and dropped into cover, a soldier again. And the bridge and the gully of bodies waited in my memory.

The Persian's Grave

The dream was all round him, smothering him. He waited, like a wrestler pinned to the mat, for his moment, and then with a heave broke free.

There was nothing familiar about this room. And for the first few seconds he stared at the shabby plaster of the ceiling, not committing himself. It might be another dream. Certainly, that heavy dread was still with him, though the grip that had held him down on the floor of the dark was gone. But then he noticed the dryness of his tongue.

'Boozer's gloom,' he said and, as if to shake it off, made to sit up. The sudden movement disclosed an ambush of pains which had been waiting for him to do just that.

'Christ,' he said and lay back again. This needed sorting out. From where he lay he looked at the room. Bare enough for a barracks. Small enough for a prison cell.

Somewhere out in the morning whose light came through a high, barred window and through the barred fanlight of the door, he heard a high, German bark: *'Halt's Maul.'*

A prisoner, by Jesus. They'd got him. So this was the end of last night's sally. After all these months to be landed like this. But how?

He looked back across the dark blank of the night. The last thing he could remember was the scatter when the patrol spotted them. But there must have been a lot after that. Some scrapping in it, too, by the look of his knuckles. And he must have been clocked by something pretty heavy, the way his head felt.

He began to pick his way back through what he could remember, looking for a clue.

First of all, Darby had brought him out, just after dark. The first time for five months he'd been outside the door of the little lean-to where they kept him hid. A tricky business sneaking through the streets, all shuttered and quiet, with Darby in front and stopping at every corner to look both ways for patrols. But they'd got to the café without any trouble and when they went through the outer room all the Greeks there, drinking coffee or ouzo or whatever it was, had kept their heads down and pretended to notice nothing. Though he must have looked pretty queer in Darby's overcoat several sizes too small for him.

And sure enough there in the back room was this other Kiwi, all right. He came to meet them in the doorway with his hand out.

'Ted Fothergill's mine,' he said, '21 Battalion. What's yours?'

'Boxer Cahill. I got hit up in the Servia Pass and was left behind at Megara when they took the hospital jokers off.'

'Tough luck. I got separated from the rest in our show up the Tunnel Pass and there was nothing for it but every man for himself and the devil take the arsemost.'

That got them over the first awkward part when he'd found his eyes watering to see a Kiwi face again and hear the good old lingo. So then they sat down to it and Papa brought them some ouzo and they settled down to plan the getaway. Darby, and Ted's Greek and a few more Greeks, sat round in a circle and watched, for all the world like the crowd listening to the Salvation Army in Dee Street of a Sunday night in the old days.

But after a while Darby said he would have to go back and see how Joan was getting on. She was all by herself and that was no good these nights. He'd come back in a couple of hours so as to make sure Boxer got home safe. And they'd be all right here in the café because George was a good man and he'd give them plenty of warning if the Germans came. But

perhaps it would be better if Boxer came now too? Now that he
and the other New Zealander had met that was perhaps enough
for one night? They could arrange to meet again soon and fix
their plans. And Boxer could see him looking at the bottle of
ouzo old George had just put in place of the one they'd got
through already.

'That's all right, Darby.' Boxer slapped him on the
shoulder. 'She'll be jake. This is the first time I've had my nose
outside the door for five months. I reckon I can do with an
hour or two yet, can't I, Ted?'

'Too bloody right. What do you call him Darby for?'

'Well, you see,' said Boxer, still with an arm round Darby's
shoulders, 'when we were at camp in Kaisariani before we
went up north Darby was a neighbour of ours and we used to
cook up our scran over at his place and have a few drinks
together, didn't we, Darby?'

'That's right, Boxair.'

'Talks just like a dinkum dig,' Ted said.

Darby smiled.

'But I still don't know why you call him Darby.'

'Well, you see, his wife's name is Joan, or something like
that.' It was one of those things that doesn't sound so good
when you explain it.

'Anyhow, Darby,' Ted said, 'don't you worry about Boxer.
Me and Boxer are in the same canoe, aren't we, Boxer? And by
Jesus we'll paddle her out of this creek and back to Alex if we
have to swim the whole bloody way, won't we, Boxer?'

'That's right, Ted.'

Darby still looked a bit doubtful and he hung round a bit
longer. But he must have seen they were settling down to a
session because in the end he went off and left them to it.

After that they knocked off the ouzos faster and faster until
Ted said he was sick of the stuff and they went over to cognac.
Things got pretty pally and a lot of Greeks from the outer
room came in to have drinks with them and somehow they
decided to leave the details of the escape till next time and
they started to swap yarns about their battalion and where
they came from back home and all that. And more and more

Greeks came in and they had to shake hands with everyone and there were more drinks and what with one thing and another they felt life wasn't so bad.

It must have been round then that Ted got to reciting poetry because the next thing Boxer could remember was seeing him standing up on a sort of stool and waving his arms about and spouting a long thing about the isles of Greece, the isles of Greece. The Greeks all kept nodding to one another and one of them who seemed to be a sort of teacher kept saying 'Veeron, Veeron', and all the others nodded their heads again and said it too.

At the same time he knew he must be getting pretty shickered because he kept saying to himself: I mustn't get shickered, whatever I do I mustn't get shickered. And if he wasn't getting shickered he wouldn't be thinking about it and besides, he wasn't in practice, not having had anything to drink worth speaking of for so long. But he couldn't stop himself from thinking another glass of cognac would be pretty good, or from having it either. Who gave a damn, anyhow? It'd all come out in the wash. They'd be all right.

> The mountains look on Marathon
> And Marathon looks on the sea;
> And musing there an hour alone,
> I dreamed that Greece might still be free;
> For standing on the Persian's grave,
> I could not deem myself a slave.

And by God, Ted was right. A man wasn't a bloody slave to go scuttling from place to place just for the sake of those Jerries. The master race, eh? Just wait till the boys got cracking again and we'd see about that. And he and Ted'd be there, too, to crack the whip.

'Fill high the cup with Samian wine,' Ted said. But this reminded him his glass was empty and he got down to reach for the bottle.

'Pretty good, eh?' he said. 'I got first prize for that three years running at the Onehunga school competitions.'

It wasn't long before he was off again. This time it was something about a maid of Athens and though he flew to Istambol Athens holding his heart and soul. He hadn't bothered to stand up for this one and he seemed to get a bit mixed up because he kept stopping in the middle to tell Boxer what a crackerjack she was and how she'd come in the boat with them.

'We'll have to get hold of a little sheila for you as well, Boxer, won't we?' he decided, seeing Boxer's heart didn't seem to be in this new idea. 'You leave it to me, boy. I'll get one jacked up for you, trust me. We might even get ourselves an island, boot the Jerries off and set up for ourselves. That'd be the right sort of occupation, I reckon.'

By this time Boxer was so full of cognac he couldn't get himself to wonder how he was going to last out at this rate till Darby arrived. And there seemed a lot to be said for this new scheme, now that it wasn't going to be just a threesome between him and Ted and one maid of Athens.

Somewhere about then, he remembered now, the little Greek with the cap over his eyes and them popping out so far they seemed to be holding the cap up came rushing in, waving his arms and gabbling something about Jerry officers outside.

'She's jake, boys, don't panic,' Ted said. 'Don't do your scones. Of three hundred grant but three to make a new Thermopylae. Pity there are only the two of us, Shelley here and myself. But, by Jesus, we're members of the Second New Zealand Expeditionary Force, sons of the Anzacs are we, and by Christ I've never been run out of a town yet and I'd like to see the bloody Hun who's going to make me start now. No fear, me old cobber General Freyberg, VC, 'd never forgive me if I did that.'

But by this time old George who'd supplied all that liquor on the house, enough to make you think you were back on the West Coast again, had got the back door open. Boxer who had just enough sense left to shut Ted up and shove him towards the door could hear the sharp strike of military boots crossing the floor of the outer room.

They must have got outside all right because he could

remember a lot of streets, dark and deserted, and himself and Ted and a young Greek who'd made himself guide. The two of them had their work cut out trying to make Ted keep his trap shut.

After that part, though, things got pretty vague. The streets seemed to go on and on and then the cold air must have caught up with him, because all he could remember was young Papadi, that was the Greek's name, saying something about a patrol, and the three of them running. And then he could remember still running but by himself now.

Perhaps he'd just passed out somewhere and the patrol had caught up with him?

No, that wouldn't account for his raw knuckles. There must have been a bit of stoush in it somewhere. And anyhow he knew in his bones something far worse than that had happened. He could feel it. He'd had plenty of hangovers in his time but he hadn't felt like this before, not even that morning he woke up in the guardroom and found he was supposed to have been drunk on guard duty and to have hit the Orderly Officer and knocked out two MPs.

He tried to turn over and discovered both his elbows were skinned as well. Keeping his knuckles as far away from the cloth as he could, he searched the civvies Darby had got him for a smoke. Not even a butt. The bastards must have ratted him. He lay on his back again and tried not to think about cigarettes or being a prisoner. That wasn't so bad but he couldn't stop his mind nosing about, going over everything and trying to work it out.

There was another thing. Had Ted got away? Jesus, what a balls-up they'd made of it between them. What a bloody awful morning to wake up to. Even worse than that morning he woke up in the olive grove at Megara and found everyone had gone.

God knows that had been bad enough, though. His shoulder had been throbbing badly and the wound needed a new dressing. And his temperature was sky-high. But it was looking round and seeing all the other evacuees from the hospital had gone that really got him. Missed him in the dark

and him too full of morphia to wake up with the racket they
must have made going down to the beach. That was the worst
of being away from your own outfit. His cobbers in the
battalion would have wakened him, morphia or no morphia.

Still, that time there'd been something he could do about it.
He lay doggo till he saw the Jerries weren't going to search the
olives and then he fossicked around till he found some bully
the blokes had left behind in the dark and an old waterbottle.
Then the rest of the day he hid under the lee of an old stone
wall, waiting for the dark and listening to the Jerry planes
overhead and the Jerry convoys pouring down the road
towards Corinth. There'd been plenty of time to think of what
to do next.

And of course it had to be Athens. Even if he hadn't always
been a city joker ever since he bolted from the old man's farm
it was obviously the place to hide. Anyhow it was the only
place where he knew someone. Darby was the bloke to try.
The boys had been pretty good to him and he knew what it
was like, seeing he had a taste of Albania. Albania'd had a
taste of him, too. It had got three of his toes last winter.

The next morning was a pretty bad morning, too. It was
bloody near daylight when he made it and for the last couple
of miles with all those houses locked up and quiet and the
streets brightly lit in the moon and not a soul to be seen it was
like one of those nightmares. Besides, he'd had a private
nightmare going all on his own with his temperature the way
it was and he had to keep telling himself that all the queer
things he saw weren't really there and those shadows weren't
really watching him and following him. For a spell he'd got it
into his head, too, that he was on his way home from a dance
in Invercargill and it'd be quite all right to sit down and wait
for a taxi. And he'd had to force himself to remember he was
on the run and wounded and if he didn't get under cover
before daylight the Jerries would have him cheaper than you
can buy a po at a jumble sale.

He'd made it all right, though, just as daylight was starting
to sneak round those cypresses and gawping at him over the
top of the hills. He'd just managed to sneak around to the

back and give a bang on the door. Then he'd slumped on the doorstep.

There wasn't a sound. Only you could tell that whoever was inside was awake and listening. A few houses away a rooster let go and a dog barked somewhere. But not a sound in the house. He knocked again. Perhaps there were Jerries inside? No good panicking. He listened. Not a sound. Perhaps he'd just shut his eyes for a bit. He forced them to stay open. His forehead was sweating and there were noises in his ears. Getting dizzy. Going to pass out. Have another go.

This time he called out. 'It's me, Boxer.'

The noise was coming up in his ears like a train. But he managed to listen for a noise outside them. Someone was coming.

The door opened a bit. He fell in, after it. Darby was looking down at him.

'Boxair.' That was the way he'd said it the night of the final party before the battalion went north.

It was a long time after that when he came to again. Next morning, it might be even the morning after. Some morning, anyhow. They'd put him in the little lean-to where Spiro used to sleep.

Mornings after that had been worth waking up for. First of all you'd hear the neighbour's rooster and then the hens in Darby's backyard would start clucking. Boxer would lie there half awake, part of him still with his dreams in the back bedroom at Rimu and his childhood long ago.

And even when Joan came in with the coffee and he knew where he was, she smiled so brightly and the coffee was so good he didn't feel altogether swindled out of his dream. At least I don't have to get up and milk the cows, he used to say to himself as she washed him and changed his bandages. And a hen sometimes followed through the door if she forgot to shut it. The hen would stand there where the sunlight with the motes in it came in and would blink first one eye and then the other at him, cocking her head to one side, and she would lift one leg up with the foot limp like an empty glove and make crawping noises.

The cat, Venizelos, used to come in too, and sit on the bed, at the foot at first. Then it would get round the other side from Joan and put up its grizzled white muzzle where there was always a drip and purr and look up at him and try to lick him. Till in the end Joan would get wild and chase the hen and Venizelos out and come back laughing and scolding in the Greek he couldn't understand yet.

That was at first. Venizelos kept on coming back but there weren't so many hens after a while because Joan kept giving him a sort of chicken broth with a lot of rice, pilaff or something, at the bottom of it.

Then in the evenings Darby used to come in and take off his boots and show where the frost had got his toes and say how if it hadn't been for Metaxas the soldiers might have had decent boots and even trucks instead of ox-carts to move about in. And they'd work out how far Servia Pass was from where Darby's outfit had been and talk to each other in a sort of lingo that was half-way between. He was a great one for news, old Darby, and he always had some fresh story of how the British had just taken Tripoli and were getting ready to invade Bulgaria through Turkey and things like that. And of course when Russia came in there was a special celebration and it wasn't only Boxer who had chicken pilaff that night, even Joan had some though she tried to pretend she didn't want any at first.

In the daytime young Spiro, who was now sleeping on some sort of shakedown in the kitchen, used to come and give him Greek lessons out of a book he had full of pictures of hens and horses and cows and cats, like the ones Boxer could just remember using himself as a kid back home. The same sort of bright colours and big, black print. Only he'd never been too hot at learning. He'd always been too keen to be out with the shearers or to help making the hay or to go and set his rabbit traps and his father had always winked, though it used to upset his mother a bit that he'd never be bright enough at school to get away from the farm.

Anyhow, this time he'd only just begun to get a hold on the alphabeta business when poor young Spiro got his omega.

Before the Russians came in, it was. Just when things had got to be blackest in Crete and even old Darby had to admit that what the Germans had to say about it on the wireless might be true.

It was when they were bringing the wounded and prisoners from Crete back through Athens from the Piraeus. Spiro and a lot of other kids had been down in the town every day passing figs and chocolate and stuff and the girls had been slinging flowers to our jokers as they went through. The kids had even scrounged cigarettes from the Jerries to give to the convoys. That made the Jerries mad because they saw the kids hadn't taken the cigarettes for the love of their beautiful blue eyes and for some reason blokes who've kicked you in the guts the way the Jerries did the Greeks always want you to turn round and say how glad you are.

So the Jerry guards got mad and they threatened the kids and tried to chase them away. That wasn't enough to stop young Spiro and he'd dived under the arms of one of the Jerries and the girls who were throwing the flowers all clapped and that made the Jerries madder than ever and one of them, a Hitler Youth bastard, whipped out his Luger and shot Spiro.

That was in the morning, too, and it was still morning when they brought Spiro home and he'd died on the way before he got there. All that day there were women in black coming in with the tears streaming out of their eyes and some of Spiro's pals looking very queer and grim for such kids and the men too talking in low voices and trying to comfort poor old Darby. And Darby had cried a bit but there wasn't a sound to be got out of Joan for days. She just walked around with a face like frozen milk. Till one evening she found Spiro's little lesson-book under the bed in the lean-to. She just sat down on the bed then and put her apron over her head and cried and cried. There was nothing for it but just to put an arm round her while she cried and feel a fool and bloody miserable.

After that it wasn't so bad though. She began to take even more trouble over the wound and Darby, who'd taken to going to the café every night and not coming home till long after the curfew, stopped going. He used to stay at home instead so she wouldn't worry about him and so he could keep an eye on her and the two of them would come into the lean-to and Joan used to drink coffee while Darby had some ouzo with his and sometimes Boxer was allowed a drop as well.

When Darby had a few in he always made speeches the way Greeks do about how Boxer was his son now and you could tell by the way Joan watched that she felt like that as well, though she wasn't such a one for saying what she thought.

But as the summer came to an end and it got towards autumn, which is a time that makes you remember things somehow, the shoulder began to get better. He started to get restless, tired of being cooped up like a bloody hen, and he wanted to get out and contact some of the boys because by that time it was well known there were quite a few hidden round about. With a couple of good cobbers he reckoned a man'd have a fair chance of a getaway.

But as soon as he began to talk like that there was holy hell to pay. He wasn't well enough, he was crazy, what would they do without him, why wouldn't he wait a bit longer when the English would come and drive the Germans back where they belonged and the Italians scurrying in front of them.

So he'd quietened down for a while. But then the RAF began to come over, going for the Corinth Canal, so the Greeks said, and the people were all out in the street, man, woman and child, or up on the roofs in spite of the curfew and shouting 'Drop bombs on them, drop bombs on them. Bomb us, we don't care, kill us. Only kill the Germans too' and things like that. And he saw it was going to be a long war and began to wonder what the hell he was doing lying there on his back and eating other people's grub when there was fighting to be done.

But by that time Darby had got it into his head that what he wanted was a girl and it was a wonder he wasn't right. So he used to drop hints that it could be fixed some time when Joan was away at the market. And she might have had the same idea or perhaps they'd talked it over at nights the way a man and his wife do. Anyhow she used to bring in a schoolteacher friend of hers quite a lot, and a beaut she was too, only Boxer felt it was a bit too much of a good thing and anyhow with his mind set the way it was there was no room for getting mixed up with women and he wouldn't come at that caper at all.

After a bit when they saw he meant business they came round to the idea and even got quite keen, saying they'd even lose their second son, which was Boxer, for the sake of Greece. At least it was Darby who put it that way. But when Boxer looked at Joan, embarrassed because he'd never known anyone in New Zealand who would say things that way even when they meant them, he'd find her looking at him the way she used to look when she was talking about Spiro and he could see she felt the way Darby talked.

So from then on there'd been new schemes every day, each one crazier than the last. And anyhow by this time he knew enough about the Greeks to know that though they had all the guts in the world they were a bit mixed up between dying for your country and making a sensible getaway to fight for it. And the one thing they were no good at was making plans that worked. Even when they agreed on a scheme each bloke always had a different idea on how it was to be done. Besides, the schemes were always too clever and complicated and depended too much on good luck. You'd have thought Greeks would have known a bit more about luck by this time.

But at last Darby had come in that day with talk of another Kiwi hiding up nearby and so after the usual false starts and breakdowns and balls-ups it'd been fixed for them to meet in George's café. And so it had all started.

Which is all bloody well, he said to himself now. But it was what happened afterwards that counted. What had happened after they were chased by that patrol? And what had happened to Ted? Had he been nabbed or what? And why did he feel the way he did, the way he felt the day they buried his mother and his old man had refused to speak to him and said he'd broken his mother's heart?

Well, it was no good lying here on the flat of his back. The thing to do was to get cracking and see what chance there was of getting out of this. Chewing the rag wouldn't get you anywhere. Time enough to feel sorry when you found out what you'd done. And it generally wasn't long before you did find out.

He heard a double set of footsteps outside. He lay back and presented to be asleep, watching through half-closed eyes from his corner.

The door was unlocked and flung open. The sudden daylight set him blinking and showed up his pretence of being asleep. One behind the other he could just make out two figures against the light. Then the one in front was given a shove and sent stumbling across the room.

'Many happy returns,' Ted said.

'So they got you, too, Ted.'

'My bloody oath they did. And I was just getting off to sleep when they pitched you in on top of me. Don't you remember?'

'*Halt's Maul,*' said the German at the door.

'Well, you were pretty dead to the world when they hauled me out this morning,' Ted began.

'*Halt's Maul,*' said the German again. '*Kommen Sie mal.*' He was looking at Boxer and gesturing towards the door. Boxer got up slowly.

'*Schnell, schnell,*' said the German. '*Marsch, marsch.*' Boxer looked at him. Did you say everything twice in German? Then he saw the German was carrying a Schmeisser.

'See you later,' Ted said. 'Keep your temper with them – ' But the German was making threatening motions with the machine pistol. Ted shrugged. Boxer saw now that he had red marks on his cheeks as if he had been slapped hard.

'See you later, Ted.'

They crossed a sort of compound. Barbed wire, Boxer noted, and sentries patrolling it. A lot of PW at the far end, some of them in shorts, though there was a bitter wind. Queueing for breakfast, by the look of the dixies. Some of them saw him and called out.

'Good on you, dig. Don't let the bastards get you down.'

He grinned back and waved. He felt less alone.

The guard went in front now and knocked at what must be

the Jerry COs door. A voice called out from inside. The guard
stood to one side, shoved Boxer and followed him in.

A table covered with a Jerry blanket. Behind it a Jerry
officer, just under the window so that the light struck over his
head and down into the centre where Boxer stood, more or
less at attention. Boxer looked straight at him. Blue, hard
eyes. There was a silence and they went on staring at each
other. Boxer did not like to take his eyes away. But he was
aware of manuals on the table, swastikas, and somewhere on
the right someone else in the room. Still no one spoke.

The officer suddenly swivelled his eyes. Following, Boxer
saw the other man, in civilian clothes and seated at another
table, the wall and a big street plan of Athens behind him.
Interpreter? He seemed too confident and the officer seemed
to be leaving him the initiative. Gestapo? The officer said
something in German.

'Won't you sit down?' said the man in civvies. He spoke
English like a tommy officer.

Boxer heard the guard behind him fetch a chair. When he
felt it shoved against the back of his knees he sat down without
looking. He would not have liked to turn his back on them or
take his eyes off them.

'Have a cigarette?' said the man. He offered a case. There
were Players in it. The first he'd seen since Megara.

'No thanks.'

Neither the officer nor the man looked at each other. But
they both stiffened and there was a sharp glint in the officer's
eye. Only Boxer felt as if it were approval. The way his father
had looked the day he refused to say who was with him when
he smashed the policeman's window. But it hadn't stopped
the old man from laying on with the harness strap.

The civvy was smiling again. Well the bastard might, Boxer
thought, the joke's on me.

'You were very helpful to our people last night,' the man
said.

'Was I?' said Boxer, off his guard and puzzled.

'Yes.' The man looked down at the table for a second and

then looked up, smiling. 'The patrol was Italian, of course, and so one doesn't entirely believe their story. According to the patrol commander you were drunk and just because he spoke to you in English you thought he was English. He seemed to think that was why you told him where you lived.'

So that was it. Bits of it came back now. Especially at the last when they dragged out first Darby, then Joan. So that was why his knuckles were bleeding. He must have sobered up then. He could remember Joan's eyes now. He'd never be able to forget them again.

'The patrol commander seems to take great credit because you struck him. I'm afraid our Allies often display a misplaced idea of what is creditable. Besides, he should not have laughed at you. That was cruel.'

Boxer scarcely heard him.

The man hesitated, watching him. Then he looked at the officer, looked down at the table and began to tap the ashtray with a pencil. He did not look up again as he went on. The officer was looking at a spot on the wall high above and beyond Boxer.

'It occurs to me,' the man said, 'you might help us a little more.' He looked up suddenly and straight at Boxer, no longer smiling. 'I think perhaps you were not so very drunk last night. Perhaps it was just that you knew what was good for you.'

Boxer set his jaw and said nothing.

'If what happened should get round the camp,' the man went on, still staring at him, 'life with your fellow prisoners might be rather uncomfortable for you.'

Boxer was trying to read that look in Joan's eyes. Surely she and Darby would know that he could never have done that on purpose.

'But there is no reason why they should know. Your friend who seems so much less intelligent than you are knows nothing about it. If you are sensible he need never know.'

If only there were some way of seeing them and explaining. He became aware of the expectant silence around him.

'What's happened to them?'

'Eliades and his wife?' The man paused. 'That rather depends on you. Nothing yet.'

Lying or not? There were only two other honest men in the room. The officer and the guard. Boxer could feel their discomfort. Of course he was lying. What would be more like a policeman? Even if he wasn't lying, even if they were alive, they'd sooner be dead than get out of it this way. They hadn't grudged Spiro, only grieved for him.

'Could I have a cigarette now,' Boxer said.

The man smiled and Boxer felt sure he had been lying. He took a cigarette from the box. The officer looked further away than ever.

The man reached out his lighter across the table, half standing. He was enjoying the officer's discomfort. Proved right again.

Boxer crouched over the lighter. He caught the man's wrist, pulled him up close, slapped his face once, twice, swung back his right and hit him on the jaw.

The guard pinioned his arms behind him. The man was sprawled back across his chair. The plan of Athens had jerked loose and was slowly subsiding on his shoulders. Only the chair askew against the wall kept him off the floor. He was out.

The officer was still sitting under the window. When Boxer looked at him the faint smile vanished from his face. He gave some command. The guard frogmarched Boxer out.

Back in the cell Ted said: 'What happened?'

'The bloody bastards,' Boxer said. Then he told the whole story, leaving nothing out.

At the end Ted came over to him and put his arms on his shoulder. Boxer could not look at him.

'Never mind, Boxer,' Ted said at last. 'I believe you, though thousands wouldn't.'

Boxer got to his feet, his fist bunched.

'Now, now, Boxer, don't start getting the pricker. I reckon I know how you feel. But it's done now. We both got shickered and it was as much my fault as yours. All right, the bigger bloody fools us. Now we've got to start thinking how the hell we get out of here so we can do a few of the bastards. Right?'

'That's right,' said Boxer.

Coming And Going

By the time I'd got myself marched into Base Camp at Maadi and fixed up with a bed I could see it was too late that night for the spree I'd been counting on having in Cairo. Too late to bludge a lift in and rouse up a few old pals. They'd all be out taking their snakes for a walk before I could get there. Still, there was bound to be someone I knew at the Mess. If the worst came to the worst there was always the duty officer.

'Where's everyone, Jack?' I said after I'd scoured the ante-room and the bar.

'They've all gone off to the show at Shafto's, sir. I expect you could do with some scran if you've only just got in?'

'It's a bit late for that, isn't it?'

'Well, the bar's not busy, you can see that. If you'll just sit on that drink for a bit, I'll soon jack you up something. Where'd you like to have it? In the dining-hut?'

'Here'll do just as well if that's OK with you.'

'Right. It'll have to have a bully beef base, though.'

So Jack scratched round in the kitchen and before long I had my entrenching tools into a fine binder of bully fritters and fried tinned potatoes, with any amount of marge and that fig jam we used to get that's all right if you're hungry enough. I was, what with the long trip up from the rest camp and only the unexpended portion of the day's ration for company.

And then Jack fetched over a big pot of tea and two cups and we settled down to a good natter about old times. He used to cook for A Company in the early days. But then he stopped one, I forget where it was, one of the Sidi Rizegh battles I think, and they found out about his age – he'd joined up to keep an eye on his grandsons, some of the blokes used to say. So they dumped him in this job at the depot until his turn came to go back home.

'Who's all here now, Jack?' I asked him when we'd chewed the rag for a bit about the end of the war and all that.

'No one much you'd know, sir. There aren't many left out of the old crowd now. Jimmy Larsen's here on his way back to the unit, he's a captain now. He got a bad one at Ruweisat. Tiger Smith's been on leave and he's going back, too. And there's Ted Tarrant just out of OCTU, you'll remember him, he used to be QM in the November '41 show. And there's Colonel Maitland, he's OC. And Bill Adair.'

'Yes, I saw him on duty when I clocked in.'

'Well, that's about all you'd know. The rest are reinforcements. It's a here today and gone tomorrow sort of place, this. Nothing much for the officers to do except take a parade or two for the look of the thing and censor a few letters.'

'Thank Christ I'll be out of it tomorrow. It sounds worse than death.'

'I suppose that's the idea. I used to think it was Christmas, having a good bludger's job, when I first got here. Now if I hear a Bren go off on the range I get homesick for the unit. And Rommel would be a relief after the sergeant-major.'

There was a banging against the wooden slide in the bar.

'Someone wants a drink,' I said.

'Always some bastard wanting something.' He was out quite a while.

'Anyone I know?' I asked when he was back in the kitchen.

'You'll know him all right.'

'Who, then?'

'Major Reading.'

'What's he doing here? I thought he had A Company.'

'So he did.' Jack got up and began to put the gear away.

I didn't take much notice, beyond spotting he didn't seem to have much time for Reading. But then none of us, men or officers, ever did and I thought it was just this that had made him dry up on me. Anyway, it was a long time since I'd seen Reading. In a long spell on your back you usually see only the chaps in the same ward with you and any of your cobbers who happen to be back from the sharp end. And I was too glad of a bit of company over a few drinks to remember that the last time I'd seen him was when we had the run-in over company boundaries the night before I got knocked at El Mreir.

'I think I'll go round and have a yarn with him.'

Jack said nothing but just gave me a sort of look.

'Thanks very much for the feed, Jack,' I added.

'That's all right, sir. It was nice seeing one of the old faces and talking about old times.'

'I liked it, too, Jack.'

Then I went out through the bar to the ante-room.

Reading didn't look up from the old *Free Lance* he was turning over. But he must have heard me and I fancy he could see me out of the corner of his eye anyhow. He was sitting on the other side of the room from the Mess piano. The wireless was on low and someone was drivelling away in Arabic.

'You don't want to listen to that, do you?' I said and I turned it off. 'Just someone telling the poor wogs about democracy.'

'Oh, it's you, Andy.' He gave me a quick look. I grinned back at him. We were from the same battalion, after all. 'Where've you sprung from?'

'Just back from sick leave. Guaranteed a new man. I've been eating so much white fish and milk pudding it was a waste not having an ulcer. What about a drink?'

He emptied his glass. 'Gin and lemon.'

I went back and knocked on the slide.

'Might as well keep the hatch open now, Jack,' I said. 'One gin and lemon, one whisky and water. Make them doubles. Have one yourself?'

'No, thanks all the same, sir,' he said.

I brought them over to Reading's table and pulled up a chair.

'Here's looking at you,' I said.

'Cheers.'

I was just going to ask him what he was doing. But he got in first.

'Seen any of the others?'

'No, I've only just got in.'

He took his glass in his hand and sat back. The cane chair gave a creak as he relaxed.

'Any of the boys back from the battle in Number One General when you were there?' he asked.

'One or two I didn't know came in just as I was leaving for rest camp. There were a few from our lot in Number Two, they said. These chaps looked pretty bashed about. A bit of an MFU, I gather. But I ought to be asking you. When did you leave them?'

'Oh, I left after the first night on Miteiriya. Have another?'

I watched him go up to the bar. He could have been back on leave, of course. But it seemed queer. After all, you didn't usually swop company commanders on the first night of a battle. Unless you had to.

There were still two wet rings where the last glasses had been. Reading fitted the two new ones in as carefully as if he was playing some kind of game, fiddling with them this way and that until he'd got them exactly right.

'You'd miss the main part of the scrap, then? There was some pretty heavy going, after that.'

'Yes,' he said.

Neither of us spoke for a while. It wasn't a comfortable sort of silence. I ransacked my mind for something to say but I couldn't think of anything. Not my usual trouble.

'Good luck,' I said, picking up my glass. It was the best I could do.

'Good luck,' he said and picked up his.

Then we said nothing again. And I caught myself planting the glass exactly in the ring, the way he had done. This wasn't my idea of an evening. It wasn't even my idea of Reading. In the old days he'd have been shooting some line about what he did in peacetime – he used to be a stock agent I think it was and he'd got mixed up with some of the big station families.

I began to wonder when the others were coming back. It must be getting on towards the end of the film at Shafto's. Reading was breaking a little thread off the left sleeve of his battledress jacket. Well, he hadn't changed that way. He was always very fussy about his togs. It used to annoy the jokers, I remembered. And he was a terrible man to fuss before ceremonial parades and all that kind of thing. Used to do his scone completely if everything wasn't just so. 'A very smart officer,' our first CO used to say before we left him behind in Trentham. The new CO wasn't so quick to make up his mind.

'I'm off back tomorrow,' he said suddenly.

'So am I.'

'No, not back to the battalion. Back to New Zealand.'

'The hell you are? Jesus, that's a bit of luck, isn't it?'

'Luck? Yes, I suppose it is, in a way.'

'Give my best to anyone I know.'

Not that it was likely he knew anyone I knew outside the army. He came from Christchurch and was the sort of chap who, when he wasn't spending week-ends up on some sheep-station, would take an interest in the territorials and all that. Chaps like him had got off to a flying start when the war broke out. Still, you had to be fair, there were some quite good blokes among them, though I'd never have believed it in peace time and took a bit of convincing when the war came too.

He didn't seem as cheerful as you'd expect, though. After all, we'd been away three years then. And if a man had a piece of luck like this thrown at him, there was more than an even chance the war would be over before he heard shots fired in anger again. What more did he want?

Still, I thought, I suppose even old Reading feels it a bit, clearing out and leaving the boys to it like this. It'd be better to be going home when everyone else did, with the feeling that you'd taken your chance right up to the last like the rest of them. Provided you weren't being left behind for good, like so many who'd had it already; Buck Travers, for instance, who got his the night I was hit.

'I expect you take it a bit hard, though,' I said, 'leaving the old battalion.'

'Yes,' he said. And bugger me if I didn't suddenly get a horrible feeling he was going to let go and bloody well cry. Why not, anyway? Just because they didn't like him much it didn't mean he mightn't like them.

'I'll fill them up again,' I said.

It's probably the gin, I said to myself as Jack poured them out. They always say it does that to you. It never did to me, though, and I've had a power of it in my time.

Where the hell were all the blokes? I could have done with someone knocking out a tune on the old piano and a bit of a sing-song with plenty of drinks on the table and the boys letting themselves go with Samuel Hall or The Harlot of Jerusalem or, when they'd got sentimental, 'To you, sweetheart, Aloah.'

Reading seemed to have pulled himself together a bit by the time I brought the drinks back.

'You work the racket all right,' I said, the way we used to talk in those days half-thinking we meant it, 'and you should be jake sitting out the rest of the war in some bludger's job in Trentham.'

He didn't seem to like this much. We never really talked the same language, anyhow.

'I don't know,' he said and his accent seemed to have gone a bit pommier than usual, or what he thought was pommy, only that was another thing that meeting a lot of pommies had made some of us wise to.

'I might ask for my discharge,' he said.

I was a bit surprised, even a bit shocked. Everyone says these things from time to time. But he sounded as if he meant it.

Just then, though, you could hear the trucks pulling up outside.

'Here they come,' I said, 'the dirty stop outs.'

'It's time I was off to bed. An early start in the morning.'

'Come off it,' I said, 'you might as well stay till you finish your drink, at any rate.'

'Yes, why not?' But when he said it he set his jaw the way you'd think he was sitting on one end of a tug-of-war.

Well, the door opened and a lot of the blokes came in. I didn't know any of this first lot and so I didn't take much notice when, after one look at us, they went straight to the bar without saying anything to either of us. I did think it a bit funny, though, the way they all quietened down suddenly when they'd been talking their heads off outside.

Then in came Jimmy Larsen, Ted Tarrant, Tiger Smith and several others I more or less knew. They glanced over our way. Tiger called out 'Hello, Andy,' and the others waved. They joined the rest at the bar.

This struck me as a pretty queer way of going on. And, of course, dumb as I was, it wasn't hard to guess there was something the matter and the something was Reading. I looked at him. He'd gone white in the face and as I watched him he slowly went red again, red all over.

Now I'm not a joker to kick another bloke when he's down but I'd sooner have been back in hospital, back in El Mreir for that matter, than where I was then. I couldn't think of anything to say to Reading and I don't think he was even trying to think of anything to say to me. He was just staring into his glass where there were a few little husks of lemon floating about on a thin wash of drink.

How the bloody hell was I going to get out of this one? Say what you like nobody much wants to be with someone everyone else seemed to think lower than a snake's testicles. If it was a cobber that might be a different thing. But Reading was a bloke I wouldn't have given you two knobs of goatshit for, even in ordinary times. Not my kind of chap at all. Yet I couldn't very well clear out and leave him flat, all on his lonesome like that.

'Good night, Andy,' he suddenly said.

I was relieved, I've got to admit. But at the same time I felt ashamed at feeling relieved. So I asked him to have another drink, though I must say I was pretty sure he wouldn't.

He didn't seem to hear but just got to his feet and walked straight out of the room. The other blokes didn't look at him and he didn't look at them.

I didn't like to get up and join them even then. Too much

like a rat leaving a sunk ship. I felt in a way as if Reading was still there. Besides, I was damned if I was going to start explaining myself to all these jokers, a lot of them I'd never even seen before, just new chums and red-arses.

'You know I don't like to see my little Andy boy in bad company.'

It was Tiger Smith and by God I was glad to see him standing there and grinning down at me. He was the sort of joker everybody likes and if a thing or a chap's all right with him then it's got to be all right with everyone or he'll know the reason why.

'What's he done?' I said.

'What I always thought he'd do some day. Cleared out. Ratted. Buggered off. Said he had to report back to battalion. There was a counter-attack coming in. You know, just when the light was right for them. With tanks, too. Luckily the sergeant-major, old Dick Coster, was on the job. But it's mafish for Reading. The high jump. Of course, no one could prove anything. But Dick got killed and later on when Larry took over he got killed too.'

'Court martial?'

'No, no court martial. As I say, you couldn't prove anything. I don't suppose anybody'd want to. Nothing like that ever happened before in the battalion.'

'No,' I said. 'Not in the battalion. The bastard.'

Jim Larsen and Ted Tarrant had come over by this time. 'Come on, Tiger,' Jim said. 'We're all going back tomorrow. Let's make a night of it before the flies wake up and get us. Get cracking on the old piano, Andy.'

It was late when we broke up. I was still clear in the head but pretty shaky on my pins when I left the others and cut across the parade ground for my hut. You know what those huts were like, all the same size and all alike.

Anyhow, I found mine at last. I thought I was the only joker there but as I passed the end room I noticed a light coming under the door. Naturally, I thought it was one of the boys, so I knocked and went in.

'Hello, Andy,' Reading said.

He was sitting on the edge of the bed. All his kit except what he'd need in the morning was packed up. On top of his tin trunk there was a hurricane lamp and a bottle of gin and a mug.

'Sorry,' I said, 'I thought you were Bill Adair.'

'Sorry to disappoint you. Sorry to disappoint everybody. Have a drink.'

I didn't see how I could get out of it. And anyhow I felt sorry for him sitting there drinking with the flies when all the rest of us had been over in the Mess singing and wrestling and slapping one another on the back, the way we used to in those days.

I sat down. He fished out another mug from his kit, rinsed it with some water out of the seir, and poured me a stiffish gin.

'No, I'm not Bill Adair,' he said. 'I'm not Tiger Smith, either, or Ted Tarrant. And I'm not sorry I'm not. I'm damned glad.'

'You're glad you're not Dick Coster, too?' I couldn't help saying.

'They've told you all about it, of course.'

'Yes.'

'Self-satisfied bastards. Anyone'd think they'd never thought of doing the same. A hundred times, every one of them.'

'They never did it, though.' And I remembered all the times I'd had that feeling in my own guts as we went forward under the barrage, or waited shivering in the half-light for the counter-attack to come in.

'No, they never did it. Brutes, clods, that's all they are. You think it's guts. But it isn't, I tell you. It's only that they're afraid of what people'll say.'

I said nothing. But I was remembering how on mornings before a big parade he'd be nagging at his batman because his trousers weren't properly pressed and giving his platoon commanders hell if the men's gaiters weren't blancoed and every other bloody thing just exactly so.

'And anyhow I wasn't well, I tell you. I hadn't slept for

nights before that.'

I still didn't say anything but that didn't worry him. He just went on and on, in a mixed up kind of way, sometimes saying he hadn't done anything and other times saying he couldn't help doing it, anyone else would have done the same and anyhow he was sick. I felt very embarrassed. At the same time I'd sobered up and I was tired and sleepy. I remembered the batman was to give me a call at first light.

From time to time he'd pour himself another but after the first one or two he forgot to offer me any – it wasn't really me he was talking to but himself. And I didn't tell him I could do with another because I knew I was too tired for any amount of gin to jack me up and besides I was looking for an excuse to get away. In fact I was so busy trying to find one that I almost missed it at first when he started off on a new track.

'I suppose they think that the only thing for a chap in my position to do is bump himself off. I suppose that's what you think too. You think I won't be able to go back to my old job because the blokes'll be back sooner or later and they'll tell the story round and people'll begin to pretend they don't see me there either. You all think that's what I ought to do, don't you?'

He wasn't shouting at all, but the way he was staring at me I could see he was looking for some kind of an answer. I felt all dopey with a hangover coming on and being in need of a bit of sleep and I didn't know what to say. And as a matter of fact I couldn't help feeling he could do worse. But I didn't say anything. Only I thought it really was time I cleared out. So I got up.

'Yes, that's what you think, the whole bloody lot of you,' he said, sitting there with the mug in one hand and the other hanging down the way you could see he was up to the eyes in booze.

'But you're bloody well mistaken,' he suddenly shouted at me and his hand came up so hard that the gin splashed out of the mug. 'You needn't think I'm going to do anything of the kind.'

'I don't,' I said. 'But look here, I've got to get to bed. I'm off back in the morning, remember.'

'That's right,' he said. 'And I'm off back, too.'

He said this so quietly I thought this was my chance.

'Good night,' I said.

He said nothing, didn't even look at me. I felt bad somehow, so I said, 'I'll look in before I go.'

'You needn't bother.'

So I left him sitting there, staring at the floor.

After I'd put my light out and was just getting off to sleep I heard someone trip over my shoes.

'It's only me, Andy,' Reading said. 'I just came to say good night. And good luck.'

'Thanks, Cliff, and good luck to you.' It was a bit of an effort but I managed to call him by his first name.

I heard him stumble back in the dark towards the door.

But I must have slept very heavily after that because I didn't hear the shot and it wasn't till the batman rushed in and told me at first light that I knew anything about it. And the Adj insisted on me staying for the court of inquiry though what the hell there was to inquire into I don't know. It all seemed plain enough to me. Anyhow by the time I got back the Div was getting ready for the left hook round Agheila and before we had time to stop and think again no one felt much interest in what had happened to Reading.

In Transit

As soon as we boarded the train at Naples the four of us had each selected a corner of our wagon and unrolled our beds. Jimmy Stapleton and Hori, the big Maori, had taken the top end, Bill and I the lower. We had all joined the draft in Egypt, Bill from a staff course, the other two from OCTU, myself from leave.

At the first stop Jim and Hori hopped out and began to collect bricks from the station's bombed relics. It wasn't till then that I realised how far Bill and I had come since the days when we were second lieutenants like them and still close to the ranks in time. Now that we were going back, he to take over his company and I to a bludger's job on Div. HQ while they were going back to that perilous business of platoon commanding we'd got over before we knew how bad it was, a man could see the difference between them and us. It wasn't only that they were veterans already where we'd been green. No, it was that they still had that rankers' knack of making yourself comfortable which we'd imperceptibly forgotten. Batmen had not yet interposed themselves between them and the hard floor of living, relieved them of that constant need to foresee each day's discomfort.

But there were no batmen here. So we'd soon joined them and the fireplace that flamed tonight in the centre of the truck was floored and walled with bricks. We'd all helped collect the store of wood, fragments of the broken houses at every stop along the way.

We'd sat over that fire as the dusk's returning tide began to cover the fields and hills through which the train wound our draft from Naples to base near Bari. We'd brewed our tea over it and eaten our bully and afterwards plugged at the big strawbelly of Chianti. But it hadn't been enough to dissolve so soon the slight awkwardness between two generations of officers, the knowledge that all we had in common was a journey and the Division, that we had seen different friends die.

Their life was still large with the vitality of the ranks, not yet contracted and controlled by the responsibility of not being able to grouse and of leading others in places where men died. Perhaps they did not yet realise that though the enemy was still the same old Hermann the conflicts they were going back to would be more complex.

Besides, Bill, always a little silent, was more so tonight. Perhaps his mind was ahead of him, an advance party for the efforts of one more campaign. Or perhaps it was still back in Haifa where the staff course amused itself of an evening in cool hotel lounges with outside the smell of orange blossom.

So when the wine was finished and Hori had built up the fire against the night, cold like all the nights of all the war's long winters, we had gone to our corners and climbed into our bedrolls.

Jim and Hori talked for a while. From time to time between the clatter of the wheels and the engine's demented scream at crossings I caught snatches of their talk, mostly those shared recollections of the OCTU which remain vivid for a bit, like the memory of a dead or transferred friend, then fade. But soon like Bill they turned their faces to the wall and turned into themselves till gradually sleep was sealed about their consciousness and inside that intimacy time and identity and place lost their daylight compulsions and gave way to dreams.

But in spite of the heavy steel wheel, separate from me by board and inches and a physical law and throbbing in its revolutions the monstrous catchword it had jerked from a past that lay very near to dream – *vae victis vae victis vae victis vae victis* – I could not sleep.

Scenes and fragments of the day repeated themselves against a blood-bright curtain if I closed my eyes; if I opened them, against the foreground of the dark. Again we marched down the cobbled streets of Naples, damp and dark like an eel's back. In first-floor windows girls gaped with American soldiers. If you smiled they waved back gaily as they must once have waved to their own men marching to captivity or meaningless death in Libya. Or to their late and hated allies tramping in arrogance towards the crude barbarity of German dreams. Small boys, always international, and old people, too tired now to be partial, watched our column from the foot-paths and then turned back from its irrelevance to their purpose and play. Our passing interrupted the road crossing, and the crowds bunched on both sides waited for us to go by as we have all waited for the war to go by, thinking we can suspend or postpone living and not knowing that in war the heart grows older than it does in dreams.

And I saw again that marginal comment to it all, consequence to the blind bomb, the small boy. One arm poked in the rubbish of a levelled house, the other clutched a stick and balanced between it and his only leg a starved and ragged body. Over the other leg's stump the flesh had closed and puckered. What end of tyranny would give back that leg on which gaiety should have run? Liberty demands two legs. And even I who have two legs could not look at this oblique consequence with comfort.

Then the relics of the Naples station, with the old men wandering in it like shifty ghosts, the small boys and girls too real in their noisy proffer of apples and lemonade and too realist in their quieter murmur: 'Signorine?' And the staggered rakes of carriages, rust already caking the burnt blackness, and the weeds as patient as barbarism to rear their heads between the rails.

No, with all this to square with principle it wasn't easy to sleep. The fire itself, that Cassius, seemed to have thoughts as another piece of wood toppled from the edge into its heart. The flames writhed up again and wrestled with the shadows, tumbling them from their gentleness into the truck's dark corners. They challenged even the soft serenity of the moon whose subtle shaft pierced the open doorway but whose straightness adapted itself like water to every jolt and jump.

The moon at least has forgotten how to burn, I thought. Its age is content with light and that discreet.

I got up and pulling on my greatcoat walked, stockinged, through the acrid smoke to the door. We had left it ajar but little of the smoke found it worth while to leave the truck's protection and lose entity in the cold dark.

Nor leaning out over the iron bar could I blame it. We were climbing in a slow curve so that the train's whole length was visible. Far ahead the engine stack vomited a red fan of fire into the dark. Beyond that fan a few sparks shot up, slowed as if to exhort the rest on the road to nothing, paused and seemed to glow more intensely, then vanished and were nothing. From the open doorways of each truck the firelight burst into freedom, but reaching only to the track's edge lost virtue and halted, lighting up the passage of stone and shrub.

Behind me the light from the trucks was brighter, more regular. That was the engineers' draft. They had liberated a lighting-plant from a neighbouring train in Naples. I smiled. The pioneers had not died, these men had still the trick of coming to terms with circumstances.

Times had changed. Once, to travel like this in a snake of flame would have been suicide. All of us here had crept through the night in Greece, in Crete, in the desert, our long convoys dark and muted and the tension such that we whispered as if we might be audible to the pilots far above who sat over their throbbing engines and hunted us.

Now they were gone and we fought not in sand but in a country whose wounded and winter earth contained a sure promise of green. Yet, though the years of defeat had passed and carried us to green countries and the rain, though the graves we would make this spring would silence but for a week the murmur of the grass, none of us would forget the dryness, the sand and the shallow holes where we had buried friends and hopes. Even if this spring the dappled leaves should shelter our minds from the moon's pale echo we would still remember how once they were sheltered by our skulls only from the day's sun and the night's stars and never from what we feared and what we remembered.

I went back into the truck. The fire was dying. I heaped on some more wood and got into my bed-roll. The fire had not yet grappled with its new victim when the wheel's refrain became only a murmur and I fell asleep.

When I woke it was with that perfect poise of body and nerves that comes sometimes from sleeping in the open. The train had stopped. The moonlight still lit up the first two feet of the doorway. The fire was blazing. But on the door-sill dark figures pressed and scrambled trying to climb in and excited Italian voices, most of them women's, chattered incomprehensibly. I waited, trying to understand.

But suddenly from his dark corner Hori arose. He was in bare feet and wore only a vest. As he came forward, rapidly and only lightly crouched, the firelight caught his towering legs vaulted above the wood-heap and his strong, broad-nosed face was still shadowed, remote and very fierce. Behind him the shadow of his legs formed a huge triangle on the wall and his back blotted out the low ceiling.

He picked up a stick and padded quickly to the door between the fire and the moon. Cursing in Maori he began to lay about him with the stick. But already the women were fleeing back in terror as before an apparition.

We were all awake.

'What's the trouble, Hori?' asked Bill.

'Bloody Ites,' he said, 'trying to get in here.'

'No harm giving the poor bastards a ride,' said Jim.

'No harm,' said Hori. 'That'll be the bloody day. Those bastards got my brother on Ruweisat Ridge. He was caught on patrol. Cut off. He surrendered and as soon as he'd given them his gun they shot him. Te Awa Thomson saw it. Don't talk to me about bloody Ites. I know all I want to know about them.'

'OK, OK, Hori, don't get off your bike. You can have them for all I care. Probably would have kleftied our gear, anyhow.'

I was too awake now. I began putting on my boots.

'Where are you off to?' Bill asked.

'Going along to take a dekko at the boys.'

'Hang on and I'll come with you.'

We walked along the track. Everywhere just off it dark figures with parcels squatted. American MPs with torches and sticks patrolled up and down the train.

A few of our draft still sat in the doorways, still interested in seeing pass the land that might yet bury them. But most were bedded down, packed in the gross discomfort somewhere deemed good enough for soldiers and made bearable only by the soldier's grousing patience, his humour, his stoic adaptability, and least but still a little by his officers' helpless solicitude. When they saw us, those who were still awake neighed like horses, baa-ed like sheep, moo-ed like cattle. We laughed and they laughed.

'You know how it is boys,' we said.

They laughed again, without irony.

'We ought to by this time,' one said.

'We'll have to have the next war in New Zealand and get it run properly,' another said. And we all laughed.

'Goodnight,' we said.

'Goodnight.'

As we walked back we met an MP. He did not see our pips in the dark.

'Who are all these people?' I asked, pointing to the shapes and their bundles.

'Why, it's like this. They've got a black market down there in Potenza, it being a kind of agricultural centre. And there ain't no transport so all these townspeople are kinda trying to bum lifts down there to buy eats.'

'Rotten job you've got, chasing them off.'

'Well, you get kinda used to it. Ain't bad at times, either. You get a nice dame sometimes. You say you'll get her a lift if she goes to bed with you. After a coupla nights when she gets sort of troublesome you tell her to scram and get yourself another.'

A policeman, impervious to hate. No good, therefore, to stare at him.

The train gave a warning scream. We ran back to our truck.

Hori had been squatting watchfully in the doorway. He helped us on as the train slowly laboured from inertia to motion. We took off our boots and got into our bed-rolls.

The train was now clear of the station. Hori stood up and looked over the night-smooth velvet of the fields.

'Bastards,' he said.

Then he began to piss out of the doorway, rejecting the land, its moonlight and its people. We, further from our hates, no more aware of our revenges than the red pine knows its fat, white grubs, slept.

The day that followed was divided by its hours, not by its stopping places. These were all the same, the ruined station, the loiterers in the army's dishonoured rags, the silent proud as hungry as the voluble who begged, the ragged children, the mothers whose eyes were nobler than the words need wrung from them. So that the journey seemed to become an allegory, a sneer at the futility of movement, a mockery of living.

Once Sergeant Graham brought me a scrap of dirty paper.

'Where did you get it?'

'Well, you see, we hid an old woman in our truck last night from the MPs. This morning we gave her some breakfast and dropped her at Potenza. She asked for a bit of paper and wrote this on it. We thought you might tell us what it meant.'

I translated it for him.

'The Signora Julia Albieri wishes to give a thousand thanks from the deeps of her heart to the brave and noble New Zealand soldiers who gave her shelter and food in a night of winter. When they come again to Naples she will count it a blessing if they will call at 10 Via Firenze and allow her to repay even a little from the poverty of her home to the richness of their hearts. If they should never come her heart will go with them and she will pray to the Blessed Virgin and Jesus her Son that safety should follow them along the hard roads of battle. Signora Julia Albieri.'

'Jesus,' said the sergeant, 'poor old bitch. Say what you like, they've got good hearts. And what do they know about the war, anyway. Would you mind writing it down so the boys can read it?'

I wrote it down for him. Hori had been sitting in the doorway. He said nothing.

Towards evening we stopped at another station. The bleak day was hurrying towards its end as if it could hardly wait for night to relieve it from an unwelcome duty. The grey dome of cloud was closing in and the mists crept towards us from the horizon. The cold dwelt in us more deeply than the dark soon would.

Hori and Jim were leaning over the doorway's iron bar. Bill and I sat on a low stone wall.

Two boys came towards us from opposite directions. One was fat and stoutly built, his clothes quite good. His eyes were too small in his head and his mouth was already pursy. He came to us boldly, like a boy who has not yet been afraid. The other was younger, frailer in build and face very pinched. He wore only a ragged pair of shorts and old army boots too big for him. He slunk towards us sidelong and did not meet the other boy's eyes. He knew early the guilt of being poor.

'What's your name?' I asked the fat boy.

'Iulio.'

'And what does your father do?'

'He is a lawyer.'

'And you,' I said to the other, 'what's your name?'

'Carlo,' he said, his eyes still cast down. 'And my father is dead. My mother does washing.' He looked up at me, sombreness behind his placating eyes.

I smiled at him. 'Have you any brothers and sisters?'

'Two brothers, and three sisters?'

'Hey, bambino,' called Jim.

They swung round to him and he tossed them the packet of biscuits he had been eating. They both reached for it. But Iulio was there first and Carlo bounced from him and fell. He got up and calling to him I gave him a packet of biscuits.

Iulio was watching and there was greed in his eyes. He

would have them too when we were gone.

Hori had said nothing. His face was very sulky, his thick lips pursed.

Suddenly he moved back into the truck. When he returned he had a drill shirt, a pair of shorts and a pair of socks over his arm.

On the other arm he swung under the bar and dropped to the ground beside Carlo. The boy recoiled from this dark, powerful man but then stopped and looked up at him. We looked too. Hori was smiling and his eyes had all that Maori gaiety.

'Come on, bambino,' he said. And he sat down, the boy on his knee, and dressed him in the shirt and shorts and socks.

'There you are, bambino,' he said.

Then he turned to me: 'Tell Carlo to run home as fast as he can to his mother while I hold on to this little Italian bastard.' And he grabbed Iulio.

I told Carlo. He smiled at me, touched Hori as if to assure himself that strength was sometimes right, said 'Grazia', smiled again and ran towards the houses.

Iulio was wriggling in terror but still holding his biscuits. When Carlo was out of sight Hori let the boy go. He ran off after Carlo, never looking back.

The train gave its derisive whistle, mocking us, mocking poverty.

We climbed aboard. As we drew out of the town the MPs ran alongside it, knocking Italians off the steps and couplings with their sticks, throwing stones at those who climbed on to the flat roofs.

'Bloody busybodies,' said Hori, 'bloody MPs.'

I was afraid Jim would begin to tease Hori, but he said nothing. Jim, Bill and Hori sat around the fire, over the thudding wheels. Near us the fields scudded by and further away they swung in a slow circle to the past.

'Those bloody Huns,' said Hori, 'they've got a lot to answer for. A cold day like this and no shirt.'

He looked at each of us, challenging.

'Do you remember,' said Jim, 'how cold it was that night in

November 41 when we first crossed the wire?'

I leaned over the iron bar. The train wound upwards in a slow curve to the right. A burst of singing came down from the trucks in front. The boys must have got hold of some more plonk. The red fan of fire belched up into the dark and the engine dragged us on with our narrow hearts to our scattered fates.

Mortal

·

Sunday morning, when the battalion wasn't in the line, was always a bit of a break. And this morning was particularly good because the morning before all they'd cared about was a decent sleep after a night that had gone first of all in the tricky business of being relieved and then the long, slow trip back to rest area by the Volturno. But last night had been quiet and a man could sleep in peace, his wife's letters under the pillow or in his battledress pocket and perhaps, with the warmth and the temporary escape from danger, the woman herself coming across time and the seas, warm and loving enough to deceive even doubting hands in that reality of dreams.

In the little casa they had taken over from Fred Murray, when his battalion relieved them, the Colonel and the MO were looking through the batch of New Zealand Weeklies that came in with every mail, and Pat, the Adjutant, was re-reading his letters. As Lew took away the breakfast dishes none of them looked up. But the Adj. gave a last look at his girl's 'lots of love'. Then he put the letter back in its envelope, stuffed it in his shirt pocket and said:

'You can take my mug, Lew.' He turned to the Colonel. 'I'm going over to the Orderly Room for a spell, sir.'

'OK, Pat, I'll be over shortly. I'll just finish this pipe first.'

The Adj. went out.

'Always on the job, young Pat,' said the MO.

'He's good, all right, Ralph. Gets on well with everyone. I'm only sorry we'll have to lose him soon. He's due for that company.' He drew on his pipe and sighed. 'Well, I reckon he won't disgrace the old hands.'

'No, he'll do all right, Jim.'

They looked at each other for a moment and then looked away. Five years together had given them much in common. Each knew the old hands the other was thinking of were dead. Each remembered those dead as living and could have named without pause all those company commanders who, stepping into one another's boots, had helped bring the battalion through from one battle to another and then dropped in their turn, so that to name Olympus, or Galatos, or Sidi Rizegh, or Minqar Qaim, Ruweisat, Miteirya Ridge or any of the bloody hours which the long curve from Greece round North Africa to the Sangro and Cassino had cost, was to call out echoes of other names, the names of fallen friends, and raise, for those who wandered still, ghosts whose smile was always the smile it had been before the minutely pelting rain of Greece bruised the dead face to putty or the diamond sand gritted its way through and the sun polished the bone.

Jim Winters took a gulp of the thick, sweet tea, drew at his pipe and, putting his elbows back on the table, returned to his *Auckland Weekly*. The Canterbury-Wellington cricket match. Yachting clubs. Annual carnival of the Amateur Swimming Club. The elegant strength of the yacht sails leaned out from the page like a gull's wings. The batsman looked at the ground as he came out from the pavilion between the grass and the sun. Hands behind their backs, the swimmers dominated the camera with their thighs, those smooth swimmers' limbs, round contours masking the muscle, muffling the flesh with a skin that had borrowed something of its sleek rubberiness from the seal, mammal of the sea.

He turned the page. Death was drawn up there in rows, military. Ten rows of them, five portraits to a row. Dead mostly, but some wounded or missing. He scanned the faces. Shorty Wallace, in civvies, judging by the collar and tie. Must have been taken before the war. You wouldn't have known him if the name beneath hadn't pulled your eyes back to find behind that pasty, paper-deep smile the grimness the camera hadn't prophesied. No hint there of the Shorty they'd known on the Sangro the night they attacked through the vineyards hung with S-mines.

And Con Talbot. And old Bill. And that Air Force joker was surely Paddy Peters. Hadn't seen him since 1937, never thought of him even. DFC and bar too. He'd been a grand half-back. Paddy, quick behind the scrum and sure hands.

None of the Cassino faces here yet, though. Too soon for photos and heroism. Their mothers would still be crying as they hung out the washing or got the old man's dinner, would still be remembering them as their little Willies. It takes less time to get killed than to become a hero and your own wounds will heal before your women are cured of them.

He knocked his pipe out on the table edge.

'My paper's full of bloody bathing girls,' he said. 'To think they've still got a bit of summer back there.'

'Mine's the same,' said Ralph. 'A bastard, isn't it?'

'A bloody bastard.' He shoved the pile of *Auckland Weeklies* and *Free Lances* over to one side. 'I'll have a look at them later. I'd better go over and give the Adj. a hand now. How was your sick parade this morning, by the way?'

'Not bad, Jim. They're all in pretty good nick, considering. Shagged, of course. A short time's a long time on Belvedere.'

'Yes, I'm glad we're out for a bit. It's been a tough winter. And they don't like having to sit still while Jerry slings mortar at them all day. Not that the night's any better, what with patrols and all the rest of it. Anyhow, at least they've got a chance to get dry now and read their mail.'

Jim got up and went to the door of the casa.

The sun felt stronger. Almost a Sunday morning's sun back home towards September. Shelagh would be getting ready for eleven o'clock Mass. But Sunday was lie-in morning for him. She'd be putting on her gloves by the dressing-table and smiling at him in the mirror now, that slightly puzzled smile.

'What do you want to put powder on for?' he would have teased her. 'Your husband is in bed and you're only going to church.'

'You old pagan,' she'd say as she leaned down to kiss him.

'Why don't you come to Mass with me? It would do you good.'

He sighed and moved away from the door-jamb. Poor Shelagh, no good arguing with her. That was the nearest they ever came to having a row, when he tried to explain how unnecessary he felt it was, all that stuff about hell and the immortal soul. It just made her think his own soul was on the way there. As if she could know anything about hell. Hell was the day before yesterday on Belmonte, or those last days on Crete or that bad time at Ruweisat when the unburied corpses out in front were swelling in the sun.

And heaven was here and now, today, not having to use men like money, spending some here to save others there. At least it was enough to be going on with till some Sunday morning when he'd be back in that bed again and Shelagh in front of the mirror and him smiling while she fretted about hell and his immortal soul. But that would come all the quicker if you didn't think about it.

Yes, a nice day. Not exactly spring yet, too close to the mountains still. But the grass was beginning to make a show, especially down where the Volturno skirted the camp's edge, yellow and turbulent wherever the gravel banked. The olives had had it to themselves all winter for green. But spring wouldn't be long now.

Outside the casa he looked down the long row of olives with pleasure. Nearly every tree had its bivvy, some of them from habit or from caution dug in against the strafing that never came now. On the left in the transport lines the trucks were well hidden by both trees and nets. Everywhere blankets hung over the ropes and signal wire the boys had rigged between the trees. Beneath them the men sat, mending, scraping their boots, most of them in khaki drill while their battledress, the caked mud washed from it, hung out to dry. War had domesticated them where wives would have failed. Here and there a man sat screened by scrim on the latrine, reading his mail. Oblivious, taught by similar necessities, Italian women wandered among the bivvies, collecting scraps, empty bottles, cast-off clothes, dallying to smile at the love of being alive which rang behind the broken phrases of soldier Italian.

Bill Reynolds, OC D Company, called out as Jim went by:

'Any use giving the Ites some washing, Jim?'

'Better not, Bill. Don't know how long it'll be before we're in again.' He came closer. A guess from him would soon swell to a detailed rumour, if overheard. 'I don't think we'll get more than a day or two at the most, Bill.'

'Thought it was too good to last,' said Bill. He spoke half bitterly, but the sun leaned through to where he sat in the open back of his truck and put a smile into his words.

'You might tell that young Adj. of yours I'll be finished his bloody returns sometime this morning, if he's lucky,' he added.

'OK, Bill.'

Jim went on. To the left in the transport lines he could see a group of men stoop, look up as if watching a flight of invisible birds, look down, and stoop again. They were a group, but while the coins were in the air each man was alone with his luck. Well, their two-up was like their fighting that way. You acted together; what you felt about it you had to yourself. And what happened to you was largely a matter of luck there too. So two-up was a kind of training in taking what was coming to you. Though what wasn't the view King's Regs. took, another Bible you took with a grain of salt.

Some of the players had seen him and were getting uncomfortable. So he looked away and walked on.

Padre O'Halloran's jeep was in the car park. RC Church parade at 10.30 hours, he remembered. He looked at his watch. 10.30. The Padre was always on time. A good fellow. He used to be captain for Marist in the old days and he'd been a tough scone in the scrum. What the hell he ever wanted to become a priest for – . Well, he must have had his reasons. But it was a nuisance sometimes. A good bloke, especially in the field when the stoush was flying, a chap you'd known for ages, who could take a drink with you and referee a game or a fight. But when it came to the pinch they could never go all the way with you. In the field, fine. But in Cairo in the desert days, or in Naples now, you always had to dodge a padre in the end, even if you'd known him for donkey's years. And they could never understand that. Back in Cairo at the Club there'd be plenty of chaps to have a drink with the padre but damned few for him to spend the evening with, except for other padres. It was this bee they had in their bonnets about women; always going for the boys about the brothel business. As if that wasn't the only bit of a break the boys had, their only way of proving they were alive.

As he reached the three-tonner which was the Orderly Room Padre O'Halloran came towards him through the olives, walking fast.

'Morning, Padre.'

'Morning, Jim.'

'Everything OK? Full house?'

'No one from HQ Company. I've got ten tykes in that company and not one of them has shown up.

The Padre was angry. The bluff, man-to-man geniality was gone. He was the church militant, affronted. Hair greyer, Jim noticed, though he was only thirty-five. Heavier, too. You felt the impact of his anger.

'Pat,' Jim called into the truck, 'did you put it in orders that there'd be an RC church parade at 10.30?'

'Went out to all companies yesterday, sir.'

'Runner.'

'Yes, sir.' The runner on duty dropped his paper-backed book and came running to that bark.

'It's you, Hawkins? Good morning. Go over to HQ Company and tell Captain Mair I want him. At once.'

The runner fled through the olives.

'Sorry, Padre. Some balls-up, I expect. We'll soon fix it.'

'It's not your fault, Jim, I know that. When'll you be putting in an appearance yourself? I know we'll rake you in one of these days.'

'Think so, Padre?' The Padre was close to him and smiling now. His breath smelt decayed. Must be fasting. Yes, of course, they made a great song and dance about that. Bad for the temper, though. Luckily, when Shelagh made her monthly communion she always went to early Mass.

Tom Mair appeared. He looked at Jim and decided to call him 'sir'.

'You wanted me, sir?'

'Now look here, Tom, why the hell haven't you got your Micks on church parade?'

'Aren't they there?'

'No, they're not and it's your business to see that they are.'

'They must have thought it was a day of rest.'

'It doesn't matter what they thought. This is a parade. Take a truck and go and fetch them.'

Mair looked at him. Jim knew that this was one of those moments when you've got to show who cracks the whip. They didn't come often in a battalion as good as this. But often enough to find out if you were weak. And oftener, if you were.

Mair's eyes fell.

'Sorry, Padre,' he said and went off to get his truck.

Jim watched him go. An intelligent apology, he thought. Mair would be all right. Hadn't had his company long enough yet. Still wanted to be too popular with the boys. He'd remember later that the only man who is popular in a scrap is the one who knows what to do and insists on its being done.

'He'll have them here in a brace of shakes, Padre. You might as well go on over.'

'Thanks, Jim.' The Padre went back to the flat place by the river where each company's small contingent stood grouped, waiting. Before and after Mass they were A, B, C and D Companies. And HQ Company. But during Mass they were his, souls rather than soldiers. No, they were always souls, always God's. But in this interval that gave them a moment to contemplate and pray in company he, kneeling in front of them, felt himself most of all their guide and leader and felt that the Latin he intoned gathered and interpreted the aspiration united behind him and without him only half articulate.

Jim climbed into the truck.

'Anything new, Pat?'

'This signal, sir.'

'What is it?'

Pat looked down the truck to the clerks bent over the bench, eyes intent on their papers, ears alert.

Jim read the signal in silence.

'I see,' he said. 'Right. Get all company commanders. I'll tell the MO and the IO. Conference in the casa at 11.00 hours.'

He walked slowly back. It hadn't been long, the washing, the drying, the stretching of cramped legs, the freedom from immediate fears.

Well, there'd be no recce to do. At least they knew the ground. There hadn't been time to forget it.

The jeep belted through the lower skirts of Acquafondata. The moon came up and silvered the sturdy village to a two-dimensional fragility.

'Are you warm enough there, Padre?' asked Sammy, the driver. 'My greatcoat's in the back.'

'Right as the bank, thanks, Sammy.' But he gathered himself more closely under the wind-screen.

'You were right about the moon,' said Sammy.

'Yes.'

Or rather Harry, the IO at Div. HQ, had been right. Another pleasant evening had turned its swift turtle into danger. He had been sitting in the 'I' truck after mess, having a gossip and a cognac. Then Lance Simmonds, the IO at Brigade, had phoned through. That was about nine o'clock.

The G3 'I' had swivelled in his chair.

'Trouble brewing in your parish, Padre. The Jerries have been putting down mortar and stuff on Jim Winters' right company all evening. Must have dropped to it there was a change-over last night.'

'What Jerries are there?' asked the Padre.

'Second Battalion, 132 Regiment. Not much good, mostly Austrians. But they're nervous and they haven't managed to get a PW from us yet. And they can't make much of a guess what is happening on the front unless they know who they're dealing with. Last time they put down stuff as heavy as this they sent in a strong fighting patrol. On Bill Reynolds' company it was. They didn't get their PW but they gave us a couple. I wouldn't be surprised if they try again tonight.'

'Jim's boys will deal with that all right.'

'You bet.'

The phone rang again. Mick scribbled on his pad. Then he rang off.

'An attack in about company strength came in on D Company's forward platoon, Lance says. About half an hour ago. Things are a bit confused, but it looks as if we took a PW and chased them out again. Lance'll ring through as soon as he gets an identification from the PW. It's bound to be II/132, though.'

'Shall I tell Ops, Mick?' said Harry.

'No, they know already. We'll wait for the identification and then ring.'

The Ops phone rang. Harry answered.

'Yes, Lance told us. No identification yet, but we've got a PW. What? What a bloody shame. Jim Winters? That's too bad.'

The Padre stood up, waiting for Harry to finish.

'What's happened to Jim?'

'Got walloped, apparently. A stray mortar. Ops don't know how bad but think it's pretty bad.'

'I'll get going,' said the Padre. He called down to Sammy who was drinking tea in the canopy.

'Be right with you, Padre,' Sammy shouted back.

'Which way are you going, Padre? Top road or through the Inferno track?' asked Harry.

'There'll be less traffic on the Inferno.'

'But the moon's not up. That's why they raided so early,' said Mick. 'Here, Harry, pass over a moon table.'

They looked at the chart. Moon rise at 10.29 hours.

'It's 10.15 now. It should be up before you get to the Inferno, Padre. Try and get in ahead of the jeep train. They leave this end at 10.45. If you get stuck behind them you'll only be able to go their pace, though that's none too bloody slow.'

He had put on his leather jerkin and tied the heavy scarf about his neck. Luckily the viaticum was with him, the pyx snug in his battledress jacket.

Outside Sammy had started up the engine already. The phone rang again and the padre paused at the door. Mick put his hand over the receiver. 'Nothing more about Jim, Padre. It was II/132 all right,' he added for Harry.

And the Padre had climbed into his jeep. The Casale valley was a lake of darkness as they hurried across its floor.

But now the moon was up. They had left the jeep train still forming by the roadside near Acquafondata for the nightly run of supplies. There was nothing in front and the Provost on duty, expecting the jeep train, would let nothing on to the one-way track at the other end. Sammy gave the jeep her head.

Poor Jim, the best of all the colonels. And he'd promised Jim's wife that if anything ever happened he'd be there, to make a Catholic of him at the last. A good girl, Shelagh. She'd done her best with him. But behind those FDLs of good nature he was terribly stubborn. Didn't seem to think religion mattered. As if any man had a hope in a world like this unless he had God's grace to help him. But he was a fine fellow for all that, a clean-living fellow.

Where the gradient was one in five the jeep clattered over the netting put there for grip. On the right the verge dropped sheer to the pines. On the left was the hill out of whose face the Free French had cut the track in mid-winter. Good Catholics many of their officers were.

His hands were telling the rosary in his pocket but his mind ran on beneath the repeated prayers. Anxiety like this was itself a prayer. So was the whole journey, for that matter. If only God would not let it be in vain.

Jim had got on well with the French when they were neighbours in the line. His own kind of bravery had something French about it. He had a boy's notion that courage was like money — you mustn't be mean with it, at least not with your own. Too brave he was, really, for a CO whose job was to be alive just as much as to be brave.

Now that they had the stretch on the floor of the valley Sammy was letting her go some. He'd been in Jim's platoon in Greece, before flat feet had pulled him back to transport.

The wind whipped past them up the valley, its speed as urgent as theirs, as if it too pursued a soul. War, thought the Padre. When would it end? He avoided the thought that this was better than the humdrum round of the parish and that this drive, for example, at the mercy of providence and Sammy's hairbreadth judgement was good also. Certainly men were better here in the field. No women to degrade them and make them mean.

They were in the last of the Inferno now, twisting and threading. At each hairpin wrench the jeep swung skidding on the gravel, back on her haunches, her brakes fixed, travelling on momentum.

What a loss to the Div. if Jim were a goner. Their youngest and most brilliant CO. Such a grand fellow. And a good influence. That business about church parade, for instance. He could set an example to many a Catholic.

Out into the Bowl now with Belvedere in front of them, a looming mass and beyond it, less immediate, Monte Caira about 5,000 feet. Still snow on the top. And there on the right was Cifalco, cold and jagged.

But it was to the left he looked longest where Monte Cassino showed the broken pride of its monastery, open to the night like a wound. Like stigmata, like Christ's wounds; bleeding between the two armies as once between two thieves.

Slower going now as they began the steep climb. If only they could make it in time. No good hustling Sammy. Nobody could get more out of a jeep than he could.

'The Terelle Terror Ride,' said Sammy as he felt down for the gears.

The Padre nodded. They came round the first leg of the staircase road. A climb of two thousand feet in about the same distance. A Jacob's ladder. Not all angels, though, that climbed it.

A real angel of a woman, Shelagh. 'Look after him, Father,' she'd said at the farewell party. Five years ago, 1939. She had handed him his glass and another to Jim, a two-pipper he was in those days. Jim had laughed and said: 'She'll have me a doolan yet, Father.' He'd gone over to the piano then, to the rest of the boys. They were singing: 'To you, sweetheart, Aloah.' Not yet drunk. He'd go before they had too much.

'I must be off, Shelagh.'

'Already, Father?' Only with God would a priest be finally at home. 'Well, goodbye, Father. You've promised you'll keep an eye on him, remember.' Her blue eyes had darkened. It was from her Irish mother she got the sadness of those eyes, their smile. And her faith, too. The women knew how grief always came behind gaiety and at the end you had only God and your immortal soul.

'We'll skip Brigade,' he said to Sammy. 'You remember Battalion HQ?'

'Same place?'

'That's right.'

They drove on till Colle Abate darkened the sky above them. Then they parked the jeep in a gully and the Padre walked on.

By the KOd tank he took the track to the battered casa. Men had been born there, had brought back their wives there from the church in Santangelo or Terelle, lived out their age there and died at last, tired. Now the trellis work was broken, the vine's torn length lay shrivelled by the wall. In front the windows were blown out and a shell had bitten off one corner of the house. No births or marriages now. Strangers came here to die.

Ralph was in what had been the kitchen, talking in low tones to the orderly. He looked up.

'How is he, Ralph?' asked the Padre.

Ralph shook his head. 'Unconscious just now. He's in the back room. Padre Craufurd is with him.'

Craufurd, the Battalion chaplain, a Presbyterian. It should have been himself. But Jim was C of E on the forms. You had to be something.

'He's in a bad way,' Ralph was saying. 'He won't be able to hold out. He ought to be dead already. Anyone else would be.'

A hard man, Ralph, and war had made him harder. A Scot. They had had it out many a time together in the Mess, hammer and tongs. Army brothels, birth control, the infallibility of the Pope and, if they had had enough to drink, the existence of God. Jim had laughed at both of them, not needing either. He was never sick. 'God and medicine,' he used to say, 'are all right for those who believe in them. They're just another name for hope when there's no sense in hoping. All right, too, I suppose, for those who need to give things fancy names.'

Well, he was a friend of them both. And because of that, and because he was dying, they were friends with each other.

If only he'd come to and could be persuaded to take Extreme Unction. The Padre caught the MO's eye and felt guilty. And it was hard to believe it might help a man recover when everything else failed. Yet it sometimes did, oh yes, of course it did, sometimes.

'The bloody fool would go down and poke his nose into it,' said Ralph. 'As if Bill couldn't have handled the Hermanns on his own. He got it before he reached them, even. A mortar, an over, in the chest.'

The Padre went in. Jim lay on a stretcher. The blanket was drawn up to his chin. His face was beaked with pallor. The cheeks, falling away, emphasised the strength of that nose and chin. The beard was more noticeable than usual, dark. His breath came in shuddering gasps.

Padre Craufurd got up from the old twenty-five pounder box where he'd been sitting. The two of them looked down at Jim, so far from them.

'Morphia,' said Padre Craufurd. And the breathing did seem to have that heavy quality, driving up like a geyser from some depth below consciousness where everything was effort and mindless pain.

Ralph came in and turned back the blanket, gently. The blood had soaked through the bandages in a great stain, black in the mellow light of the hurricane-lamp. Ralph took his pulse.

'Not long,' he said.

Padre O'Halloran stooped over Jim. Padre Craufurd stayed where he was. Too late to squabble over whose heaven should have him. And they had all been friends.

Jim's hand stirred. Long ago at Minqar Qaim he'd been hit
by a fragment of 88. The tendons of the hand were still
buckled outward like an umbrella half-folded. That had been
a lucky wound.

Then something seemed to catch in his throat and he tried
weakly to scoop it up with his breath. Wet blood joined the
caked brown about his lips. He opened his eyes.

They were looking beyond the Padre to where a tiny
movement of the blanket blackout threw a large shadow on
the wall. Then they focused, with an effort. He recognised the
Padre and out of his last strength, smiled.

'No, Padre. Tell Shelagh – '

The breath caught at the blood in his throat and did not
come again. The light went out of his eyes. The smile which
had framed the light, remained about his mouth. A friend's
smile became a dead man's.

The Padre made the sign of the Cross and closed the eyes.

'Poor old Jim,' said Ralph.

'The Lord have mercy on him,' said the Padres.

Ralph led the way out of the room.

'A cup of char before you go?' he said to Padre O'Halloran.

'No, thanks, Ralph. I'd better get back to Brigade.'

Outside all was quiet. On the two slopes of Colle Abate
enemies absorbed this night too into themselves and their
past.

If only I'd been able to make it in time I'd have got him.
Which way now was his soul gone? And what should he tell
Shelagh? A lie? Was that what Jim had wanted?

Inside the dark room Jim's body stiffened slowly and fixed
the smile. But the light in his eyes had gone with his life,
wherever that had gone. The Padre walked towards his jeep,
left behind, alone.

Psychological Warfare at Cassino

I woke up with that feeling of panic and looked at my watch. False alarm: it was only 0655 hours and so I hadn't missed the seven o'clock news. I switched the set on and waited. After the time signal the announcer began. Koniev had got across the Bug and was bashing on towards the Dniester. Malinovsky had taken Khersen and cut off the better part of an army. Zhukov's left wing seemed to be striking south from Tarnopol. The impassive BBC voice went on to give astronomical figures for German dead and prisoners. I noted them down. This was the stuff the General could never hear enough of. Nothing about our own Cassino front, of course. We were waiting for the weather to be right for the big bombers.

My bed was one of the two benches that ran along each side of the Intelligence truck. When I got up it would be a desk again. I lay there for a bit, warming my hands under the khaki blankets. The bench on the other side was piled high with sit-reps, all sorts of other reports, maps and mapboards. The Badin and Bukra trays, as we called the in-trays, were full. Plenty more paper would come pouring in after breakfast. There was a stink of kerosene from the extinct heater. Rain was dripping through a hole in the roof on to my 'aqueducts' – two tobacco tins, a dirty glass, and a very dirty old vest. Away towards Cassino our guns had opened up with a routine early morning hate. The German guns were almost silent. They were short of ammunition and knew they were going to need what they had.

Smithy, my batman-runner, slept in the lean-to canopy beside the truck. The wireless must have wakened him. I could hear him pottering about as he got the benghazi boiler going for my shaving-water. Time I was up. I slid out of my sheath of blankets, swivelled on my bottom and shuffled into my socks and trousers. Then I sat up and lowered my feet into my wellingtons which I'd left on the floor beside the bench, right way round. Smithy wasn't much of a housekeeper and there was mud a wet inch deep on the metal floor. Then I stood up, put on my battledress blouse and leather jerkin and was almost ready for the day.

Smithy brought in a blast of cold air and a bowl of hot water. He cleared a space among the papers and set the dish down.

'Morning, boss. Still raining. How are the Russkis?'

'Going like a marble clock, Smithy.'

'Good on them. We'll be back in God's own Kiwiland for Christmas at this rate. Well, I'll go and have some breakfast, if there's nothing you want.'

'Nothing, thanks.'

I cleaned my teeth and then shaved in the Italian mirror Smithy had liberated somewhere back along the trail. Then I went out and stood on the tailboard of the truck, examining the dismal day. Above the tops of the olives I could see the Monastery, where Apollo had once had a temple, frowning down at us. Like the Church, it was built upon a rock. Would it stand in our way for ever, forbidding our passage, dominating us?

I set off for C Mess, watching out warily for the General as I passed his caravan. No sign of him yet, though.

The General and I were not on very good terms, just then. I wasn't long back from a three months' leave in England that had taken six months – half of it on troopships dodging submarines. Des Cassidy had held the fort in Intelligence all that time and the General had become devoted to him. Des was supposed to go on leave as soon as I got back but the General had found one pretext after another for hanging on to him, until after we'd had our first shot at gatecrashing

Cassino, just a month ago. Then Des at last managed to get away. For days afterwards the phone used to ring. 'Is that you, Des?' 'No, sir. It's me.' 'Oh,' he'd say in a changed voice, and ring off.

After a bit of that, I'd made up my mind to teach him a lesson. This compelled a dangerous change of tactics. Des and I had always worked on the principle that our independence and efficiency must be based on going direct to the General and not through Sabretooth, as the colonel in charge of Operations was accurately nicknamed. Operations and Intelligence were supposed to work together like Siamese twins but we'd found that there was a one-way blood circulation. We gave the gen all right but they had a tendency to hold out on us. They were regular staff officers and mistrusted us amateur intellectuals; a pious lot who trusted their training manuals like prayerbooks. We called their office, an Armoured Carrying Vehicle, the Tin Chapel. Our own flimsy unarmoured vehicle was the Café or Bistro. People came to us at all hours of the day and still more at night for a dash of irreverence, strategic fantasies, political prophecies, arguments about 'Life'. Ours was a place where you could have a dram and a dream without being wakened up too harshly. Our occasional carousals were tolerated by the members of the Chapel, partly because they themselves were occasionally tempted to the relief our ambience afforded, partly because we were very good at our job; and mainly because the General cherished us. One night when Alexander had been to visit, he and the General had passed our truck late. 'What's that appalling racket?' Alexander asked. 'Oh, that's just Des having one of his tangis.'

All this I was putting at risk when I decided to change tactics and work direct to Sabretooth. I couldn't play the General as joker in the pack any more. And Sabretooth could be very fierce ... He prided himself on not being 'one of you clever, educated blokes.' So it was rather trying when he queried the style of my intelligence summaries, or wanted me to spell Italian place-names the way he pronounced them. We nearly broke when he tried to get me to substitute 'San

Angelo' for 'Sant' Angelo'. But I grew to like him. You could
wake him any hour of the night and he wouldn't bite your
head off, even if your news turned out to be a mare's nest. He
hated bullshit and could forgive almost anything to a man
who did his job well. And it was a pleasure to listen to the
pure, cold ferocity of his voice when he rang up his opposite
number at the higher formation over some cock-up, and tore a
strip off him, senior or not. He was afraid of nothing, except
losing men's lives when they needn't be lost.

Still, it wasn't the same as working direct to the General.
Apart from the fact that he was a more subtle character than
Sabretooth, with more curiosity about things outside the
military world, a more interesting man to talk to, there was
the hard fact that you had lost mana. So long as you were
known to have long conversations alone with him, you had the
prestige of being thought to know what was in his mind,
things no one else knew. Now all this I'd thrown away.
Brigadiers no longer dropped in and became indiscreet in the
hope that you would do likewise. And the blokes in
Operations showed signs of thinking that because you took
Sabretooth's orders you ought to take theirs. If he was away
somewhere, you had to put up with officious questions from
acolytes who tried to pull rank on you and didn't seem to
grasp that the extra pips only made some people even bigger
pipsqueaks. So I was waiting for my chance to switch back to
the old relationship.

Unluckily it was a quiet time on the front, while we built up
for the new attack on Cassino. 'Unluckily' and 'quiet' in very
special senses, of course. Nothing much was happening:
which meant that every day some poor bastard was stepping
on a mine, hundreds of blokes were freezing wet in slit
trenches and not able to move about by daylight, the odd
mortar bomb was always crashing on someone, engineers
were bulldozing under fire in Mortar Gully, MG bursts were
always liable to whizz around the FDLs, and the Jerry
artillery, with superb observation from the Monastery and
Monte Caira, was apt to take on anything that moved along

the roads. And at night things got pretty fierce, with fighting patrols from both sides out and trying to get prisoners for identifications.

Still, from the Intelligence point of view, it really was quiet. The devil finds work, of course. So, bored with no enemy goings-on to report or predict, I decided one night to write an Intelligence Summary that would be an appreciation from the enemy angle. A good idea, I thought, to give our boys a notion of what it looked like from the other side of that bloody great hill. I rather went to town on it. When I finished it some time after midnight, I was downright proud of my objectivity.

The General, though, was enraged. What would his battalion commanders feel like, when they learnt what the enemy had in store for them, put as plainly as I'd put it? So there was the very devil to pay. By the rules of the little game he and I were at, however, a game I guess he understood very well, he couldn't have me up on the mat and give me a rocket. And old Sabretooth, to do him justice, stood by me and said it was only right that the chaps who would have to fight the. battle should know what they were up against. But that put me all the more in his debt: in his debt now as well as in his power. I even had to put 'Monte Cairo' into my Summary, once, instead of 'Monte Caira', to please him. Only once. I avoided mentioning it after that.

But now the General played into my hands. The brigadiers started to ring me up and ask me what was all this about the German paratroops leaving the front. Of course, I told them it was all balls. Where did they get a bull-shit yarn like that from? From the Old Man himself, they said. I didn't believe for a moment he could be right. First Para Div. was the cornerstone of the Cassino defence. Nothing else had a hope of standing up to us. The Germans weren't going to be such mugs as to shift them. After all, it was because they'd identified us on the Cassino front a month ago that they'd moved the paratroops in from the Adriatic front.

But then I began to have my doubts. What about that visit from the Eighth Army Commander the day before? I'd watched his staff car drive up to the General's caravan. There was a ritual about these meetings that I always relished. This time the form didn't vary. General Oliver Leese, a very large man in a sheepskin coat, stepped out and stood facing our General's caravan. Our General came to the caravan door, paused, and they beamed at each other. Then they approached at equal pace till they were about a yard from each other. They flung out their arms. 'Oliver,' said our General. 'Bernard,' said the Army Commander. They rushed together and embraced like two huge brotherly bears. Then, our Old Man doing the honours, they disappeared into the caravan, and I was left speculating.

So now, to be on the safe side, I rang my friends at Eighth Army. We weren't under their command for the Cassino battle but if there was any top level intercept information they'd know. There wasn't and they didn't believe the story either. So I thought again and decided the General must have made it up or got it from US Fifth Army under whose command we were. The Yanks were always suckers for wish-fulfilment stories, especially Mark Clark's lot. Anyway, whatever the General's source, I knew he was wrong and had given me a trump card. The problem was how and when to play it.

I munched that problem along with my breakfast of little Italian pullets' eggs, tinned American bacon and burnt toast that morning in C Mess. And I smoked it over a couple of cigarettes and cups of black New Zealand tea until it was time to get back to my truck and do some work.

On the way there, I spotted the General outside his caravan. He was pacing up and down, as he always did after breakfast, waiting for the right moment before he made a dash for his special latrine, 'GOC Only'. As I always used it myself I'd made a special study of his bowel and other movements. And in the old days we had usually had a chat, walking up and down together, till he suddenly made his dash. Nowadays, though, since our estrangement, he always pretended not to see me, and to spare him embarrassment I changed direction this time as usual so that our tracks wouldn't coincide.

But this time he himself altered direction and prevented me from slipping past.

'Oh, there you are, "I",' he said, with such formidable geniality that I thought I must be properly in for it.

'Good morning, sir,' I said, distantly and dissembling my trepidation. It was the first time we'd spoken for nearly a fortnight.

'And how's your leg?' he asked.

This was a ritual question that went back a long way. It was three years since I'd been wounded but he always acted as if I'd just come out of hospital.

I assured him the leg was fine and thanked him for asking.

'Aren't you glad I got you out of that horrible Headquarters in Cairo?' This was the second question in the routine and equally baffling. It was now nearly two years since he'd discovered I was seconded to British Intelligence at GHQ, Middle East. He knew nothing else about me then, but on the principle that, if the British wanted me then he must, he had winkled me out and back to NZ Div.

'Very glad, sir,' I said. I waited to find out what he was up to.

'Anything on the news this morning? How's Malinowsky?'

I told him about Khersen and Tarnopol and the advance on the Dniester.

'What about the Germans? Have they lost much?'

'11,000 prisoners, and 5,000 killed, sir.'

'Killed, the announcer said killed, did he?'

'Yes, sir, killed.'

'Killed, eh, 5,000. Good.'

This was all very well but I knew from his ADC that he listened to the news himself every morning, the same early news as I did. So he was only enjoying hearing it over again or trying out my accuracy, or both. Even though he was obsessed with the Russian front, envying the scale and sweep of the Russian operations and their room for manoeuvre and jealously aware that the outcome of the whole war was really being decided there, this couldn't be what was in the forefront of his mind now. He must be leading up to something else.

'And what's happening on our own front? What's he up to? Anything new? What are 1 Para Div. doing? Are they still there?'

My problem was solved. Now was the time to play my trump. I stared him straight in his blue eyes.

'Of course they're still there, sir. We're listening to them on intercept every day. Kesselring would be mad to move them. But someone's been spreading a rumour that they're leaving the front. A fifth columnist, I expect, unless it's wishful thinking on somebody's part.'

He continued to return my gaze but he knew what I meant and I could feel it was an effort for him not to look guilty.

'Very well,' he said, calling me by my first name. 'It's always as well to know the worst. Thank you.'

I kept a straight face and went towards my office. Out of the corner of my eye I saw him making his dash. If I knew my man I'd had an apology. Tactics could now shift back to normal and I could revert to direct relations with him.

There really was a hell of a lot to do at that time. We'd been made into an ad hoc Corps when, in preparation for the mid-February attack on Cassino, we'd taken 4 Indian Div. and 78 British under command. Now we had a Yank armoured formation as well which was supposed to be rushed through into the Liri Valley as soon as we'd bashed a road through Cassino. All the bods in Operations and the other bits of HQ did a sort of amoeba stunt and the half that became Corps staff all went up a rank. I hadn't been paying much attention, partly because I was cut off by my tiff with the General. The result was that Intelligence stayed the same. I was Corps Intelligence General Staff Officer and simultaneously Div. Intelligence General Staff Officer; two hats, one head. It was cheaper that way and it made for a wonderful concentration of energy. When I woke up to what was going on I did manage to get myself an extra Intelligence Officer from one of the Brigades and I also used the opportunity to get a trained interrogator from my pals at Eighth Army – an Austrian Jew named Hans Zweig. He could give the prisoners the time I couldn't spare and didn't suffer from my little weakness of liking front-line soldiers from either side better than anyone from Base.

We'd originally been going to crack down on Cassino within about a week of the failure of our first assault. But a tremendous bomber concentration was an essential part of the plan. So we had to wait until the weather was good enough for Fortresses and Mitchells to get off the ground. But the weather kept being bloody awful and forced one postponement after another. That's why a special Met section began to appear in my Intelligence Summaries about that time: in the old days you just poked your head out the door or the slit trench at first light and assumed everyone else would do the same. But that was in the desert and the weather wasn't hard to predict there. Full moon, first light and last light, were all you had to worry about.

Anyway the big show kept being put off day after day and we were all getting pretty nervy. One good thing was that the newspapermen had got bored with us, except for a few cunning old hands, and they weren't such a nuisance as the famous ones who flew in like buzzards from New York or somewhere and took it as a personal affront that we didn't mount the offensive at once for them.

Besides inquisitive newshounds – bloodhounds, some of them – there were the liaison officers from every other formation sideways and backwards, the enemy intercept chaps and own troops intercepts, all of them with a tendency to turn up without rations, beds or blankets and expect to be looked after. Then there'd be a sprinkling of politicians, the most tiresome of the lot, who seemed to think that their next election depended on our being ready to get on with the killing. And there were the poor sods whom the American OSS kept sending for me to brief: the idea was that I would tell them what we specially wanted to know about what was happening behind the Jerry lines and they'd go across on dark nights or be dropped by parachute and come back and tell us the answers. They were interesting blokes to look at – not because I knew I'd never see them again; for I'd seen too many friends of mine going towards the sharp end by now and known I'd never see them again. No, they were interesting because one could make almost any sort of guess about their ultimate motives and probably be wrong; whereas the motives of one's friends were much the same as one's own: to get on with the job and get the war over and done with. These OSS jokers were usually Italians and some of them looked pretty fishy customers while others looked as simple-minded as the Yanks themselves. Anyway, I didn't have any confidence in their future and I didn't tell them anything that the Germans wouldn't have guessed for themselves. Once in the hands of the Gestapo, where most of them were bound to land up, I reckoned I myself would have been a pretty poor security risk and I didn't think they would be any better.

The trouble with all these visitors, of course, was that they took up time and talking to them was completely non-productive – didn't shorten the war by a single second. So I passed them on to one of the IOs, whenever they weren't such VIPs that they'd be insulted. And sometimes I dressed Smithy up in captain's pips and let him deal with them. He might be a rough diamond but they'd think he was a typical example of the down-to-earth Kiwi. And, being a man of imagination who could keep a straight face, he'd spin them endless yarns of heroic behaviour on the part of our chaps that made good copy for newspaper articles and politicians' speeches.

Meanwhile, I'd hide in the canopy and get on with my paperwork: trying to sort out the information that came in from all quarters, decide what was reliable and set about making sense of it, get to the guts of it and emerge with a picture of the enemy situation that might be of some use to our blokes on the ground. Good hard stuff about where the enemy mortars and machine-guns were or what was the latest type of anti-personnel mine they were likely to come up against, or new Jerry weapon, that kind of griff meant more to them than any amount of bullshit about the relations between Hitler and Jodl or how our bombing was affecting the morale of the German worker.

Because of all the postponements, though, things were pretty quiet in the office that morning after my talk with the

Psychological Warfare at Cassino

General. I had good reason to believe that next day was the day, but the story hadn't got around yet. So there I was, safe in my truck, answering telephones, and marking the latest identifications on my mapboard. I had a hunch that I Para Regiment was being brought into the south-west corner of Cassino and perhaps on to Point 193 as well. Toby Grayson had reported a couple of PW taken during the night but he couldn't get them back to Brigade because of the shelling and I was trying to think of some way of speeding things up. So when I heard the splutter of a motor-bike outside I took it for granted it was a despatch rider with some gen – the phone had gone adrift and every time it rang I had to deal with a mad linesman from Corps Signals with no roof to his mouth.

Smithy came in. Behind him I could see the white under-bellies of olive-tree leaves turned upwards by the wind and passing showers of sleet.

'There's a Yank major outside, boss. Says he wants to see you.'

Someone from Fifth Army, I thought, who imagines he's going to win promotion by coming back with some really special plum of information from the horse's mouth. Was it advertising or Hollywood that made them that way? Anyway, I'd take a look at him before I let him in.

I went out and stood on the tailboard, my apron stage. He was standing just below, at the foot of the steps. Young and biggish, face pale and fat, the way the Yanks got from sitting for hours in those overheated tents of theirs. He looked earnest and full of zeal, the sort of look that made you see why Custer's last stand happened, and not sorry either. He was wearing one of those Hudibras helmets and he had a huge Colt .45 pistol at his belt. We were a peaceful lot ourselves, at Div. HQ. And we never wore helmets or pistols, for fear of what visitors from the battalions would say, real soldiers who had a genuine use for such things.

'Is this your G2 Command Post, sir?' he asked.

I supposed he was giving me the 'sir' because he was a southerner and a stranger to me. But I had an uneasy feeling it was because he thought I was older than he was. I dare say I looked it. I probably was, too, in many ways.

'Yes,' I said. 'This is the Intelligence truck and I'm the boss.'

'Sorry,' he said. He knew he ought to have remembered our name for it. He blushed and I felt sorry for him.

'Come on in,' I said.

'Thank you kindly.' He climbed up and in through the canvas flap, eyeing my muddy floor doubtfully. I cleared some papers off the second revolving chair. 'I'd leave your coat on if I were you,' I said. 'I like to work in the cold but it's hard on you people who're used to central heating.'

He had a thing stitched to his arm with the initials PWD. I knew I knew what they meant but couldn't remember. Something to do with prisoners of war, I guessed. I hoped he wasn't going to bellyache about the way we treated them, or complain we didn't get them back to the Army cage fast enough. Whatever it was, I'd find out soon enough.

'Have a drink?' I said. 'I've only got vermouth, I'm afraid, or a drop of Italian cognac, if you'd prefer that.'

'No, thank you, sir. It's too early in the day for me. I'd sure like a cup of coffee, though.'

Smithy, always inquisitive, had kept hanging round the door. 'We've only got tea, boss.' He didn't approve of coffee. Or Yanks. Their planes had killed a cobber of his in Tunisia, when they dropped a load on 24 Battalion by mistake. He held all Yanks responsible.

'OK, Smithy,' I said. 'Let's have some tea, then.'

The Yank's name, it turned out, was Elmer Glass, and he was from the Psychological Warfare Department, Fifth Army. I asked him if he knew one of the G2 staff there, Colonel Buckley. I didn't add that I privately called him Buckley's Chance.

Indeed he did know Colonel Buckley. It seemed that the colonel had a truly amazing grasp of German strategy and ability to size up what the enemy was up to. Having once heard the colonel talking to us about the Anzio landing, I could hardly concur. So I dropped that subject.

Smithy brought in the tea. I took mine straight. The major

wondered if we had a slice of lemon and was disabused. We found him some condensed milk. Even then, the tea stayed a dark brown. The first mouthful seemed to quench poor Elmer's thirst.

We got down to business. They'd had a big idea at Fifth Army. They'd filled some mortar bombs with propaganda leaflets. Our forward units were to fire these things into the FDLs of 1 Para Div. The front-line paratroopers would read the leaflets and, profoundly moved, would wait for darkness and desert to us in droves. Just like advertising, really.

I kept a grave face. There are always a few lunatics around at army level. It's a bit like modern art. Nobody can be sure after a while what's mad and what isn't. It's only near the front line that people have a criterion: what's going to help you stay alive.

Friend Elmer had got me into a sticky position, all the same. There wasn't a snowflake's chance in hell that his pamphlets would bring over a single parachutist. And the chances of anyone on our side being willing to try them out weren't much better – say a snowflake's in purgatory. The very thought of what Sabretooth would say sent a shiver down my spine. It would never get as far as the unit commanders but I knew what they'd think of the idea and of me for passing it on. It was hard enough to look after your mortars when they were firing real stuff which did at least make the Germans keep their heads down. If they fired these wads of paper the only thing that would come over after dark would be a pattern of moaning minnies, brackets of 88 airburst and a pasting by mortar bombs that had something more convincing than paper inside them.

On the other hand, I'd rather taken to poor Elmer. I didn't want to be the one who took away his toys. And he was one of our great allies, after all. I couldn't have him going back to Army and telling them what a cynical, uncooperative bastard I was.

I indicated a few doubts, so as to prepare him for what was coming. It wasn't a decision I could take, I explained. It was more a matter for Ops than for Intelligence. He'd have to talk to the Brigadier General Staff. 'We call him Sabretooth,' I warned him, 'and he hasn't got that name for nothing.'

So I rang Sabretooth's next man down the ladder, rather a solemn sort of bloke himself, and told him I was sending Elmer over, though I was pretty vague what it was all about. I thought it prudent not to go with Elmer. I was afraid of guilt by association. And, to be on the safe side, as soon as he'd set off, I rang up Ops again and squared off by explaining that I felt this was high-level stuff and too much a matter of policy for a humble fellow like myself. They lapped up that kind of thing.

It wasn't long before Elmer was back again. He was flushed now instead of pale and I could have sworn there were tears behind those steel-rimmed hexagonal spectacles. He picked up the mug of tea he'd hardly touched before and had a good swig. It seemed to make him feel better.

'The BGS didn't think much of the idea?'

'I'll say he didn't. Gee, he must be hard to work with, that guy. I thought he was smiling, at first.'

'He doesn't smile often,' I said. 'But he looks just the same when he does. The last time I saw him smile was when the Corps Commander's latrine was shelled in the desert. It was a mistake, though. He thought the Corps Commander was in it, at the time. He must have blamed himself for thinking that for once life had lived up to his expectations. White Fang is another of his nicknames round here.'

Elmer gave a sort of smile himself at that, but pretty wan. 'I thought he was going for my jugular,' he said.

I was pleased with the way he was coming on and so I tried to cheer him up. 'He may have been in a specially bad mood this morning,' I said. 'I'll tell you what. You leave some of those propaganda bombs of yours with me and I'll see what we can do. You never know, he might change his mind.'

Sabretooth changed his mind a good deal less often than Smithy changed his shirt, and that wasn't very often, but I didn't think it would help to say so.

'Will you? That's mighty kind of you,' Elmer said. His face cleared like a nice child's. 'I'll go and get them.' He went down the steps and over to his motorbike. He unstrapped a box from the carrier and brought it back to me. 'There's half a dozen in there,' he said.

'OK, I'll look after them.' I'd come out to the tailboard so as to keep him from getting back into my office and wasting too much time converting me to psychological warfare. I had my own views and didn't want to explain it was best reserved for internal use.

'Thank you kindly,' he said. He looked at the box as if he were an unmarried mother leaving her first-born on my doorstep. Then he set off back to his motorbike, got astraddle, pulled down his helmet over his forehead, shifted his pistol out of his groin and back on his hip where it belonged, started his engine and spluttered off through the mud.

Smithy was grinning at me from the flap of the canopy. 'Put those bloody things under your bed or somewhere, will you, Smithy,' I said. 'I'll think about them some other time.'

Naturally, I forgot all about them from that moment onwards. The phone was ringing. It was the General wanting me to come over to his caravan. Here we go, I said to myself. We're back on the old system already.

Then the other phone went. It was from Brigade. The two PW had come in and been identified as from II Battalion of 1 Para Regiment. I marked this up on my mapboard and took it with me to the General.

'There's a conference on at Fifth Army in an hour's time,' he said. 'What's the latest picture?'

I told him. I didn't think it was very cheerful but I let the facts say that for me. I didn't labour the new paratroop identification either. The General knew a hawk from a hand-grenade better than most. And I could see from the glitter in his eye that things were going to start happening at last. His spirits always rose as soon as he smelled action.

I went back to the truck. The sky had cleared and the rain had stopped. I sat on our tailboard with Smithy and we watched the bustle and ceremony while the General and his ADC piled into the staff car and the PA fussed around handing them mapboards and papers.

They'd hardly got away when my phone started up again. It was Colonel Buckley at Fifth Army. My heart sank: more psychological warfare. But no. 'We've got a conference on here in an hour's time,' he said. 'The Commander-in-Chief's coming as well.' He made it sound as if God was coming. Still, old Alex did have a touch of God about him. An Anglican God, out of the top drawer of gods.

'How exciting for you,' I said.

'They'll want to know all about the enemy situation from the G2 angle,' he said. 'You're closer to the front than I am. What's your view of things?'

Poor old Buckley's trouble was that he had hundreds of chaps collecting thousands of facts with a map reference for every time a shell landed or a sparrow farted but he hadn't a clue how to cut out what didn't matter, concentrate on what did, and come up with something that made sense about what was happening or might be happening. We were all fighting the same war, though, and it wasn't going to help if I held out on him. So I told him roughly what I'd just told the General, spelling it out a bit for him. For dignity's sake, he said that was exactly the way he saw it too. I indicated gratification.

Late that afternoon the General came back. My phone went soon afterwards, and his voice crackled in my ear. 'You'll be interested to know that Fifth Army takes the same view of the enemy situation as you do,' he said.

I'd planted a few characteristic phrases on Colonel Buckley which I was pretty sure the General would spot as mine. Otherwise, if he'd thought that Army's view had been reached independently of mine, he might have felt less confident in mine. For I was pretty sure he'd have taken Buckley's measure long ago. He was a crafty old scamp, the General.

Well, after that, things really got humming. There was a special Orders Group conference of the brigadiers and what have you and I had to say my piece all over again – no joke with all those pairs of gimlet eyes fixed on you and tough brains behind them checking how many paratroops there were in front and where, how many guns, how many mortars, exact locations of minefields and dug-in pill-boxes, all that sort of thing. Then the General went over his plan again, with timings, and the dope about how the Fortresses and Mitchell medium bombers would come in first at 0830 hours next morning to saturate Cassino and the defences before the infantry got cracking.

Just before I went to bed that night, 14 March, a runner brought me a note from a friend who had one of the forward companies and was to go in with the first wave of the assault. '800 yards from the Monastery; 400 yards from the town. Losing weight fast. Regards. Jack.' I thought of him a lot before I went to sleep. At first I thought I knew how he felt. Then I realised I only remembered how he felt.

Well, the newspaper boys were round in swarms by 0630 hours and at 0830 the bombers went over, and after that the infantry went in. We were as busy as bees and yet there wasn't much we could really do, except wait. And it was much the same for the next few days. Vesuvius started erupting the third day after the battle started but we hardly noticed we were so intent on Cassino. We'd got Point 193 but couldn't be sure how long we'd be able to keep it. Jack's company, or what was left of it, had taken Hangman's Hill and were so pinned down that we had to supply them by parachute. The Maoris had taken the ruins of the Continental Hotel and then got bogged down in the rubble of the bombing and so did the other battalions.

Our plan to punch a road through the centre of Cassino and then pass the American armour through just wasn't coming off. The paratroops kept hanging on to the last crucial few hundred yards. The bulldozers couldn't get cracking to shove aside the masses of fallen masonry. The ruins made wonderful cover, there was no way of outflanking them, and no room to bring in superior numbers and go over the top of them.

Our Photographic Interpretation Unit had picked up signs of a possible alternative defence line being prepared by the Germans, a Riegelstellung. Our chaps had taken quite a haul of PW, in the first assault, especially the Maoris, and so I asked Hans Zweig to see what he could find out about this possible switch-line. Once I found him talking to a red-haired corporal. Hans was plugging away at him about the Riegelstellung. The German seemed to know something but wouldn't talk. Hans tried a new tack.

'Is it your duty to obey your officers?'

'Yes, sir.'

'Am I not an officer?'

'Yes, sir.'

'Then listen closely and answer my questions.'

You could see by the way the German scratched his crutch and wrinkled his forehead that he felt there was something wrong with the logic but couldn't quite put his finger on it. He asked why we wanted to know.

'Because of the archives,' Hans said. 'The battle is over and your troops have had to retreat. This officer is an historian. He wants to know, for the archives, where they would have made their second line if they had had time.'

The German was impressed. Hans put the map in front of him. The prisoner drew his finger across it. The switch-line was where we had thought.

I thought I'd better pass this one to the General, though by now I was pretty sure we weren't going to need the information, not this time, any more than the enemy were going to need the switch-line. On the way I noticed Smithy hanging round the cage where we kept the PW after we'd finished with them, until Fifth Army took them on to the Army cage. He was trying in his matey way to make conversation with the prisoners. He was always interested in whatever was going on. In fact, his problem was the same as mine really. How to be near enough to the big bosses to know what was happening and at the same time avoid getting chewed up by the machine. I must be to him what the General was to me, transparent as a child and inscrutable as fate. At the moment, though, he didn't even notice me. Probably too absorbed in the prospect of doing some sort of trade in watches or Luger pistols, if any had escaped frisking on the way back from the Maoris – which wasn't likely.

A few more days went by and we were no further ahead.

Stalemate in Cassino was what the journalists called it. The troops had other names. Where we were, in San Pietro, it was quiet enough, though depressing after the first hopes had become disappointment. The Jerry artillery had scored a hit on the Chief Engineer's petrol dump the first night and that encouraged them to drop a few more shells on us every night afterwards. I used to go my rounds most evenings. I'd find the off-duty intercept chaps talking about Kafka and playing chess. When that palled I'd go along to the PRI section and they'd show me the latest air photographs. Then I'd mooch off back to my truck where there'd usually be visitors. We'd try to cheer up over the poisonous stuff we called cognac. The fumes from that and the oil heaters and the cans full of burning charcoal would drive us out for a bit of fresh air on the tailboard and then the sleet and rain would drive us in again. I would be scratching an I Summary together from whatever bits and pieces of information I'd picked up. Sometimes shells would pass over and drop fairly near and we'd all bend our heads, as if that was going to do us any good. But there was some help in having at least a bit of danger. It used to make me feel less bad about not being with my old battalion down there in the rubble of the smoking town.

By the beginning of the second week it was as plain as a bull's bum that we were stuck. I hoped the General wasn't going to hold that earlier appreciation of the enemy situation against me. In or out of your own country, it's dangerous being a prophet. Then, one afternoon, shortly after Smithy had reported that Alexander's staff car had arrived and Alex himself had gone into the General's caravan, they called for me.

As I came in, mapboard under my oxter, the General's bright blue eyes and Alexander's very cold blue eyes drilled into me. What did I think of the enemy situation? I told them. They said nothing for a bit. It wasn't news to them. Then Alexander asked me, in his clipped, dangerous voice, what I thought the morale of the paratroops was like.

My spirits sank. When generals start asking you about

enemy morale it means they're getting pretty desperate. I told them: the morale of I Para Div. wasn't likely to be shaken, even if Monte Cassino fell in on top of them. Besides, they must know that if we hadn't got through by now, after trying with everything we had, we just weren't going to. That would be enough to keep up the peckers of most troops, let alone paratroopers.

They were silent again, both staring at me, as if I were some sort of shifty Delphic oracle. I began to wish I could think of something more cheerful and could see my head on a salver. Still, there was nothing else I could say. They'd have to like it or lump it. I needn't have worried. I was merely confirming what these two tough characters thought already. In fact, the General put his arm round my shoulder as he saw me to the door.

That night they called the battle off. I hadn't, for some days now, expected anything else, and I'd never been too hopeful. Whenever I was tempted to think we might bring it off I always remembered the morning Des left after we failed the first time. 'You'll never get into the Liri Valley this way,' he had said. 'If you go on trying you'll still be here when I come back.' Now it was all over, though, I felt pretty depressed all the same, just like everybody else.

Next morning I was sitting in the silence, the telephones quiet at last and the hordes of visitors dispersed. We were about to revert to being the good old Div., instead of being a Corps. Those who had gone up a rank would lose it again. Sceptre and crown were tumbling down. I had a hangover, after drinking too much with Jack who'd somehow or other got his remaining men down from Hangman's Hill to safety, temporary safety, and been relieved. We had gone over the battle again, touching all its sore places: our failure to get Point 516, losing surprise and strength on Point 468, the fact that the bombing had made the job harder instead of easier by giving the paratroops almost impregnable cover and completely blocking up the only road through. And we had gone over the names of friends who had been killed.

Wisps and echoes of our talk were in my mind now. I remembered the General's face as he said to me, sadly, that he was tired of war and that he was always thinking of the young battalion commanders, friends, who had been killed in these gruelling Italian battles. Then he had smiled an apology for the momentary weakness of sharing his feelings and we had broken off to talk about the Russian campaign. But I had had a glimpse of his burden. To cheer myself up now, early though it was, I poured myself some of the horrible cognac. Then I heard a motorbike pull up outside. I peered through the door-flap and saw it was Elmer. This was a bit much, having to put up with him again. What had we done with his infernal propaganda bombs? But he had spotted me and it was too late to get Smithy to say I was out. He came up the steps, beaming. 'May I come in?'

'Of course. Have a drink?'

'I don't usually take a drink so early. But I will this time, thanks. Is there any ice?'

'Only out in the puddles,' I said. 'We don't use it much round here.'

I poured one out for him all the same, wondering why the hell he seemed so cheerful.

'Here's to you,' he said, as he raised his glass. 'And thanks a lot.'

He couldn't have been thanking me for the cognac, not after the way he put it down, screwing up his face.

'Thanks what for?'

'For what you did.'

I said nothing, scratching my brains. What the hell had happened to those mortar bombs?

'It was a great success.'

'Was it?'

'Yes, when the prisoners got back to Fifth Army Cage we searched them and every one of them had a propaganda leaflet. Colonel Buckley in person congratulated me and I'm being made a half-colonel myself and put up for a decoration. Not that that matters so much. What I care about is the way we've showed them, all those people who wouldn't believe us. Now they've just got to believe us. Psychological Warfare does really work. I'm writing an article on it for Washington. And we'll get all the backing and the staff we need. General Mark Clark is really behind us now.'

'Well, well.'

'So I thought I'd just come along and thank you kindly for what you've done to help win the war. We can't look back now.'

I didn't say that I was expecting to do quite a lot of looking back myself. There was plenty to look back on, more than plenty. So I just thanked him and said it was nothing, really.

He began to go on about English modesty and all that. It was very embarrassing and I didn't have the heart to tell him I wasn't English and was a bit sceptical about most forms of modesty anyway. I don't think I ever knew a grown-up man who made me think of more things it was impossible to say than Elmer. I concentrated on getting rid of him instead.

Eventually he went off, still bubbling with enthusiasm. When his motorbike was out of earshot I went to look for Smithy. He must have taken off smartly at the high port as soon as he saw Elmer but I ran him down in the end, skulking in the Public Relations section.

'Looking for me, boss?' he asked, innocently and superfluously.

'Smithy, what did you do with those mortar bombs?'

'What mortar bombs?'

'You know bloody well what mortar bombs. The ones the Yank left.'

'Well, boss, you didn't seem to be much interested and so I thought I'd take a gander and see what was inside them. They were full of leaflets printed in German with pictures of foreign workers in bed with German women and things like that. Pretty spicy some of them were. I knew you wouldn't want them, not your sort of thing at all. And when I saw all those Germans in the PW cage, looking so down in the mouth and with nothing to read or pass the time with, I felt sorry for them. So I gave them all those leaflets to take their mind off things, poor buggers. Not that it seemed to cheer them up very much, though.'

'I don't suppose it did,' I said.

The General and the Nightingale

With two bivvies joined together and open along one side
Plugger Holmes, the General's batman, had made himself a
snug little shelter. After today's surprise shelling he'd thought
he might have to move to some place with a deeper soil under
it. But when he dug down he'd found there was enough depth
for a shallow slittie before you got to solid rock. So he was
staying on. It wouldn't have been easy to find another spot so
well sheltered from the wind and tactically it was nicely
placed. Without getting out of his blankets he had observation
on the three vital points, the General's caravan, A Mess, and
the Car Park.

Not that there was any need to keep an eye on them just
now. The GOC was still away at Brigade. When he did come
back he'd probably make straight for the Mess where the
Mess Corporal could be relied on to look after him for a while.
And Plugger had guests, the AQ's batman and the GI's
batman, especially invited to sample the latest parcel from
home. A panful of whitebait fritters was already crackling over
the Primus under Shorty's care and Pongo Rose was just
bringing the water to the boil. As host, senior batman and
provider of the rations, Plugger had nothing to do but
supervise.

'Billy's boiling, GI,' he announced. 'Make the tea, will you?
And, AQ, I like my fritters well done on both sides. You'd
better turn them over, hadn't you?'

It was the General's voice and manner, exactly mimicked

but with asperity slightly exaggerated. And there was something of the original's authority.

'There we are, sir,' said Shorty Evans, caricaturing his own master, 'We'll just give her a minute to draw and she'll be jake.' And he set down three mugs beside the black boiling of tea, took out the twigs which plugged the two holes in the Highlander Milk tin, and tapped the sides of the billy with the handle of his knife. The leaves began to settle down from the surface where they had floated like the debris of an ants' nest.

'Come on, AQ,' said Plugger, sitting up on the blanket he had disposed over the edge of his slittie and letting his legs dangle. 'Can't wait all night, you know. They look well enough done now.'

'Yes, sir, yes, sir,' Pongo began to shuffle the fritters out on to three enamel plates. Fortunately, they divided evenly by three and there was no argument.

'Shall we have our plonk now, sir, or wait till afterwards?' Pongo added, looking at his mug.

'What sort of Mess were you brought up in, Pongo?'' said Shorty. "You know the General never takes red vino with his fish.'

But like all great men Plugger didn't like to think he was an open book to his subordinates. Or to be anticipated. He eyed the half-full demijohn. 'I don't see why we shouldn't make an exception this once,' he said. 'Hardships of the field, you know. Eh, AQ?'

'Yes, sir,' assented Pongo with enthusiasm.

'I suppose you're right, Plugger,' said Shorty, and he pushed forward his mug, too. He wasn't very good at this game, not as good as if he'd been General, and he constantly forgot the rules.

'You know, GI,' said Plugger, who never forgot, eyeing the last of his fritters sadistically, 'I really think it's time you went back to your regiment for a spell. After all, it's selfish of me to keep you away from your men and regimental life so long.'

'That's right, sir,' said Pongo. 'He'll never get the VC here. And you've given him the Other Bastards' Effort already. I don't suppose he wants to be mentioned in dispatches again.'

Pongo was apt to labour his points. 'Nothing like the regimental life,' he went on, after another look at Shorty, 'keeps you close to reality.'

'Nothing like it,' Shorty's lugubrious emphasis gave the phrase a more sinister meaning.

But Plugger believed in the balance of power.

'Yes, AQ,' he said, 'I suppose you do miss the excitements of the old life. The friendly shells screaming by, the comradeship in danger, the old nebels. Those were the days, eh?' He picked up his mug of tea, blew on it and gazed reflectively towards the Car Park.

'Jesus,' he suddenly said and put down his mug. 'There's the Old Man's jeep. He's back early.'

The others stared in the same direction. The sun was already down behind the Casole hills which the French had bitterly fought for that winter. But there was still enough light in the basin that held the camp for them to make out the Divisional Commander's flag on the bonnet of the jeep. And as the jeep passed the Provost on point duty saluted with unmistakable smartness.

'Well, his bed's made and everything's OK,' said Plugger. But care had returned to his face. Once the General was within the borders of the camp he was Plugger's responsibility. And Plugger had to watch him like a hawk to make sure he was kept in good trim and didn't want for anything. It wasn't a sinecure because the General combined absent-mindedness with considerateness so that you couldn't tell which was which. And he had a trick of asking you what you would do if you were Kesselring, which was a bit tough, especially before breakfast. So you had to keep on your toes. Anyhow, if he hadn't kept one jump ahead and been thinking while the General was taking off his trousers which ones he'd wear tomorrow, Plugger would have felt the way the General himself would feel if one of his brigades went short of ammo or lost more blokes in a scrap than they need have done.

The General had got out of his seat beside the driver. The GI and the ADC vaulted from their perch in the back of the jeep and then bent over it again to get their map-boards. All three began to climb up the slope towards 'A' Mess. The driver, left alone in the jeep, swung her round and drove off towards the Car Park. Plugger and the other two watched him get out there and stand for a moment looking towards the men's cookhouse. There'd be something kept hot for him. But then he half turned and his gaze swivelled across the slope. It stopped on them. He began to walk firmly in their direction.

'Nose like a bloody bloodhound,'' said Plugger. 'Well, here goes for the last of the whitebait.' With resignation, no longer General, he began to prepare more fritters.

'We've got the wood on him tonight, anyhow,' said Pongo. 'He can't come that Terelle Terror Ride stuff on us once he hears we've been getting pasted ourselves.'

But the other two shook their heads and Shorty said sourly: 'That'll be the bloody day when Alec lets himself be trumped. What's an 88 bursting in Rear Div. cookhouse to his imagination? Just a provocation, that's all. If he'll even listen.'

'Well, you pack of bludgers,' was Alec's greeting. 'Can you spare a bite for a front-line troop? Nothing fancy. Anything will do for a man who's been in the saddle since dawn.' His eye had taken in the frying pan and his nostrils were twitching.

'Bludgers, what the hell do you mean, bludgers?' said Plugger. 'You're the bloody bludger round this outfit. Touring round the country all day and bludging their rations off the brigades and now you come and take their last bite from your old cobbers who used to know you when you were nothing better than the sanitary corporal's assistant. Don't think you're getting a clean plate, though, even if you have been hobnobbing with the big shots. You can pig it off mine.' And he flapped a couple of fritters on to the plate.

'Good old Plugger,' said Alec. 'Too old to be anything but a base-wallower himself but never lets the fighting-man down.'

'Jesus, just listen to him, will you,' Shorty reached over for the loaf of bread Plugger had scrounged. 'He'll be telling us he's a soldier next.'

'He wouldn't be talking so big if he knew what a day we'd had here, would he, Shorty?' said Plugger.

'My bloody oath he wouldn't. D'you know what those bloody Teds have been up to? They've been bloody well shelling us. Air-burst at that. On top of all the nervous strain of an important HQ job we've got to put up with air-burst. Takes a man back to Sidi Rizegh, doesn't it, Plugger? But, of course, you were only a bloody redarse in those days, weren't you, Alec?'

'So that's it,' said Alec. 'I thought I noticed a lot of new holes dug. Place looks like a Klondyke gold rush. Suppose no one thought of digging one for me?'

'Well, you know,' said Plugger, 'you being such a glutton for it and all that, we thought you wouldn't want us to bother.'

'Not after today. I'm a changed man.'

'Why, what happened today? You ought to be used to the Terelle Terror Ride by now. We are, hearing you talk about it every day since we got here. Hey, Shorty, go easy on that Cocky's Joy. It's not every day my old woman sends me a tin of that stuff.'

Shorty went on spreading the Golden Syrup. 'She wouldn't send you any at all if she knew what you did with the last tin,' he said when he had finished.

'Have a heart, Shorty, the poor girl was starving.'

'Lonely, too, I suppose. She seemed to need quite a lot of company, even after you left Naples.'

Alec had finished his fritters and skipping the tea, which by now had an oily film on its surface, armed himself with a mug of plonk. He put this beside him and began to roll a cigarette from Plugger's makings.

'So nobody's interested in my day of peril,' he remarked bitterly.

'Not if it's one more of those yarns about how with a savage twist of the wheel you wrenched the jeep away from the bursting shell and tears came into the General's eyes as he thanked you,' said Pongo. The others said nothing.

Alec looked at the three of them sorrowfully. Clearly he would have to shift the emphasis of his speech away from himself.

'You know he's a queer old cove, the General,' he said and

took another dip into his mug. When he looked up the others were watching him. He had his audience.

'What's he been up to now?' Plugger asked.

Alec was away.

'Well, you know how it is,' he said. 'There we were as usual this morning at sparrowfart, me with the jeep pulled up in front of the General's caravan, the GI hurrying across from the Mess and wiping the bacon fat from his mouth, the ADC scuttling about getting the map-boards together and covering them with a ground-sheet so the sun won't shine on them when we come under observation from the Jerry OPs on Cifalco. Then out bursts the GOC from his caravan, looking at his watch. Time to get cracking, he says, come along GI, come along, Harry. And all three of them bundle into the jeep. Then he spots one of the Intelligence blokes shaving outside his truck. "What's the news, 'I'," he shouts, "anything fresh?"

' "No, sir," says the "I" bloke, "nothing much. There was a raid on the International Post early this morning, that's all. We took a couple of PW and lost no one. They were from II/132, as I thought."

' "Good," says the General and rubs his hands. "Tell me all about it when I get back tonight. But what about the Russians?"

' "Rokossovsky's rounded up another Corps, sir. Claims 10,000 killed, according to the BBC."

' "Good, good," says the Old Man. "Killed, eh? You did say killed?"

' "Killed, sir."

' "Good, good. Drive on, Alec. Thank you, 'I'."

'And so away we go with him sitting beside me, that jaw of his as set as if he meant to go off and get 10,000 on his own.'

'And he would, too,' said Plugger, recognising the will for the deed. The General had so often made the two identical.

'Well, we decided to go by the Inferno track because old Ted's been knocking hell out of the top road lately. Got all those loops absolutely taped. So the next thing we're belting through Acquafondata and then on to the Inferno. I thought the General might kick up a bit about the way I took that one

in five down grade part but there wasn't a murmur out of him.
He never did like wasting time. But it was bad luck on old
Harry and the GI in the back. They were bouncing about like
fleas.

'At that rate, it wasn't long before we were at the Hove
Dump. You should have seen the glare the Old Man gave at
all the burnt-out trucks and stores. As if he'd like to have
wrung the neck of the Jerry that got his guns on to the dump
that night.'

'He would, too,' said Plugger, and the others nodded their
heads.

'Well, from there it wasn't long before we were out in the
Bowl. I must say, it looked as pretty as a picture. All the
mud's dried up now, and the corpses in that knocked-out
Sherman have stopped stinking and there are poppies all over
the place. You could see Cassino as close as if you were
looking through glasses and the old Monastery up on top
looked as if it were full of monks instead of Fritzes. But I must
admit I wasn't thinking much about the scenery just then.
That's the worst part of the trip, just round there. There's no
cover, just the flat and the road going through it and you know
you're in plain view of every OP he's got from the Monastery
to Mount Cifalco. Not to mention that bloody great Mount
Cairo. Makes you feel very queer in the guts, believe me, to
think that if the OP officer has had a bad night on the booze
and wants to work it off on someone he can bring Christ
knows how many guns down on you in a God-awful stonk.'

'Not for just one jeep,' said Shorty. 'He can't spare the
ammo. At least, that's what Geordie, the IO's batman, says.'

'All bloody well for the IO's batman. You wouldn't catch
him out in the bloody Bowl by himself though, let alone with a
General in his jeep. Anyhow, that's what I was saying to
myself, too: It's not worth their while to crack down on a
single jeep. But when I saw that stretch of flat all round us, as
bare as a baby's bottom, and thought of those bloody Jerries
up there watching us through their glasses and perhaps
getting a fire order ready just for fun, I put my foot down on
the old accelerator and gave her the gun just the same. And

just as I was thinking to myself: only another mile and then the Terelle staircase road and we're jake till the return trip, what do you think happens?'

He paused.

'You hear the whine of a shell. With a savage twist of the wrist – .'

'Don't be a bloody fool all your life, Shorty,' said Plugger.

'I hear the GOCs voice,' said Alec, ignoring Shorty. 'And he says: "Stop, Alec, stop."

'Well, you know, when the Old Man gives an order there's only one thing to do about it – do what you're told. So I stopped. And there we were, in a miserable bloody jeep under all those guns, a sitting shot. No one says a word. I couldn't see how Harry and the GI were in the back but I could sort of feel they were thinking along the same lines as I was. As for me, my ears were pricked waiting to hear that shell coming and my eyes were swivelling all over the place looking for some hole in the ground to make for when the time came to bolt.

' "Listen," says the General, as if we weren't listening already. I reckon we could pretty near have heard the Jerries sliding the shells into the breeches of those guns of theirs. We could hear them eating their breakfast sausage up in Belmonte. I could hear Kesselring say to his own ADC: "Isn't that Alec Kane down there?" Yes, we were listening all right. We must have been sitting there a full minute, as stiff as statues except inside, listening.

'Then the General pipes up again: "Was that a nightingale I heard?" he says.

'Well, I thought to myself, it comes to us all sooner or later, I suppose. Only most of us don't have to start hearing little birds to know it's a mug's game. But he deserves a rest if anyone does. He's had a tough war, two tough wars, in fact. And then the Sangro and Cassino on top of everything else and a stinking bad winter. Making this Terelle Terror Ride twice a day every day this month has just about sent me crackers myself.

'But I wasn't so crackers I wasn't still listening for that bloody stonk to come screaming down on us.

' "I think it was a blackbird, sir," said Harry at the back of me. Good for you, Harry, I thought to myself. You're not an ADC for nothing. Humour him, that's right. That's the presence of mind that makes an officer. If I had my way I'd make you GI. Now we can get cracking to hell out of here.

'But I ought to have known the Old Man better. And the GI too, for that matter. He was too shrewd to make Harry's mistake. Because, of course, it only made the Old Man determined to prove he was right.

' "Nonsense, Harry, nonsense," he says. "I know a nightingale when I hear one. Of course it was a nightingale. Listen!"

'So we start listening again. As if we'd ever stopped. Suddenly I gave a jump and so did the two in the back. It was only a mortar away over in Mortar Alley but all strung up like that we didn't have time to stop ourselves.

' "Keep still, will you," says the Old Man to me. "You'll frighten the bird."

'I ask you, frighten the bird. When I was in such a state that I'd have taken off myself if only I'd had the wings.

'And then out of a bit of a bush about fifty yards away we hear it. And it's a bloody nightingale all right, singing away as if he'd burst. I haven't heard a nightingale sing like that since that morning we skeltered through Athens trying to get to the beaches before the sun and the Stukas were up.

' "There you are, Harry," says the General. "I told you so. Didn't I, GI?"

' "That's right, sir," answered the GI in that poker voice of his. "Drive on, Alec," says the General. And, believe me, no one ever got into top gear quicker than I did and, by Jesus, we were half-way up the Terelle staircase road before I remembered to change down.'

'The old scamp,' said Plugger with delight. 'Isn't he an old scamp?'

'Well, I suppose I might as well have another jorum of your plonk before my hair turns white,' said Alec, reaching out.

A low-flying plane grumbled slowly overhead, looking for a target. It was now quite dark. The General must have come to the door of 'A' Mess. They could hear that peremptory, carrying voice.

'Put out those lights.'

They covered their cigarettes. All over the camp chinks in the blackout suddenly disappeared, the way a life goes out.

'The old scamp,' said Plugger.

Not Substantial Things

A few miles beyond the village we came to a blown bridge the way Amedeo had said we would. So we began to have some confidence in him. Perhaps he did know a way through the minefields and round the demolitions after all.

But it was well after midday by now and we thought we might as well stop here as anywhere else and have something to eat. So Terry and I helped Ned get out the scran-box and then we left him to master the Primus and brew up while we took another look at the map. Amedeo skipped round helpfully at first. But we'd worked out a technique of putting a feed together in the past few years which didn't allow for spare parts like Amedeo and so in the end there was nothing to do for Amedeo but sit sadly on a stone while Ned brought the billy to the boil.

I still didn't really feel as if my heart was in the business. When Terry drove into HQ that morning and suggested a day's liberating I'd jumped at the idea, thinking it would be a change from just hanging round and chafing at the bit. Jerry had pulled out a couple of days before and was going North hell for leather to shape up on his new line above Rome. But the Div. wasn't being allowed to follow. The big shots were cooking up some new job for us and according to current latrino-gram we were going to be given a rest and then put in to crack a hole in the next line. Whatever it was we were all pretty browned off. We weren't allowed to follow up now we had him on the run, there was nothing much to do and there was no leave yet to Rome.

In fact, liberating in the territory old Jerry had vacated was about the only diversion there was and everyone who could lay his hands on a vehicle was cruising round looking for some village that hadn't been spoiled by other liberators getting in first. That would have been enough by itself to make Terry welcome when he and Ned turned up in the Brigadier's car.

But there was another reason. I'd thrown a farewell party the night before for my batman, Bandy Grimm. He and I had been together a long time. And now he was off to New Zealand on his three months' leave. With the Jerries rocking on their heels the way they were the odds were they'd have taken the count before he got back. Somehow it wasn't the way you expected to see the last of a bloke in this war. You got used to them pushing off for a while to Base or a hospital, but you knew they'd turn up again. And you got used to them setting out on some offensive when you knew there was a good chance they wouldn't turn up again. But somehow to realise all of a sudden that a chap you'd got as used to as Bandy was going for keeps, and going home at that, was different. It meant times were changing. Change and decay, in fact. You had to face up to it that you were probably going to survive after all. All these years you'd been thinking that as long as you hung on and didn't let your cobbers down and took the rough with the smooth, it didn't make much odds what else you did because there was no guarantee you wouldn't go back to the battalion any time, and then you'd soon reach the end of your ration of tomorrows. You'd have had your firkin, in fact.

But if blokes like Bandy were getting out of it alive, going home and all, then the chances were you would yourself. And then what the hell would you do?

So when we saw Bandy off in the jeep for Rear Div., all his traps along with him, and he leaned out and shook hands and the jeep roared out with Bandy looking at the HQ sign and the serial number for the last time, and raising a last crack for the Provost on point duty, I turned back to the Mess tent feeling pretty low. And breakfast didn't help any. It just reminded me

I had a hang-over as well and that I'd been pretty offensive to the G2 at the party, calling him a bank clerk in battle-dress. Which he was, but that's another story.

So Terry's arrival couldn't have been better timed.

All the same, the hang-over, or whatever it was, wasn't as easy to shake off as all that. And Avezzano, our first stop, didn't help. There were a couple of armoured cars in the main square and the Div. Cav. had roped off a section for themselves. A few blokes were sitting on top of the cars reading the NZEF *Times* and a few more were brewing up alongside. The Ites were crowded round the ropes, gaping. The usual kids had got to close quarters and were cadging biscuits. Wally Riddell was in charge.

'Hallo,' he said, 'you bloody base-wallopers. Is the war over? Or are you doing an advance guard for AMGOT?'

'No, Wally,' Terry said, 'just showing ourselves to keep up the morale of the forward troops. AMGOT'll be along when the mines are lifted.'

'Poor old Ites,' said Wally. 'They've had everything. Ostrogoths, Visigoths, and all the rest. And now AMGOTS.'

'Don't blame us, Wally,' Terry said. 'We're just a couple of liberators like yourself.'

Wally gave us a bit of a look, as if to say: Not so like as all that, you come along afterwards. But he didn't need Terry's MC ribbon to remind him we'd had our share and he said nothing. Besides, a hell of an uproar broke out in a side street just then and so we all strolled over to have a look.

A crowd of Ites was struggling down the middle of the road. In the centre we got a glimpse of a woman they were dragging along and she was certainly getting a rough spin. She must have been quite good-looking, but her face was all scratched now and one old dame in particular kept grabbing her by the hair, peroxided it was with the peroxide beginning to fade, and trying to yank it out by the handful. The equivalent number of Gyppos could hardly have made more noise than this crowd.

'You speak Itie, don't you, Mick?' Wally said. 'What the hell's it all about?'

One of those bright kids you always find on the edge of a crowd explained.

'Well, what's he say?'

'Seems she and the local Jerry commandant went in for a bit of horizontal collaboration. He dropped her in the getaway and she's been hiding out. The general idea is to tear her to bits.'

'Oh, Jesus, here we go again. That's the second today. Where the hell's that Field Security bloke? I have to do all his dirty work.'

'Well, you'd better get cracking, Wally, on your errand of mercy,' Terry said. 'Remember her only sin is that she has loved too much.'

Wally glowered at him and shouldered his way into the mob, a couple of his men after him.

There was no point in hanging around and so we went back to the car where Ned was waiting for us.

'Popular as a bag of measles, poor bitch,' Ned said as we watched Wally's boys escorting her towards the Field Security place and the Ites trailing after like wolves.

In the next village we came to we were still a novelty and the wine was shoved through the windows at us in vast quantities. The usual Ite who'd been to the USA came and demonstrated his English and we pretended to understand him till all his cobbers were convinced he hadn't been lying all these years and really could speak English.

'He'd have been a top-sergeant if he'd stayed in the States,' said Ned.

'Why top-sergeant?' I asked.

'All Yanks are top-sergeants,' said Ned.

Just then I picked out what seemed to me a bright-looking youth and he turned out to be this joker Amedeo. According to him all the roads out of the village were blown. But he reckoned he could find a way through to his own village which was a few miles north-east of us.

'The only thing is,' Terry said then, 'I feel the call of Uncle Spam.'

I wasn't sure whether it was hang-over or hunger with me

but I felt pretty hollow myself. And, anyhow, I was keen to get away from one particularly unpleasant bloke in a blue suit who kept telling us he was a bank manager and inviting us to lunch. I've always maintained there must be something wrong with people who can look after all that money without spending it and it was pretty clear Blue-suit was no exception because the rest of the crowd kept their eyes on him the way a horse does when there's a fly he doesn't like hanging about. In fact, it was obvious he was one of the local Fascist johnnies and the crowd were still scared of him and wanted to see if he could make his marble good with us.

'This joker's a bit of *non buono*,'' said Terry, who'd smelt him too. 'Let's get out of here into the fresh air.'

So we put Amedeo in the back with the plonk we hadn't been able to drink and driving East we came to the blown bridge.

But the plonk hadn't had time to take much effect yet and my mind kept running over the day's bad marks: a hang-over, old Bandy's face when we shook hands, that crack of Wally's about base-wallopers, the poor scragged whore, the Ite from the USA and the bloody business man. A poor catch so far.

'You know, Terry,' I said, 'what say we call it a day and go home?'

'Don't be a piker, Mick,' he said. 'I know it's not been much chop so far but we're only getting started. Come on, take a pull of this plonk.'

So I knocked back a bottle and sure enough what with that and the smell of some eggs frying that Ned had scrounged, and the sun shining on the nice colours of the 1/200,000 map with the roads marked in yellow and red, I began to feel better.

On the broken bridge someone had splashed up in tar: Viva Stalin, Viva Churchill.

'Wonder why there aren't any Viva Roosevelts?' said Terry.

'Too hard to spell,' Ned said, looking up from the pan.

'Suit them better to defend their bloody bridge rather than paint it after it's down,' I said. But I didn't really mean it any more. And I'd just realised from looking at the map that the drained swamp on our right was the setting of Silone's *Fontamara*. The wonder was that they still had the heart to splash up even the names of hope.

After that pretty nearly every bridge and culvert was blown. And we weren't very anxious to go near the ones that weren't. Even as it was, creeping down into the gullies and skirting along the faces or tacking up them, we always stood a reasonable chance of going up on a Teller.

Once we came on a mule with its guts blown out but still alive. Terry got out and finished it off.

'Jesus,' he said as he put away his pistol. 'And to think we're doing this for pleasure.' So I could tell he was feeling the way I was. And I remembered he and his truck had gone up in one of the Ruweisat battles when he was an LO. He still had a bit of metal in his bum.

It wasn't so bad for Ned. He had all he could do keeping the car going and right side up. She was one of the few vehicles left in the Div. with the old desert camouflage and she had a mileage behind her that was nobody's business. Ned was very attached to her.

'One thing,' Ned remarked some time after we'd passed the mule, 'if we do go up I can always blame you jokers.'

Of course it soon turned out that Amedeo had no idea where the mines were. But he was quite happy and like most Ites he put all his brains into finding reasons for staying that way. He sat on the roof and dangled his legs in front of the windscreen. He had confidence in us, he explained.

Eventually we struck a good bit of road and were able to hit her up, keeping well clear of the verges. Every time we passed one of those little Itie farms the kids dropped everything and rushed out after us. But the old people just waved and went on with whatever they'd been doing as if they'd got to the stage of not caring who drove by in fast military cars, Germans or anyone else. They knew they'd never do any riding themselves, by this time.

Well, it all took time and it was late afternoon when I poked my head out the trap in the roof to see what Amedeo was screeching about.

'Ecco, ecco,' he was shouting. 'Castel di Goriano.'

And sure enough, a couple of miles away you could see a village perched up on top of a knoll. And very nice it looked too, so old it was the colour of the ground and sitting up there soaking the sun into itself the way a lizard does.

'He says it's Castel di Goriano,' I said, pulling inside again. 'It's really in 5 Corps territory, I should think.'

We checked up on the map and sure enough it was.

'First come, first served,' says Terry. 'The poor old pongos are probably still indenting in triplicate for mine-detectors.'

By this time we were climbing up the last slopes and had had to slow down. There were swarms of partisans all round us, banging off those Itie tommy-guns. The roof was covered in kids and Amedeo had moved to the bonnet. At the main gate we found the whole town had turned out to meet us and there wasn't a dog's chance of getting the car through. There was nothing for it but to abandon ship.

The next thing I knew was that I was being hoisted shoulder high and carried up the main street. I got my head round long enough to see that Terry and Ned were aloft too and even young Amedeo for good measure. So I didn't feel quite such a fool. Besides, I was tickled at Ned's face. You could see he was worrying his head off about the car. But I wasn't going to worry, because I'd seen a hefty partisan with a carbine sitting on top of it and it was obvious that it would have been high treason for anyone to start monkeying with it that day.

Well, as we go up the street we're pretty busy what with keeping our balance and catching the wreaths of flowers tossed up by the girls and taking a swig from every bottle that was pushed at us and kissing all the babies their mothers kept holding up to us. And there was an old woman who kept kissing me on the boot. But the other two didn't notice, thank God. They had troubles enough of their own.

As a matter of fact, once you got used to it, it wasn't at all unpleasant. Of course, we knew we were pretty phoney heroes but the Ites wouldn't have believed us if we told them and, anyhow, it's amazing how quickly you get to take this sort of thing for granted. In fact, if you had enough of it you'd always want more. That's the way old Musso went, I expect, and a good many others before him.

At the town hall things were slightly easier. All the big shots were there and they weren't bad blokes for big shots. They seemed to be under the impression one of us was General Montgomery but they weren't at all upset when we explained it was only us. They weren't weeping tears of joy like most of the people outside and they had a tendency to keep the thing rather dignified and ceremonial. But that suited us all right because we weren't very tight. And the glasses kept coming overhead in a continuous chain, which was the main thing. I haven't seen the booze flow so freely since the old days at Wallacetown pub after a Southland-Otago match.

In fact, all was as merry as a marriage bell until Terry got the notion into his head I ought to make a speech, since I had a smattering of the tongue. The idea took on like a house on fire and I must say I didn't put up as much opposition as I might have done what with the plonk and the feeling I had at the time that there was a good deal to be said for the human race. It almost seemed worth it that day, all the good cobbers that were gone, the hard backward fighting in Greece and Crete, the boredom and sweat of Maadi, and all the scares a man had had in the desert.

So the next thing I find myself out on a balcony with a great red carpet over it and the mayor holding forth explaining what was going to happen the way mayors always do. Then he bows to me and I go forward and put my hands on the balcony. And below me in the piazza is the whole population, man, woman and child, all absolutely crammed, with their faces turned up and waiting. When I saw them my heart jumped into my mouth and in spite of all the plonk I was so dry I could scarcely move my tongue.

'Give her the gun, boy,' says Terry by my side.

So I lift up my hand.

'Popolo di Castel di Goriano,' I paused and I could feel the silence go shuddering over them like the sun on a hill side and over me too and I knew I had them.

'Popolo,' I began again, 'popolo questo giorno libero.' A simple trick, after all. But it worked and I thought that one word 'free' had sent them mad. The applause went roaring up out of that narrow square and past my ear like a rocket.

Meanwhile Terry spots I've shot my bolt for the moment and am working out my next sentence and so he starts up a yell in the background: Viva il Maggiore Michele. Of course, that was all they needed – a handle for me and away they went. They like things personal.

When he saw I was ready Terry leans forward and lifts his hand: 'Silenzio per il Maggiore,' he says.

And then there was the sort of silence Shakespeare must have heard waiting for him over the centuries when he wrote the first line of one of his best spellbinders.

'Siamo venuti,' I said, 'noi, il terrore del mondo, i novozelandesi, i diavoli e cannibali, i rubatori, i negri – come vedete.' And I threw my hands out wide like Abraham and smiled my sweetest smile.

Well, give me the Ites for speed at picking up irony. They jumped to that one all the faster because the Jerries had been doing a special line for months on what scoundrels, cannibals and niggers the Kiwis were. And since Terry and Ned and I were only just a bit off white the 'negri' part underlined the nonsense of the rest.

By that time, I'd got properly into my stride and what with Terry leading the cheers whenever I stopped to think I had plenty of time to think the thing out into Latin and then work out what the Italian words must be.

'Siamo venuti,' I repeated, 'soltanto tre; perciò possete vedere come forti sono i tedeschi.'

At that there was a terrific burst of booing which had me puzzled till I saw it was the mention of Jerries that had started them off. But then I thought of a further refinement. You see, they were a bit narked because only three of us had turned up and not a battalion or so and it was a bit delicate to explain.

'E perciò possete vedere,' I went on, 'che il vostro futuro è per voi stessi.'

Of course they jumped to this immediately, too. We didn't

want to overawe them but just to suggest by our fewness that now they were their own masters.

'Siete liberati dei tedeschi,' I began to develop the idea, 'si deve adesso liberarvi di voi stessi, del tyrannismo ancora rimasta, dei fascisti, e si deve fare per voi stessi uno governo di libertà, di giustizia, di ugualità, di fraternità.' By this time I was well away and that little man who sits on your shoulder and sneers when you're talking English was completely out of it. Danton had nothing on me.

'Restono cose difficili per il popolo Italiano.' That hushed them a bit. They didn't like the sound of difficult things ahead much. So I came in again with a swing.

'Ma, senza dubbio, questo popolo Italiano col suo corragio, colla sua onestà, la sua fortezza, va fare una vita piu bella, una vita chi saro conforme colle tradizioni splendidissime di questa patria, questa patria piena della grandezza passata e in questo momento gravida d'una grandezza piu magnifica, uno futuro digno del madre della civilizzazione.'

I'd got pretty tangled in my nouns, what with all those genitives, but it didn't seem to matter. The older people were all weeping and the younger all cheering. The vivas were deafening and above them came sharply the crackling of enthusiastic carbines where the partisans were grouped on the fringes of the square.

'Siamo soldati, uffiziali forse, ma ciònonostante soldati, soldati semplici, come i vostri eroici partigiani.' I had to stop there again. The partisans were not at all modest and joined more vociferously than anyone in the vivas for themselves. I made a mental note of that as another useful motif to use when things got dull. Meantime I wasn't going to be cheered away from my joke.

'Non siamo oratori,' I went on, 'non piu duci.'

The allusion got them. 'Abbasso il Duce, abbasso il fascismo, abbasso Mussolini.' The roar was deep and angry. The was the first time I'd ever roused and heard the anger of a crowd.

Well, it went on in that fashion. I'd worked out the keynotes. The Jerries and Musso when you wanted rage, the glorious partisans when you wanted to cheer them up a bit, the glorious allies for terrific applause, the distant past of Italy for sentiment and the difficult future for sobriety. My difficulty now was to find some way of stopping.

Then during one particularly prolonged bit of cheering I leaned over the balcony and was watching them. As a matter of fact, I was thinking to myself that I could understand old Musso's point of view a bit better now. There was something that got you about having all those people below you there in the piazza and feeling your mind one jump ahead of your voice all the time and your voice being able to produce whatever emotion you wanted out of them. It was very exciting. And you felt it was dangerous, too. Something like taking risks with a very powerful car at top speed. At the same time you felt a certain phoneyness in your power, the way when you're shickered you know in the back of your mind things aren't really as good as they seem.

As I was staring down at them like that and trying to think of how the hell to finish without an anti-climax, I suddenly spotted the parish priest in front of the crowd and immediately I saw my end all cut and dried. I started into a peroration about the magnificence of the alliance of which Italy had now proved herself worthy, drew them into a series of vivas for Roosevelt, Churchill and Stalin and then when I'd got them at the top of their pitch, pointed suddenly at the priest and said: 'Now the time has come when the lion can lie down with the Lamb of God, the Te Deum can be sung in Moscow, and here in Castel di Goriano, as a symbol of the glorious alliance which is winning us freedom and the future, the parish priest can join with us in singing "The Red Flag".'

And so out it comes in those magnificent Italian voices: 'Bandiera Rossa trionferà,' and I must admit I was so moved myself that I forgot to look to see whether the priest was singing with us. And it was a good moment to make my getaway.

'You didn't say which got up again,' said Terry, 'the lion and the lamb. Or just the lion.'

'Where's the plonk?' I said. I needn't have troubled to ask.

And that was the programme for the next hour or two except that from time to time one of us had to show himself on the balcony just so that the crowd wouldn't feel they were out of it. Then when we thought it was time we got going, the mayor wouldn't hear of it because they'd jacked up a special liberation dinner for us and the widows of all the partisans the Jerries had shot before they left were invited as well.

Well, by the time that dinner was over, and a pretty queer dinner it was, with lovely girls waiting on us and the widows bursting into tears from time to time and a stream of people coming in and out all the time to shake our hands, and gallons of plonk and more speeches, I was just about done. I had just enough sense to stop Ned abandoning his seat of honour towards the end and sneaking out with one of the women. Not one of the widows, though.

Anyhow, that settled it and in spite of all the protests we decided to get cracking. So we had a last round of speeches, nobbled Ned and made for the car.

The cold air must have got me then because the last thing I remember was thinking it was midnight and wondering how the hell Ned was going to get us first of all through the crowd and then through the minefields and wishing the partisans escorting us wouldn't fire off their carbines so much. Then I must have passed out.

The next thing I knew it was bloody cold and there was a rooster crowing somewhere and I had an iron throat. I tried to pull up my sleeping bag and it wasn't there. That brought me to and I saw we were still in the car and it was just cracking dawn.

I felt so depressed I didn't care where we were or how we'd got there. I reckon that most of the time we've got ourselves so organised that we only see as much truth as is good for us. Just the way our bodies only get as much air as is good for them. But all the time all sorts of muscles are probably at work stopping the atmosphere from closing in and squashing us. And that's the way with truth. The muscles of a man's mind are constantly engaged in keeping it back and only letting in a trickle at a time. But when he's exhausted or got a hangover, which is the same thing, he can't keep the truth out and it all bursts in. And that's what we call being depressed.

Well, that's the state I was in. The bloody truth came pouring in like water into a diver's suit. I saw that what we'd thought was good fun was deadly serious for the poor old Ites. They really believed the things I told them. And of course in theory they were true. But they weren't true, all the same.

Nothing is as simple as that. And nobody can risk being as simple as those Ites. Even after all these years they hadn't guessed what was coming to them, the steady disappointments, the gradual realisation that nothing had really changed, because they were still men and women and so still vulnerable. Only it would be less easy for them now because they were rid of the enemy outside themselves, the scapegoat. They'd been reckless enough to hope and they'd have the rest of their lives for a hang-over.

But it wasn't only that. I could see what was coming to me as well. I'd got a glimpse of it the day before when old Bandy went. The fact was that chaps like me had got older without noticing it. We'd never give anything again what we'd given the Div. We'd never bring the same energy to anything that we'd brought to things like the break-through at Minqar Qaim or the assault on Cassino. And we'd never be able to make friends again the same way or drink and laugh and die the same way. We'd used up what we had and we'd spend the rest of our lives looking over our shoulders.

Yes, that was it. The best was over with the worst. There was nothing left now except the dragging of some wretched whore through the streets in Avezzano yesterday, in Castel di Goriano today perhaps, and in the rest of the world tomorrow. Now that we knew the war was won, it was just a question of a lot more people dying for another year or two. The real excitement when you might lose was gone. And the peace everyone had felt while the war was really on was going too. A man'd soon have to start up again all the old fights with himself that used to go on in the days when there was no danger to his skin.

Terry stirred beside me and woke up.

'What the bloody hell are we doing here and where the hell are we?' I asked.

'Jesus, it's cold,' he said, 'listen to those bloody frogs. Petrol, we're out of petrol. We missed Avezzano in the dark and then when the petrol ran out we had to stop here.' He looked out the window. 'A mist, frogs, and it's pretty flat. We must be in that Fucine Swamp of theirs.'

'We're in the bloody cactus, in fact,' I said. Not that I cared much but it was a pleasure to think of something else.

'We'll be jake,' he said. 'We'll rustle up some breakfast and then make tracks up to the main road. If there's an armoured car about or a boy with a bicycle we can easily get a message back for petrol.'

'Yes,' I said.

But we didn't stir. Neither of us cared much for the thought of Wally's jokes when we passed through again.

'I could do with a drink,' I said. The muscles of my mind were doing so much work I could hear them creaking. But there was still too much truth getting by.

Ned opened his eyes. 'I saved a couple of bottles,' he said. And he pulled them out of the front pocket.

We sat there drinking in the early morning and the cold seeped into us like reality.

'Never mind, Ned,' Terry said. 'It was all that third gear work that used up the petrol.'

'Shouldn't have happened all the same,' said Ned.

'Anyhow, it was a great day,' Terry said. 'She's been a bonny war.'

'She's been a bonny war,' I said, and took another swig at the bottle.

III

A Return

Of course I didn't show it but it was all a bit of a shock to me. I'd heard bits and scraps of news from time to time while I was away – that Martin's old man had died the year I left, that Martin had come back and had married the O'Halloran girl whose father owned the stud farm up at Morton Mains. But none of it meant much, what with Munich and a war brewing and then the war itself. It didn't prepare me, anyhow, for a new house in what used to be the front paddock, with an electric stove and a washing-machine and all sorts of things Martin's old man would have sweated blood to see.

So I was rather relieved when I got outside with Martin by himself. Though for a start neither of us had much to say; picking up the threads, I suppose.

It was seeing old Glen that gave me the first link; apart from Martin himself, of course.

'Surely it's old Glen,' I said, as I bent down to pat him. 'Do you remember me, Glen, old boy?' But he didn't know me. It was too long.

'That's him all right,' Martin said. 'Nearly blind now, poor old chap, aren't you, Glen? I'll let him off the chain and he can come with us.'

We walked on down the drive and Glen came along behind us, close at Martin's heels. Don, the new dog, a smart black and tan collie, heard us and came frisking out from behind the woodheap.

'Now there's a dog for you,' Martin said. 'He knows more

about sheep than I do myself.' And he began to tell me stories
of Don's brains, much the same stories that used to be told
about Glen, except that in the old days it was always cows, not
sheep, that gave a dog on this farm a chance to show his
intelligence.

But I was only half-listening. My mind was on the past and
I seemed to be seeing things double, as they were now and as
they once had been. This drive under our feet still ran down to
the old house I could see ahead of us, crouched among its trees
the way it used to be, but empty now. To that house, built
with his own hands, and along this drive old Martin must
have come when he first brought his wife there in the years
before I, her sister's son, was born. And along it, after she had
had young Martin, the last of her sons, the old man had driven
her in his trap that cold November morning when he took her
to the dentist in town, twelve miles away. They had come back
the same night, she with all her teeth out and muffled – but
not enough – against the bitter wind. Her last journey till the
one not long after when they took her to the cemetery, dead
through the chill she caught.

And in the years that followed, as one child after another
grew old enough to rebel, each of them had come along this
drive in the night, just before daybreak, making his way to the
gate, the main road and freedom. At the last the old man
himself had come along it to join his wife, worn out by work
and his own harshness to himself. Only Martin had come
back, alone of all that family. And now the old house was
empty, the drive was a path that led only to the past. Grass
grew between the wheel ruts.

'What's happened to the gorse hedge that used to be here?'
I asked. For the wind came straight across the paddocks,
ruffling the backs of the ewes and cutting at us through the
bare, wire fence.

'Had it all yanked out,' Martin said. 'I got the tractor on to
it. You can't beat a good wire fence. Tight wire and sound
totara straining posts and you're jake for ten years.'

I looked at the hedge that wasn't there. The thrushes used
to fly out of it bursting with alarm as the ferret threaded his

way in and out among the dry, twisted roots before vanishing down another burrow. In spring the whole hedge was saddled in gold.

'That fixed the rabbits, too,' he said. 'Not one on the whole place now. No, I'm well rid of the hedges.' He changed his voice suddenly. 'Get along with ye now, what way is that to cut a hedge? It's as crooked as a dog's hind leg. Give me that slasher.'

He had his father to a T. I gave a jump when he said it. For I'd had the lash of the old man's tongue myself in my time.

'Remember?' he said. 'And he wouldn't be satisfied, either, till you could have run a spirit-level along it. By God, what a tiger he was for work, the old tyrant.'

'Well, I've changed all that,' he went on. 'No hedges, and no cows either. Sheep, that's the thing. No more slavery for me. Look at that mob of sheep now out there, worth four guineas a crack, every blasted one of them, not counting the lambs they'll have.'

I looked at the sheep, bunched out in the paddock, heads down and backs to the wind, cropping.

'Here, Don,' he said to the dog. 'Way back.'

Don ran out towards the sheep and, answering immediately to every whistled command, shuffled them about for me to get a good look at them.

'Hullo,' Martin said. 'What's the matter with that one?'

We got through the taut wire and went over. The ewe didn't move as we came up. There were two lambs beside her.

'She's had it, poor bitch,' he said. 'Still, we'll rear the lambs all right. We'll pick them up on the way back.'

Out on the drive old Glen, who hadn't followed us into the paddock, fell in behind again.

'I suppose I ought to shoot him,' Martin said. 'But he was a good dog in his day. He's never been the same since I got rid of the cows. Once a cattledog always a cattledog. Though he'd be too old for that now, anyway.'

I said nothing. The Glen I remembered was a young dog, out in the morning chivvying the cows in for the milking, the dew flying up at his heels.

We were coming into the backyard of the old house now. The kitchen garden on the right was wild. There was no movement in the macrocarpa hedges that once bustled with hens. No trail of geese came marching in convoy from under the five-barred gate. The cartshed seemed to have staggered, got smaller. What had been the stand for the milk-cans was a crumpled heap of boards with docks growing round. The old spring-cart we used to drive in with the milk to the factory had fallen on its knees.

'We'd better take a look at the old house,' Martin said, 'before it gets dark enough for ghosts.'

He fished out the key from under the tankstand, the old hiding-place. The door gripped a bit on the floor but gave to a shove. We went in, Glen following.

We wandered from room to room, our feet echoing. And in all the rooms it seemed as if the old man's presence dominated still. In the kitchen where the family used to eat, his fearful silence still ruled over the absent table. In the sitting-room the emptiness, the bare boards, were less real to me than that clear picture from the past where he sat with his legs stretched before the log fire, boots still on, the boys scarcely daring to whisper over their homework and no other sound but the occasional knock of a pot out in the scullery where the girls would be washing up.

But most of all you felt him still in that room where Martin and all the others had been begotten and born, where their mother had died, where the old man himself had died, reconciled to no one and alone.

Something about the timid way we peeped into it as if we half-expected him to stare up at us with his fierce, green eyes roused Martin to the defiance which was the mainspring of his life.

'And what brings ye in here peeking?' he suddenly shouted. 'Can't ye find anything better to do than hang round here waiting to see when your father will die? Aren't there cows to be milked and pigs to be fed? Is there no ploughing that you can be idling away the good days that God made for the land? Get away with ye now to your work before I get myself up from this bed and show ye who's the master here.'

Glen looked up at Martin uneasily and went skulking down the passage to the back door.

'You were always a devil for the mimicking, Martin,' I said.

He grinned. 'Wait and I'll give you another one.'

He crossed the passage to the room where old Paddy used to sleep, his father's only friend. We used to hide under the bed in there and frighten him, pretending to be ghosts.

There was silence for a minute and then I heard old Paddy's high-pitched brogue.

''Tis the fairies, Martin, 'tis the fairies that are after the living soul of me,' the voice shrieked and Martin came rushing out as if he were indeed Paddy and were fleeing from all the ghosts of Ireland.

I followed him down the passage and through the thickening memories.

At the next door on the left a new voice awaited me. It was Norah this time and how well I recognised that passionate storming of God that you might have heard any night and any time of the night in the years when this house lived so long ago.

'Oh God in Heaven,' the voice was surging, 'have mercy on us all, have mercy on us all, all of us, oh God, except those wicked devils, my own flesh and blood, that never leave off tormenting me with their teasing and talking and tattling, and you, oh Holy Mother, do you save me from that lost soul, O'Connor, who's forever watching me at the dances and in the very church itself in the middle of Holy Mass is moving his terrible eyes at me.'

But another voice took its turn now, the voice of Rose, the bold and domineering, daughter of her father, a strong voice full of jeers.

'For Heaven's sake, Norah, won't you be quiet now and leave us in peace with your O'Connor. It's ashamed you should be howling and praying at all hours and all over a man that's nothing but a red-haired gorilla when all's said and done and would never have looked at you twice if you hadn't put the idea into his head yourself by asking him to dance in

the Ladies' Excuse Me, if it's in anybody's head but your own,
that is, and him a married man and all.'

There was an even wilder shriek from Norah at this and as
the door flung open it was all I could do to believe that it was
not Norah herself I saw holding it closed and shouting back
through it.

'Not a minute longer will I stay in this wicked house, I
swear to God I won't. I'll go to him now with all I have which
is myself and tell him I've been driven out of my own house by
my own sister. I'll disgrace the lot of you, that's what I'll do,
but at least I won't have to stay on here among a lot of
scheming, jealous devils that have the making of nothing in
them but drunkards and old maids. So put that in your pipe
and smoke it.'

All the men were out of the house that night at the lambing,
I remembered. She had gone, and I wondered that the
memory of that alone and what had happened to her
afterwards was not enough to quieten Martin. But he was in
the grip of his art now and perhaps, too, there was something
in all this that helped him shake off the past that had driven
him to the new house and new ways, bold man that he was
ever to have come back to that place so full of terrible
memories.

'Look,' he was saying now, having drawn me into the back
bedroom where he and his two brothers, Neil and Con, used
to sleep, after Ned, the oldest son, had gone off to his death in
the first war, and before Neil cursed his father and went off to
Australia and Con shot himself in the back stables. 'Look,' he
said, 'There's the window we used to climb in at after the
dances long ago or after all night round a keg or a bottle of
Hokonui whisky, and sometimes we'd hardly be under the
blankets before he'd come roaring in with that whip of his.'

He began to shout in his father's voice again.

'Up with ye, up with ye, ye lazy omadhauns. Isn't it nearly
daylight already and the cows out there with their bags
bursting and devil the one of you caring a tinker's dam but
lying there like gentlemen pensioners. Oh, it's a fine parcel of
useless brummocks and Lady Janes I'm rearing and no

mistake. Out of bed with you now before I tear the blankets off
you and lay this whip across your bare backsides.'

Martin leaned against the wall and looked round the empty
room, bemused.

'Ah, poor Con,' he said. 'Will I ever forget that night? It was
after the milking and I had just put the cows out and come up
with the buckets from feeding the calves when I heard the
clamour of it. "And what brings you home from the seminary,
my lad?" the old devil was saying when I got in. And there
was poor Con, still in his black suit the way he'd walked up
from the station, leaning back there in the corner by the
window. "I've decided I haven't got a vocation," he said, as
quietly as I'm speaking to you now. And the old man came up
on him, and little fellow though he was, it was frightening, I
tell you, because of all that devil was in him.'

' "So that's it," he says at last, quietly this time. And then
he suddenly lets out a bellow. "I'll give you vocation," he says
and hits Con across the face with his open hand. Well, you
know how I liked Con, I wasn't going to take that. And poor
Con was the last man in the world to stick up for himself. So I
caught the old man by the shoulder. And what does he do
then but take a crack at me, if you please. So I hit him. And hit
him hard. That was the night Con shot himself. And I lit out
for the North that same night, not knowing.'

'Aye,' he went on. 'And Rose wasn't long after me and none
of us have heard so much as a whisper of her from that day to
this, whatever happened to her. Aye, there was a devil in that
man, even though he'd whip you for not knowing your
prayers. Comfort was a sin for him and he died as hard as he
lived. Well, I hope he has a better time in hell than he gave us.
And yet, you know, when I look back on it all I feel sorry for
him. God only knows what was the matter with him, but I
think he was fond of us in his own queer way.'

He led the way towards the back door.

'Yes,' he said, looking back into the dark kitchen from the
failing light outside. 'He was a queer old fellow. But he was a
hard worker and we were a wild lot. It was a good farm he left
behind him at any rate. And he made it out of nothing.

Perhaps if she had lived things would have been different. It might have been the devil in himself that he was trying to whip out of our backsides.'

When we got through the fence to pick up the lambs he bounced his hand on the wire. It didn't satisfy him and he took hold of the straining stick to give it a couple more twists. 'I'm glad I got rid of the hedges,' he said. 'A man's got to keep up with the times.'

And as, each of us with a lamb under his arm, we walked up the drive again towards the roughcast house where the electric light was already shining and where hot water and a meal and a wife were waiting, I saw that it was not only Glen and I whom the times had left behind, not only us for whom this new, efficient factory, its wire fences and its sheep, were not quite real, not only us for whom youth meant the old place behind us where there used to be room for gorse and rabbits and ghosts and where life had toiled and twisted round its own frustrations, a coil of passionate wills driven not by comfort but by love and appetites and dreams.

First Flight

1

It was the last day of my visit. After my mother's death, my father had sold the old house and nowadays he lived in digs. So, to be independent of friends, I'd put up at the *Grand*. That way, I'd been able to get around by myself a bit, though I'd been seeing a fair bit of the old man as well. He really was something of an old man by now, just how much over seventy I wasn't sure, but wearing well. Retirement didn't seem to have got him down at all, though he liked talking about the old days on the railway – especially the time that I could remember best, nearly twenty years before, when he used to be on the Invercargill-Dunedin run. He didn't really miss it, though, and he was quite happy, as far as I could make out, living on his pension and keeping his hand in by digging gardens for people who knew what a slogger he was with the spade.

This last day of my visit he was having lunch with me at the hotel before I caught my plane – only I called it dinner when I was talking to him in case he'd think I'd got stuck up all these years away in England. When coffee came, he sat back in his seat and watched me light a cigarette.

'You ought to throw off that rotten habit,' he said. 'It'll do your lungs no good at all. Expensive, too.'

I didn't answer. I was working out how long it was till the plane left. This was probably the last time I'd ever see him.

And I couldn't think of anything to say. It didn't seem worth while to argue about smoking. I was too old myself now, and had been too long my own man, to get annoyed by that sort of advice the way I once would have.

'You know,' he said, 'I've got a bally good mind to come with you as far as Dunedin. I've never been up in an aeroplane. I nearly went once, just after the other war, when they were charging a fiver a time out at the racecourse. But your mother wouldn't let me. A waste of money and you might get killed, she said.'

He was like me, the way he often seemed to be coming out with a sudden idea when he'd really been turning it over in his mind for a long time. I guessed this one must have come to him when he saw my plane coming down to land three days before. He was like me another way, too, or perhaps like any man who's been married a long time. The reason he would give for wanting to do something wasn't always the real reason, or at any rate the only one. If you gave your real reasons, you often found yourself landed in unnecessary arguments.

'Why not?' I said. 'I'll pay your fare. You could do with a holiday. Or a bit of a change, anyway.'

'There's nothing to keep me here since your mother died. I could look up a few old friends.'

'Come on, then,' I said. 'If we get a taxi now there'll be time to pick up whatever you want from your digs. I expect there'll be no trouble about getting a seat. There was only one other passenger when I came down.'

I waited in the taxi while he went into the boarding-house in Tweed Street to get his bag. I used to pass the same house on my way to the school in Clyde Street when I was a kid. It looked even more the worse for wear than I did.

There was an east wind blowing across the airfield from the estuary. I remembered the tidal flat that used to be there before they reclaimed it; the mud and the little crabs scuttling to their holes. The whole of Invercargill and the people who lived there were like that, I used to think in those days. Not only Invercargill, I knew now. My father didn't seem to feel the cold but I did. Autumn coming. But it would be spring when I got back to England.

There'd been no trouble about getting a seat on the little Rapide. The only other passengers were a young man and a girl with confetti in her hair. We had seen her mother crying at the edge of the field, and a lot of other people cheerful with wedding breakfast. They were calling out now and the girl was looking back. Eurydice, but not for the underworld.

We were both wide, heavy men. They stowed us up front, my father in one seat on the left of the gangway and me across from him and just behind the pilot. The young couple were right behind us. The man watched me show my father how to fasten his seat-belt and then leaned across to show his wife. She had been waving a wet handkerchief at the window but now she turned to him and let herself be taught. His hands were red and strong. They looked as if they were used to harness. But I remembered things had changed since I left New Zealand. It would be tractors he knew about, not horses.

The pilot was a large man, too. He worked his way along the narrow gangway and took his seat at the controls. He took off his cap and loosened his tie. He'd probably had a good lunch. He didn't close his door. The instrument panel in front of him didn't look much more complicated than a motor-car's.

We took off without much fuss. My father was looking out his window, with that sort of fixed grin he had when he was excited and interested. I watched Invercargill's rectangular blocks turn into an almost vertical plane and then go flat again. I was not sorry to be going. My life there had been over long before I returned. The house I had been born and reared in was surrounded now, hemmed in by other, new, houses. Other people lived in it, unaware of all that had happened there. Thinking of this, I realized we were over the cemetery already, with my mother's grave.

He shouldn't have married again, so soon after Mum died, my sister had said. It was an insult to Mum's memory.

She felt too much, poor Nora. She had loved him, perhaps even more than she loved her mother, if that was possible. She had probably been jealous, too, without knowing it. There had been no point in trying to explain, and anyhow she had a nice nature. She'd get over it. I thought I knew how it must

have happened myself, though I hadn't been there and with a
man as reticent as my father you didn't get much to work on. I
guessed he was in a state of shock when he found that everything was over and he was by himself in that empty house, the
house he'd built himself when they were first married.

He was hard in many ways and probably while she was ill
he thought he'd be able to take it all right when the time came.
And then the time came and he couldn't take it at all. So when
the widow, Maisie, turned up, at some euchre party or other,
and they'd taken a bit of a shine to each other that must have
seemed the answer. It wasn't an insult to Mum at all but a
compliment, if anything, thinking that was the only way for a
man to live.

Besides, it must have looked quite a promising set-up. She
had a pretty good farm out Edendale way and her only son
was doing well in Australia with a family of his own. The old
man had always wanted a farm and he was good with
animals. At the time, he was still only in his early sixties and
still as tough as a goat's knees. It must have looked like the
answer all right. It might have been, too, if the son hadn't
taken fright about the property and come tearing home.

I took another look across at him but he was still staring out
and down. He hadn't talked to me about the big quarrel, only
about my mother. He behaved as if the thing with Maisie had
never happened. He knew he could count on my not asking
questions. That had never been my method of finding out
about things. In a way, I suppose I didn't care enough, either.
I liked him, as I knew he liked me. Whatever had happened, it
was his business, and it probably made plenty of sense once
you saw his side of it. So best leave it at that.

I looked away from him again and found myself staring at
the pilot's back. An old RNZAF man, to judge by the glimpse
I'd had of his medals. In his middle thirties now, with a
married set to his shoulders. Beefy tanned neck, and a honey-
comb of deep lines above the collar. In quincunxes. Had Sir
Thomas Browne thought of that one? Pity the way one
couldn't help thinking in literary allusions. Occupational
syndrome. You had to keep that sort of thing to yourself in this

part of the world. People would think you were showing off.

I felt my father was looking at me and I turned towards him. He spoke but the noise of the engine was too loud. I cupped my left ear and leaned over. He raised his voice and it came through as a shout.

'These aeroplanes don't go anything like as fast as I expected.'

'Faster than you think,' I said, and I looked nervously at the pilot. Blood had flooded into the tan network of his neck. He probably hated having to fly this miserable little machine for a living anyway. In his own mind he'd always regret that he wasn't back in a Spitfire or a Wellington or whatever he'd flown when he was a youngster, the speed and dash of a fighter or the mighty throb of a bomber. He'd mix it up with regret he couldn't acknowledge for the days when he was a kid, the tension before a mission, the extreme excited calm of being up and over the target, the relief afterwards, the mess and the drinks, the fast cars across the tarmac, the beer and the popsies whose tomorrow you didn't have to worry about because you probably wouldn't have one yourself.

Or else he'd resent being wakened up from a fantasy of flying a Thunderjet or a stratocruiser or whatever was the latest thing. Perhaps WAAFs on the tarmac in Korea or BOAC stewardesses in smart uniforms, with disciplined but promising breasts. And millionaire passengers aboard, of whom he was master.

And perhaps anyway he was devoted to his little crate. They were probably things you could get fond of, like a pony that understood you and answered all your hinting movements.

My father was looking out the window again. I thought of the book in my pocket. But he had always hated me reading. And even if it was too difficult to talk over all the noise, and there wasn't much anyway that either of us could say, I felt it would be rude to cut myself off from him by reading. Silence, for him, was still a way of talking, so long as a book didn't spoil it.

What plans did he have, I wondered. I'd been going to take

a room at the *Majestic*. He'd probably want to stay somewhere cheaper and less showy, even if I offered to pay, as I easily could. Would it be all right if we went to different hotels? And would he let me pay in any case? He hadn't made any objection when I bought his ticket and I didn't suppose he had much money, though he'd probably picked up all he had when we stopped at the boarding-house to get his traps. I had no notion of whether my mother had left a will. Anyway, whatever savings they'd had would have been in common. I seemed to remember that even in the depression years she had always managed to stow something away in the Building Society Savings Bank. She was one of those who always think that there'll be even worse rainy days. And he must have got a bit of hard cash when he sold the house. He'd probably come off pretty badly when the thing with Maisie went bust but he couldn't have lost much and he didn't have to support her, since she had plenty of money and she was the one who'd technically deserted him. Well, if he needed money I'd know soon enough.

The plane was losing height, I noticed. We couldn't be as near as all that to the Dunedin airfield, could we? I peered out the window, and down. That wonderfully clear New Zealand air. Perhaps I missed that more than anything, expatriate in a country where even light was a compromise. My father was tugging at my sleeve. When I looked at him he gestured downwards. I went across and looked down over his shoulder.

The pilot had flattened out again and we were coming in fairly low over what must be Wingatui racecourse. The grandstand was full and the rails crowded. My countrymen and their religion. A race was on. We were too high to upset the horses but flying in line with the course. There were three out in front, the rest bunched, except for a straggler or two. As we watched, the shadow of the plane, about a hundred yards wide of the course, drew level with the horses and passed them. Then they were out of sight behind the wing. It had all happened in the second or two I stood beside my father. I went back to my seat and he grinned at me gleefully.

In front of me the pilot was immobile. He must have been

tempted to look round and grin but he didn't. Then my father was plucking at my sleeve again and pointing.

I looked down. We were flying above the main trunk railway. Away in front and below, a train was moving towards Dunedin. We overhauled it quickly and left it behind.

'That must have been the Express,' my father shouted across to me. 'To think I spent all those years on her and I thought we made a fast run.'

Something in the pilot's back told me he had heard; I guessed he was satisfied. The plane was gaining height again. Soon he began to turn into the wind, getting ready for the final drop into Taieri airfield. We were to fasten our safety belts, the pale lights told us. My father didn't need any help this time. His fingers had always been quick to learn things. I took a look over my shoulder. The young man was helping his wife into hers and she was letting him. But I could tell she didn't really need help, either. He let his hand lie a moment across her upper thigh and smiled at her. She saw me looking and flushed. I looked away.

The plane landed smoothly and taxied to the arrival point. It stopped, breathing, and we waited for the steps to be brought and the door to open.

'I'll never go by train again,' my father said in the same loud voice he had used when we were in the air. 'It's a sheer waste of time. Isn't it great the progress there is nowadays? You've got to move with the times, there's no getting away from it.'

The door opened and we all got up, standing awkwardly between the seats and waiting for our turn. The pilot had turned in his seat and looked at my father, smiling.

2

My father and I stood in the bar at Mrs Blaney's. It was Saturday evening and the five till six rush hour. He had insisted we both stay in the same hotel and whenever he was in Dunedin he always stayed at Ma Blaney's. They both came

from the same part of Ireland, I discovered. Something I'd
never known in the days, twenty years before, when I'd drunk
there as a student on Saturday nights after football. She was
busy now, helping with the rush, a little old woman with high
white hair, brisk and fierce in all her movements, though she
must have been rising eighty. She had noticed us in the bar
and sent two more of what we were having.

A man of about my own age, but greying and with more of a
paunch, came up to me. 'It's you, isn't it?' he said. 'I'd heard
you were paying us a visit.' Kevin Hickey's face emerged from
under the face in front of me, young, devout. For some reason
I remembered him at the altar rails, eyes closed, tongue out,
waiting to receive the Host. He had a vocation, we all said,
and was going to be a priest. Then he met a girl and took to
the law instead. His father had felt disgraced and went to bed
refusing to get up. Kevin's brothers were said to have lit a fire
under the bed and smoked him out. What difference did it
make now?

I introduced him to my father and of course my father had
known his. There was a time when my father must have
known everyone. But after a bit we were an island of silence in
the middle of all the noise and I knew they must be thinking of
the bed business and all that, as I was.

So I said something about the old days and then got Kevin
to tell us a bit about his law firm. Things got easier and we
had another round. The noise was terrible, even after you got
used to it. The usual subjects, what they always talked about.
Football, the races. My father began to make a story out of
how we'd won at Wingatui but Kevin caught only half of it
and looked puzzled.

My father gave up trying to explain. 'Excuse me a minute,'
he said. 'I've got to use the telephone.'

I marvelled. We had never had a telephone at home and
somehow I'd assumed he wouldn't even know how to use one.
There'd been great progress, all right, in my long absence.

When he came back, Kevin had gone. The barman was
calling time. Men were buying their last-minute bottles to
take away.

'She's invited us out after tea,' my father said.

'Who has?'

'Maisie.'

It was the first time he'd mentioned her name but he knew I would know it. He wasn't one to waste time on explanations. When I came to think of it, he'd never written to me since the letter he wrote after my mother died. We were in the middle of the Cassino battle then, and so many were dying. I had read the letter and put it in my battle-dress pocket, meaning to read it again. I never did, though I often thought of my mother, that night and afterwards. She had been good to me and I was guilty that I had not been more grateful. After she died it was always my sister Nora who wrote the letters.

'We'll go and get a bite to eat somewhere,' my father said, 'and we'll go out there afterwards.'

'Let me shout you a meal at the *City*,' I said. 'I'd like to take a look at the place for old times' sake.'

'It's not as good a table as it was in Mrs McCormick's day, God rest her,' he said. 'Still, it'll be good enough, I dare say.'

We waved to Mrs Blaney as we went out.

'Don't you boys be late now,' she called to us. 'You've got to get to Mass in the morning, mind.'

I hadn't thought of that one. It was going to be awkward. But I'd find some way round it when the time came.

3

It was latish when we got away from the *City*. There were a lot of people in Dunedin for the races and we had to wait for a table. That meant a few more drinks in the lounge and as usual the old man kept running into people he knew and old-timers of one sort and another. Everyone wanted to buy a drink, of course, for their old friend Paddy – they always called him Paddy though his name was Ned – and that meant me as well. They'd ask me a few questions for politeness' sake and because, being back from the Old Country and all that, I was a bit of a nine days' wonder. But nobody really wants to talk to a nine days' wonder and my answers, like their questions, were just a sort of social sparring to show willing. They soon got back to talking about the old days with my father. After all, it's only your own life that's real, the realest part about it is the time when you were young, and the best way of being sure you haven't just dreamt even that is to talk with someone else who remembers the same things and can be trusted to remember them in the same sort of way, with plenty of detail but not too accurately.

Like a lot of Irishmen my father had always been better at talking to acquaintances, friends as he called them, than to his own family. He'd always been pretty silent at home, not necessarily in a grim sort of way, but in a way that suggested that it was only women who always had to be going on about something. When men weren't doing things, they were thinking. It wasn't till I was well grown and old enough to have seen him drinking with other men, that I realized he was really a rather talkative man. But he was good at listening, too, and he had a way of identifying with the other people while they were together which made them feel easy with him. It was quite genuine, too, I think, though afterwards when they'd gone, he'd become different again, and he'd go over what they'd said with a sort of amused mockery, often. I suppose it was a way of having his own back for the energy he'd spent in being partly inside their skins for a bit.

He was back on the old caper tonight properly and when the waiter came to tell us there was a table I had a bit of trouble getting him away. When we got down to it, though, he tucked away one of those big South Island meals without any trouble – soup, fish, roast beef, cabbage and potatoes, and a great wodge of apple pie.

Then it was coffee in the lounge and two or three rounds of whiskies with the pals who hadn't eaten yet and didn't look as if they were going to. So I began to think we were stuck there for the night, what with most of them being residents in the hotel and so no trouble about opening hours. I didn't much care myself, as I rather enjoyed listening to these tough old fellows. I'd have been bored to tears when I was a youngster, but by now I'd learnt enough to prefer long yarns about the early days to the average conversation about books which had once been my idea of how an intelligent chap should pass the time.

My father hadn't lost sight of his objective, though, as we used to say in the army and it wasn't as late as all that before he had me out in George Street again and striding north. He'd gone quiet again, in spite of all the drinks and I guessed he was working out how the evening was likely to go and how much he ought to brief me or how far he could rely on me to sort the situation out for myself.

It wasn't until we turned into Pacific Street and began to climb the hill that he evidently decided to give me a grudging clue or two. 'She's got a nice little packet salted away somewhere,' he said. 'But she's pretty near with it, though she likes to live comfortable.'

There was a flight of stone steps up to the front door. It was freshly painted and the doorknob and the knocker were shining under the light. My father didn't seem nervous, but a little bit tense and almost mischievous at the same time, I thought, as he rang the bell.

The door opened and I saw a woman, it must be Maisie, standing in the hall.

'Hello, Maisie,' my father said.

'Hello, Ned. Come in. And so this is that famous son of yours.'

'That's the one.' I realised that it was only when we were by ourselves that he took me for granted. It was one of those moments when you suddenly know that other people talk about you when you aren't there and you become a counter in their games instead of always being banker in a game of your own.

She had a service flat on the ground floor of one of those houses that used to be lived in by a single well-to-do family when I was a student. The sons were usually in the family business or medical students and the daughters were always in the social column of the *Otago Daily Times*, giving farewell parties before they went Home to be presented at Buckingham

Palace, or getting engaged to young men from the same sort of houses as their own. For some reason or other, it always seemed to be important what dress they were wearing on these occasions and who else had been present.

My father never wore an overcoat unless it was actually raining, but I took mine off in the hall and she hung it for me, using a coat-hanger. She then led us along a wide corridor to the living-room, where there was a good log fire burning under a massive mantelpiece. I noted, out of the corner of my eye, glasses and a bottle of brandy on a sidetable. There were deep, comfortable chairs, not too modern, a grand piano with photographs in frames, a procession of diminishing elephants on the mantelpiece, various brass objects, and pictures from which one immediately averted one's affronted eyes. And there was a cabinet wireless which she went over and switched off.

She stood in front of the fire and faced us. Black hair, probably tinted, bright dark eyes, a full-fleshed neck and bosom, figure well-preserved though thickish and the lines controlled by corsets. A dark red dress. A lot of jewellery. Probably in her late fifties.

'Now sit down and make yourselves comfortable while I get you a drink,' she said. She was addressing herself to both of us, but looking mainly at me. And when I offered to help she put a strong hand on me and pressed me to sit down. 'Would brandy be all right?'

'That'll do us fine, Maisie,' my father said, winking at me like a showman as she went over to the table.

I had the feeling she had been thinking carefully about the evening, what was likely to happen, what I was going to be like, what my father might be up to. She had decided brandy would make the right impression on me. It was probably her own favourite drink, as well.

They talked about people who lived near the farm, which ones were doing well and which were just working for the mortgagees, and who had sold out. He asked about her son John, who'd brought his family back from Australia and was now running the farm. It seemed he'd settled down well but the wife wasn't too keen.

I didn't say much. I just sipped away at my brandy and water, warning myself that I'd had a good deal already, and I watched and listened. My father gave no sign of what his real reason for coming might be. He managed to give a general impression that he had simply wanted us to meet each other. As I watched, I could see that there was still a physical attraction between them. They were people whose vitality had been less slowed down by the years than was usual for their age. Her bare forearm along the arm of her chair was only a foot or so away from him. The flesh of the under side, though it was rather full and flattened a little too easily, was still the flesh of a woman, not just the neutral flesh of one who had reached the age where the sexes merge. She had kept herself well and was turned out well, even if flashy and provincial. The rings on her fingers were too many, too big, and too costly. She had on her left wrist one of those bracelets which have a lot of charms and knick-knacks dangling from them. Her necklace might have been a real diamond one and the turquoise cross at the end of it hovered over the crevasse of her full breasts. She was rather heavily made up, but the lipstick and the rouge went well with the dark skin, not turning it magenta.

At the end of the day my mother used to sit, tired, at the kitchen table. She'd have her old slippers on, because of her poor feet. She carried too much weight and was too short for this to suit her. Her hands were red and swollen, the skin shiny over the knuckles. Her hair hadn't been near a hairdresser for years, perhaps never. She wouldn't have changed her dress – too tired, and nothing but her Sunday dress to change into, anyway. She never wore make-up and she and my father scoffed at people who did, especially older women.

In my mother's idea of marriage, there was no need for these things. The tactics of femininity were for girls or fast women. Absolute devotion to her family, her man, to the house and her work, this was the weapon and the armour of her simplicity. An equal loyalty on my father's part she took for granted. Her love was unthinking, inarticulate as far as I could judge and expressed mainly in worry about him in his absence and too much fussing when he was at home, but confident and quite free of coquetry.

She was right, while she lived. But my father, though he depended on her as she was and would not have expected her to be different or have been pleased if she had tried to be, must have missed all the rest – the effort to make him seem more than he was, even to himself, the little extra gestures that might give him the sense that he could be desirable to others, hard to be kept, the attention to appearances as well as the reliance on realities.

It was clear how Maisie must have attracted him: an obviously sensuous nature, a determination not too laboured to remain attractive as a woman: the alertness of the widow who still needs a man and must be attentive, flatteringly predatory. She had a kind of energy, too, and a sort of readiness of response to a man that might have looked like warmth, an affectionate nature. To my father she must have seemed rather sophisticated as well, someone who had been brought up in a convent, had seen a good deal of the world afterwards, and had travelled in the North Island and Australia when she was young. She would have seemed rather a cut above him, somehow, a way of improving himself.

That was the trouble, though, I decided, looking round the room which I gathered was called the lounge. It was furnished in a way that suggested an attentive reading of the woman's page of any and every New Zealand newspaper. For such a taste, in ruthless pursuit of refinement, my father must have seemed too crude, too rough, once the first animal drive had slackened and could no longer sustain the machinery of illusion necessary to keep two people living together in harmony.

I looked at him now. His cards weren't really very strong. He was still very much a man, it was true, and his blue eyes were lively with a sort of intelligence and life. But he was not polished, not educated. The hands that rested from the wrists on his knees were those of a man who used the axe, the shovel, and the spade. His back was too straight, his laugh too unguarded. He was not quite the stereotype of the New Zealand working-man because there was still in his bearing and manner the peasant Irish culture of another world, a dignity, a pride in being a man rather than that harassed and embattled masculinity. But his wasn't a dignity or a culture that she was likely to discern or value if she did discern it. It was the kind that a woman of her sort would be able to sense and appreciate for a while where both were alone or in an environment proper to it. It would not show to advantage in the world where she would like to shine. So she would have wanted to change him, civilise him, make him a middle-class husband in the New Zealand pattern, as she would have aspired to be a middle-class wife, superior and more genteel than he, but not too much so. And the very strength in him which attracted her, the pride, would have ruled that out. There could never have been any real prospect that the thing would have worked.

My father had been steering the ball my way, I became aware. It was time I took my cue. She was good at listening. I found, and all the drinks we had had were beginning to take effect. She herself must have had quite a few by then, and perhaps before we came, too. But she showed very little sign of being anything but the better for it.

I told stories about London, about Paris, about the war. My father led me on to something about Dublin. Her father had been a Dublin man, it seemed, and her mother had come from the North. We had more drinks and I remembered nice things about Ireland, the Old Country to both of them. There was a suspicion of tears in her eyes, a faraway look, and she folded her hands in her lap and sat up straight without realising it. So, as a little girl, she must have listened to her father.

My father took the opportunity of telling stories about his own boyhood in Galway but I could see she had heard them before and he sensed too that this wasn't what she wanted and left the going to me again. I knew somehow that I was in the vein he wanted. I sang one or two songs – my tenor was good enough to pass so long as people had had a few drinks. My father's chair seemed to have got closer to hers and their arms were nearly touching. As if their bodies at any rate were more or less ready for a *rapprochement*.

'Ah, it'd be great now to see the old country again,' my father said. 'I hope I'll get there once at any rate before I die. It'd take no time at all in one of them planes.'

He looked at me as he said this, but I knew it was meant for her. She just sighed, as if in sympathy, but non-committal. I said nothing. The old people I'd known who'd gone home to Ireland had found no place for themselves there and, when they came back to New Zealand and found themselves without a dream, they usually died fairly soon. You cannot emigrate twice.

I asked where the bathroom was. 'Come and I'll show you,' she said.

When I came out again into the corridor, she was still there, waiting for me. She took me by the arm and I realised there was still a passionate woman there. A bit tight, though. She had been drinking drink for drink with us.

'Martin,' she said, 'I don't want you to think it was my fault that things went wrong between your father and me. He's the one who was to blame.'

'I'm not blaming you,' I said. 'Or anyone else. It's no business of mine. You're old enough, both of you, to know your own minds.'

But it wasn't good enough. She insisted and kept hold of my arm, with a grip surprisingly strong. 'No, Martin. He's a very cruel man, your father. He had me and John in fear of our lives. He didn't tell you he went for my son with an axe, I'll bet.'

'He didn't tell me anything at all. And perhaps you shouldn't, either.'

'You're a very nice man, Martin, and you've seen a lot of the hard world, I know. And it's only natural you should stick up for your own flesh and blood, don't think I don't understand. But I wanted you to know how awful he'd been to me. He's a very hard man, Martin, real hard. I couldn't ever live with him again. I'm sure of that.'

'Well,' I said, 'that's up to you to settle between you. And no one's going to make you live with him if you don't want to. We'd better go in now or he'll think we're smooging with each other out here.'

'Fancy even thinking of such a thing, you naughty man.' But her face had changed and she looked pleased at being still thought possible.

As we came in my father gave her and then me a quick, curious look. He would have guessed that she was telling her side.

We couldn't get going again, somehow, after the interruption. It was after midnight and I for one had had enough, of the brandy and the situation in general. Somehow that bit about his being cruel stuck in my gizzard. He might be a hard man, and unfeeling sometimes, but whatever else he was he wasn't cruel. If he really had taken the axe to John, it must have been to scare him, and even then they must have driven him to the end of his tether.

'Well, Dad,' I said. 'What about it? We mustn't keep Maisie up any longer. It's time we got going.'

'Yes, son, it is that. Well, Maisie, it's been very nice seeing you again.'

'You're very welcome. But you can't go off and leave that little bit in the bottom of the bottle.'

She filled up our glasses, all three of them. But she didn't sit down again, and neither did we.

'Here's to your health on your travels, Martin, and I hope you go on making a name for yourself over there. It's a fine young man you've got for a son, Ned. Someone to be proud of.'

'He is that, Maisie.' And he looked very pleased.

4

My father wouldn't hear of getting a taxi and so we walked back along silent streets, silent ourselves. Only a taxi sped past us now and then, an occasional policeman on rubber-soled boots tried the locks of shop-doors, and once a drunk student was kissing his girl goodnight outside the *Excelsior*. Dunedin was already in its Sunday sleep. I forgot to wonder what my father might be thinking and thought of the early mornings long ago when I had hurried along these same streets, from a girl's bed to my own.

The front door of the hotel was closed. I was going to press the night bell when my father stopped me. 'Come round this way,' he said.

We went down a side passage and at the back of the hotel there was an iron fire-escape. My father led the way up, and on the bedroom floor a window opposite the landing was open. Mrs Blaney leaned out and looked at us. She was still dressed as she had been earlier.

'A fine time of the night to be coming home,' she said, 'for the pair of you. Shame on you, Ned, to be setting your own son such an example. Come in with you, now, and don't wake the whole hotel with your noise.'

She stepped back and my father climbed over the sill. I got in after him, half expecting to be slapped.

'Sure, we were only visiting a few friends,' my father said, and I could tell he was as scared of her as I was.

'Fine friends they must be that would keep you and the boy up drinking to this hour of night. Off to bed now, the pair of you, you scallywags, and don't be late in the morning.'

My father came as far as my room with me and sat on the bed. 'She's a great old stick, isn't she?' He grinned a bit ruefully.

For a moment I thought he meant Maisie and then realised my mistake in time. He didn't want to talk about Maisie at all, and he was using Mrs Blaney to fill the gap.

'Yes, she's a great old character,' I said. 'She's hardly changed a bit since I was a student.'

'Well, good night,' he said. 'I'll call you for breakfast.'

I was desperately tired and a bit tight. I went straight to sleep, leaving it till tomorrow to puzzle things out.

I woke about eight, pretty thick in the head and cursing Maisie and her brandy. I went along the passage to the bathroom and let the cold tap run in the bath while I cleaned my teeth and shaved. Then I stood in the bath and lowered myself gingerly, gasping. I lay back in the cold water and splashed about till I'd had enough. Then I got out and dried myself, feeling a bit better.

Outside the bathroom I found my father standing in the passage fully dressed. He looked cheerful and none the worse for wear.

'I thought that was where you must have got to,' he said. 'Come on now and get dressed. I managed to get her to open up the bar and I've brought up a couple of double-headers.'

Sur enough there were two full whisky nobblers on my dresser.

'Drink it up now. It'll do you the world of good and give you an appetite for breakfast.' He took one of them and drank it off.

I sipped mine and the taste and smell of it at that time of the morning and the way I felt made me toss my head and almost whinny like a horse. I put it down again.

'I'll get dressed first,' I said. 'I'll see you downstairs.' Funny, I had some sort of shyness at getting dressed in front of him. Because he was my father, I supposed, though that didn't really explain much.

He went out and I began to put on my clothes. Even that little sip of whisky had begun to act now, though. I took the glass and gulped the rest. Then I finished dressing and went downstairs.

There was a sign pointing through the bar to the dining-room. But in the bar I found my father talking to a large red-faced man. They each had a long beer in front of them. 'This is Pat Plunkett,' my father said. 'My son Martin, the one I was telling you about.'

We shook hands and my father went behind the bar and got me a bottle of beer. 'That's what you need now, my lad,' he said. 'A chaser. Drink that up and you'll be as right as the bank.'

In spite of the whisky the idea of breakfast was still not at all acceptable. Coffee and a bit of toast and marmalade at the most. But I drank down the beer. Somehow it was all a bit like one of those wartime mornings in the mess, when you were making an early move back to the desert.

'Well, cheerio just now, Pat,' my father said. 'It was nice running into you after all these years.'

He led me into the dining-room and we sat down at a round table in the corner. Someone had already breakfasted there. The maid came and cleared the table and laid two fresh places. 'Bacon and eggs for two,' my father said, and I shrugged inwardly.

Mrs Blaney appeared in the entrance from the kitchen and saw us. 'Good morning, Ned,' she said sternly to my father, and she managed a faint smile for me. Then she looked down and saw the crumbs on the table. She clicked her tongue. 'These girls you get nowadays,' she said.

She went away and I listened for a row in the kitchen. But instead she came back with a little tray and curved brush and swept up the crumbs from my part of the table. She didn't bother about my father's place, though, but went off again and came back with a clean linen napkin which she handed to me, ignoring him.

He didn't appear to be at all offended or puzzled by this but just grinned at me, showing white even teeth, not one missing. You could have guessed from that alone he hadn't been brought up in New Zealand.

'You can't beat old Mrs Blaney,' he said, 'for knowing how to keep a good table. Fancy her being on deck at this hour of the morning. It must have been going on for two when she let us in last night.'

To my surprise I had no trouble eating the bacon and egg after all. And the coffee was very good.

Afterwards, we sat in the lounge while I had a smoke. My father sat still and silent the way people can who never read and don't feel conversation necessary. I thought he might be trying to make up his mind to talk about the night before. But it wasn't that.

'It's time to be thinking of getting up the hill to the Cathedral,' he said.

I noticed the neutral way he'd put it. No doubt it was well known in the family that I didn't go to Mass any more and he was leaving it to me to make the running.

'I don't think I'll go with you,' I said. 'I've got some people to see and some letters to write.'

I could feel him disappointed. Perhaps he'd hoped it wasn't true that I'd left the Church. And I suppose he'd rather have liked meeting people he knew, the way he always did, after Mass, and introducing me to them. But he made no comment. 'I'll see you here about twelve, then. We'd better have something to eat here before you catch your plane.'

5

Travelling out to the airfield on the bus, I looked at the broom with its twisted black pods. When we were kids we used to hear the sharp crack they made in the summer heat when the time had come to scatter their seeds. You could hear quite small noises in those days. Now there was always a roar of engines between you and small noises, and a screen of motion between yourself and stillness. I thought of the people I'd seen that morning, after my father went off to Mass. They had all got older except me, it seemed. Their hair was grey, you had the feeling of fixed habits, minds preoccupied with the unknown experiences that lay between now and the time we had been friends. They remembered different things, or remembered the same things differently. I shouldn't have come back. They were blurring the outline of the past. It was only the broom, and the gorse, the sun on the hills, and the wind, that didn't change.

'You know,' my father said, 'she took rather a fancy to you.'

This time I knew he meant Maisie, but I couldn't think of anything to say. Looking back on last night, I'd decided I didn't like her. She obviously didn't see that my father was worth two of her and rather looked down on him. And if she'd made a fuss of me it was only because I had prestige value for discussion over tea with her friends, having come back from abroad and having my name in the papers.

'I've been thinking that one of these days I might talk her into shouting the pair of us a trip to the Old Country,' he said. 'It'd be great to see where you live and meet the children. And I'd like to go back and see who's still left in Galway.'

'We'd love to see you,' I said. 'The children have heard so much about you. When they were small, they once started to dig a hole in the garden, so as to get through to the Antipodes and meet you.'

If it ever came off, I was thinking, it would be worse for him than it had been for me. At least I had been warned by books that you could never go back. I knew what to expect not to expect. There was no need to fear, though. He'd played his cards well enough, but the hand was too poor. I was his only trump and there wasn't much he could do with me against her sort of player. Perhaps I should have taken a hand myself.

'It's not money that'd be the trouble,' he said. 'She's got plenty of that.'

I didn't much like the idea of a proud man like my father scheming to use the woman's money, even if she was his wife, more or less. I began to wish, as I did once in a while, that I'd paid a bit more attention to making money myself. It would have been nice to be able to say, 'Come on, Dad, don't worry about her, I'll shout you the trip myself.' But I'd never treated money seriously enough to have it in that sort of quantity. So there was nothing to be done.

When we were in the little departure lounge I saw a hire car pull up and Maisie get out.

'I thought I'd come and see you off,' she said when she found us.

'That was very nice of you. But you shouldn't have bothered,' I said.

I looked at my father. He was smiling to himself as he bent to pick up the luggage. 'How are you feeling today, Maisie?' he asked.

'Fine, thank you, Ned. It was such a nice day I thought I'd come out and find you both. It might be a long time before we see him again, after all, that young man of ours.'

'It might, at that.' My father spoke shortly. He wouldn't have liked that suggestion of ownership. And he was probably thinking that the likelihood was he'd never see me again.

'Your poor mother,' he said to me, 'if only she'd lived to see you come home. She always believed you'd come home some day. Even in the thick of the war, when they said you were missing, believed killed, she always said you'd come home. You were like a cat, she used to say, always so quick and quiet, and with nine lives and all.'

Passengers had been called. The others had gone out already the short distance across to the plane. I half-embraced Maisie. She wasn't a bad sort, after all. She'd lived in a hard world where you had to look after yourself, or else. I shook my father's hand.

'Good-bye, son. Forget what I was saying about that trip. I wouldn't want it to happen that way, you know.'

'I know,' I said. I did too, in a kind of way.

'I may see you some day over there myself,' Maisie said. 'You never know.'

I knew it was quite likely she would come. But I knew, after what he had said about my mother, that if she did come it wouldn't be with him, whether she wanted it or not.

When the plane was in the air, I looked back and down. There was no one waving from the airfield now, and I could not tell whether he had gone back in the car with her or was in the bus which was crawling minutely out to the main road.

The Locksmith Laughs Last

Exhaustion, social exhaustion, why don't New Yorkers suffer from it, or seem to suffer from it? Skill at dissembling? They may be as skilled as I am but can't be more skilled, surely? Good manners, better manners? But manners are part of what causes the exhaustion. Possibly business and ambition and fear, the spurs of the urban peace-time warrior?

Sweating in the late afternoon at a borrowed office in our Madison Avenue premises, I was prepared to let it go at that. And to let my beautiful, borrowed secetary go, as well. She thanked me kindly and went out to wherever beautiful secretaries go, presumably to a better dinner and younger company than I was to eat or to encounter; or to be.

One of the scourges, only one, of a business visit to New York is that it is impossible to be alone, I reflected, especially for a meal. Breakfast, perhaps, if you're staying in a hotel; but given what probably happened the night before, all that you probably feel like is a dog's breakfast. And after this particular last fortnight I'd reached the point where I seldom felt like a meal at all. Every day one too many martinis before noon – and even one martini is too many, however good it may be at the time. Then the intimidation of a business steak too big to be eaten and too expensive to be wasted. After that, appointments, conferences with accountants and lawyers, and other men with vellum faces. Then another cocktail party with more martinis and a dinner with some colleague whose wife's anxious suavity flourishes your first name when you've forgotten hers, and your own as well. The shame of not liking avocado pear stuffed with outrage, the same steak that defeated you at lunch, nothing to drink except iced water, and that salad full of carrots, cabbage, raisins and a deep-sunk reef of nuts, a vegetable *bombe surprise*. Whatever diet is currently reputed good for cardiac liabilities like the one you're rapidly becoming, all proffered with a lethally sincere and insistent hospitality.

Still, even supposing I didn't have to go tonight to the dinner to which I was doomed, wouldn't I be delighted if I were taking out Annabel, that delicious secretary I had just liberated from my bilious gloom? I was appalled to have to admit to myself that I would not. That was what I'd been reduced to by New York. By New York? No, to be candid by time as well. I looked at my watch, as if to see how old I was. Not impossible, either. My mother had given it to me for my twenty-first birthday; and, now in 1965, today was its thirtieth birthday. I couldn't speak for my watch but I knew how I wanted to celebrate: by an early bed, alone.

My colleague's de luxe telephone made a discreet but determined bid for attention. I lifted the receiver from its elegant lap. It was my colleague's wife – Eleanor, no, Elaine. Robert had been summoned suddenly to Boston. So much for that dinner, I thought, dissembling jubilation.

Not for long. She wanted me to come just the same, instead of being secretly relieved the way any hostess but an American would have been. We would have a quiet meal *en famille*, and some friends would drop in afterwards, in case she was too boring for me.

I remembered, with the speed and terror of light, that she was one of those beautiful women who must be intelligent because they seem to be listening to you and who later turn out to have no idea of what you're actually saying but are really only marvelling because you speak in period sentences with reasonably intricate but co-ordinated syntax, are thrilled at taking part in a cultured conversation, think you're cute because you take it innocently for granted that you'll be allowed to finish your sentence.

I also remembered how good her salads were – good for you – and how the last time I had dined there her two small sons had kept running in and out from the TV room and pretending they were spacemen, with suitable noises. And I remembered again that it was my birthday, though I was much too crafty to say so. So I told her I had a feverish cold and didn't want to pass it on to her nice children, the single excuse that would save me in that cellophane world where only health had priority over hospitality.

Safely off that hook, I replaced the receiver and sat there hugging the idea of a whole evening to myself. A week before, I'd fled my hotel and taken sanctuary in the apartment of an old friend. In hotels I couldn't trust myself: there the solitude I thought I longed for turned to loneliness, loss of identity, and I ran the risk of seeking out company, any company, simply to reaffirm my own existence.

Tonight I knew my friend was going out to a party and I would have his place to myself. It was the first of September and outside this air-conditioned office – inside it too – New York was as hot as hell, or as humid if moisture is allowed in hell, and almost as infinite. I would take a cab home to West 86 Street, have a shower and change my shirt, and then decide where to go for dinner. Afterwards I would return, 'Turn the key deftly in the oiled wards, And seal the hushed Casket of my Soul'. Alone and in a deep sleep I would be as safe as death.

'You from England?' the taxi-driver asked.

'From Oxford, England,' I said. I had adjusted to my original culture-shock by now, and was wary of transatlantic ambiguities. People might look the same, have two legs, wear spectacles, be called by names like plain William Smith as this driver's identity card proclaimed him. But they weren't the same, didn't mean the same things by the same words. New York refracted reality as water does a stick. You had to adjust appearances by a constant sleight of mind, for they were possessive in this city about the reality of their refraction, and easily wounded, offended even. If you went along with them, they penetrated your pretence but were kind to you for trying.

'I was there during the war,' he said. 'Were you in the war?'

'Yes,' I said. But I knew he'd want more than that and so added. 'In Greece, Crete, North Africa, and Italy.'

'You sure got around. I was in Normandy myself.'

It was clear that I'd spent my war in sideshows, not much better than a tourist. I didn't feel I need pay much attention while he went on to develop his opening into a conventional middle game – General Patton, Omar Bradley, and Ike against Montgomery. I was speculating about whether it was the humidity of New York – I could feel the sweat passing through the back of my shirt into the light fabric of my jacket – that produced peculiarly favourable conditions in the cells of the imagination for osmosis, the interfusion of reality and fantasy. Were these skyscrapers on either side of us a product of this, concrete enough and tangible, yet assaults on probability, hypertrophied fungi of the mind? Or were they themselves a factor? If they were true, and a man lived among them every day, saw them and the way they surpassed the clouds, would he not come to think that hypertrophy, exaggeration, fantasy, were themselves the qualities, guarantees, of truth?

He was on the Marshall Plan now, and how American civilisation was saving us from Communism, as if he were following my mind and providing an illustrative commentary. I doubled back on my tracks to elude him, and began to think of dinner. Not because I wanted to eat, or would want to, but because I knew I must. There was a place I'd found called Moriarty's where they served something small enough not to put you off, a thing called a Chorus-girl's Butterfly Chop. But you ran the danger of someone at an adjoining table ordering one of those steaks that the head waiter cooks alongside the table over a flame thing, and with onions. Better, probably, and safer, to go to that German place in Yorkville, East 86 Street, wasn't it, where you could get real boiled beef and cabbage. Yes, the Blue Danube, that was the place.

I looked at my watch. The minute hand had fallen off again, relaxed by the heat, but it had been about half-past five when I left the office and now it was somewhere near six. We were

crossing Broadway. 'You've got to smile on Broadway,' the
driver said, 'as the song goes. But from what they've done to it
someone must be laughing outright, on his way to the bank.'
Broadway Melody, that took me back to long before my
watch, the first talkies that came to New Zealand, and myself
a devout Catholic Irish boy looking sinfully at the delicious,
delusive mirage of that swirl of long female legs and the
maddening glimpses of their junction. Alas for lost lust. To
think that all I wanted now was to have eaten and to lie in bed
alone, and this in the very metropolis where those legs had
danced and others now were dancing.

As I got out of the taxi, it had begun to rain or, rather, the
steam they called air was beginning to condense on the
asphalt streets, and then steam back again, an allegory of life.
My friend Victor was a much-married bachelor who never
seemed to be married, except during the long intervals
between my visits to New York. His apartment was large
enough to have held all his wives but Americans prefer their
polygamy serial, and he really liked it better when he housed
no wives at all: his marital phases were aberrations, feverish
illnesses when, unlike himself, he capitulated to the fantasy
that this time was for ever, a fantasy as chronic and recurrent
in this part of the world as malaria elsewhere.

'The kitchen's clear if you want to fix yourself anything,' he
said. 'The Countess is on the phone.'

I'd seen her there, in the hall, when I let myself in with my
key, the way I saw the desk the telephone was on, without
actually noticing. It seemed the natural place for her. She was
a friend of his of long standing, like myself, and formerly a
lover, I guessed – he was not forthcoming about such things,
but there was a settled and peaceful quality about their friend-
ship, a sense of favours given and taken, of all passion spent.
She was hard up and involved in an endless lawsuit about a
castle in Liechtenstein which seemed to belong simultaneously
to her and to a lawyer. That was one of the
reasons why she was always on the telephone, having business
chats with other Countesses and lawyers in other castles all
over Europe, privately thought by me to be castles in Spain.

She also had a formula for making gold which she'd got from a Ruthenian baron who was an alchemist. That was why the kitchen wasn't available most of the time. It had to be kept constant at some tremendous temperature if she was to get the formula to work. Victor didn't care because he couldn't cook anyway and it kept her happy. Besides, you never knew, perhaps the formula might work sooner or later. Anything could happen in New York. Meanwhile, though, all the dollars she could lay hands on went into her fantasy Fort Knox. She was a sort of Midas in reverse.

'Has she struck it lucky yet?' I asked, wondering why the kitchen was free.

'No, I don't think so. Besides, she's off to Liechtenstein first thing tomorrow morning.'

'Perhaps the formula's worked and she's making off with the gold.'

'No, she's not like that.' Even Victor had that American trick of taking you literally. 'She'd have given me some of what she owes me. Anyhow, she's just borrowed fifty dollars from me towards the fare. Worth it, though. I'll be able to use the phone myself tomorrow.'

The Countess was rather deaf but she always heard the word dollars. It drew her to us now in the living-room and Victor poured her a Scotch. I gathered, was meant to gather, that the fare was costing more than she thought and the people she'd been telephoning weren't able to help. She smiled at me, a smile which had worked wonders in the past and in which she still had confidence. She was right, too. After all, we prudent, matter-of-fact businessmen have an obligation to people who live by the imagination, to historic anomalies, eccentrics and other endangered species, beautiful survivors. And, anyway, I liked her. After I'd lent her the money, she politely kept us company for another drink – Victor affectionately amused at her need to make us feel like desirable men, not creditors, and I ruefully regretting that I hadn't known her younger when I'd have been prepared to prospect the feet of rainbows for her sake. Then she excused herself with delicate regret: she must go to bed because she had to take an impossibly early flight.

Victor picked up his raincoat and we walked together to the corner of the block on West End Avenue. There we picked up separate taxis. I'd made up my mind in favour of boiled beef, though without the cabbage, and Victor had reminded me whereabouts in East 86 Street the restaurant was, since a New York driver has to be told exactly where he's going.

'The Blue Danube?' said my new driver, Joseph Maria Cellini according to his identity card and Italian by face, photograph, accent and prejudice. 'Isn't that a German joint? If you'd been in the war you'd have had enough of those bastards. What do you want to go eating kraut food for? Why don't you go to a nice Italian place? I could take you to a real nice one, real class.'

I refrained from telling him that I had been in the war, and in Italy, where I'd eaten quite a lot of Italian food and seen quite a number of Italians. Instead, I thanked him and said I really much preferred Italian food, but I had an appointment with a beautiful Swiss Italian and didn't dare to risk upsetting the arrangements. He agreed grudgingly and showed his disappointment in me by driving in silence through Central Park, where it was still daylight. When he dropped me at the Blue Danube he was still grieved and an extra percentage on the fare mollified him only a little. As a parting shot, he warned me that Swiss Italians weren't like real Italians.

The drinks I'd had at Victor's had partly revived my spirits and I was rather disappointed not to find the beautiful Swiss Italian girl waiting when an elderly fraülein took me to my table. But I took heart of grace and dispelled this Lilith from the blessed Eden of my solitude. I shielded myself behind a book of poems, modern poems, some woman friend had given me. There was a stein of beer before me and in due course that boiled beef. Afterwards, I had a second beer and was emboldened after it and after coffee to look around me at the Teutonic appetites, thinning blond hair and fat necks. Where had I been somewhere like this? In Tel Aviv, oddly enough, in 1943. And before that? In Schmidt's in Charlotte Street, London, England. And before that? In Munich, in 1938.

Telling the truth was no help against the shivers of the might-
have-been. I was an escaped prisoner on the run, trying to
escape recognition in the thick Nazi crowds of the
Hofbraühaus. The man over there in the hat and pince-nez
had me under observation. I asked for more coffee and read
some of the poems to calm myself down from a fantasy all too
easy in this ambience to sustain. The poems made me sleepy.
Like all modern poems they were about the poet's difficulties
in writing a poem. My earlier exhaustion began to catch up on
me. I remembered that the original idea had been to celebrate
my birthday and unexpected freedom by having an early bed.
I paid the check and stared back at the man in hat and pince-
nez as he lifted his head to stare at me.

'West 86 Street,' I said to the new taxi-driver, and I
refrained from telling him to watch out in his mirror and see
that we were not followed. He might be one of them, of course.
No, his licence card said his name was Kirschbaum, Leopold.
And he asked me to excuse him from talking: he was thinking
out the next move in a chess game he was playing over his car
radio with another driver. The Gestapo weren't named
Kirschbaum and didn't play chess, unless with human pawns.
Human pawns? But I looked at his photograph again and was
reassured. So gentle a face would be satisfied with ivory. I
relaxed and remembered again how tired I was. On this
chequer-board of nights and days only destiny was cruel
enough to play with men for pieces.

Yes, when I got back to the apartment into bed, it wouldn't
be those vociferating poems written by a mouse I'd read, it
would be Omar. Victor was bound to have a copy somewhere
on his shelves. I'd drift off into a delicious slumber, reading
about the stone which put the stars to flight. I lay back trying
to remember the quatrains. The driver had to wake me when
we got to West 86 Street.

'Ah, take the cash and let the credit go,' I said to him as I
tipped him.

'Nor heed the rumble of a distant slum?' he rebuked me,
and I realised I had been in the hands of the NKVD.

'What move did you make?' I asked.

'Knight to Queen's three and mate.'
'Right-wing deviationist,' I retorted and castled.

The apartment was on the fourth floor, the elevator was early twentieth-century bourgeois, and very slow. Exhausted again by my bold challenge to the Soviet police and by the beer, I nearly fell asleep again, standing. Only my claustrophobia kept me awake enough to stop the contraption at the right landing. I fished out my key, prepared to carry my sleepiness across the threshold like a bride. I turned the key in the keyhole, met some resistance, and turned it a bit harder. It turned, sure enough. At least, one end of it did, the end in my hand. The business end stayed where it was. I looked stupidly at the piece I was left holding, broken off, like a severed ear lobe, an impotent man's amputation fantasy. Perversely I remembered the accursed Omar: 'There was a Door to which I found no Key, There was a Veil past which I could not see'.

But I was no Persian mystic. Never mind, I reassured myself, manly and rejecting my fearful prescience. The man who lives in the disasters ahead of him never lives at all. The gods – there's safety in numbers – help those who help themselves. The Countess, faithful chatelaine, was within, after all. I pressed the bell. I waited. I pressed it again. And several times again, becoming more and more desperate like an unrewarded psychologist's rat, pealing and appealing. I took off my shoe and banged it against the door. But the sole was rubber, about as effective as a detumescent dildo. I tried shouting and discovered that my voice had become falsetto, the shrill scream of a demented bat, inaudible to human ears. Then I remembered the Countess was deaf. Why had evolution not provided us with some sort of personal radar?

This was nothing to situations one had faced in the war, I told myself, imposing authority on incredulity. Keep calm, and be resourceful. I summoned the aching elevator, went down and found the black doorman. We rang the telephone number, his idea. No reply. The Countess had probably taken a sleeping draught against just that seduction, no doubt some potion concocted to a secret Ruthenian formula, going back across the miasma of time to Medea herself.

Adversity, my adversity, suited the doorman. He beamed and became positively buoyant, a Mark Tapley to my Chuzzlewit. But it wasn't catching. He said we'd find the Super, which I gathered meant some sort of overlord of the underworld. Orphic, with his help, I would awaken my Eurydice. We went down into the basement. No Super. 'What about a locksmith?' I said. 'They're all closed. No, there's one over on the East Side who'll be open, the all-night locksmith.'

He sounded somewhat sinister, as well as superhuman, this creature of darkness. The sort of wizard fairy princes were sometimes forced to consult, I seemed to remember. 'Great Opener of Doors, we thee implore – ', no, that was Hafiz and he was also discredited. What was the name of this passe-partout, who held the keys of darkness? The doorman didn't know his name, didn't rightly recall it, but he did know that his name and address and telephone number were written on the wall of the basement toilet. I took heart from this: others, then, had also been benighted. Taking Wellington's advice first, and making the libation to the goddess Cloacina that apprehension and the German beer imperiously demanded, I then noted down the name and telephone number and, just in case, the address. He lived in East 86 Street whence I had just come, so innocently confident of sleep. And the house number was the same as mine. I did not find a good omen in the symmetry of this. We called the number from the doorman's desk. No reply. There was nothing for it but to set out on my quest.

Another taxi. It was dark by now. Grumbling, the driver – Gabriel Horvatz – told me we must go fast through Central Park, paying no attention to cries for help, broken-down cars, signals from damsels in distress. I asked him if he had been reading Spenser. He softened to my perspicuity and explained that he was driving a cab to get himself through college and he had a seminar on *The Faerie Queene* which was a set book. He was also temperamentally apprehensive and Central Park by night had an evil reputation. I reminded him that Colin Clout came home again, to comfort him. Exchanging quotations – mainly from Book I, I noted – we two gentle knights managed to prick our way across the perilous plain. He actually helped me to find the right number in East 86 Street and I brushed aside my fear of enchantment as I paid him and went alone to the dimly lit shop-window.

The door was locked. But perhaps the All Night Locksmith always kept his door locked, having himself no need of keys? I pressed the bell. No reply. I looked back for my taxi but it had gone. I peered at the door and saw a card with a message written on it. If he was out the All Night Locksmith could be reached at his home telephone number. In the light from the window I noted it down.

On the other side of the street I saw a bar. If I was to survive the trials of this night much longer I would have to have a drink, and the bar would have a telephone. It was a bar full of large Germans, one of those places where everyone is a regular except yourself and they all think a stranger must be a policeman. At first I thought all the drinkers must be deaf and dumb but then I realised the silence was too unnatural for that. I bought a double Scotch on the rocks, reconnoitred past those glaucous eyes, and saw the telephone on the further wall. I had a great fear of American telephones and until tonight I'd always managed to avoid using a public one. So far, there'd always been someone else's office or someone's secretary. As time went on I got more skilful in disguising my shameful weakness, like one of those truck-drivers who've never learned to read but can find their way anywhere without being detected. Now I had reached the testing time.

Nonchalant, resisting the powerful desire to have another drink first, I sauntered over to the evil instrument, trying to remember how I'd seen people like William Powell do it in films about detectives and newspapermen. Even though I didn't have the right sort of hat, and the smoke of my cigarette butt kept getting in my eyes, the trick worked and I was as successful as a somnambulist. I heard the ringing-tone sound, as the besieged at Lucknow heard the Campbell pipes.

A feminine voice replaced the ringing, a wife's by the sound of weary resentment in it, resentment not just against me – for I, whoever I might be, was merely another pawn in the fingers of a hostile fate who always played white and always won.

This was no time to meditate on the miserable life of a woman married to the All Night Locksmith, however. And she dispersed my cloudy sympathy at once when she told me he was out on a job. What was my trouble? She'd tell him when he returned. Could I leave a number?

I left the number and returned to the bar, found a seat, and bought a double Scotch. In that inimical and continuing silence I began to feel it was my only friend. Why did we have to live in a world of locks and keys? Because of Property, Kirschbaum, the NKVD man, murmured in my ear. No, I told him, I had heard there were locks and keys, and warders too, in the Promised Land. No, indeed. Wasn't life itself a locked door, waiting for the All Night Locksmith to come and release us all? Were we trying to get in or to get out? Which side of the door was the prison? These reflections were unsatisfying. The real question was which side of the door was my bed. And the answer wasn't in doubt.

The telephone rang and I rushed to it. If someone else got there first, it would be for him. At the same time I knew that if I got there first it would be for someone else, or a wrong number. In fact, no one moved, though their eyes all followed me and I was conscious of a rapt attention I might have been glad to command in other times and places.

A voice that was patient, old and wise, a voice that had unlocked many doors, told me, yes, this was Peter Rock, and asked me to confirm my name and address. Then he would be there in half an hour. We synchronised watches, as we used to do in the war, though mine had lost its minute hand. I could have built a church on Peter Rock, on or for him. I almost told him of his impending papacy but managed to confine myself to something more conventional. He severed my gratitude, locksmiths were used to it presumably, and told me it would cost me twenty-five dollars. Cash. Wildly, I promised. Cash.

Wildly, indeed. For the Countess had cleaned me out of most of my cash and, thinking I would be back in bed so soon, I hadn't troubled to replenish. Dinner, the further taxis, the two double Scotches, had left me distinctly anaemic.

Normally, I allowed for the haemophilia of the hip pocket endemic in New York, and carried in my wallet all that was necessary for emergency blood transfusion. Under the attentive but averted gaze of the people in the bar I counted what I had left. Enough, with luck, to pay for the next taxi. *Solvitur in ambulando?* No, I was too exhausted to walk. Even if I hadn't been I couldn't have walked it in time.

Time? It was well after eleven, at least my surviving hour hand was. There was already a hole in that half hour.

But I had traveller's cheques, of course. I took the folder from my trouser fob and inspected it. Three left, each for twenty-five. I looked up at the barman, who'd been drying the same glass for quite a while as he kept me under observation.

He shook his head. 'Not here, sonny,' he said in a voice of withering compassion. He must have abandoned some time ago his suspicion that I was a policeman. Now he had clearly thought of something much more suitable, but worse. I decided to leave before an ambulance was called to take me off to wherever the psychiatrists were, waiting in their white coats.

The new taxi-driver was very large. His shoulder muscles beetled over into the back seat, menacing. His fists on the wheel were the colour and size of hams and they made the wheel look like a child's toy. I sat back and pondered. I couldn't help looking at the meter all the time, the way some people keep looking at their watches. I'd forgotten again exactly how much I had but began to feel more and more certain the fare was going to be more.

We had entered Central Park. I regretted my friend of the Spenserian stanza, only driving a taxi to get himself through college, a timorous gentle intellectual like myself. Still, this new man wouldn't easily let himself be robbed by whatever demons dwelt hereabouts, not even by the Blatant Beast should he be abroad. Or by me, either. More likely to rob me. And he'd be quite capable of taking his disappointment out on me with those great paws, too, when he discovered how little money I had. I began to feel marginally better as my latest apprehension, the worst for some time, elicited my last

emergency supply of adrenalin. Or perhaps it was belated
Scotch courage.

In a particularly badly lit stretch the taxi began to slow
down. I couldn't see any distressed damsels. I must be the
nearest thing to one there was. I wouldn't be able to sell my
life dearly, or even cheaply, but I was damned if I was going to
give it away. I leaned forward, tense, ready to jump out when
he stopped and at least meet him on my feet. If I could get a
left into his stomach, then connect with a right as he bent
forward? Or perhaps he had very short legs, all giants had
some weakness, and I could outrun him.

He was watching me in the driving-mirror, my fingers on
the doorhandle. 'I wouldn't if I were you,' he said. 'Not here.
It's dangerous round here.'

'What is?'

'Doing what you were going to do. I'd hang on a bit longer
till I got home, if I were you. The Vice Squad might get you
for doing it here.'

'Then what have we stopped for?'

'Are you interested in trinkets?' he said.

I paused and thought. The usual double malentendre was
possible. Perhaps 'trinkets' was New York slang for girls. If so,
I couldn't very well explain I was worried enough about the
fare already clocked up, let along having money to spare for
trinkets. Still, at least it would be one way of getting to bed?
It would be embarrassing, though, even humiliating, to have
to explain to the trinket that in spite of your overwhelming
passion for her you only wanted to go to sleep. She'd want
cash, too, sleep or sleep with. Better, all things considered, to
keep my date with the everlasting locksmith. Anyway,
perhaps trinkets weren't girls at all.

His back was still there, stolidly expecting an answer, a
back not to be trifled with.

'It depends on what you mean by trinkets.'

'That's what I mean,' he said, not looking round but lifting
his left arm in the air. His unbuttoned sleeve fell back, mystic
white samite and all. There were about a dozen wristwatches
strapped around his forearm, their straps straining, one above

the other. Gold, silver, and steel, they glimmered like Excalibur.

'Watches,' I said. Apart from being obvious, the word didn't seem adequate to my astonishment.

They didn't seem adequate to him, either. Not worth a verbal reply, in fact. He brought his left hand back to the wheel, the watches disappeared beneath his sleeve, and he restarted the engine.

'Thanks all the same,' I said, 'but I've got a watch already.'

He made no comment and we pressed on once more. I sat back, one set of fears at rest, but my mind ticking over. Like his meter, and his watches. It was true I had a watch already. A careful study of its faded face reminded me that its thirtieth anniversary would soon be over. In less than half an hour. With luck the locksmith and I would keep our tryst at midnight. 2359 hours, even, a time with some highly disagreeable associations. Zero hour for night attacks. Wasn't that the time we went in at Alamein? A difficult time, too, for people like Cinderella, Hamlet. For the Nazis as well, that last year.

I looked at my watch again. The luminous paint had long since flaked away. The loss of the minute hand forced me to eat time by great coarse gulps, instead of with measured delicacy. Sometimes it just stopped, too tired to go on, like an old horse. A week before the battle began in Crete, the mainspring had broken and a watchmaker in Canea, a frugal Greek who looked like my idea of Daedalus, had mended it. He had no new mainsprings, he said. So he'd used the longer of the two broken pieces. Ever since, I'd had to remember to wind it twice a day: at six in the evening because long ago in New Zealand six, the time the pubs closed when I was twenty-one, was an easy time to remember; and at whatever time first light came in the morning because, ever since the war, that was when I awoke.

How long was a year in this life of a watch? Did watches compare with dogs? If so, my watch was very old. Or with elephants and parrots and tortoises? If so, the watch was young and it would be cruel to have it put down. The state of my poor watch seemed to argue for a comparison with dogs, or with horses.

So I did need a new watch. But, even if I'd had the money, could I really be such an ingrate to an old friend? It would be like taking a second wife because your first had worn herself out in your service, at bed and board. Besides, it would be betraying my mother's memory.

On the other hand, when I told this taciturn giant I didn't have enough money for the fare, he might beat me up in such a way that my own mother wouldn't have known me. She wouldn't have liked that. Neither would I.

Supposing I offered the watch as security? It was gold, after all. But this great troll was no connoisseur of watches. Another night his arm might glitter grotesquely with diamond bracelets. And he was an American, valuing only what was new. What odds to him that the steed I offered was an Arab, if it was broken-winded and long in the tooth? Or, again, he might simply keep it, and then I'd have no watch at all.

Then I thought of my traveller's cheques. An idea began to form that would solve all my problems: pay him, pay the locksmith, provide me with a new watch. But those watches of his must be stolen property. Was I going to set up as a receiver of stolen goods at my time of life? And on my birthday, too. Replacing my mother's birthday present and being an accessory after some almost certainly larcenous fact, how would my mother have liked that? Well, there were a lot of things in my life that my mother wouldn't have liked. I didn't very much care to think of them myself. Besides, we had come through Central Park underpass already. It wouldn't be long before the moment of truth arrived.

'How much do you want for one of those trinkets of yours?' I said.

He pulled into the side of the road again, just short of where it left the Park for lighted places where policemen walked with big sticks and large revolvers, inquisitive men.

'It depends which one you want.' He had swivelled in his

seat. I took my eye off his broken nose, not wishing to be uncivil, and looked at the banded galaxy glittering on his anaconda of a forearm.

I rather liked the look of a stainless steel self-winding one. It seemed less treacherous to my patient gold Griselda to go for something plain. And it would be cheaper.

'Fifteen dollars.'

'I'll tell you what,' I said. 'If you'll cash two twenty-five dollar traveller's cheques, it's a deal.'

'Hot traveller's cheques?'

I explained they were OK, with a confident lucidity that dissembled my instant conviction that they were duds, forgeries, and that he would spot me at once for a confidence trickster.

'Let's have a look at them.'

He examined them the way a savage might have scrutinised an explorer's bead necklace. He could see a certain beauty in them. And, fortunately, they were American Express. That seemed to impress him with their probable reliability. I began to be afraid that, like some imperious native chief, he would refuse to give them back, pretend they were presents.

'What do I do with them?'

'Once I've signed them — but not without my signature — you can cash them anywhere. I'll give you my office telephone number and address in case you have any difficulty.' It was the office address that got home to him. All my colleagues drove Cadillacs. While he reflected, I had to struggle with a vision of his being arrested with the stolen goods, one watch missing, and my traveller's cheques signed, and my office address, in his possession. I won the struggle.

He took a good look at me and decided I was a sucker but, as suckers went, an honest sucker — worth an uneven break. A man who talked the way I did, a limey, couldn't possibly be smarter than he was. He unstrapped the watch. I signed the two cheques and handed them over with one hand while I took the watch and then the residual thirty-five dollars with the other. The cab started up again and I changed watches, guiltily putting my discarded friend of so many years in my trouser fob pocket along with my last traveller's cheque.

There was complete silence until we reached Columbus Avenue. I was getting my mind ready for the next catastrophe: his discontented wife, a real Xantippe, would have persuaded the All Night Locksmith that it was better for me to stop out all night than for him to do so. A Vivien to that Merlin, she had blackmailed his spell out of him and now had him imprisoned in their wooden bed.

'What I don't get,' the taxi-driver said as we waited for a light, 'is why you had to change two traveller's cheques when all you had to hand over for that watch was fifteen dollars. One cheque would have been enough.' His voice was low and sad and puzzled, like that of Heurtebise in *Orphée*. I like men who suffer discomfort from difficult problems and cannot rest until they are answered. That's what's got us where we are, God help us. But, after all, if we hadn't been lunatics, we'd never have got into space and wouldn't be hoping to get to the moon.

I explained about the All Night Locksmith. It occurred to me that in real life perhaps the taxi-driver was Haroun-al-Raschid. That would explain a lot. I was having my intellectual discomforts, too, about this night's work.

'Do you mean to tell me,' Haroun said, 'that he wants to take twenty-five dollars off of you, just to get your door open?'

I explained that almost anything that would get me to bed would be cheap, if I could pay for it.

'It's daylight robbery,' he said. 'Here, I'll tell you something. When we get there, I'll come up with you and I'll get you in for nothing, before he gets there. I can't have a visitor to New York treated like this, just because he's a stranger and a limey and has to go to bed.'

I was too tired to explain I wasn't a limey and anyway I'd never been able to convince any other taxi-driver I wasn't. Moreover, I thought to myself, how do I know that once you've found the way you won't come back some other night? Victor didn't have a large supply of watches, as far as I knew, but he did have a few trinkets of another sort. And supposing Haroun made his entry some time after the Countess had come back from Liechtenstein and succeeded in making gold?

So I declined with thanks. Haroun pressed me. I declined again, telling him I had to keep my promise to the All Night Locksmith but not telling him I was now convinced that the great opener of doors would fail to appear. I had a vivid picture of him, lying in that oaken bed with his malignant wife Vivien. His forehead was wrinkled and he was fretting at not having kept his tryst, at having betrayed the Locksmith's Oath. His wife was saying, 'Aren't you glad, honey, I didn't let you go out and help that man with the limey accent? I'm sure from his voice he was a gentleman burglar. Anyhow, he can't be up to any good wandering about at this hour of night when all decent people are in bed. Do you love me, honeybun?'

It was too revolting and I averted my mind from their enseamed sheets. The driver was watching me in the mirror. He caught my eye now and shrugged. I was obviously mad. He was still shaking his head after I'd discovered that I had just enough for the fare after all and had tipped him an extra five dollars. I felt him watching me as I went up the steps of the house, and then I heard him drive off, my only friend.

This time there was a little wiry man with the black doorman, a sort of vizier whom I guessed to be the Super.

'I'm the Super,' he said, reading my mind. 'Having trouble with your lock, Hiram tells me.'

I explained, untruthfully in a sense, that I was expecting the All Night Locksmith in ten minutes. The new watch, eager to ingratiate itself, confirmed that he still had ten minutes before not coming.

'How much is he going to charge you?'

I told him.

'It's robbery. I'll get you in myself for nothing. Come on. We've just got time before he gets here.'

'But I promised I'd meet him.'

'Come on.'

I was too weak, morally and physically, to resist the impetus of this fiery little firbolg. We got into the elevator. After all, that faithless locksmith was stewing in bed somewhere over on the East Side, betraying me with his wife. Some people had all the luck, being in bed. Served him right, though, that he wasn't alone but had to share the sheets with that scrawny, demanding bitch.

I tried the bell again, just in case the Countess had insomnia, or had wakened up with a new idea for making gold. No reply. The Super picked out the other half of my key with one of those things you use to take out stones from a horse's hoof, if you have a horse. 'Reckon the keymakers and the locksmiths are in the racket together,' he said, looking at the bit he'd taken out and the bit I'd given him. 'Made of peanut butter.'

I squatted on my heels, too tired to stand up any longer. 'Wait here,' he said, as if I had anywhere else to go. I closed my eyes. Against the screen of my eyelids I saw my bed. I lifted back the covers. There was a clean, white pillowslip. I got into bed.

I was just getting off to sleep when he returned. The film ran backwards and there I was again, squatting on this landing. The Super had a long white strip of celluloid in his hand.

'What's that?'

'It's a loy, of course.' He spoke in the sort of voice that nurses use to explain a bedpan to a novice, or kindergarten teachers use when they explain about cats sitting on mats.

He inserted his loy into the slit between the lock side of the door and the frame and began to work it up and down, very tenderly like a young man with a girl. It seemed to come against some resistance and he worked it to and fro. There was a sort of click. I felt like a voyeur. 'Got it,' he said and tried the door-handle. Nothing happened. He worked the loy further down and met resistance again. But this time there was no click. The girl must be a Crusader's wife, fitted with a chastity belt.

'A double lock,' the Super said. 'I'm always telling him he ought to leave a duplicate key with me. The trouble is that no one trusts anyone in this man's town.'

I moved from despair to anaesthesia. The locksmith's time

was past. That awful little wife had won. She must be younger than he, and sexually attractive in an awful sort of way, to him at least. Old men are always said to be uxorious. Perhaps I'd better kip down where I was, on the floor. After all, I'd slept on floors before. Yes, but thirty years ago.

Then I heard the elevator coming up. 'Don't want him to see my loy,' the Super said and darted out of sight somewhere off-stage.

The door of the elevator opened and out stepped the All Night Locksmith. He was young and tall and lean, rather like an extra in a Western who's going to be the star of the next one, the new Gary Cooper or James Stewart.

Then I was aware he was not alone. Behind him from the elevator came a blonde, almost equally tall, young and very beautiful, and carrying a bag of tools.

'You the one who's locked out? Meet my mate.'

I looked puzzled.

'My wife, get it? She doesn't trust me going round all these swell apartment houses by myself. She thinks I'll be asked to unlock the bedrooms for too many dames. Sorry we're late. We always have a bit of a lie down before we go on the rounds.'

So she took Ovid's advice as well, without knowing it, and made sure he was in no state to yield to any temptations when she wasn't watching. Whatever it was, they were beaming at each other, as if it were the end of the Western and they were going off into that sunset. I took it as a good omen. The sooner they got me into bed the sooner they'd be able to get back to bed themselves. But I felt rather excluded even jealous. The fact was, though, that I really was excluded. There was no good feeling like a minotaur when I couldn't get back into my labyrinth without his help. Why did some people have all the keys? Was her name Ariadne and his Theseus?

He produced a sort of spiked mace from the bag which she opened for him, a fearsome object. In the middle of the spikes there was a hole, like the mouth of some bizarre metal insect. He fitted the hole over the lock, and the spikes stuck out on either side like one of those crown of thorns starfish which envelop and devour a succulent piece of coral on the Great Barrier Reef.

'No you don't,' said the Super, suddenly reappearing.

I looked at him with equally sudden hatred. Then at the All Night Locksmith, for salvation. His mate was looking at him too; had been all the time.

'Why not?' said the locksmith. I was disappointed in him. I felt he knew the answer already and was merely fencing.

'Because I know what you're going to do with that thing. You'll get the door open all right but it won't lock afterwards. And I'm the sucker who'll have to take the lock off when you've finished with it and carry it all the way down town to the makers to get it mended. That's why not.'

The locksmith looked at him, looked at his mate, and then looked at me. The Super looked at me as well. It was evidently up to me. I weighed getting to bed at once against the ruin of Victor's lock, for the Super had convinced me. The locksmith knew he was right, too, of course. Only he wanted to do the job the quickest possible way and get back to bed with his mate. It wasn't jealousy of them but the iron law that binds guests as well as host that made me come down on the side of the Super.

'OK, then,' said the locksmith. 'Is there an outside plug on this landing?'

'No,' said the Super, 'but I can reach one. Leave it to me.'

The technological mysteries had now approached a climax and I looked and listened at their further doings like a weary dog watching a game of chess. I was comforted by the suspicion that the Lady of the Lock knew as little as I did, but she was better at looking as if she knew all about it. I wasn't in her league at the game. I dare say she had had more practice, though, and her eyes and smile would always get her a ten yards' start in any Caucus Race where men were doing the handicapping.

The Super returned from some remote part of the labyrinth – the secret recesses where he kept his loy, no doubt, and who knows what other strange devices: a fiery furnace perhaps, and a tame iceberg, a universal bugging system, a closed circuit television by which he could tell when the Countess was asleep and when she was making gold, a portable fire escape.

This time he was carrying a series of rubber umbilical cords, each with a navel at one end and three prongs at the other. When he reached the end of one of these things, he'd plug the prongs into the navel of the next. I imagined the whole series snaking back to some placenta of power, perhaps at the core of Mother Earth, via some mohole or other. The last bit of this flex, as they call it, with the ultimate plug dangling from it like a mechanical sexual organ was within easy reach of the door.

The Super now delegated the power to Peter Rock, Lord of the Keys. He was handed some weird gadget by the priestess of the locks. He fitted it onto the sexual plug and at once the whole apparatus began to breathe. He placed his breathing thing over the keyhole and we all held our own breaths. The thing, or the lock, I couldn't be sure which, or perhaps both of them, with a unison of which Marie Stopes and Dr Kinsey would have approved, gave a kind of gasp, and seemed to relax. The All Night Locksmith turned the handle and the door opened.

'Twenty-five dollars,' said the All Night Locksmith, barring my entrance.

I counted out Haroun-al-Raschid's notes. The Super looked on, like Maxentius acknowledging the victory of Constantine. The mate looked at her watch. Soon she and her man, for he must be a man, would be murmuring sesame together in their own magic dwelling, and afterwards they would relax and sleep, breathing deeply. Meanwhile she took apart the connection and the stallion thing. They sighed and then stopped. She packed the business part of it into the kitbag.

I sighed, too, and looked at the new watch – I couldn't quite call it mine yet. It was half an hour after my birthday.

The two of them got into the elevator and it bore them away, downwards yet somehow ascending. Angels watch their locks by night. The Super, subdued, looked at me.

'I've still got five dollars,' I said. 'And I'd like you to have them. And thanks very much.'

'That's OK. You go in and close the door. I want to make sure the lock isn't broken. I ought to have checked before I let them get away.'

'But you must take the money.'

'Don't worry about that. I didn't get the door open for you, did I?'

I realised he was suffering in his amour propre, the amateur's jealousy of the professional.

'You'd have managed all right if it hadn't been a double lock.'

'That's it, I guess.' He must have been feeling bad to accept comfort from me. It was obvious I'd never even heard of a double lock before tonight.

I went inside and closed the door. I heard him trying to open it and failing. 'Good night,' I called through the door. 'And thanks.'

'Good night,' he called back.

I had just enough strength left to get undressed before I got between the sheets.

It was daylight when I woke. Victor was standing by my bed. I looked at my watch and wondered why it was different. I had slept late, no doubt because from now on I wouldn't have to wake at first light to wind my old watch. Already it was nine o'clock.

'Where did you say you left those pieces of key?' Victor asked, rather grimly.

'When did I say I left them anywhere?'

'Last night when I came in. You got up and told me a long drunken rigmarole about Haroun-al-Raschid and the Super and an All Night Locksmith. Not to mention the Gestapo, the OGPU, Duessa and the Blatant Beast, and God what knows what else.'

I faintly remembered now. We had been in the living-room, I in my dressing-gown and he in his light raincoat.

'In the ash-tray on the dressing-table,' I said.

He took away the pieces without explaining. I lit a cigarette. In ten minutes he was back. 'It's no good,' he said. 'They can only make a duplicate from a whole key.'

'Who?'

'The locksmiths, of course. There's one across the street.'

'But what about your own key, the one you got in with last night?'

'The Countess must have taken if off the hall table when she left. That's where I always put it and it isn't there. Her flight will have taken off by now.' He went out morosely.

I got up and had a hot shower, then a cold one. I didn't feel like singing but the cold water helped with my traces of hangover. I peered into the living-room. He was reading and didn't look up. A bad sign.

I went into the kitchen to poach some eggs, enough for both of us. Food ought to help. The Countess's researches had taken over most of the equipment but there was one small saucepan in which to boil the water and drop the eggs. There was some sinister mixture in the kettle, with an odd smell. So I kept the eggs hot on a plate while I washed the saucepan and boiled water again for coffee.

After he'd eaten and had a cup of coffee he was able to speak, though only in very short sentences. He was trying to work out a routine by which having no key wasn't going to mean that one of us would always have to be at home. It didn't seem a very promising line to me. So I took a different tack and thought intensely about the precise details of our meeting the night before – no easy task for a man with my amnesia.

'I suppose I could always ask Harriett to come in when we both had to be out,' he said.

'Harriett?'

'Why are you always asking questions. My last wife.'

'Weren't you still wearing your raincoat when we sat in here last night?' I said.

He looked at me and understood. He went out into the hall and came back with the key in his hand.

'Where is this locksmith's, did you say?' I said. 'I'll go this time.'

'No,' he said. 'I'll go. You made the breakfast, after all.'

I insisted. I found the locksmith's across the street, on the corner. When he looked up I felt myself go pale. It was the All Night Locksmith. He gave no sign of recognising me. I wanted three copies made, a magic number. 'You'll have to wait a few minutes,' he said. I waited and watched while he did the job at a bench, his back to me.

A tall, dark woman came in with a tray from the back of the shop. 'I've brought your coffee, honey,' she said.

I studied her carefully. She had all the lineaments of satisfied desire – so did he – but she was not the wife I had seen last night. And, looking again at the locksmith, I saw that he was fair-haired, a daylight locksmith. A practiser of white magic.

As I went out with the triplet of new keys and their parent, I looked at the name above the door. I hadn't been dealing with warlocks and witches, after all. The name was Paul Rock. They must be brothers.

When I handed Victor the keys, he gave me one back and took a second for the spare. 'I think I'll give this one to the Super,' he said.